HEXEN'S CROSS

D0746631

HEXEN'S CROSS

J. KOWALLIS

Columbus, Ohio

Copyright ©2018 by Jernae Kowallis.

Published by Gatekeeper Press

Cover design by Lauren Crest Illustration

ISBN (Hardcover): 9781642370430
ISBN (Paperback):9781642370423
eISBN: 9781642554038

For my own ancestors:

I literally wouldn't be here without you.

CONTENTS

PRONUNCIATION GUIDE

Nouns

Æsir	ICE-ear
Alemflu:	ah-LEM-flew
Craniarann:	crown-EE-ran
Cúchulainn:	ku-hoo-LIN
Deireanhexe:	DEER-an HEKS-eh
Gea:	YAY-uh
Gee Bulg:	GUY-bowl-ugg
Gungnir:	GUNK-neer
Gylfaginning:	GEEL-va-GIN-ing
Himilæsa:	HEEM-ah-LAY-seh
Le do thoil, tá suíochán:	LAY-doe-hoil, toh SEE-oh-hoan
Meoxhus:	meh-OAKS-hoos
Móraí :	MORR-ee
Mo sféar:	moh-sFEER
Ragnarok:	RAHG-nuh-ruck

Ruhmactír:	RUHM-mack-teer
Schippete:	shee-PET-the
Víðarr:	*vee-THAHR*
Wælcyrie:	veyl-KAHY-ree
Yggdrasil:	EEG-dreh-seel
Zonne:	ZONE-eh
Zwielichtgötter:	ts-VEE-lik't-goe-tr

Spells

Spell	Pronunciation	Purpose
Bása tás (Tás)	*BOH-suh* TOHS (TOHS)	Instant Death (Death Spell)
Klariea gei anru frien	*klair-EE-uh gee AHN-roo FREE-en*	Peace/Central Clarity
Dúbla	DOO-blaeh	Copy/Duplicate
Sehe dein knechte, heile magie.	SAY-eh dine NEK-teh, HIGH-leh MAH-jee.	Ancestral prayer
Cosai die eine,	kahs-EYE-ee dee EYE-neh,	
tabhai uns kraft.	tab-EYE-ee OOns KRAHFT.	

Fuil dere eine.	FOO-eel DAIR-eh EYE-neh,	
reveille sie mærke.	rev-EYE-leh see MAIR-keh.	
Áilleacré. Dekore mi.	ALL-yeh-AHK-reh. de-KOH-reh mi.	Common Summoning & Command
Gransui	GRAHN-swee	Dry
Freo i nomeit	fr-AY-oh ee NOH-mit	Freeze Object in Time
Kénlas arn min shisern,	kch-YEN-laws AHRN meen SHIS-earn,	Intelligence summons
pase i une chumig.	PAHS-ee oon KOO-meeg	
Machéan doie ang curen ane	MAH-kchen doy AHNG-koo-ren AH-nuh	
draie da hæirein	DRY-yay da HIGH-ren	
Tacht, tacht. Folay die rinnea	TAh'kt, TAh'kt. FOH-ley dee REE-neh-a	Spiritual guidance
im Feue.	eem FUH-yeh	

Lave, Lave. Siste i atme,	LAH-veh, LAH-veh. SEEST-eh ee AHT-meh,	
kenne die rinnea	KEHN-eh dee REE-neh-a	
Ó somme til Winte.	OH SOH-meh teel VEEN-teh.	
Ó doma toh hayer.	OH DOH-mah toh HAHY-er	
Ó stranzer toh cinsire.	OH st-RAHNT-ser toh seen-SEER-eh.	
Es ruhte in doman	ehs ROO-teh een DOH-mahn	
Tá er anse, visay veje	Toh AIR AN-seh, FEE-say FEH-'jeh DOHM	
dom beala seo,	BAY-lah SEEo	
som vi forlo a mui an lámhái.	sohm fee VOR-low ah MOO-ee ahn laym-HAHY-ee	
Mina til mina. Eje til eje.	MEE-nah teel MEE-nah. EYE-yay teel EYE-yay.	Vision/memory share

Mala af bille. Mar sina re lom.	MAH-lah av BEE-leh. mahr SEE-nah rae LOHM.	
Baen	*BEHN*	Milk summon
Tóa mi	TWAH mee	Physical guide
Heileigh	HIGH-lee-eh	Heal
Besaint ag skjoth	BEHS-sent AHK sk-YOT	Protection/ Hiding
Nyrte	NYUHR-teh	Strength
Tiaseal:	tee-AH-sil	Travel
Afslochtan	afs-LOK-tan	Reveal
Flagibet	fla-GEE-bet	Auditory Amplification
Mutaraigh leabenett	moot-AR-eh LAY-ben-et	Mutation/ transfigure
*Datter an nature, Sone mac tíre,	DOTter awn NAH-too-ruh, SOHN mack-TEER	Unlocking spell for the Daughter of nature and the Son of the wolf
Cinniúi af begetre, agne	keen-NEEW ahf beg-ET-reh, an-yeh	

zeris af tolód.	TSAIR-ees ahf tol-WAT	
Ahne hor lineh, lag din i.	AH-neh or LEE-neh, LAH-dee-NEE	
Vie ama sul tuer, anoi almar kin.	vee AH-mah sool tway, AH-noy al-mark EEN	
*Sturfa	STEUR-fah	Storm Summons
*Fanliv hos mi. Táir sar en.	fah-leef OHS mee. TORE sah-wren	Claim *Craniarann*
Churraick	kuh-RAY-ick	Implosion
Actuve	AHK-tuh-veh	Body Possession
Lochel	LOCK-uhl	Sever nerves
Schosynt	show-SINT	Magic Binding
Cuimhure cé were hiem	KEWM-burr s-yeh VER-eh EYEM	Memory Restoration
*Argærts	are-GEHR-ts	Call to the past
*Stallifte sa kraft	STAHL-eef-tuh saw krahft	Magic Removal (tearing genetic power from another Hexen. Only possible with *Craniarann*.)

Deiparsiú	die-pehr-SEE-oo	Repair
*Ceade san mi	kee-AY-duh sahn MEE	Oneness
Eighlase	eeg-LAH-suh	Unlock
Fiehe ana Morrigan	FIGH-ya ah-nuh MORE-ee-gun	Search (for Morrigan)

ONE

FATHER DIED. AGAIN.

I blink back the globs of tears that have now dried into a thick paste and rub my sore eyes. The raw skin at the corners burns like lemon juice and sandpaper exfoliated my tear ducts. I roll over in bed; tired muscles protest and the cream-colored sheets pull back, tangled around my legs. I reach for my phone plugged into the charger near my bed, my long dark hair falling in my face.

3:20.

Three more hours until I have to get up.

Lost in the darkness of my bedroom, my eyes wander around, and I debate leaving the confines of a hot—slightly sweaty—bed. If I try to fall asleep again, even for a few minutes, I know I'll be taken right back to my dream: A little girl stuffed in the ancient, cold, dark cupboard that played host to a colliding symphony of chamomile, lavender, baneberry, milkweed, hemlock, and so many other different herbs that assaulted my nose. The man, standing in the shadows that approaches my father and asks him over and over, "Where is it?"

1

Just like my young mind remembers, and just like every night for the past three months, my father never answers. That's why he's always killed. *Bása tás,* the man says. The next thing I know, my father's lifeless body hits the ground with a soft thud. It's the same nightmare I have nearly every time I close my eyes. While it might seem like just a dream, with each passing day I feel it getting more and more vibrant. What's worse, the images and memories become harder to shake.

I don't want to get out of bed. Even so, I know I'll never be able to fall asleep again. I don't want to.

"Ugh, Taran," I say to myself, my groggy morning voice cracking in the bleak darkness, "you say that every morning."

I sigh and push the restricting sheets off, kicking them to the bottom of the bed. Rolling over, I sit up and brush my tangled hair out of my face. The warm wood grain floor kisses my feet and each step toward the bathroom feels heavy and labored.

Sleeping at night is more of a chore and I often wake up feeling more tired than I did when I shut my eyes.

When I walk into the bathroom the light switch flips on with a gentle wave of my arm. I flinch at the glaring lights and hide my eyes with my long fingers. Slowly, my hands lower, the marking on my right hand stares back at me. A perfect circular pattern, right in the center of my palm. Mom told me the scar came from a hot tailpipe that four-year-old me tried to grab. I don't believe her, though, and I never have. It doesn't help that *Mórai* always tried to correct her and Mom would shut her up.

I squint into the mirror. My waist-long raven hair is knotted and damp around my hairline, yesterday's curls can still be seen in the ends. Red creases, the branding of my bunched linen pillowcase, paint a map-like pattern on the left side of my face and the delicate ivory skin below my eyes is inflamed.

"Oh, hell," I whisper. "I look like death."

After stripping off my satin camisole and sleep shorts (my attempt at staying cool in this abnormally hot summer climate) I climb into the shower and let the cool water rain down on me. Each bead of water dissolves the exhaustion, the heat, and the anxiety, twirling the cloudy soup of emotions down into the drain.

Oils that smell of citrus bergamot and lemon, and evening floral jasmine. Soaps of palmarosa and sandalwood. Half-assed attempts of my emotional younger self to attract healing, love, luck, and success. Herbs I picked to counter my low self-worth, and a slew of horrible junior high-school friends. Even all these years later, they're my scents. My magic.

The suds follow, then the razor. The entire process feels like work, even if it's the only thing that helps me feel like a human being before I . . . well, linger in my home for the next two hours before I go back into the world and enter the realm of work.

My skin changes from its creamy tint to a salmon pink under the scalding temperature of the hard water. The moment I feel my head start to spin from the heat, I turn the water off. Streams of water trickle from my hair into my face and onto the porcelain tile floor. I lean over, resting my elbow on the wall.

Deep breath. Close my eyes.

Bása tás. The words of the death spell rotate in my mind.

"Let it go, Taran. *Klariea gei anru frien.*" I feel the spell work its way through my mind and body and the moment the clarity sets in, I take a deep breath and push away from the wall dripping with water that's quickly getting colder.

Standing straight, I wrap myself in a towel and take a second look at my face in the bathroom mirror. The imprint on my cheek, the puffy eyes—mostly gone. Staring back at me is a pair of bright violet-gray eyes with their typical golden-brown ring around the pupil. With a wave of my hand over my reflection, the dark shadows replace the inflamed tissue, my eyes sharp with scrutiny.

"I know how you feel," I mutter.

After slipping into a pair of black high-waist wide-leg trousers and a jade-green blouse with black lace detailing, I stand in front of my full-length body mirror and study my face and hair. A quick snap of my fingers simultaneously and my hair dries into blown-out waves, the fringe of bangs framing my oval face. Very Brigitte Bardot retro-chic. Apparently, it's all the rage on the runways this year. At least that's what my sister, Lotte, says.

A touch of minimal makeup appears on my cheeks and lips, while a thick line of black liner accentuates the brilliant cool color of my eyes. Behind me, my bedroom door swings open and I leave my room to find a kettle of boiling water already whistling its monotone melody.

Hexen.

That's what my father told me and my sisters before he died. Like him, his mother—my grandmother, Marlis—and all their ancestors including both of her parents, we're all born into the same calling—a lineage supposedly descended from Woden, the hexen historically and mythically known by most as the Norse god, Odin. Zeus. Jupiter. Cú Chulainn. Take your pick. Every culture recorded their own name for him. His power and . . . proclivities for a variety of women kept him traveling across the known world. His real name, over time, became lost in myths and legends and stories so grand they couldn't possibly be true.

I pull out a mug from my cupboard and rest it on the counter. After pouring the boiling water over my own Earl Grey loose leaf mixture of rooibos, bergamot, blood orange peel, and jasmine, I add vanilla syrup. I stick a small teaspoon in the cup and allow it to start stirring on its own while my magic mixes up a bowl of warm ginger cookie dough. I'm a witch who still enjoys my comforts.

With my less-than-adult breakfast, I sit in my living room and light the few candles on my coffee table with a wave of my hand. Etched into the side of each snowy candle is the cross of Woden. A simple circle with a large cross—a line descending from the top of the circle to the bottom of the circle, and a second line connecting the west wall of the circle to the east, lying horizontally through the middle. It's been our family crest of sorts.

I lick a large spoonful of cookie dough while I study the cross, the smells of citrus tea filling my senses.

Until the age of five, I heard all the stories of Woden, his sons, their accomplishments. Víðarr was my sixtieth great-grandfather. Ancient records spoke of him, specifically in the Norse Gylfaginning, one of the more fantastical depictions of his life. It took me a while to understand what it meant. Móraí and Dad only ever rehearsed it in the old tongue—a language never written. Then, in my first year of undergraduate school, I found an English translation for it:

The second son of Woden is Víðarr, and good things are to be said of him. He is best, and all praise him; he is so fair of feature, and so bright, that light shines from him. A certain herb is so white that it is likened to Víðarr's brow; of all grasses it is whitest, and by it thou mayest judge his fairness, both in hair and in body. He is the wisest of the Æsir, and the fairest spoken and most gracious; and that quality attends him, that none may gainsay his judgments. He dwells in the place called Bryden, which is in heaven; in that place may nothing unclean be.

After all these years, it's never made sense to me. White grasses, light, he dwells in heaven . . . if anything, the words have always reminded me more of the Christian deity, Jesus Christ. Still, there are so many differences between the two figures. I could blame my ancestors for not being great record keepers, in part, because they weren't. The biggest problem: the human race. Some prophecies have even been seriously tampered with and no longer make sense to this day.

I've spent a good deal of my professional career studying the ancient family line. For my Master's thesis, I tried to tie it into my work. Then, my advisor, Dr. Farrow said, (and I quote), "There's no way to prove this. Please remove and rework this section as it's more fantasy than fact."

Like everything else in the Grim family, the stories and knowledge have really only been passed by word of mouth, and sometimes not even then. More secrets have gone to the grave with my ancestors than bones. Cremation has been a way to destroy truths, and ancient coffins are more like prisons for mysteries than holding boxes for corpses.

Performing my craft—or what little I regularly engage in—I hum a simple tune and watch the flames of the candles dance back and forth in the dark midnight ebb. The shapes of the flames turn to forms of other figures. Obscure at first, and undetectable. I continue to hum to bring out their clarity.

A face in one. Male. I can't make out the details. Another flame shapes into a crude rune. Horizontal bowtie, meaning "the day." The flame directly next to it forms into what others might consider a lightning bolt—maybe even the same mark associated with a popular fiction wizard. I know better. It's the sun. The day and the sun. The image shifts and begins to form into another shape. From within the center of the flames I swear I can see a hand beginning to form. A hand reaching out to me from within the hottest white of the flame. The fingers are spread wide and in the center of the palm is another rune. Ice? No, ice is vertical. What is that?

A jarring melody pulls my focus away from the candle and

I look to my cell phone that I must have brought out into the kitchen with me. I leave my bowl and cup of tea on the coffee table and hurry over to look at the screen before answering. Mom.

"Mom? What are you calling so early for?" I ask.

"Early? What are you talking about? You're always up by now." I look at the clock. Seven thirty in the morning? How did four hours go by that quickly?

"Besides, I have to have a reason to call my daughter?"

"At . . ." my voice fumbles, "seven in the morning? Yes." I smile nervously, the loss of hours sending a shock through my system. What in the world just happened?

I hear her soft laugh on the other end. "Fine. I'm calling about your grandmother."

"*Mórat?* What's going on?" I frown.

"She's grunting about something and I can't figure it out. The only thing I know is that I can't tell you how many times during the day she says your name. Marlis keeps asking to talk to you, calling your name like she thinks you're in the next room. I'm getting a headache."

I quickly peel back the curtains of my living room and look out the window. Murky morning sunrise colors are forming on the horizon, breaking over the headline of the Stanford cityscape and filtering in through the wide-open bay doors looking out of the apartment, setting a golden glow on the room.

"I didn't realize she was getting that bad," I respond. How? How in the world did this happen?

"Her lucidity comes and goes," Mom's voice cuts through my inner freak-out. "But, Taran, I'm telling you, it's like living with an old witch."

"She is an old witch," I chuckle, nervously.

"Why do you think I said that?" She sighs. "I just wanted to see if maybe you could make out something for me."

"Sure. Go ahead."

"She keeps mumbling something about crown-erie-ran? I kept thinking she was saying 'come and ran,' but every time I 'come,' she near bites my head off."

I laugh, the anxiety still coursing through my heart. "I actually swear I used to hear Dad talk about something like that. Could she possibly be saying *Craniarann?*"

"That's what I just said."

"Well, the *craniarann*," I look around my apartment, the fear beginning to increase—nothing is out of place or unusual—"isn't a name I typically use. In my field, we call it *Gungnir,* or *Gee Bulg.* Both are just different names for the mythical weapon belonging to the Norse god, Odin or the Celtic god, Cú Chulainn."

"Oh no. Not your grandfather, Woden?"

"One and the same." I reach for my patio door and slide it open, allowing the fresh air to infiltrate the smell of heavy burning candles and clear my panic. "Although, Dad never called it that. He called it *Craniarann.*"

I take a deep breath and try to clear my head. How could I have been in a trance for nearly four hours? I'd only sat on the couch for a few minutes.

"Taran?"

I walk back into my apartment, my sandals clipping across the tile hallway, then over a detailed Persian rug covering the entry that leads out of my apartment. "*Craniarann* was the family name for the spear since it was formed using the wood of the Himilæsa tree."

"And . . . what's that?"

I quickly grab my satchel and my keys before heading out the door, locking it behind me. "Himilæsa is what the Norse called Yggdrasil or the gallows. It was a," I motion with my hands, knowing full well that she can't actually see me, the keys jingling at the same time, "gigantic tree, essentially, whose roots connected all nine Norse worlds. Dad always just referred to it as the gateway to the afterlife."

Mom sighs again on the other end. A sound I've become accustomed to over the years. That happens when you're the only human one in an entire family of hexen witches. "I don't think I'll ever understand all of this. I call you and it's like taking a history exam. So, why is Marlis mumbling about a tree?"

"Not the tree, the weapon made from the sacred wood of the tree."

"Whatever."

"Well," I jog down the stairs from my apartment and step outside, "I don't know. Have you asked her?"

"You think I haven't tried?" she balks on the other end. "I have, and then she glares at me and says, 'No. Taran.' Sweetie, can't you take a weekend and come up here to see her? I know finals week is coming up soon and you'll have tests to administer and papers to grade, but," she sounds desperate, "I need some help."

"What about Alina? Can't she come over and talk to *Mórai*?"

"You know your sister."

I find my CR-V and quickly climb in the front seat. "Yes, I do. Can't she just leave Carl at home and go talk magic without him?"

"She's got kids, Taran. Unlike you, I might add. When do you think you'll be able to rectify that?"

I roll my eyes and start the car before pulling out of my parking spot alongside the road. "I thought that this was a conversation about why *Mórai* is talking nonsense. Not you."

"Oh, and suddenly wanting to see my oldest daughter married with children is nonsense?"

"You know what I mean, Mom." I set my phone down when the Bluetooth capabilities in my car take over, allowing me to talk without compromising my steering abilities.

"A single woman like yourself doesn't need to be fixed. I get that. But, would it hurt you that much to marry Alex and settle down? It doesn't even have to be Alex. Just . . . someone. Someone who makes you happy. Even if you want to live in sin for the rest of your life."

I burst out a laugh. "Live in sin?"

"You and your father might be Hexen, but I'm still Christian. Look, don't get me wrong, I like Carl, and I love my grandkids. It's just . . . I hate the fact that he won't let them come over here. It's as if he thinks Marlis has a disease and the children will catch it. It's embarrassing."

"That disease is called 'magic,' Mom. Alina knew he was like this before they got married. You did too, might I add."

I turn a few more streets before heading up a steep hill toward campus.

"And you made everyone very aware of the fact. Believe me, I remember." There's an accusatory note in her voice.

"He made her sign a contract, Mom! I mean, I understand wanting to lie low. Hexens don't really have the best history when it comes to normal people. Pendle Hill, North Berwick, and Salem come to mind. That doesn't mean that he has to give her a gag order."

"She loves him."

"Right." I roll my eyes. "It's *Bewitched* all over again. She's the lowly fifties housewife and he's the bumbling, controlling, manipulating—"

"Taran," my Mom warns me. "Besides, it's not like you use magic all that often."

I take a deep breath and pull to a stop at the next red light. "I'll take a look at my schedule, move things around, and see what I can do to make it up there this weekend. I can't promise anything about Alex, though."

"Thank you."

I hang up the phone and drive the rest of the way to the university. Once I arrive, I haphazardly gather my junk and walk toward the side entrance closest to my office.

A man walks directly in front of me, having turned the

corner from another direction, sharply dressed in a tailored grey suit, golden tie, and a cigarette pinched between his fingers. His eyes graze up and down my body before he takes a drag on his cigarette and walks on, talking on his iPhone. I tuck my leather satchel under my arm and walk into the entrance of the building.

"*Gōdne mergen. Lang fierst besēað nā*," I greet David, the student staffing the front desk of our department this morning. He nods to me.

"I hope that was Martian because I didn't understand a word that came out of your mouth."

"Aren't you studying Old English this semester?"

"Yeah." He curls his lip in self-loathing.

I smile. "All the more reason to practice."

David chuckles. "I'm trying. But, um, Dr. Grim, someone is here to see you."

I stop mid-step and fumble with my belongings. "Oh?"

David motions to a man who'd been sitting on the waiting bench. When the man looks up, I note the streaks of gray at his temples and laced throughout his dark hair and trimmed beard. With eyes like onyx, he stands and holds his hands clasped behind his back. Against his cool white skin, his black suit—most definitely custom made—creates a very stark contrast. Premium polished black leather dress shoes. A large 18-karat gold ruby ring placed on his right hand, the middle finger. He's not a penny pincher.

"Dr. Taran Grim?" he asks, stepping forward, his voice laced with a thick Gaelic accent.

I tuck my bag under my arm and reach out my hand. "Yes. I am. And you are?"

"Michael Donovan. Yeh can call me Mr. Donovan."

I narrow my eyes. I swear I've heard that name somewhere before. Not anytime recently, though. It's almost like someone my mother would have mentioned once upon a time. "Donovan? My apologies, have we met before?"

The man grins underneath a bulbous nose, his onyx eyes sparkling, and shakes his head. "No."

"Sorry. It's just . . . your name is familiar." I clear my throat and shift the bag under my arm again. "What can I do for you?"

"I'm under the impression that yeh . . . teach European occult in this university, correct?"

I nod. "More specifically, its relevance to mythology and the impact on the religious beliefs of the common man. Have you already spoken to someone about my work?"

"My contact in London told me about yeh. And this good young man informs me," he nods to David, "you are currently teachin' a class called Anglo-Saxon Myths and the Roman Occupancy?"

"I am. Well, actually, it was originally Dr. James Cavill's class. He's on sabbatical this semester, however."

"Wonderful." He claps his hands together. "Would yeh have time to meet in your office for a few minutes this mornin'?"

I shuffle the bag under my arm again, trying to keep a grip on everything before it comes tumbling out onto the floor. "I'm sure I can move some things around. Please follow me."

After taking him through the large glass door, and a few paces down the carpeted hallways, I unlock my office and escort the wealthy mystery visitor inside. Decorated in old European fashion with touches of Norse and Gaelic traditionalism, I breathe in the smell of the bergamot and jasmine wax—relaxation, peace, and love—pooled in the warmer on the corner of my desk and shut the door behind me. A detailed Viking shield replica—a wooden design, modeled after a real piece of war antiquity, originally intended to be an offering to one of the ancient gods featuring the simple design of a sea monster—hangs on the wall over my pre-fabricated desk. It's paired with two copies of pagan runes once found etched into stones in Northern Britain (they also just happen to be potion recipes. A fact that all scholars have missed). Beige armchairs, and books piled on books piled on books line the manufactured steel shelves, all completing my attempts to cover up the basic "teacher" furniture the university provides.

"*Le do thoil, tá suíochán.*"

"Ah, you know Irish," he says, taking a seat across from my desk.

"Gaelic, Old English, Danish, and German." I leave off the fact that I know a fifth, undocumented language. It doesn't bode well when people hear you speak Hexen. "My father learned from his mother. And he taught me." I take another glance at my guest and sit down in my chair. "So, what can I do for you?"

Michael Donovan leans forward on his knees and carefully

studies me. "Fascinatin'." His eyes scan every inch of my face, staring directly into my lavender eyes.

"I'm sorry. What is?"

In what seems like a change of topic, his focus shifts. "The fascinatin'. Have yeh ever searched for or studied what the rest of the known world would call 'the fascinatin'"?"

I frown. "What do you mean?"

He smiles. "Have yeh heard of *Gungnir*?"

My eyebrows lift and I try my best to keep myself from pushing back in my chair. My heart beats wildly and I nearly choke on my own tongue. The spear of Woden. The same weapon *Mórai* has been mumbling about? If my bloodline has taught me anything, anything regarding myth or legend is rarely coincidence and to have this object mentioned by two separate people to me in the last hour with no provocation from myself is sending me into a startled curiosity.

I try to mask my rising interest. "What mythologist, historian, or scholar hasn't? A spear, crafted by the wood of the Himilæsa by dwarves. It's the weapon of Odin. One, legend says, he's to carry in the final battle of *Ragnarok* to fight Fenrir. Myths not so well-known also claim that the spear is still residing in the mortal world. The contracts of Odin that are inscribed on it give the user unimaginable powers—the ability to access the nine Norse worlds—and of course, the ability to kill Fenrir."

The full story is, of course, one of the floating secrets that mostly seems to have been buried with my ancestors. The son of

Woden, the legend says, who hid the spear is the very ancestor my father told my mother he came through: Víðarr.

"So, yeh know much. What if I told yeh the spear was real?"

I smile, feeling my pulse thump in my neck and into my ears. I finger the edge of my desk, the plastic edging digging in between my nail and finger. Dad only once told me about the spear. He spoke about it like someone would talk about a family heirloom, not a legend.

"Mr. Donovan, while that might be very thrilling, the existence of such objects, including the gold helmet and chainmail Odin is prophesied to wear during the war, all of which were—again—claimed to be hidden by his son, Víðarr, are merely myths. Stories concocted by uneducated peoples in order to make sense of the world around them. Unfortunately, they're no more real than . . . a *wælcyrie's* daughters."

The man smiles. "The Valkyrie. I notice you reference the old English forms of the legends."

"Excuse me?"

"*Wælcyrie's*? The Himilæsa? These are not the Norse terms."

"Your point?"

"Listen, I understand your hesitation to believe, and I'm not asking yeh to. All I need is your expertise. Yeh see, I've been searchin' for this piece of history for a good portion of my life. I've been on excavations in Denmark, Germany, England, Norway, and parts of Sweden since I turned seventeen. It's been forty-five years and I still have nothin' to show for it. Havin' your eyes on my findin's would help me immensely."

"Your findings?"

"Runes, jewelry, wall art . . ."

"Again," I breathe deep, giving a kind smile and reaching for the glasses in my bag, "it's a myth, Mr. Donovan."

"Please, Ms. Grim." The smile on his face falters; the crinkles around his eyes soften. "All I'm askin' for is a li'le time. I'll even pay yeh."

"You'd have to," my voice deepens. "Unfortunately, we're coming up on finals week and I just don't have the time you need. Can you at least tell me why you think this spear exists?"

Michael Donovan reaches into his suit pocket and pulls out a stone, roughly the size of a man's palm, and slides it across the desk towards me. I hesitantly pick it up. I look down at the stone in my hand and my fingers brush over the worn etched surface.

It's a rune stone. From my experience, I guess the stone's age to be roughly late first century. Using a magnifying glass on the edge of my desk, I hold the stone underneath it and make note of the faint drawings and rune symbols all carved in fading lines and shapes. It's been broken off from something larger, perhaps a wall or larger rune stone; the writing mentions an unusual famine from the year it was carved. Then, another image along the side edge grabs my heart, strangling relentlessly, and refusing to let it pump.

Two hands shown separately first. The next image shows them clasped in a joining embrace. One seems smaller than the other, giving the impression of a woman's. The hands are mostly inconsequential on their own—since the hand represented a way of meaning "by the way of one's hands" or "by these actions."

No, it's what's on the hands that closes off my throat. Carved on the larger hand is a straight line across the palm. It looks . . . familiar. Something too close in similarity to a shape a saw extending through the flames of my early morning candles.

The smaller hand, though. A round shape circles around the center of the palm.

It's my hand.

TWO

MR. DONOVAN SITS BACK IN HIS CHAIR AND THE movement registers in my peripheral vision.

My hand. That can't be my hand.

"Is there a problem, Doctor Grim?"

My eyes flick back to him and I force myself back into composure, quickly hiding the pink scar on my left hand. "It's most definitely genuine. The, uh, piece is from the first century, most likely, or possibly the second."

"Yes," he nods. "I know this. Do yeh see the symbols near the bottom?"

I'd been so preoccupied with the hands on the edge, I hadn't even finished looking at the piece of stone. I pick up the magnifying glass again and look closely at the bottom. Mention of an ancient village, one not familiar to me in my studies, depiction of water, and a weapon. Directly next to the weapon, a long stick, is a faint image of the cross of Woden. My family crest.

"Yeh see the mention of Odin next to the ancient weapon."

"Yes," I shake my head, avoiding his eye contact, "however, this could mean anything, Mr. Donovan. I'm sorry, it's . . ."

I purposefully drop the stone on the ground beneath my desk and quickly reach down for it. "Oh no! I'm sorry."

"*Dúbla*," I whisper. In my other hand appears an identical stone. Same markings, same stone. For all intents and purposes, it's the exact same. When I sit back up, I reach the original out to Mr. Donovan, using my left hand. "I'm so sorry for that. Unfortunately, it's just not enough grounds for me to take time out of my schedule to study the possibilities of a myth. I'm sorry you flew all the way out here to waste your time."

Michael Donovan's face turns hard and he purses his lips, reaching out for the stone. "I understand, doctor. Thank yeh for your time."

He moves to stand and I hesitate to open my mouth again. I do anyway.

"Mr. Donovan. Can you tell me where you found that piece?"

The man slowly turns, his face straight. "It's a family object. Given to me by my father. I couldn't tell yeh where he found it. Good day."

With that, he turns and exits, leaving me alone in the silence of my office. Quickly, I lean back down and grab at the stone I'd created. It's just an artistic element the original carver used. It can't be my hand. It can't be.

Except—what really peaks my curiosity, my worry—images carved for mere artistic effect rarely happened. Everything told a story. Everything represented something. What's even stranger is the fact that the hands, when clasped, form a mark not seen often in pagan symbolism. An incomplete cross of Woden.

I look down at the pink circle on my palm. My fingers shake.

The circle, a symbol of the female entity, and a straight line, the male representation, and the coming together. One larger hand. One smaller hand. Male. And female.

This doesn't make sense. It can't be.

I set the stone on my desk and reach into my bag for my cell phone. "Siri, call Evangeline."

"Do you mean Evan-gah-line Cook?"

I roll my eyes. "Yes."

I wait for the dull ringing on the other end.

The phone rings three times before she picks up.

"Good morning, Taran!" she greets me cheerfully. "Why are you calling me this early?" One of her four children wails in the background and I close my eyes. She must be in the middle of breakfast.

"I'm sorry, Evangeline. I just needed to talk to you. You free for lunch today? You can bring your children if you need."

"Of course! Actually, my sister and mother-in-law are coming from Boston to see us today. I'll let them watch the kids and I'll come meet you."

"Well, if your husband's family . . ."

"Stop it, Taran!" her voice sounds hard. Almost pleading. "I'm coming. Don't even think about canceling on me. You know how I feel about them."

I smile nervously, my eyes, still locked on the stone. "I know.

'Nosey Toilet Leeches' you called them once. Do you want to meet me at the university at noon and we'll go?"

"Yes!"

A loud high-pitched scream pierces my ears and I flinch.

Evangeline starts to yell at her children, "No no! Take that cookie out of your brother's nappy!" Then, with a calm voice she speaks back into the phone. "Want to make it eleven?"

I chuckle. "Sure."

I hang up the phone and stare at the stone, sitting undisturbed on my desk. Evangeline and I have been friends for nearly twenty-two years, having met in grade school. Her parents, British expats and working in Stanford, moved back to Leeds last year. The separation has been difficult for her, especially since her mom often helped with the kids.

She's also the only friend I have in the city who knows about my alternative . . . way of living—aside from my youngest sister, Lotte, who's a student at the university and only wants to chat if she needs money or a car to borrow.

Right now, I have to talk to someone.

Quickly, I turn in my chair and walk over to my office door, swinging it open. The first class of the day, a basic US History 1050, would normally have been enjoyable. Near silence while the class took a section review test. Today, however, my curiosity and wondering are drilling a hole into my head, the silence simply giving the thoughts more power to drill deeper. When the hour finishes, I hurry out of the room even faster than my students and quickly jog out of the building and across campus until I find myself in the back rooms of the library's collections department. After some begging, and a . . . eh . . . small threat, the next thing I know, I'm looking over Zain's shoulder. The man's long curly black hair is tied back into a bun and he keeps squinting at the computer screen over his wide nose.

"Mind telling me why I'm looking for these again?" he asks, glancing at me.

"Yes, I do mind," I murmur impatiently. "Just keep looking."

"Late first century?"

I pause and shake my head, thinking back on Mr. Donovan's request. "Yes. Include the second as well."

"Okay, well, there are thousands of results coming up that involve Odin from that period. I need a little more to narrow it down."

I put my hands to my hips and bite down on my lip. "Look for anything mentioning Odin's spear specifically and maybe any other unidentified hieroglyphics. Particularly anything that involves hands."

"That helps a little more." His fingers fly over the keys and when he finishes, a new list of results populate the page. Only a few hundred. Only.

"You want to search the original documents or browse the microfilm? Some originals are here. For the most, though, we'd have to put in a req to offsite locations."

I look down at my watch. 10:55.

"Can you send me the digital microfilm files? Include any references to off-site documentation too. If there are any citations or documents at the local museums, or available through request from anywhere else, I want them. Just send them right to my secure online access files. I have to head out and I want to start looking on my phone."

"Can do."

He hits a few keys and I squeeze his shoulder. "Thank you, Zain."

"You going to tell me why you're looking for this stuff?"

"No," I smile and start backing up. "That's what's so great about living in the free world. I don't have to tell you anything."

"You whore."

"Oh, cry me a river." I grin at him before leaving the room.

When I get back to my office, I quickly gather up my bag and hurry for the front lobby of the library. Sitting on one of the side benches, waiting patiently for me, is my best friend. Evangeline's blonde hair is perfectly set into a crown braid with a burnt orange headband and her eyes are painted with a brilliantly beautiful shade combination of teal and gold, perfectly playing off the pink shine on her lips.

Since her husband, Josh, is a banker, I know she can afford a daily blowout like Kate Middleton's signature locks. Though, taking care of four children under the age of eight means she's usually clothed in sweat pants and a t-shirt with creamed peas smeared down the front. For some reason, today's different. A coral-color blouse and pencil jeans with gold-hooped earrings, gold rings and brown ankle boots finish off her look.

"Evangeline," I smile, approaching. "Look at you! I don't think I remember the last time I saw you . . . out of sweats."

"I need this. Don't give me your lip."

I laugh. "Sorry I'm late."

"Don't be. I'm used to you being a few minutes late. Oh, the life of a busy working single woman."

I sigh, slumping my shoulders. "It's not all glamour. Most of the time it's like a horror movie. Where should we go for lunch?"

Evangeline tucks her purse under her arm and grins. "I was thinking Sprout. It's been decades since we've been."

"Decades, huh?" I smile.

"I listen to Dora the Explorer for five hours a day. That roughly translates into what feels like two weeks. If you do the math, it comes out to a few mental decades of children's shows, tantrums, nappies, and potty accidents."

We both leave the University and jump into my CR-V. During the drive to the restaurant, Evangeline drivels on about Benjamin's teething, Phoebe's potty training, Charlie's star performance in *Annie,* and his twin brother Martin's math failures. I smile absentmindedly when she mentions the "treatie system," in the back of my mind, though, all I can think about is that stone. The hands—possibly, my hand.

I think what troubles me most about it is the fact that I've been having the strangest sense of déjà vu. Even stronger than when I met Michael Donovan. While others might brush it off, I know better. You see, déjà vu is associated with things my dad always called "truths." Though everyone experiences the feeling from time to time, for hexens, it's more like a compass. That sense of familiarity is a magnetic pull, pointing you towards truth or a particular path.

This feeling . . . somehow, I've seen this, or at least heard of this all before.

"Taran?"

I look up from the digital microfilm information scrolling on my phone and into Evangeline's face.

"Are you going to order?"

Shit. I haven't even realized we stepped out of the car and now stood on the damn sidewalk. "Sorry," I smile and step up to the order window of the small barely-noticeable sandwich shop that's become a favorite of ours. After talk of a vegan Barbacoa burrito, a zucchini cookie, and bottled water, I pay and follow my friend down toward the outdoor seating area that's gracefully covered by emerald oak leaves fluttering above. Along the sidewalk, others line up to order their lunches while cars and bicycles wheel by on the road. A slight breeze rustles the leaves and tangles its fingers through my hair.

Without hesitation, Evangeline leans across the table.

"Spill. Something's up with you. I heard it in your voice when you called, and you've got this disconnected," she twiddles her fingers in my face, "*thing* going on here. It's like that time you broke up with Brandon . . . or was it Kyle . . ." She pauses to think it over. "Anyway! It doesn't matter. You'd broken up with 'Brandyle' back in uni and you didn't want me to know about it, yet you begged me, subconsciously, to ask you how bothered you were. So, why'd you really call?"

I playfully glare at her and sigh, my voice calm. "You know me too well." I set my phone on the table and reach into my bag. With a solid thud, I set the replica stone on the table. "That's why I called."

Evangeline glances at the rock, then back up at me. "You wanted to show me a rock?"

"Look at it."

She reaches out for it and turns it over in her hands.

"Do you see the picture on the far right? Looks like two hands that come together?"

She squints and raises an eyebrow. "So?"

I raise my right hand and push my sleeve back, revealing my palm. "Look familiar?"

When her eyes widen, I push my sleeve back and lower my arm.

"Taran . . . are you saying this is your hand?"

"I don't know. Something odd is going on. I've been having senses of heavy déjà vu all day today. Something weird happened this morning with my candles or my magic. Or maybe it had nothing to do with them. I don't . . ." I shake my head, a real feeling of real I'm-way-out-of-my-league confusion washing over me for the first time. "Evie, I lost about four hours of my morning."

"As in, you got busy and lost track of time?"

I shake my head. "As in, I must have been in a trance, and when I came out of it five minutes later, four hours had gone by. Not only that, this older gentleman who came into my office with that rock couldn't stop staring at me."

"Perv."

"It's not just that. He's looking for a weapon my ancestor

is fabled to have owned and his son, my—like, sixtieth great-grandfather—was forced to hide."

"Does this creep know you're a . . ."

I shake my head. "I don't think so. You, Mom, *Mórai*, and my sisters are the only ones who know about our hexen bloodline. Technically, Mom doesn't even know you know, although I think she may have an idea. I wasn't all that great at keeping secrets as a teenager."

"So, what are you thinking?" she rests the rock on the table.

I look at the rock and back at Evangeline. "I think I've met Michael Donovan before."

"The man?"

I nod. "I also think this weapon he's looking for actually exists."

"What's the weapon?"

"Evangeline!" a girl calls.

My friend's eyes continue to stare me down, oblivious to the fact that her name is being summoned by the sandwich girl.

"Evie." I nod toward the window.

"Oh!" she jumps up to grab her order the same time my own name is called. Once we're both settled down once more, Evangeline shoves the end of her barbecue chicken sandwich into her mouth and while chewing, squints at me and asks, "Da eppon?"

"The weapon?" I ask.

She nods.

"It's a spear. Apparently, it's also a term my grandmother

started mumbling repeatedly over the last day or so. Ironic, no?"

Evangeline's eyes widen. "Your grandmother's been talking about it too? What does that mean?"

I swallow my bite and shake my head, thoughts tumbling around like clothes in a dryer. "I don't know. What's even more odd is the fact that Dad never called it *Gungnir*. He always called it *Craniarann*. It's the same thing, just the ancient English version of the name our family's been passing down from generation to generation."

Another group of young college kids take their seats across from us and I lower my voice. "*Craniarann* is sort of like Thor's hammer. But, it was his father, Woden's—or, Odin's—weapon."

"Oh, I love that movie! Chris Hemsworth? Like, can I lick him all over like an ice cre—"

"Evie, can we stay on point?"

"Sorry." Evangeline clasps her hands and leans in. "So?"

"Anyway, my dad used to talk about this spear. Not in the story-time way, but in the 'pay attention because this is going to be on the test' sort of way. And I can't help it. Something is really making me feel weird. I mean, that does look like my hand. Doesn't it?"

Evangeline picks up the rock once more and takes a close look. "You know I'm not the person to ask about this stuff, right? I mean, I spent two years working on my communications degree and never even finished. I decided to get married and start making human beings instead."

"Just . . . humor me, idiot. Doesn't that look like my hand?"

"Maybe it's just artistic?"

I nodded. "I thought the same thing at first. Mostly in denial, but pagan art was rarely just artistic. There was always historic, symbolic, or prophetic meaning behind everything they recorded. That image is found nowhere else in regular symbols of the time. One hand? Yes. The cross of Woden? Yes. But to have two hands with only a partial cross of Woden imprinted on them? No."

"Are you thinking there might be someone out there with the straight birthmark across their hand?"

I glance at the rock. Memorizing the simple image of the two interlocked hands. The connecting symbol, and the feeling of insecurity mounting in my stomach.

"I don't know."

THREE

I LEAN BACK IN MY OFFICE CHAIR, MY LUNCH sitting uncomfortably at the bottom of my stomach. The phone rings three times. Finally, she picks up.

"Is that you, Taran?" my mom asks.

"Yeah. Sorry, am I bothering you at all?"

"Of course not! I just had a major argument with Marlis and I could use the break."

"About what?"

"Oh," she sighs on the other end, "she found a book underneath my pillow."

I smile. "What kind of book? Don't tell me you're kidnapping her grimoire."

"No! Just a regular book! It's . . . just a book." Her voice trails off as if she thought about telling me more, and in the end, decided against it.

"Why was she upset about the book?"

Mom groans. "Okay, it's called *Circe's Passion* and it's written by this woman, Sara Clancey or Lara Clooney . . . something like that."

"*Circe's Passion*, Mom? Like one of those grocery store novels with the man showing his nipples on the cover?"

"Don't judge me."

I chuckle while swiveling in my chair and caressing the stone on my desk. "Let me guess, *Mórai* thought it was beneath you."

"Surprisingly, no. She said that if I . . . missed that kind of stuff, then I should stop dabbling in fiction and make it a reality. The old woman actually suggested a spell, some kind of tincture made with bull semen, and a pair of men's boxer shorts. I told her I'd die first, she called me a prude—well, actually she called me an *schippete* or something like that—and one thing led to another and now we're not talking. How is work today, dear?"

The broad grin that's spread across my face slowly fades. I look down at the stone in my hand, my finger gently rubbing its surface. "I'm not sure. Weird." I squint, thinking about how I'm going to phrase this. "I had a man come to see me this morning. Have you ever heard of a Michael Donovan?"

Mom hums on the other end of the phone. "I can't say I have. Who is he?"

"I don't know." I sink back into my chair, the rock plunking against the desk when I release it. "I swear I've heard his name before. Anyway, he came to see me today. Older gentleman, wealthy, and he asked me about the spear of Woden. Sound familiar?"

"Oh, dear," she sighs. "Not the same thing Marlis was groaning about all evening and morning?"

"One and the same. Did Dad ever talk to you about it?"

"Taran, your father told me so much about his hexen line, and none of it ever made sense. I think Alaric did that on purpose so I'd lose interest and stop asking. It was his way of openly keeping me in the dark, I suspect. He might have been good, handsome, and honest, your father. Still, he was infuriating when he did that."

I smile and play with the peeling edge of my cheap desk.

"What about it?" she asks.

"Well, this man, Michael, he handed me something today." I glance down at the dark stone, its old and worn carvings, and feel a weight press down on my chest.

"Well, what is it?"

"A rock. Do you think *Mórai* would be lucid enough for me to talk with her?"

Mom clicks her tongue. "You can try." She pulls the phone away from her mouth and says in a slightly louder voice, "Marlis, Taran wants to talk to you."

Mórai complains in the background. I notice her raspy voice and the fiery attitude.

"Tell her it's about the *Craniarann*," I say.

"Taran says she wants to talk with you about the *craniarann.*" At that, I hear no response and then next thing I realize, an old worn voice is speaking to me from the other end.

"You know," she grates. It's not a question, or the beginning of a sentence. It's a statement of fact.

"Know what?" I ask, almost afraid to hear her answer. And I don't even know why. So, I skip forward without waiting for her response. "*Mórai,* do you know anything about the old symbols and runes?"

"Of course, *mo sféar.*" *Mórai* says, calling me by her pet name she bestowed on me the moment she held me in her arms for the first time. It literally means "my circle" and it feels heavier than it used to.

The image of the two joined hands and the incomplete cross of Woden stare back at me. "Have you ever seen a rune that resembles an unfinished cross? Like the cross of Woden, our family crest, with the circle and only one central line?"

There's so much silence on the other end, I wonder if she's thinking over my question.

"What about a symbol of two hands clasping?" I retry. "One of the hands has a round shape in the palm, and the other hand has a solid line?" I absentmindedly rub the slightly raised pink skin on my palm.

Again, *Mórai* says nothing.

"Maybe it's . . ."

"You must go home." *Mórai* interrupts me.

"Right now? I need to finish out the workday. I have two more classes to teach and I . . ."

"Go home."

"*Mórai,*" I sigh, feeling impatient. "Do you know what the symbols are?"

"Yes. You must go home."

"Why do I need to go home? Did you cast a spell on my apartment?"

"Not your home. *Our* home."

"In Jessen? You want me to come see you?"

"No!" she shouts. "To *Bryden*. To Asgard."

I blink a few times and lick my lips. Asgard. The place where Thor, Odin, and Valhalla await the warrior dead. Bryden, the heaven where my great war-faring grandfather is supposed to be residing. My grandmother wants me to go somewhere that doesn't exist. This is perfect. The best way to end an even more confusing day. Senseless woman rambles about a spear, mystery man believes in the spear, and the senseless woman wants me to go to a fictional land.

"*Móraí*, Bryden isn't real," I say calmly. "Are you using a figurative name?"

"No. Go there. And don't tell me I'm being crazy. I read your mind like cling wrap."

I sigh and lean forward in my chair again, glancing at the clock. I have ten minutes until my second class. "Can you tell me why I need to go to this place?"

"No. Not over the phone. Maybe you should come see me."

"I'm in California, *Móraí*."

"Now, Taran." She uses a tone I'm more than familiar with. It's the tone that would stop my sisters and I from fighting even if each of us ended up screaming at the top of our lungs about the same Popples doll. It's the same tone that would spurn my father into doing just about anything she asked him to do. It's the same tone that Mom said almost kept him from marrying her.

"I'll leave tomorrow morning. I can only stay overnight."

Mórai hangs up the phone without even saying goodbye and the line goes dead.

"*Mórai?*" I ask, thinking there might have been a chance that the line just cut out. I sigh and gently rest my cell phone on my desk. After a brief glance at the clock, I realize I'm five minutes late to my class. I quickly gather my tablet and satchel before heading out the door. Early Medieval European History 2350.

As expected, the next hour drags on like a dentist at a pagan religious ceremony . . . long and confusing for the students, while I feel like I'm pulling teeth from not-quite virgin sacrifices.

"What's even more shuddering is the fact that these early Celts, it appears, offered human sacrifice as a way to prevent their clans from being wiped off the face of the earth. Killing to survive. You see, the Romans invaded their lands and this was a group of people that seemed so alien to these sheltered pagans, and this desperate will to believe that if they appeased the people they believed to be gods, and in many cases, ate the marrow out of the bones of their human sacrifices, that they'd be blessed with the power to defeat this new enemy. Of course, all of this came crashing down as life began to change.

"Can anyone tell me what was the culminating event around the year 1000 AD that changed the course of Celtic and Norse paganism? Specifically in areas like Iceland and the rest of Scandinavia?" I ask, trying to lead the young twenty-year-old students toward the right answer. With a classroom of dead stares and about half of them staring at their "hidden" cell phones beneath their desks, I smack my hand on the nearest desk. The entire classroom jumps. A single hand shoots into the air.

"Yes, Mr. Deveney."

"Christianity?"

"Exactly! Thank you. You are the only one who gets a gold star today. I'm glad that at least one of you is paying attention." The class offers me sympathy chuckles. "And that leads us into Monday's discussion on the effect of Christianity's spread across Europe."

I continue to talk over the students shoving their books and notebooks into their bags. Over the tops of their heads I see a man standing in the back of the room, leaning inside the doorframe. Alex. His Latino skin is even darker than usual due to his weekend summer hikes. His warm brown eyes seem to melt like chocolate at the sight of me. It makes my adrenaline peak for a split second—though not in the way others feel it. For some reason, his sweet gaze just sends me into slight anxiety mode.

"On Monday, we'll finish out with the High Middle Ages: what happened to ancient beliefs and then on Wednesday, do *not* miss because we'll be completing a review from mid-terms up 'til now before your final during the next week. That's it for today. Please be sure to have your final papers in by next Friday! One week."

"Thanks, Dr. Grim," a young girl says, sliding out of the row in front of me. I give her a tired smile. "Bye, Cassandra."

My eyes slowly slither up to Alex while I grab hold of my tablet. He smiles at me and shoves his hands into his dark jeans—an ensemble that's finished off with a Stanford Fire Department shirt hugging his chest and pair of white Nikes.

"How was class?" he asks.

"Ugh, they're at the end of the semester and their brains are already having a tawdry affair with summer. That's all I need to say."

Alex chuckles.

"What are you doing here?" I ask, giving him a warm smile.

"I just got off of my shift down at the department. Thought I'd drop by and say hello to the most beautiful woman in the world before I head home and dream of her. I miss you."

I offer a somewhat forced smile under his saccharine gaze. The over-wrought sugarcoated compliments that I get from him on a daily basis are just part of who he is. I keep telling myself that other women would love to have a man this sensitive and affectionate. I'm lucky.

"Well, I'm glad you came by," I sidestep his compliment, kicking myself when I see the flicker of recognition in his eyes. I heft my bag and other things into my arms and saunter toward him.

"You want to come over tonight? Around nine, after I wake up? I'll make your favorite: fettuccini alfredo."

About a year ago when we first started dating, Alex made me the most disgusting fettuccini I've ever had. Between Alex's bulked Latino looks and my own desire to seduce him, I didn't want to ruin my chances. So, I told him I'd never had pasta that tasted so amazing. I mean, I went on and on about it. Now it's eleven months later and he's still making me fettuccini that I have to hex to make it edible.

"Actually, it looks like I might have to go out of town this weekend."

Alex frowns and crooks his index finger around my waistband. "Really? I was kind of hoping to actually spend time with you. I haven't really seen you for three weeks. It's like I don't have a girlfriend these days."

"And whose fault is that?"

"It's not my fault we've been fighting spring fires. Blame the idiots who thought they could camp with an open pit fire and not put it out during a draught year. Come on." Alex leans in and kisses my neck. The moment he does, I realize how long it's been since he's been over. I might not be a complete fan of his clinginess or sappy compliments, but oh, does this man know how to use his lips . . . (I moan when his hands curve around my backside) and hands.

I realize my hips are pressing harder against his pelvis and I quickly snap out of it. "I have another class."

"Skip it," he smiles before digging his fingers into my waist and parting my lips with his.

Sometimes I've often toyed with the thought that Alex might be some sort of sorcerer who specializes in lust. Then he spouts phrases like, "every second I yearn for my Venus flower," and my entire body recoils in disgust. It's like that twinge you get when you bite into a dessert that's too rich and the overwrought cloying taste forces you to drop the fork after two bites. It's been eleven months of cloy, okay? You'd think he could stand to be apart by now!

I pull myself away and clear my throat. "I can't. I'll see you on Monday. Okay?"

Alex loosens his grip and drops his arms. "K. Can I at least call you tomorrow?"

"I'll be in Jessen. You know how the reception is up there."

He nods, and I can just see it in his face: he knows I'm pushing back. "Yeah."

"But," I reach up and brush his smooth jawline, "I'll make you the best meal of your life on Monday when I get back. That is, if you're not saving babies from building fires."

He growls low in his chest and glares at me. "You better. Now, hurry up, goddess. The sooner you get moving, the sooner I'll see you again."

I really have to force the smile this time. When I turn around and head out of the room, it takes all of my energy not to roll my eyes and add "frigid witch" to the growing list of names he should actually be calling me. Ugh, this is why my mother keeps asking about him. I'm the worst.

It's all right, though. I'll just push it aside for now—like I've been doing for months. I've got a class, I'm headed out of town for the weekend, and I don't have to worry about him again until Monday.

* * *

"Stay here, Taran. Don't make a noise, don't move, don't speak, don't even cry. No matter what you hear."

"Daddy?"

"Promise me! If you move, you're going to be in big trouble!"

"I promise."

Dad shuts the cupboard door behind me and I hear the pounding on the door again. BAM, BAM, BAM. From behind the thin crack between the two cupboard doors I see my dad move for the front door.

"Where is it, Alaric? You're hiding it! Where is it?"

The next thing I see is a bright red flash. A loud thud. A tall man is silhouetted by the residual scarlet light in the room and he stands still in the doorway. I bite down on my lip while a tear slides down my cheek.

My eyes flutter open to find that my pillow is damp. Not again. I roll over and pick up my cell phone. The blinding light of my screen illuminates half of the room it seems. I rub my eyes, waiting for them to adjust. It's only two fifty. Every night, the nightmares come earlier and earlier. I can never fall asleep after them, either. Sooner or later, it's going to start playing behind my eyes before I even put my head on my pillow.

This isn't going to work. Not tonight.

I know what *Móraí* would say. Dreams are manifestations of waking stressors; the mind attempting to expunge and massage out the mental kinks from our day. Beyond that, repeated dreams are messages—alarms from our subconscious or even from our ancestors.

I can't stay in bed. I can't even wait until morning.

It only takes me ten minutes to charm my hair into a functional top knot, get dressed, and grab my weekend bag. The nightmares, Mr. Donovan, and *Mórai's* muttering words. I'm a hexen, and I know none of it's coincidence.

"Come on!" I hiss under my breath to the obnoxiously slow car driving down Fourth. I can't handle it anymore. With a few muttered syllables under my breath and some working of my skills, the car's blinker begins to flash and it pulls over to the side, allowing me to pass. Once on the interstate, I can hardly keep my heart from pounding out of my chest. I continue to mull the circumstances around in my mind, trying to fit it in with everything I've learned, everything I know. All I can seem to conclude is that my dad never told me everything. What terrifies me more is that I'm part of this. From *Mórai's* warning, to the nightmares, the lost time, and to the stone from Mr. Donovan . . . I'm shaking.

It takes ten hours of dead silent driving down the interstate, weaving around traffic, and maneuvering through back-city roads. Not a song on the radio, or another word out of my mouth. Once I'm about a half hour outside of Boise, the road hits a switchback that continues to take me past Idaho City and into the soft mountains surrounding the valley.

Like Idaho City, Jessen resides in the midst of the Boise National Forest. Secluded and hidden away from the eyes of the world, and not by accident either. According to my *mórai*, and all my own research, our ancestors left Europe in the year 1620. And for good reason. Farther to the north, in Pendle Hill, eleven women had been killed for witchcraft, including my own ancestor, Natty. After we left, ten more burned across the valley for the same charge. The only problem was, the rest of them were innocent. Twenty ordinary women had gone to their death.

My hand grips the steering wheel.

When we arrived in America, it was only seventy-one years before we packed up and left again. The last place an entire coven of Grim hexens needed to be living was Salem, Massachusetts, and the remote American Indian lands of what would one day be Idaho seemed like a safe bet. Especially considering one of the local tribes had a hexen spiritual leader of their own that seemed to understand the need for peace and seclusion. It would still be over two hundred years before the Basques even arrived.

My CR-V dips and bumps over the unfinished road taking me up further into the mountains. I can almost smell the wood-burning fire of my childhood home, the white sage stuffed inside one of the logs. The moment the old brick home comes into view, I feel a tightening in my chest.

My grandmother knows something. The only problem is, I'm not sure I want to hear it.

I pull in next to the home and turn the key, listening to the engine die off suddenly. Growing over the tops of the cedar shakes are large Ponderosas, blanketing the old home in cool shade. A collection of needles and pinecones have collected in the gutters and crevices of the roof, while uncharacteristic ivy (a feature magically created by *Mórai*) creeps up the north wall, framing the side windows. The forest green trim of the house, the moss on the ground, and the smoke traveling out of the tri-chimney make me feel like a little girl again. It's the first and only home the Grims have ever lived in for the past three hundred and twenty-four years.

My hands grip the steering wheel again nervously and I glance at my right hand. On the underside of that palm rests the circle—a mark my mother claimed originated from a childhood injury. If that actually happened, I'd have remembered something so painful. There's not a single childhood memory that even hints to a time I would have injured myself that severely.

I think back to the stone, to the images carved on it. The worst part is I already have the answers, at least the answers to the big questions. I just need to hear it.

Pushing open the door, I climb out and step onto the crunchy pine-needle-covered ground. The smells of nature, sage smoke, and baking bread invade my mind. Memories rush back to me in a torrent of emotions and images. It's now that I realize just how long it's been since I've come home.

Nearly four years. That's not right is it?

I think back through everything and try to make sense of it all. Yes. Four years. The last time I walked through that Dutch front door, tears stained my cheeks, and fear of unemployment haunted me. I was twenty-five at the time, and I'd seemingly bombed my interview at Stanford. *Mórai* sat by me all night. Her words, and partial calming spells, kept me from falling apart. The next Monday I got a call from Dean Reeding with an offer for a full-time position. To be honest, I've always wondered if she cast any other spells that night—ensuring I'd get the job. I've just always been to grateful for the outcome to care.

I take a deep breath and start walking toward the door. Before I can even lift a hand to knock, the top half of the door swings open and standing in front of me is a woman who looks more ancient than old. *Mórai* Marlis has her thick, long, white locks braided into a single plait that falls in front of her shoulder and down her front, nearly hitting her waist. She wears a charcoal dress, slightly cinched at her small waist and a soot black shawl over her shoulders. Her face, just as unchanged as the last time I saw her is drawn down into a permanent frown and her lavender eyes, almost identical to mine, cloud over with a storm that breaks into my soul.

"You're late."

Any other person would ask, "How did you know I left?" In our family, however, the answer to that question is clear.

"It's a ten-hour drive."

She "pffs" and rolls her eyes at me, turning around and walking back into the living room of the house. "Any grandchild of mine would have been able to be here in the blink of an eye."

"I don't think it's necessary to use magic for everything, *Mórai*," I say, leaning forward and unlatching the bottom half of the door.

"*Gea*," she responds in old English. "You and that rotten husband of Alina's." She mutters something under her breath that I can't quite catch. Something about one of us being a "*meoxhus*." A toilet.

"Taran! Is that you?" Mom yells from the cellar. Her footsteps chug up the wooden staircase that drops into the cellar before her head pokes out from the kitchen. "It is!"

Mom's short blonde hair is styled with her signature 1970s feathering that she's somehow completely managed to turn into a chic modern look. Her jeans are filthy on the knees and her blue t-shirt shows signs of water splatters.

"Pipe bust again?"

"I told Marlis I'd take care of it."

"Nothing ever broke in this house until you all stopped using the craft!" *Mórai* bellows from her bedroom.

Mom rolls her eyes and then smiles at me. "As if you girls could keep this house running." She then shakes her head in disbelief. "I'm so happy to see you. Come here." Mom opens her arms and I lean in to hug her.

"I hate to do this," I pull back, "but I need to talk with *Mórai*."

"I understand. Go, go. I'll just be downstairs."

She turns around and I take a step toward the south end of the house.

"Oh, Taran?"

I turn back.

"How's Alex?"

I nod and plaster on a convincing smile. "Good!"

At that, Mom dives back down into the cellar and I mentally prepare myself to enter *Mórai's* bedroom. A room that's been unchanged for the last two hundred years, it feels. It looks like a shrine by those who didn't know any better. Generational portraits of great grandparents and owners of the craft, dried herbs and flowers hang from certain windows and specific crevices—both out of sentimentality and to ward off dark energies—candles burn at every hour of the day, and incense encircles the ceiling with fragrant smoke. The blankets, curtains, and rugs have been meticulously cared for. Not manually, of course, but by the use of ancient practices.

I reach the door, rosewood with runes and detailed designs carved into its surface, and tap my knuckles against it.

"Come in, Taran."

I push open the door to find *Mórai* sitting in her rocking chair facing the window to the east. Her wrinkled hands are clasped over her stomach and her eyes fixate on anything and everything outside while a white curling of smoke rises from the incense jar on the small table next to her.

"You want to know about the dreams."

I open my mouth to respond. She beats me to it.

"You're curious about the *Craniarann*. You've felt things."

This time, the usually ridiculous question involuntarily shoots out of my mouth. "How do you know?"

"My granddaughter shouldn't have to ask that."

It's the second time she's alluded to her disappointment in my skills. When I graduated from high school, she wanted me to stay home and learn the depths of the craft, perfect my skills. I wanted to learn the history of it all—the connection to mankind. I was already behind in that regard.

I wanted to teach.

I still remember promising her I wouldn't give up my

practice. The only thing I didn't quite realize about school . . . it takes up a lot more time than I'd thought. After the Bachelor degree, then followed the Master's. Then the Doctorate's. Before I knew it, I'd forgotten how to cast a simple peace spell and had to rely on herbs.

A guilty sigh accompanies a shake of my head. "You know I've been trying to relearn."

"My granddaughter should never have to relearn. It should be constant. It should be inherent. Habitual." Her voice is hard with disappointment. I close my eyes and step closer to her.

"*Mórai*, I lost four hours of my time yesterday."

Her chair quits rocking and her body holds deathly still.

"I was toying with the flames of my crest candles and the next thing I knew, three o'clock turned to seven and it felt like only five minutes had past."

"What did you see in the flames?" she asks.

I sink down onto her bed. The soft worn quilt smells like her—earthy and mixed with patchouli and ginger.

"A face. It never fully formed. A couple runes. I also made out a hand . . ." my words cut off. The hand. I remember the hand. It had a mark on it. A line. Just like the hand from the rune stone.

"A hand, *mo sféar?*"

The old, well-kept wood floor creaks beneath my feet when I move toward her. Using a summoning incant, I conjure the stone into the palm of my hand from within my bag that I've left in the car. Holding it out to her, I say, "*Mórai*, I saw a hand with a line burned, or marked into the palm. Just like the one here."

She looks down at the stone in my hand, her wrinkles folding in between her eyes.

"Mom said you were talking about *Craniarann*. Before that, I saw this hand in the fire. Then, a man came to me."

Her eyes widen and the violet shade of her irises flash bright amethyst. "A man?"

"At work. I had a visitor that day. His name was Michael Donovan."

Mórai narrows her eyes. "No, that's not him."

Him? All I can do is crouch down low and look up into her face. "*Mórai*, he gave me this rune stone. Tell me, is this my hand?" I hold out the rock, placing it into her lap while holding the palm of my right hand up, showing her the circular mark in my skin. The half-scowl resting on her lips falters and her breathing becomes deeper, slower. "It's my hand isn't it? The female's."

Mórai looks away and knots her fingers, avoiding my gaze.

"What was that for?" I ask, curiously.

She sighs and her eyes dart toward me, her lips still not talking.

"What did Dad know? He knew about our family history, he taught me everything I know, but I'm getting the feeling he didn't tell me everything. And neither are you."

After clearing her throat, *Mórai* licks her old soft lips. "Alaric was obsessed with the staff."

I feel a jolt behind my stomach, a twitch almost. That doesn't sound like the records I've studied. "Staff? *Gungnir* is a spear."

She shakes her head. "In legend, yes. The thought of a stick being the hero's weapon of choice was . . . unromantic."

"It's not a spear?" My head swims. It's not just a weapon. It's a hexed distaff. "So, what does it have to do with the hands?"

She shakes her head. "No. You're not ready."

"*Mórai!*" I nearly yell in irritation, catching myself before it erupts too loudly. "Tell me."

Shadows press deep into the hollows under her eyes while she talks. "He knew of the prophecy."

Taking a deep breath, and trying to remind myself that she's even more obstinate than I am, I ask, "What prophecy?"

As if attempting to push me off topic, she looks out the window again. "Shortly after he and your mother got married, she asked him to stop looking for it. You were only two and Alina was on the way. She complained about him. When he was here, he wasn't here. He was in his study or on the phone with a museum, working with his friend."

"What friend, *Mórai?*"

She shakes her head absentmindedly. "I don't know. I assumed a friend at the museum. Someone who had . . . admittance to the information he needed." *Mórai* breathes in deep and lets it out slowly. "The research. The spell books and papers were always everywhere. 'Clean it up!'" *Mórai* spontaneously shouts and it shocks me out of my hunker. I nearly fall onto my back. "She always yelled at him like that."

"What spell books?" I gather my composure and lean forward again, holding onto the rocking chair armrest.

"Your father's. He was always making notes, detailing the findings he'd found. And when your mother gave birth to you . . ." *Mórai's* eyes soften and she looks at me. "She's not like us. She couldn't do it alone. She told him their children, you, needed him. For nearly two years, he stopped looking. He gave it all up. Never touched it again."

"Because they were busy raising us?"

She nods. Beams. "*Mo sféar,* you should have seen him when you were placed in his hands. I thought he'd never stop smiling. He'd just hold you for hours, only letting go of you long enough for your mother to breast feed you. He'd hold your hand, kissing your tiny fingers over and over. Then," she frowns and a look of nausea takes over the curves of her mouth, "We came home after a weekend in Coeur d'Alene. It was the eclipse. Your mother and I and your two sisters had gone up north for the hexen rite. You'd stayed with Alaric because you were sick and he asked to watch you."

Mórai shakes her head and her bottom lip quivers. "Dead," she over pronounces the word, "on the floor. You cried and wailed inside that small herb cabinet."

My eyes widen at the images of my nightmares and memory coming to the surface. I swallow down the pressure building in my throat. "I've been seeing it."

Her head slowly tilts back toward me.

"For the past two weeks, I keep having dreams of that night. Why?"

Mórai's lips purse together.

"Do you think another hexen could have . . . killed him for something he knew?"

"Not something he knew. Something he had." Her hard gaze drills into me. "He was protecting you. It's why he wanted to watch you."

"Me?"

Mórai's hand lashes out and she grips my wrist, holding my right hand into the air. The raised pink skin formed into a perfect circle into my palm is visible to both of us. She only looks at it for a moment before catching my eyes. "Yes! That is your hand. And you're not ready." Her words hiss from her mouth. I can feel the fear, the reverence in her tone, laced deep underneath the tension.

Wind rushes through the room and I feel my hair tickle my cheek.

"Ready for what?" I dare ask.

"*Deireanhexe.* End of the hexens."

FOUR

MY MIND SPINS LIKE A CYCLONE, WHILE MY hands, firm and unrelenting, grip a kitchen knife, attempting to cut through the carrots lying on the cutting board.

Deireanhexe.

Norse mythology has its own word for it: Ragnarok. The Germans too: *Zwielichtgötter.* Twilight of the gods. End of the Hexens. It's all the same. I keep trying to pin point the details of the myths and legends, figure out what I already know about it. The problem is that most recorded stories are human versions of the tales, and not necessarily truth.

Blackened sunbeams. Homes painted in the blood of man. Brothers fighting brothers. The wolf age. The death of Woden to Ruhmactír—the first half of the brothers Geri, the other being Frec.

Chop, chop.

It doesn't make any sense. Woden is already dead.

Chop.

The carrots become soft under my touch. The knife carves downward with a sickening crunch and a soft warmth.

Ruhmactír. The shapeshifter line of hexens. Wolves. Carrots. Cut. Cleave. Through dirty bloody fingers. Wait. Fingers?

Slice.

"Oh, sh—" I bite down on my tongue and the knife drops to the ground, clanging on the stone tile floor.

"Did you cut yourself?" Mom leans over from her stance near the stove to look at me. Blood flows from the tip of my finger in a crimson stream, dribbling on the floor. A few drops fall on my shoes and the countertop.

"Yeah," I moan. I wrap my right hand around the tip of my bleeding finger. "*Heileigh,*" I whisper. Immediately, the painful stinging sensation from the smooth cut ceases. I rub the excess blood away from the magically healed skin.

I sigh, running my hands under the warm water and rinsing all the blood down the well-kept, yet ancient, stone sink.

"Is everything all right?" Mom's voice is full of concern and care.

"Yeah." I turn the water off, the image of the carrots turning into fingers . . . my knife slicing through them—and rip the dishtowel off its post on the wall. "I'm just distracted." A hitch in my breath preludes, "Do you think Alina would come up to visit if I asked?"

"At the last minute?" Mom shakes her head, turning back to the other vegetables she's sautéing over the stove. "No. She'd need at least a week to plan ahead, make sure she could come up with a suitable excuse, find baby sitters for the kids, and explain why she couldn't answer the telephone."

I roll my eyes and toss the towel up onto the counter. "I hate that man."

"He's good to her."

"He's stifling her."

"Well, I don't know what to tell you, Taran. She chose what was more important."

It's the truth. We all did. Alina chose Carl, Lotte chose sociality, and I chose academia. *Mórai* was right. None of us have really kept up what we should have. If it keeps going like this, we won't even need a war. *Deireanhexe* will happen all on its own.

I take a deep breath. "Mom, do you mind if I take a break? I hate to leave you with dinner."

"Go ahead. Something's bothering you, and to be honest, if it's hexen stuff, I don't want to know. It keeps me from sputtering it out when I'm talking with Alina on the phone. Just be aware, Marlis might be sleeping. Don't wake her up unless you want a tempest."

I weakly smile and rub her shoulder before leaving the kitchen and slowly pacing to the staircase situated close to *Mórai's* bedroom door, behind which, she's been silent. Most likely napping on her large bed.

Pulling hard on the banister, I drag myself up the stairs and to the south attic bedroom. My bedroom. When I reach the final step up to the landing, I see light. The crack between my door and the frame is illuminated by a gentle licking of a dim flame.

In the quiet darkness, a voice chants. An altered Germanic

tongue. It only takes me a single breath to realize who it is. Barely a snap of the latch sounds when I push on the heavy door. My *mórai* sits cross-legged on the floor directly in front of a medium-sized mirror that she's pulled down—a mirror my junior-high-school self once framed in pictures of Brian Littrell and Freddie Prinze Jr.—and propped up against the wall.

Surrounding her are photographs and painted portraits that used to hang on the wall of her own bedroom, the images of my ancestors all looking at me while I walk up behind her. Crest candles float in the air around her in a circle, taking on the pattern of Woden's cross. Her position at the center of the cross is illuminated by the flames snipping at the air around her.

"*Sehe dein knechte, heile magie. Sehe dein knechte, heile magie. Cosai die eine, tabhai uns kraft. Cosai die eine, tabhai uns kraft.*"

With each line, her hands push against the air over the candles, then pull it back like a dance of rhythmic breath. Pulling the energy in and exhaling it out. The candle flames devouring the negativity.

"*Sehe dein knechte.*" See your servant. Push.

"*Heile magie.*" Heal the magic. Pull.

Repeat.

"*Cosai die eine.*" Protect the one. Push.

"*Tabhai uns kraft.*" Give us strength. Pull.

The air in the room feels like it's moving, even though not a strand of my hair dances, not a chill on my skin prickles my nerves. Physically stagnant air moves with an undercurrent of rushing waves. Waves only hexen blood can detect. I close my eyes and listen to the words, allowing the energy to wash over me.

I absentmindedly mouth the words along with *Mórai*. The moment I do, I feel the wave beat harder within the room. Beneath my growing whispers, I nearly miss the fact that *Mórai* is chanting a new stanza.

"*Fuil dere eine. Reveille sie mærke.*"

Blood of the one. Awaken the power.

"*Cosai die eine, tabhai uns kraft. Cosai die eine, tabhai uns kraft,*" I whisper.

"*Fuil dere eine. Reveille sie mærke. Fuil dere eine. Reveille sie mærke,*" *Mórai* rasps underneath.

My hand begins to burn and I hiss, stepping back and looking down at my skin. The circle etched in my skin is now pale like snow, hotter than the center of a flame. Though I've stopped rehearsing the lines, *Mórai* pushes forward. The pain in my hand continues to get worse and I grit my teeth, breathing hard through my nose.

When I look up, *Mórai* stares at me through the mirror's reflection and inside it, a throng of people appear behind me. I recognize all of them. Especially one.

"Dad?" I whisper, whirling around. He's not there. When I turn back around to look into the mirror, the images fade and the glass across the mirror cracks. The building energy within the room breaks forward in a physical wind and the candle flames extinguish, leaving me standing in my dark room, my hand no longer burning, and *Mórai* staring directly at me.

"What was that?" I ask.

"With regular intensive practice, you would have recognized the ancestral prayer for what it was."

"Ancestral prayer?"

Mórai grunts, pulling herself to her feet. "You can't do this alone. You need help."

I distractedly rub my thumb over the burning circle in my palm. "Help with what? You keep saying that, and I have no clue what you mean. I want answers, *Mórai.*"

"I cannot give them." She gazes at me from the shadow near my bed. "You must go home."

This time I understand what she means by "home."

"To *Bryden,*" I say.

Mórai nods.

The tingling of curiosity builds in my mind and I step forward. "Do you realize what you're asking? *Bryden* is not in this world."

"Yes it is."

"Actually, it's not. So, enough with the puzzles. I need answers."

"No, you *want* answers. That is different. I cannot give them to you because I do not know."

"You don't . . ." my voice chokes off. "You don't know?"

Mórai drops her head. "My *modor,* ancestors bless her soul, knew the prophecy better than anyone. She only told it to your father. I suspect because she, unlike others in our line, could read the imminent. She knew you would eventually be born to your father and he would need to know." *Mórai* sighs and falls down into her rocking chair, her braid flopping over her shoulder. "From the day he turned eighteen, he dedicated his life to finding the pieces of the prophecy, determined to save you from your fate."

"What fate?" I lift my arm, showcasing the white mark on my palm. "*Mórai*, I need you to start talking clearly. I need full explanations. Everything you can give me, because I don't understand! What does any of this have to do with the prophecy?"

"You were forsworn, *mo sféar*, by the fates. The blood of Woden. The blood of Ruhmactír."

"Ruhmactír? The head of the Geri clan? What does that mean?"

"I don't know, fully. Your father knew."

"Then where are his spell books? Where are his findings? You said he collected . . . papers and books all the time. Where are they?"

She looks away from me and takes a deep breath. "Hidden."

I roll my eyes and push my hair away from my face. Of course they're hidden. Why wouldn't they be? I think to myself sarcastically.

"I have to know what it means. My hand is on a piece of rune stone that is thousands of years old. If *Craniarann* is real, if Bryden exists, I need to know what my part is. I don't . . ." my voice trails off, thinking over my words carefully. Nothing seems to be the right thing to say. Finally, all I can verbalize is, "I can't do this."

Mórai shakes her head. "Of course you can't. Not by yourself, and not with the meager training you've had. Which is why I called on the ancestors. My Alaric always said he would be safe. He swore he could do it." The last two lines, she says more to herself than to me. Like it's a conversation she's trying to remember.

"Where? Where are the journals?" My voice is deep, a weight of responsibility pressing on me. I try to keep calm while still communicating to my grandmother how important this is to me, while honestly, she probably feels the urgency more than I do. "If this man, Michael Donovan finds the spear . . . the staff, I may never see it. I may never find out why I'm a part of this. And maybe this man understands more than he's letting on. Maybe he's someone that Dad knew and I need to talk with him about it."

"No!" she barks.

"But, if they were both looking for it for years, it stands to reason that their paths would have crossed. Come on, Dad worked with someone . . ."

"And he died."

The chill in *Mórai's* voice stills the air and the energy I once felt is stagnant—submissive to her command.

Mórai sighs and her eyes close with a weight I don't fully understand. "I don't know where he hid his work. All I know is that Alaric made a final trip to the motherland the week before he died. To Bryden. That is all I know."

A flash of interest—of excitement pulses through me. "He went to Bryden?"

"Dear, it's not as far as you might believe. It's in this world. Legends have turned it into a spiritual haven. It's only land."

"In England?"

Mórai nods. "Though, the ancestors ensured it would be difficult to find. It is there."

I put my hands across my stomach and pace in a half circle. Dad was in Bryden. *The* Bryden. If Dad went before he died in an attempt to hide his journals, he had to have gotten help. "You don't know if he contacted any business associates?"

"No."

"Friends? Family?"

With a shake of her head, I know I'm on my own.

"Our family no longer lives there. Opportunity and circumstance drove us out. Fools, we were. And since he was my only child, there was no one in the family to assist him. I suppose he may have been working with someone else, perhaps an *alemflu*. He never told me. Just said he had something to take care of."

An *alemflu*. Non-hexen. Human. Mortal. Dad? No, he wouldn't have pulled in someone who didn't need to be involved.

I sit down on the bed, slump my shoulders, and look up at the ceiling. White, and trimmed with wide crown molding where it meets the pale green walls that I used to decorate with posters of boy bands, puppies, and flowers from the wrist corsages of proms and homecomings I wore. Accompanied by shelves once filled with random knickknacks and things

I'd found in the forest—shelves now empty and topped with dust.

Dad's final months involved *Craniarann*. Why? In the end, he died because of it. At the hand of someone else who wanted the information.

I close my eyes, envisioning what I can remember about him, combined with the pictures I used to spend countless hours looking at. Skin that became pale from working indoors under an old ancient rooftop, and still rich in its olive tone. Wide lavender eyes. Like mine. A carefully groomed goatee and mustache. High cheekbones. Hair darker than soot.

Dad, what did you do?

"*Mórai*," I whisper, opening my eyes. "Where is Bryden?"

She nods. "Near Betchworth Castle—the home we left behind. Before we settled in Lancashire."

"You mean," I frown, "we left Bryden before 1620?"

She confirms it with another nod. "You know the story of Rheda?"

"Yes." My voice is still and breathy. "Dad used to recite it to me before bed."

"After the sacrifice of Rheda, and the receiving of her prophecy, Bryden went under the rule of the clan of Ruhmactír Geri. He and his brother, Frec, were the heads of their clan, and close associates of Woden's, along with the Ravn clan led by—"

"Shíl and Mindier. They were a hexen clan known for their command of thought and memory and their ability to communicate with animals. I know that part of the legend. Most humans know them as the pair of ravens that accompanied Odin. While the so-called "wolf" Geri brothers served at his feet."

After taking a long deep breath, she sighs and nods. "Yes. You can see why when Rheda recited the prophecy during the symbolic sacrifice, Ruhmactír attacked Woden. Humans saw the Geris and the Ravns as foot soldiers of the Grims—not their equals. And, in truth, I think their clans felt it. That the Grims treated them as their *unseirneach*—their serfs. The attack ended Woden's reign as High Hexen. The Geris took possession of Bryden and since then, we have no access to it."

The nightmares, the coincidences—they're all colliding in a deafening storm. The history, the stories, starting to fit together. A lifetime of tales that I've considered mere legends and historical events are more than just that.

"I'm . . ." I feel my way through what I want to say, "fated to do this. Aren't I?"

I don't even need her to answer, and she knows that.

The answer is yes.

Ever since the nightmares began, ever since Mr. Donovan, *Mórai's* mentioning of *Craniarann*, and the crest candle's flame, I've been pulled deeper and deeper into an event I don't understand. What scares me most is how unprepared I am. And no number of scholarly findings will give me the tools I need to face this—thing. Whatever it is.

"This is more than just a prophecy, *mo sféar.*"

I look into her stark violet eyes. They've gone dark and hazy with a strong piercing focus that swallows me.

"It's your destiny. You were born for this, and it can't be completed by anyone other than you. And right now, you aren't ready."

FIVE

AFTER A CONFUSING AND STIFLING WEEKEND,
and about fifty missed texts and phone calls from Alex that
I still haven't responded to, the rest of the week drags on
slower than the entire semester. I keep thinking I should have
simply finished out the year with a substitute. It's my curse
that logic always takes over, reminding myself that I don't yet
have tenure and could easily risk losing my job with that kind
of . . . *cavalierity*. The moment my last test of the semester is
graded and entered into the system, I rush to gather my things
and straighten the office. I'm nearly finished shoving the last
book on Celtic paganism into my bag when I hear a soft rap
on my door.

I'm not sure why I'm surprised to see Alex leaning in the
doorway, his arms folding slowly. He's dressed in his typical
jeans and—this time—a simple black tee. He must have just
gotten off shift too. His hair is wet.

"You're not rushing out of here so you can come to see me,
are you?" he asks.

I squint, confused, before realizing I completely spaced
it. We made plans a while back for me to meet him at the

station when he got off today. On top of that, my bags and materials are encircling me, looking like I'm more prepared for a backpacking trip through Taiwan than a nice evening with my boyfriend.

Despite *Mórat's* reminder that I'm not ready, I'm still going to England. Blame my stubborn attitude or my natural curiosity. Either way, I never told him I'm leaving.

Shit.

First, last weekend I took off for Jessen. Then, the entire week, I disregarded every contact he sent me. Texts, a couple phone calls, even a Facebook message. Now, I'm leaving the country and I'm pretty sure he's the last person to find out.

My head drops and I sigh, pushing my long black hair over my shoulder. "Oh, Alex. I'm so sorry. I . . . I've been so preoccupied with—" He holds up his hand to stop me mid-sentence.

"I know." His voice is deep. Buried under the surface is a tone. The tone. The tone I heard with Brandon, the tone I heard from Kurt, Kyle, Jason, and so many others. "Taran, I don't think this is working."

I sigh and let the heavy book in my hand rest on top of my desk. Did I really expect anything different? Over the past few months we've been seeing each other, I've been hot and cold, and unable to communicate promptly. Or . . . chosen not to, is probably closer to the truth.

Though I don't know why, for a few moments, I actually feel like trying to save this. Until I realize I don't really want to.

"I'm sorry, Alex. I know I've been swallowed up in work and everything and with finals—"

"You think it's not working out because you're too swamped with teaching? This isn't about the hours you spend on your job. It's about the hours you spend mentally checked out. I don't know . . . it," he sticks his hands in his pockets, "it feels like you don't want to be in a relationship with me. I don't know. Or maybe you don't know how."

That stings. I can't help myself from rearing back—both angry with him and myself. "That's a bit patronizing."

"Sorry. I don't know. Maybe we're just not compatible like we used to be. Maybe I thought this was more special than it was." Alex glances at the floor.

"It's not you. And you're not wrong about . . . some of it." I look up at him, weighing his words. The truth of the matter is, he's not what I want. He never has been. I just can't say that to his face. "Maybe you're right. We're . . . not compatible, and we've been trying to make something work that wasn't meant to."

Alex pinches his lips and nods. His dark eyes feel colder than usual; even his stance is closed off. "Well, I guess there's no use dragging this out."

My heart sinks a few inches, and I nod. "We still friends?" I ask.

He shakes his head. "No offense, Taran. I don't need more friends. And I don't really want to stand by and wait, hoping that one day you'll appreciate me. I just can't. I don't hate you,

I hope you know that. Actually, despite everything, I think you're one of the greatest women I've ever dated."

Ouch. Don't say that. Tell me I'm a witch with a capital "B." Tell me you hope I die in a pit of boiling oil. Tell me you can't wait to be with other women because I never made you happy. Tell me anything except that.

Alex smiles. "Good luck with everything." He holds out his arm, welcoming me into a casual hug. I take it, and nearly regret it. I can feel his energy shaking and because of that, he only holds me for a brief amount of time then steps back with a twitch.

"Bye."

I wave weakly and the one thought that trickles through my mind is, *another one bites the dust.*

What is that? I ask myself. Strike ten? Fifteen?

I collapse down into my office chair and close my eyes. I can't even keep a relationship going. How in the world am I supposed to find Bryden, search for a magic object, figure out a prophecy, and possibly fight to end the battle of Hexens?

I chuckle lightly to myself and look up at the ceiling. I never thought I'd be asking myself that question. Maybe that's just the way it is. How it's meant to be.

Out of the corner of my eye I see the last remaining things I haven't yet packed. The rune stone, my cell phone, and my personal grimoire. Although, it's more of a doodled-on notebook that I haven't looked at in over seven years compared to the pristine leather-bound copy *Mórai* keeps in her possession.

My eyes flicker to the stone sitting next to it. The runes and symbols stare back at me. There are two hands there. Not just mine. Despite *Móraí's* warning, something tells me I won't be completely alone.

* * *

"You're not ready to *tiaseal*," *Móraí* said the day I left her, rehearsing spells and writing down incantations. To *tiaseal* is to travel, or appear, from one place to the next. The closest comparison would be to "apparate" a term invented by a fictional sensation that trivialized, in many ways, the real world of the hexen craft. Don't get me wrong, though. It's a *fantastic* work of fiction. I simply can't let *Móraí* know I think that.

Although I should be advanced enough at my age to be able to travel without the aid of technology, I've let my skills slip. So now I grab the notch of the airplane window cover and lift up. Tired muscles, puffy eyes, a sore back, and dry skin. That's what I get for neglecting my craft. Even so, all of that can't steal the beauty looking back at me. The British landscape sails below, the moors stretched out beneath a golden pink sunset and roads with insect-sized cars all driving on the wrong side of the road.

The airplane lurches, kissing the ground and the air roars over the wings. The man next to me elbows my arm for the fifty-third time since we boarded, hastily trying to gather up his bag and coat. Perhaps sitting next to him wouldn't have been so bad sans the smell of salami and cigarette smoke.

Allowing the other passengers to exit, I finally reach for

my own satchel, squished under the seat in front of me before slinging it over my shoulder and getting the hell out.

Baggage claim is an absolute disaster. Passengers from three other flights are pushing forward to find their own bags.

"Excuse me," I whisper, catching the eye of the woman next to me. I smile I step forward, lashing my hand around my suitcase which—thanks to my DNA—just happens to be the next bag to enter the carousel.

With a smooth turn, more so in my mind than in reality, I crash into a man who'd been barreling in my direction. His cell phone flies out of his hand and snaps against the tile floor. Even without flipping the gold-colored phone over, I know the glass is broken. I think there's a charm to fix it, but I don't dare attempt it with this crowd, and the stranger so close to me.

"I'm so sorry!" I gasp repeatedly, trying to situate my own bag, and lean over for his phone. "My apologies, I didn't even see you there," I repeat.

"Dammit, woman! Are yeh kiddin' me?" he responds with a heavy Irish accent, beating me to his phone and standing up. "Are yeh an eejit? Can yeh not walk straight?"

"*Excuse* me?" I cower back, offensively. "It was an accident. I'm sorry for that, but if anyone can't walk straight, it's you."

The man scowls back at me with rich amber eyes. His black hair is slicked back, shaved tight on the sides, and everything about his clothing (estimated $500 denim jeans, and a $90 Kanye West white t-shirt) screams to me that he's more of a wealthy playboy than educated gentleman.

He opens his mouth a second time and my initial assessment is proven correct.

"Why's that? Because you're the queen of England and everyone should kiss your arse? I know yeh may not understand this; I've been workin' my own arse off and I'm not in the mood to have my phone shattered on the ground by some stupid screamin' bitch."

He flips the phone around. Spider web cracks have traveled across the screen, making it nearly unreadable.

"Shite," he says. "You understand that this is a £3000 phone, right? I may piss money, but I don't like to just flush it down the shitter."

"I'm sorry," the words ooze sarcastically. I attempt to take a calming breath to control my words, "are you trying to intimidate me with your crass vulgarity and your over-bloated pounds? Or are you always just an ignorant prick?"

"Go to hell." He turns around and crams the phone into his back pocket before stomping out of sight, his expensive leather messenger bag slung over his shoulder.

I roll my eyes and stride forward with my bag rolling behind me. I didn't even have a chance to mutter a curse before he disappeared. Now, *that* hex would have been worth it. I would have had a good one for him, too.

"You go to hell," I whisper to myself, heading toward the exit doors and angrily tucking my jacket under my arm. "Overcompensating . . . I'd like to shove sandpaper right up your fu—"

"Whoa, Taran," a warm American voice addresses me. "I

sure hope you're talking to someone else with that kind of language."

I look up to see Pete. His blonde hair is mussed, and his eyes are wide headlights. Just like I remember him, he's wearing his Harvard t-shirt and a pair of very cheap jeans and sneakers. While his father may have paid for his college tuition, Pete fancied himself more of the thrift store type. I don't think he's updated his wardrobe since I saw him in grad school.

I sigh and smile, embarrassed. "Fff-uun loving smile," I falsely complete my sentence. "Pete. It's so good to see you."

"Geeze," he says, leaning forward for a hug. "I take it your flight didn't go well?"

"Actually, compared to what I just went through, I'd go through Mr. Salami Cigarette fifty times over."

"Who?"

I wave my hand, dismissing the issue. "Oh, don't worry about it. I don't want to talk about him."

Pete leans forward, his blue eyes sparkling, and takes my bag from me. "Are you reluctant to tell me about what has you cursing like a Russian submarine commander?"

While we walk to guest parking, I rehearse the entire story with the phone idiot and then stop dead in my tracks. Pete unlocks a rusted bucket of metal and throws my bag into the trunk.

"What's this?"

"This handsome devil is a 1979 Volkswagen Golf. My car." He smiles.

"I don't think I can call this a car. What happened to the Beemer you drove around in college?"

"My dad's car? That piece of junk was nothing compared to this."

I skew my eyebrows and grimace.

"Okay, fine." He shrugs. "He's a little rough. That just makes him a true European classic, right?"

"Or a European landmine. The driver door is blue."

"So?"

"The rest of the car is rusted out. And red. You really drive around in this?" I adjust the bag on my shoulder.

"What?" he smiles, opening what would be the driver's side door for me—if we were still in the states.

I step forward tentatively and look inside. The plastic seats are cracked and torn, their foam showing and yellowed while large holes have been gouged out with someone's fingers, or a stick. A dark stain coats the passenger-side floor, and garbage from three months' worth of street food litters the rest of what I can actually see.

"You couldn't clean it up either?"

"You're my friend, not my mother." His eyebrows rise.

"What if the engine sparks?" I grin. "All that garbage. It's just kindling."

"Get in the car, Grim," he growls.

Showing Pete just how sickened I am with the expression on my face, I slide carefully into the seat, hugging my bag to me. I'm afraid if I rub up against anything, I might just catch a disease.

Pete sighs and slams the door closed on me. He gives me a wink after he climbs into the driver's seat and starts the car.

"By the way, whatever happened to your 'gender theory?'" I ask, narrowing my eyes.

"Gender theory?"

"Wasn't it you who once said, 'A man's car is his woman?' I could have sworn you just referred to this rust trap as a he."

Pete nods, the memory dawning on him. "Ah, yes. Well, you see, Clifford has a twisted tailpipe. It kind of hangs down between his hind wheels back there."

"Pete," I look at him. "You're thirty-three, a husband, and a doctoral graduate."

"Your point?" He turns out of the airport parking lot.

"My point is, aren't you a little too grown up to be referring to car parts as genitals?"

"Taran, first of all, a man is never too old for genital jokes. And second, this is *my* car. Not my dad's, not my wife's. Cassie says I can do whatever I want with it. At least I know how to loosen up."

I chuckle. "Believe me, it's been a long time since I've loosened up. That doesn't mean I still can't throw drinks back faster than you ever could."

Pete's eyebrow arches and he gets a look of intrigue and competition flashing through his eyes. "Care to make a bet on that one?"

"Deal."

Pete pushes harder on the gas, speeding through what looks like run-down English countryside complete with graffitied building shells and brick walls covered in moss and ivy, getting us to the St. Pancras Hotel nearly five minutes faster. When we pull into the drop-off zone, I find myself pressing my nose against the glass to get a full view of this old gothic building. The towers, the lights, and the spirit surrounding it are absolutely breathtaking. The dark red facade casts a sense of wealth with its gray towers, arched windows on every floor, and golden light spilling from them.

Even though the streets and the neighboring St. Pancras station is flooded with people, it's magical.

Damn. Trip Advisor was right about this one.

"All right," Pete says behind me. "Here's the deal, Grim. You go inside, check in, put on your sexiest number and be back down here in an hour. Cassie and I are going to show you how to party. London style."

I glance back at him with a laugh and throw open the door. "You've got yourself a very weird date."

After helping me with the remainder of my bags, Pete speeds off again, the engine clanking the entire way out of the hotel drop-off zone and down the busy street. The immediate waft of car exhaust fills my lungs, with a touch of cold night air. Additional food smells, cigarette smoke, and inland English air swirl together in a cacophony of oddly comforting scents.

I turn and enter the hotel. After checking in, performing a quick cleansing spell over my living area, and showering, I slip into the nude stilettos and one nice dress I packed. The amethyst sequin fabric plunges low in the front, and rests on my skin with its lined silk. With a snap of my fingers, my hair forms into loose waves, my bangs draping the tops of my violet eyes. After finishing off the look with smoky eye shadow and deep violet-tinged lips, I realize I don't have any jewelry to go with this dress.

"Oh, crap."

A summoning could work. After all, it's only for the night, and it can't be the worst thing in the world. Since hexen magic pulls from the surrounding elements, and creations, a fully formed and crafted jewelry set can't just appear out of nowhere. I'll have to get it from somewhere.

From within the side folds of my suitcase, I pull out the three crest candles I brought and set them on the dresser top in my hotel room. After waving my hand over them, the wicks illuminate and I motion for the electric lights to power off. I step in front of the large mirror, the glow of the candles shining in the soft darkness, and close my eyes. I form an idea in my mind. A set of chandelier earrings and a drop necklace. Simple, with a statement to make. Then, I whisper the words, "*Áilleacré. Dekore mi.*"

Cold dewdrops of metal slink around my neck, and a feeling of fringe falls from my earlobes. When I open my eyes, I look at the borrowed jewelry. Where it's come from, I have no idea. That doesn't mean it's not perfect.

I take a deep breath. Mom would have killed me for this. It is a special occasion, and by morning, they'll both be returned to their original owner.

Over on the bed my cell phone rings and I whip around. Grabbing it off the comforter, I see Pete's name on the front.

"Are you here?" I ask.

"You bet your sweet tush we are."

I chuckle. "I'll be right down."

I hang up and take one last look at myself before taking up my black clutch and hurrying to the hotel lobby. I catch a final glimpse of myself in the reflective brass panel in the elevator and smile. I need this. Between everything with Alex, the rune stone, finding out about Dad, *Mórai*, and the prophecy . . . whatever it is . . . I need this time. I need to pull myself away from all the complications of magic and my love life before I sink inside and get swallowed up.

The doors open and my heels click on the decorative tile until I turn the corner. Pete turns around at my approach and his eyes widen. "Holy flip, Taran."

I take in his black slacks, shoes, and navy-blue V-neck t-shirt. At least he's not in his traditional torn jeans and sneakers. He actually cleans up quite well.

"Holy 'flip,' yourself, Mr. Evans."

He smiles, dimples forming in his newly-shaven cheeks. "Should we get this party started?" Pete offers his arm and I loop mine in his, a sly smirk slowly forming on my lips.

"I thought you'd never ask."

After greeting Cassie, and chatting for a few minutes, the drive to the club doesn't take long. When all three of us pull up to the club in Cassie's slick Mercedes, the valet looks at us and holds out his hand.

"Treat her well," Pete's younger wife says to the man to whom Pete tosses his keys. Her platinum white hair is stylized into a fauxhawk while her silver earrings sparkle against the city lights each time she moves her head.

Pounding music thrums in my ears and Pete walks his wife up to the bouncer. "Hey, Kamal!"

The large man, whose arms are easily the size of my waist, nods at us and gives what looks like a smile. After stepping aside, he allows us to walk right through.

"He's a student of mine from two years ago," Pete whispers in my ear.

"Student?"

He nods. "I taught three years of lower level British History at the University. He got the highest grade in the class. Come on. You, are going to love this," he says to me, grabbing his wife's hand tightly. The music vibrates in my bones before we even enter the main club area. Up on the walls are illuminated windows with the silhouettes of dancers moving in time with the music, whipping their hair and bracing the walls around them.

The decor combines an edgy modern luminescence with homages to England's past. The walls are sparsely lit with areas of fluorescent wavy steel tiles that curve in and out from each other. Giant oval columns of etched glass feature modern artistic coats of arms, backlit by a ruby-red neon glow at the top and base. Other ancient patterns are etched into the surrounding ceiling edges, illuminated by white neon lights.

Pete swaggers to the bar and leans toward the bartender. "One Guinness—on tap, a Pinot Blanc, and—" he turns to me.

I smile at him. "Guinness for me too."

"Another Guinness for the lady," Pete finishes.

"I wondered if we'd see you tonight!" a booming voice travels over my head and I turn around. A tall brown-skinned man stands behind me, his arm around a woman not much younger than myself. Her eyes are made up very dark and her red glittering top turns the color of blood under the red neon lights. With honey blonde hair and a bright red lip stain, she looks absolutely killer. The man with the giant voice has a jawline that's wide and sharper than a knife. He must be nearly six-foot-six. His black pants, sharp black shirt, and pristine gold watch tell me he's not just another clubber.

"Garrit!" Pete turns around and hands me my glass while holding his own beer in his other grip. The men share a handshake and Pete extends his hand toward me. "I'd like you to meet a friend of mine. This is Dr. Taran Grim. From California. She and I attended Harvard together."

Garrit, holds out his free hand and takes mine. "It's a pleasure, doctor." His Scottish accent is thick.

"Garrit runs this club," Pete shouts over the music, which has now changed in tempo and hands me my bottle of beer. "This is his girlfriend, the lovely and intelligent, Emilia Donovan."

She and I exchange smiles. Like a bolt of lightning, the realization of what Pete just said nearly knocks me off my feet. "It's good to meet you. Did Pete say your last name is Donovan?" I ask lowering the glass from my lips.

"Yes," she grins, answering with a distinct Irish accent. "Have we met?"

"No. I know it's a little farfetched, seeing how Donovan is probably a much more common last name, but you wouldn't happen to know a Michael Donovan, would you?"

A dark look passes over her face and she narrows her eyes. "How do yeh know my da?"

"He's your father?" My eyes widen. "Well, according to Mr. Donovan," I glance at Pete and then back at Emilia, "he said he had a contact here in the city that told him I could help with some research. He met up with me in Stanford just a couple weeks ago. I work at the university there and he came looking for some professional help."

Emilia rolls her eyes. Her jaw shifts. "He definitely needs professional help." Then she glares at Pete. "Evans, I told yeh not to help him."

I turn on my friend. "It was you?"

"*Donovan*," he responds in the same tone Emilia used, in a mocking fashion, "I told you I'm only a professor. I don't get tied up in your family drama. And yes," he faces me, "I happen to think you're brilliant and if anyone could have answered his questions, you could."

Emilia purses her lips and shakes her head. "I'm surprised he traveled all the way to the states." Quickly, she changes expressions and smiles. "I'm sorry. It's him, not you."

"Emi," Pete jumps in again with a glint in his eye, glancing at me while I lift my glass for another drink. "Where's Coll? Is he coming tonight?"

"Who's Cole?" I ask.

"My idiot brother." She waves her hand. "His full name is Collens."

"Oh," I nod. "Coll . . . not C.O.L.E."

Emilia nods with a soft smile. "Sounds the same, I know. Anyway, I don't think he'll make an appearance tonight. If he does, he'll be horrid. Apparently, while Collens was at the airport, some lady practically plowed him over because she wasn't payin' attention and broke his cell phone while she was luggin' around all of her shite."

I gag on the beer I'm part-way through and try to spit what I can back into the glass.

"Whoa, Taran! You doing all right?"

I set the glass on the bar, nodding, and with my back to the other three, cough the remaining liquid out of my lungs.

"Are yeh makin' the ladies sick already, Peter? I thought they didn't normally vomit until after yeh shared your pirate joke."

The deep familiar voice, now playful and friendly, doesn't seem to erase the fact that less than two hours ago, the same voice bellowed at me in the middle of baggage claim. I quickly gain composure and hand the glass back to the bar tender. "I need something stronger," I groan to him. "Scotch, please."

"Where have you been?" Emilia exclaims.

"Finishing up a meeting with Adrian."

"At the London Crown?"

He mumbles an affirmative hum.

"Coll," I hear Pete say underneath the pounding of the club

music, "this is an old friend of mine from my graduate years. Taran Grim."

The bar tender hands me my glass and I slowly turn around, keeping a solid, composed, and equally pissed-off look on my face. When Collens Donovan gets a good look at me, his smile fades, and even in the dark, I can see his pale ivory skin flash red.

"Or as Coll likes to call me, 'stupid bitch.' But maybe that's just a term of endearment for him."

"You two know each other?" Pete asks, his own smile flickering.

"Do you want to tell the story, or should I? I'm sure your sister would be interested in hearing the other half. You know, the half that's not completely fictitious."

Coll's dark eyes narrow on me, his mouth curving at the edge.

"You're the woman at the airport?" Emilia exclaims, pulling away from Garrit's side.

I stare Coll down, slowing drinking my scotch, daring him to retell his story that makes him look like the poor victim.

He stares right back, until his eyes glance to my necklace and earrings. "Say, Emi, don't yeh have a jewelry set like that?"

Briefly derailed, the conversation turns. Emilia looks at my conjured necklace and earrings and squints. "I do! The same exact set! Where did yeh get yours? I thought Rabi was the only designer who made those!"

"And you bought those in Alexandria, didn't you, Emi?" Coll leans against the bar, holding up a finger and ordering a Lagavulin.

"Yeah, about two years ago. Have yeh been there before?" she asks.

I try to hide the irritation in my eyes and I smile. "No."

Coll looks smug, yet confused. As if he's trying to study a cornered animal.

"So, how did yeh . . ."

". . . my mom. She purchased them for me and shipped them to Stanford for my birthday."

I look back at Coll. He scans the yellow bandage-dressed-body of a woman next to him. Her bleach blonde hair keeps falling down her silicone cleavage.

Coll grins and bites on his lower lip before buying her a drink. Pervert.

"So, how are you liking London so far?" Garrit asks.

"What?" I ask, my gaze still locked on the game of silicone vs. testosterone next to me.

"Is it your first time here?"

I turn my head. "In London? Yes. However, I spent three years in Bristol and Northern Ireland back during my doctoral years."

Emilia notices my distraction and I can tell she's scrutinizing me. "What brings you here?"

"Historical research. I'm working on a . . . project. Well," I correct myself, "I guess it's more like family history research."

"Really?" Garrit looks intrigued and he squeezes Emilia closer against him. "What are you looking for?"

"Yes," Pete jumps in. "What are you looking for? You never told me."

I chuckle and brush my hair back. "Well, have you ever heard of *Gungnir*?"

Pete smiles. "Of course."

"What is that?" Cassie asks.

"*Gungnir* is the key to world domination." Coll, who has been relatively uninvolved since the plastic doll arrived, switches his attention back to me, and brushes off the woman's hand that's desperately trying to pull him back to their conversation.

"Actually, that's not entirely correct. The legends of the weapon claim it will be the tool used by Odin to battle Fenrir. A pagan bedtime story to scare children." Knowing this man is the son of Michael Donovan, I can't let them know their father's search is being tailed by my own. "It's a symbol. A caveat to let mankind know that their hunger for god-like power will be their own downfall."

"Or so the legends would have yeh believe." He reaches out and takes a drink of his whiskey and rests the glass lazily in his right hand.

His hand. My gaze catches on something on his palm.

"So what does this have to do with your family history?" Pete asks.

The music in the club diminishes to a fuzzy muffled beat in my ears, I can barely even make out the words Pete's mumbles. All I can focus on is the scar I briefly saw. Only, no . . . it's not a scar. It's a birthmark. A straight line runs from the bottom of Coll's pinkie to the bottom of his thumb.

It's the same hand I saw on the rune stone. It's him.

SIX

"NO!" I HISS, SLAMMING THE BATHROOM DOOR
open. I reach out for the sink to turn the water on and splash
cold water on my face. Then the automatic function on the
faucet turns the water back off. Before looking at myself in the
club's bathroom mirror, I take a deep breath and let it out.

Not. Him. *Anyone*, but him.

Collens Donovan, the son of Michael Donovan, the man
looking for my family's staff. Coll has the imprint of the cross
on his hand?

Obviously, it must be a coincidence. It has to be. It's not
possible that Coll's hand is the same one painted on that set of
runes I've been scrutinizing since Michael brought them into
my office over a week ago. I chuckle at myself in the mirror.

"Oh-ho-ho," I shake my finger at myself. "You're all very
slick. But your sense of humor sucks," I whisper, whether or
not Dad and the rest of the ancestors are listening to me.

Michael Donovan has to know about the symbols. It was his
stone to start with. If that's the case, he'd know his son's hand
features the male entity on it, and he must have seen the female
element on my own, unless I'd managed to hide it well enough.

I shake my head. I shook Michael's hand when I met him. He would have easily seen it. I think I even remember him looking at my hand before he took it.

It has to be the reason he showed me the rock in the first place.

The door to the bathroom opens and I whisper, "*Gransui*," drying the water off my face and instantly fixing the damage to my makeup where my mascara melted into smeared ribbons on my cheeks. I look up to see Emilia walking in. In the harsh lights of the bathroom, I see just how crystalline and brilliant she looks.

"Taran? Are you all right? You looked like you saw a ghost, then bulldozed your way through the crowd."

I manage a smile. "Maybe your brother was right about me."

She frowns, confused.

"The airport. I bulldozed him over there too, obviously," I add sarcastically, "too selfish to politely move around anyone or act like a decent human being." I shake my head when I notice her looking at me like I'm insane. "I'm kidding."

Emilia smiles and nods. "Between you and me, I'm sure he was textin' some woman he'll hook up with in the next couple days and then never speak with again. You probably did him a favor. Her as well." Her eyes even smile. For a moment, she's silent, most likely trying to understand this strange woman standing in front of a mirror with water dripping down the sides of the sink.

"Are yeh all right?" she asks again.

I nod, brushing my bangs out of my face. They have the

perfect ability to appear in my eyes, tickling my eyeballs and making me water up at the most inappropriate moments.

Emilia takes the irritated tears to be emotional waterworks and steps closer. "Are you sure?"

I wipe the water away from my eyes, smearing my eyeliner, and chuckling. "Oh, yeah, it's just . . ." I catch myself, trying to search for the perfect excuse for why I'm crying and storming away in the same night, "I'm on my period." I shrug. "You know how it goes. You're up, you're down, and to make matters worse, I think I'm actually bleeding through my tampon." I groan, feigning my frustration, while actually allowing my real anger to seep through. "Maybe I ought to just go home."

Emilia's face changes from confusion and concern to genuine understanding. "I know what you mean. I'll tell yeh a secret. If you stop by the coffee shop two blocks down, they're still open. Their mix box of pastries will cure any mood issues you're havin'. Trust me. Garrit brings me a box every month. Of course, I do have to warn yeh that you'll put on ten pounds each time yeh eat it, so . . . watch out for that."

I laugh and sigh. "Thank you. Can you tell the group I'm going to head back to my hotel? Just make up a believable excuse for me. I have a headache or something. Pete will tease me, which is something I'm willing to deal with."

Emilia smiles and nods. "Of course I will. Do yeh need a ride? Garrit has his driver available for yeh. If yeh need it, I mean."

"I couldn't ask you to do that."

"Please, it's my pleasure. You've had a rough day. Between

my brother's shite attitude and now this—believe me, I understand."

I nod. "Thank you."

The back seat of Garrit's private car is more luxurious than my bed. Leather seats that swallow you whole, a mini bar, and a television built in. Though, none of it matters. The entire ride to the hotel, my forehead rolls back and forth against the warm glass while I watch the darting lights of the city shoot by like neon streamers.

I have to go back to my room and look through the files Zain sent me. There has to be something in the archives that details what my relevance to the prophecy is. Anything that important would have been documented by a pagan leader. Perhaps even something that can disconnect Coll Donovan from the equation.

The driver drops me off at the front of the hotel and I slowly walk inside, the tapping of my stilettos on the tiles cutting into my ears like a dull metronome.

Once in my room, I reverse the spell I used to borrow what seems to have been Emilia's jewelry, and change into the powder blue satin shorts and camisole I brought. Lounging on my bed, I pull open my laptop and search for the email Zain sent to me the day I met Michael.

The email has a link, which takes me to a cloud server of the university's, and I'm able to find the files that Zain held aside for me. There are three files all together each containing nearly a hundred gigs of information.

Curses. I'd better get started.

I open the first file. For two hours, I search through photographs of hieroglyphic wall art, carefully examining photos of excavations and ancient pagan weapons and shields, and studying references to other historical rune stones. Zain even included references to books we have in the department, all of which I make note of. I'll need to have him send me digitized versions. Especially Fowden's *The Anglo-Saxon Hermes: A Historical Approach to the Late Pagan Mind,* one of the books I constantly found myself studying during my doctoral years. I just don't remember anything in it mentioning the hands and the partial cross of Woden. Though, seeing that it showed up in Zain's search, it must mean it's been catalogued for some reason.

I bite into my lip and continue looking through the files. There are research excavations to Copenhagen, Jutland, even the Black Forest in Germany, and the list goes on and on.

I reach for my cell and quickly make a call. It rings three times before there's an answer.

"Taran? Why are you calling me so late at night? Isn't it like midnight over there?"

"Zain, are you still at the university?"

He groans. "Maybe. Maybe not. You realize I have a life, don't you?"

"No, you don't. If I know you like I think I do, you're still sitting in front of your computer in archives with a half-drunk mug of black coffee—it's five o'clock and you should be heading home, so only God knows why—and your shirt tail's untucked."

There's silence on the other end for only a few moments. "I'll have you know the cup is full. I just filled it."

"I need you to do something for me."

"What?" he nearly whines.

"I need you to send me links to all of these books you sent me."

"The entire library? You know I can't. They're not all digitized."

"I know. Just send me what you can."

Zain grumbles again before agreeing.

"Perfect." I give him the list, including Fowden's book and two others that have been published more recently. "See if we have those. Would it also be possible for you to include more information on the excavations of the burial grounds of Jutland back in 1979?"

"Sure thing. You know, it's a good thing I like you so much."

"I wouldn't take advantage of you like this if you didn't." I smile. "Can you have that sent to me in the next five minutes?"

"I'll upload them to the same cloud server. You can just pull them off there."

I thank Zain again and end the call, my fingers returning to my laptop. After a few minutes, I return to the file link and find the newly added files, opening them up and beginning a search for the symbol that's been haunting me since Michael arrived at the university.

My father's death, Mr. Donovan and his rat bastard of a son, our birthmarks, and all of this aligning at the same time. It's all connected. If I could just find out the entirety of the prophecy; get ahead of what I already know.

I minimize the current screen and start scrolling through the records detailing the 1979 excavation. Pictures, notes, findings. My fingers flit over the keys and then finally I see it. Zooming in toward an image of a man with sunglasses, I look at the chunk of rock in his hand. While the man isn't familiar, the rock is. It's the same chunk that Michael brought to me in the museum.

I reach my hand out to the side. "*Áilleacré.*" The replicated stone appears in my hand, having left its secure place in my suitcase. Holding up the rock to the screen and comparing the two, I find that they're indeed the same rock. Checking the footnotes to the image would give me a detailed run down of all the symbols, all of the notes the archeologists made when they catalogued the piece. I scan the references, my eyes burning through the screen, and pause.

Wait. Where is it?

I start at the top of the list again and scroll down with my finger. It's not here. Nobody ever catalogued it.

I search through the list of the artifacts and pieces listed in the findings to see how in the world this piece of antiquity never found its way into the record.

"Everything else was sent to the University of London under the direction . . ." I search through the text, "of Dr. Christian Scholtz. The library."

Pete would know. I'm going to have to see to see him again tomorrow.

I save the file pages to my laptop and continue looking through the books. After about two hours, I summon my reading glasses—a rescue effort to save my eyeballs that are now so exhausted I can barely see straight. I continue. The search results tell me which pages in the books reference unusual hand symbols. I go to those pages first. It isn't until I pull open Simon Turner's *Ancient Norse Paganism: Symbols and Mysteries of the Old Tribes* that I find myself staring directly at a vivid image of the symbol I'm looking for.

Two hands, clasped together with the unfinished cross of Odin imprinted in their skin. The only difference is both hands grip a long stick between them, their fingers nearly intertwined. The more I look at and study the symbols I realize that with the stick—"*Craniarann,*" I say to myself—with the staff, the cross is complete. One circle, which represents me. One vertical line, representing *Craniarann*. And one horizontal line—Coll Donovan.

I run my eyes down the page until I see the mention of the symbol and I begin to read slowly.

"Only recently have historians become aware of a symbol whose use is so rare it's only been noted on fewer than half a dozen findings. The 'Hand Cross' is represented with two hands embraced in a simple clasp. Though research has not been solidified, the meaning of the symbol is still being debated among those who have studied its depiction. Some believe the included fragmentary cross is merely the depiction of a man and woman in ancient historical accounts that may have been significant members of pagan society. Others believe it may have deeper, more spiritual, or richer prophetic meaning to the religious dogmas of the ancient world. One such meaning has been put into context by . . ." my words die in my throat. "Dr. Alaric Grim."

Dad?

Dr. Grim believes the Hand Cross tells of a legendary future event where a prophesied pair born with the mark of the parts of the cross will be instrumental in securing the location of the fabled Gungnir—*the weapon wielded by Odin during Ragnarok. According to Grim's studies, the seers of various tribes foretold the coming of a time when the heir of Odin, and not Odin himself, and the heir of Fenrir would unite in preventing what the world now calls* Ragnarok, *and the pair depicted in the Hand Cross would render the power necessary to either facilitate or decimate the army of Fenrir.*

"In at least two accounts depicting the appearance of the Hand Cross, the tale of *Gungnir* is rehearsed in detail. What makes these accounts unique are the mentions of prophecy, meaning the tale is not one of the past, but one of the future. While ancient pagans deeply delved into the history of their gods, they were obsessed with the future, including their lives after death and facilitating communion with the gods in Asgard."

I click through to the next page, hoping to find more. Instead, it quickly moves onto describing other rare hieroglyphics.

My fingers rest on the keyboard, the tips becoming colder, my breath stiller.

The power necessary to either facilitate or decimate the army of Fenrir. What does that even mean?

Two accounts depict the mention of *Gungnir* in future prophecy.

I hit the return button and read back to see if that line referenced any other citations or studies. A minuscule number fifty-two and fifty-three float on the page at the end of the mention of the accounts and I make a note of the books it mentions. One is a reference to a rune stone photocopy and the other to the tomb of an unmarked tribe leader. Of course, neither are included in the gigantic sum of files Zain sent to me.

Great.

I sit up straight and pop out the stiffness in my spine. It's not a lot of information. Still, it's more than I used to know. Dad really did investigate this piece of history, that much is certain.

The air conditioning blasts back on again and the air begins to move once more.

My eyes slowly graze back to the laptop screen, my focus running over the words again. My father spent most of his life researching this. *Craniarann*, the hand cross. Years and years of study. I need his books. I need his research. Without it, I don't know what the hell I'm doing.

Then, another thought hits me.

Dad recognized my birthmark the moment he saw it. *Mórai* confirmed it. Perhaps his attempt to hide me the day he died was not merely a choice he made to protect his daughter. Maybe it had been more than that. For him, he wasn't just protecting his daughter, he was protecting the knowledge of my existence.

In a stretch of reality, he was also protecting Coll, someone he also believed existed, even if he didn't know him.

A bubbling discomfort rolls in my stomach the moment reality hits and I want to swallow it down. No matter how hard I try, I can't shake the feeling. I need to see Coll Donovan in private.

SEVEN

THE BRIGHT MORNING SUN COATS THE CITY OF
London in a brilliant golden glow. I step out of my hotel into
the bright sun rays, resting the strap of my leather satchel over
my shoulder and greeting the cab that's arrived to pick me up.

"Where to?" the driver asks me.

"Senate House. Malet Street."

Gripping my cell phone, I duck into the cab and pull my
satchel over my lap. Cars, busses, vans, and various bicycles
are already out in full force. The clouds in the sky are turning
a dark gray, and threatening to split open and ruin this perfect
morning. They look exactly the way I feel. Dark, heavy, and
coming in unexpectedly from the east. Oddly, that doesn't
stop the glow of the morning from sparkling off the buildings
around me.

I'm too distracted, thinking of everything I researched last
night that I forgot to grab something to eat or drink. It doesn't
matter. I need more answers before I approach Coll, and that
is the only thing on my mind. To walk up to a stranger, who
verbally assaulted me in the airport and is so entirely full of
his own ego, with a simple, "Hey, guess what? That birthmark

you have? I think it means we're supposed to fulfill a magical prophecy. You in?" honestly wouldn't go very far. At best, I predict he'd shove me out of his apartment and get a restraining order. At the worst, he could approach his father about it, and I'm not entirely sure I know enough about the Donovans to trust any of them.

Flipping my phone open, I redial the last number I called and press it to my ear. The man on the other end sighs and responds with a languid, "Yes, Taran?"

"I'll be there in five minutes."

"I figured you would be," Pete answers. "You only said that five times already in various texts and emails. I should be getting off the elevator when you walk in."

"Perfect. See you soon."

When I arrive at the university library, I pay the cab driver in the required British pounds before I step out and jog up the elongated steps before entering the building.

"Taran!" Pete waves at me, stepping out of the nearest elevator. His blonde hair is perfectly brushed back and he's dressed in the signature professorial garb: a navy cardigan with a blazer sporting suede elbow patches. "Good gods, girl. You contacted me nearly ten times this morning. Is everything all right?"

"You have a research room open?"

"Yeah," he nods. "You'll have to tell me specifically what you're researching though. And where in heaven's name did you go last night? Emilia said you had a migraine?"

"Yes," I lie, my bangs falling into my eyes. I brush them

back. "With finals week and everything else I'm researching, it's been a while since I've gotten a decent sleep. They sometimes come and go."

Pete places a hand at the small of my back and leads me back into the elevator. "Well, I hope we can get you answers to at least the 'everything else' today. Come on."

The elevator doors close behind us and Pete eyes me. "Blab, Grim. It's time you really tell me what you're researching."

"I already told you."

He grins. "*Gungnir*? You were being serious about that?"

"What?"

"You came all the way here to research a fictional weapon that's had the crap researched out of it already?"

"Just humor me, Pete. I think I have some new information for you. At the very least, an interesting connection to it."

His eyebrows rise and he reaches out to hold the elevator door open while I step off onto the right floor.

"Follow me." He takes me through a series of display areas where grad students from the university are studying ancient documents on computer screens. "In here."

Pete steps into a large research area with its own bookshelves, cataloging computers, and artifacts on display. After closing the door behind him, he turns, folding his arms. "Okay, now that we know that this is a life and death situation dealing with . . . the weapon of Odin . . . what are you looking for?" he teases.

I set my bag on the nearest table and pull up a tall chair. I have to start at the beginning. I begin with Michael Donovan, his visit to me in California, the stone with the image—with no mention of the mark on my hand—the involvement of my father's research, and everything I found last night. When I finish with the prophecy, Pete nods.

"So, you're doing this as a tribute to your dad? Continuing the work he never finished?"

I glance at the floor. "Mostly. I feel like there are things in his life that I never knew about and now that I've found out how much he . . . was interested in this subject, my curiosity has been piqued. More than that though, The Hand Cross? I have a very strong feeling that the prophecy may not entirely be . . . fictitious."

"Well of course not. To the pagans of the day, these prophesies and revelations, so to speak, were perceived to be real. To them, they weren't just telling stories or hallucinating, they were foretelling truth. Or at least what they observed to be truth."

I nod my head slowly, realizing I'll never really get Pete to understand exactly what I'm saying. "Right. So, you know what I'm . . . talking about. Look, I have to ask, why have we never documented that image before? In all of my graduate studies I never came across this symbol."

"Do you have it on you?"

Reaching into my bag, I slide out my laptop. After opening last night's files, I point to the area of my screen where the symbol appeared on the rune stone in the man's hand. I also pull open my father's explanation of the symbol's history.

"See how the two hands, once joined, form an imperfect

Cross of Odin? And look here, my dad explains this addition which completes the cross, making it the symbol we're more familiar with." I point to the vertical line. The staff. "When combined with the staff, *Gungnir*, we have a complete cross within the circular frame."

"The sun cross."

"Right. So, do you think we've been interpreting the sun cross wrong? I mean, all these years, we thought the sun cross represented the sun and the wheel of the solar deity that these civilizations worshiped. What if we got it wrong, though? What if this is some prophecy of the . . . end of the world? At least a massive battle. An apocalyptic event we call Ragnarok?"

Pete straightens to his full height and places his hands on his hips. He squints, considering what I'm suggesting and then clears his throat. "What do you mean? How can this relate to Ragnarok?"

I explain the pagan symbol that I'd found and lay out the interpretations I've been able to conclude. The female, the male, and *Gugnir* and the weapon's connection to the end of the world, including the explanation from my dad's findings.

"What do you think?"

Pete holds up a finger and then looks me straight in the eye. "Wait right here. I think I have a book that might shed a little more light onto this."

I nod before he leaves the room. It doesn't take more than ten minutes for him to return. In his arms is a large, brown, leather-bound book. The lettering on the cover has been mostly worn off. "What's that?" I ask.

"This," he says, setting the book on the table, "is a book of Celtic pagan rituals and prophesies mainly performed by tribe seers and Druids. All of these recorded by Romans. So, I don't know how much you can really trust the validity of the records, although they do tend to follow a pattern. All of them are organized by region. If there's anything relating to this hand cross, slash, sun cross idea of yours, it would be in here. It was compiled by a bunch of scholars at Cambridge about seventy years ago."

"Is there a section on pagans in the Surrey Hills region?"

His head turns to me out of the corner of my eye. "Here? You mean just outside of London?"

I slowly raise my eyes to him in jest. "Fantastic as you are, I didn't fly thousands of miles to London just to party with you."

He grins. "Are you telling me I'm more of a distraction than help?"

I lightly laugh. "If this book gives me more answers, you're more helpful than you know. I made a list of a few books I really wanted last night, but I don't have access to them."

"Really? What are they? Maybe we have them."

After giving him the name and author of each text, he takes off to search. Taking the book he's already brought, I open it up and flip through to the beginning table of contents to see how the information is organized. Unfortunately, the table of contents is not structured by area.

I flip the pages to the back and search through the index.

Topic.

Keywords.

Region.

"Ah," I say to myself. Dragging my finger through the index. "East of England . . . Bedford, Cambridgeshire . . . Sssssssssssouth East England," I search. "Surrey." I finally find it, turning back through the book until I land on the exact page before reading in my head.

prophecy of Baduhenna

prophecy of the Conquering of the Franks

prophecy of Deireanhexe

prophecy of Ziu

"There!" I point to the third in the list.

The door swings open again and Pete has one book in his arm. "There, what?" he asks.

"The prophecy of Deireanhexe," I explain with a smile.

"I thought you were looking for Ragnarok. Or the Sun cross." He sets the second book down on the table.

"We are." I pull the book around so it's angled toward both of us. When I've got it on the right page, I search through the text. I feel Pete looking over my shoulder. He must be wondering what the hell I'm looking for.

Do you seek the end?

What will become of treacherous weather?

Harsh world, whoredom rife,

Once proud brothers will battle their foe

And defile their bond.

I pause. Once proud brothers. That could be Frec and Ruhmactír. Of course, there's also the possibility that it could be referencing the Ravn brothers, Shíl and Mindier. The likelihood of that is minimal, though. The only reason I think that is because of the Donovans. They're the literal descendants of the Geri line and if they're involved in this, Coll specifically, the odds of the "proud brothers" meaning Frec and Ruhmactír are pretty high.

"Their foe?" I whisper.

"What are you thinking?" Pete asks.

"The Geri's foe were the Grims."

"Who?"

I ignore him and continue reading to myself.

Sisters will clash.

A staff, a sword, a tablet is riven.

A magic age—a wolf age, before the world falls

In the summers that follow.

I frown. Shit. It reads more like modernistic poetry than anything else. Poetic prophecy. Just not the prophecy I need.

I continue scanning through. So far, nothing about the cross. Nothing much about the joining of hands or anything except a slight mention of the "staff" which could be Woden's staff, or it could be a completely different weapon. The brothers . . . after talking about the sacrifice of Rheda, and the death of Woden before coming here, *Mórai* and I talked about the Ravn and the Geri clans, both lead by a pair of brothers. One of the other two clans is involved in this. Which one, I can't say for sure.

"Wait," I whisper, my finger tickling the rough page.

Hexen will battle the invader. The betrayer.

Ruhmactír clashes with his heir and descendant of Woden

who wields the Craniarann.

I guess that answers that question.

In my life, coincidence doesn't exist. Déjà vu, fate, these things are common and often parts of everyday things. Knowing my life doesn't involve coincidences, irony, or mistakes, I'm going to take a wild guess and pinpoint myself as the descendant of Woden. Another wild guess would place the role of Ruhmactír's heir on Coll.

Perfect.

I continue to look, finding nothing more than that. Nothing more than I already knew. I close the book and pinch my lips together, glancing back at Pete. "Which book did you get?"

"Ah!" he lifts his eyebrows. "Unfortunately, the only one we have on hand is the second one compiled by Dr. Grant." He hands me the book and I try to rehearse in my mind which reference included Grant's *Incorporated Collection of Great British History*.

The rune stone photocopy.

"Can I check these out?"

"Taran, these are both held in special collections. We don't check them out."

"Pete, I'm a professor. What am I going to do to them? Tear out pages and roll up a doobie?"

"A doobie? What are you sixty?"

"Pete." I cock my head and let my eyes do the talking.

He sighs. "No."

"Pete!"

"No!"

"All right," I break. "You leave my no choice."

Pete looks dubious. "What?"

I bite my lip nervously, chewing on the skin, then take a breath. "I'm sorry for this, Pete."

"What are you talking about?" He looks confused.

"Freo i nom," I say, waving my hand in front of his face in a fan. Left to right.

"What are you doing?" he frowns and takes a step back.

"Shit!" I whisper, when I realize I said it wrong. I attempt to smile and play it off as a joke. When Pete doesn't get it, looking at me more like a lunatic than a colleague, I roll my eyes and sigh.

"Freo i nomeit." I say correctly this time.

I quickly gather my things, and the book I want, while Pete stands there in a stupor, unaware of anything else happening around him.

I hug my bag and the book close to my body. After a brief search on my cell browser, I memorize the address and hustle out of the room. The moment I leave the library, I hail a cab and I tell the driver exactly where I'm going.

"Please take me to Moon Street 12." I take a breath. "Collens Donovan."

EIGHT

HUGGING MY BAG AND THE BOOKS TO MY CHEST
I look up at the apartment building in front of me. Eight floors
of windows, balconies, and a perfectly clean stone exterior. The
doorman gazes at me from the front entrance, and I can tell by
the look on his face that he's wondering why I've been standing
in the same spot for over five minutes. The truth is, I know I
need to talk with Collens. I just don't want to.

"Miss?"

I look at the doorman again. His thick dark eyebrows
arch, his body language unsure. He stands stiff and almost
leans toward me, questioning whether or not he should offer
assistance.

"Yes?"

"Can I help you with something?" he asks, his cockney
accent skipping.

"I'm here to see Collens Donovan."

"Ah, Mr. Donovan is home. Should I ring his flat?"

I shake my head. "Can I just go up?"

"I'm sorry, no. I can't just let you up without approval."

I take a deep breath and rethink my decision. On the one

hand, I really, *really,* don't want to see him. A part of myself would rather soak my own face in lye. Additionally, what if it gets back to Michael Donovan that I'm talking with his son? I don't even know if Michael should be trusted. Hell, I don't even know if Coll can be trusted. If I don't go up, I could keep looking on my own. Maybe find more answers. But at the same time, I might be putting myself at risk.

Coll is unfortunately part of the prophecy. Even more unfortunately, so am I.

"Okay," I nod, taking a few steps forward until I reach the few concrete stairs that lead up to the front entrance. The patient and confused doorman might even be looking at me with pity now. "Can you tell him Taran Grim needs to talk to him?"

The doorman presses the button for apartment 8A and after a few seconds, a voice responds. "Yeh, Karl?"

"Mr. Donovan, there is a woman here to see you. Her name is Taran Grim."

"Uh . . . nope. I'm sorry, I don't know who that is," he answers. There's just enough lilt to his voice to let me know he's bullshitting.

I sigh, irritation waving over me. I bite at my lip in an attempt to keep from clamping my teeth onto my tongue. "Tell him it's the airport bitch."

Karl the doorman looks questioningly at me and then repeats what I told him.

"Oh," he says with a light chuckle, almost like an egotistical Santa Claus, "right." Coll's voice melts like honey. Entertained, amused that I'm standing at his doorstep. "Send the woman up."

I roll my eyes and then bite down on my lip again. At that, the doorman opens the door for me.

"Elevator is at the end of the hall. Flat 8A."

"Thank you, mister . . ." I wait to hear his last name.

"Davis."

"Mr. Davis," I repeat. I reluctantly trudge to the end of the hallway where I find a brass elevator. After pressing the up button and riding it to the top floor, I step out, only to find I'm now standing directly in Coll's apartment.

The penthouse?

I look around the entry to the living room and find myself standing in a thousand-square foot room. It's decorated with wide black leather couches circling a blob-shaped coffee table that looks like some gum I might have stepped in once. Candles litter the center, unlit, while three large screen televisions rest on the wall in the place of art. To the north, an entire wall of sky windows that look out over London. A polished Steinway piano resting peacefully in the center.

"Well, well, well," a voice says from above, the Irish lilt saturated with sugar.

My eyes swirl upward to a balcony overlooking the main living area. Coll Donovan stands in the center, wearing only a pair of dark green jogger sweats. Both embarrassed and admittedly a little turned on, I force myself to look away from his chest-hair-outlined pectorals and sharply carved abs. He looks like a ridiculously well photo-shopped Scott Eastwood with darker hair. And he knows it. I glance back up at him and he smiles. In his hand rests a mug, steam floating from the top.

"Miss Grim. Oh, wait, I'm sorry," he corrects himself, even more of his Irish accent oozing out, "I meant *Doctor* Grim, friend of Peter. What can I do for yeh this fine Saturdee mornin'?" Coll lifts the mug to his lips and sips.

"I'm sorry to bother you on a weekend, especially after everything that happened yesterday, but," I try to look anywhere else, anywhere that's not his abs each time he purposely flexes, "I've been doing some research and I think you might be able to help me with something."

"Really? Well, talkin' 'bout yesterdee, I'm not really sure why I should. After all, yeh broke my phone, and then insulted us the night you stormed off from the club."

My eyes slink up toward him, the Matisse copy painting hanging on the north wall moving out of my view. There's more than irritation now. Annoyance? Vexation? Either way, I try hard to let my stare burn into his sockets. "Let's straighten out a couple things here. You ran into *me* as I turned around, as, I'm sure, you sexted with an 'important' one-night stand, your eyes glued to a digital screen instead of the floor where you should have been focused. Second, as I believe Emilia told you, I got sick. I had to leave, and I know it's shocking," the word bursts from my mouth, "that I didn't make a decision based on you, but the fact remains that I—and the general population—don't really care what you think."

The venom saturates my lips. I lick them and look away before something else comes flying out. For a while, Coll simply stands on the balcony overlooking me. Slowly, the corner of his mouth curls up and he chuckles before turning toward a circular staircase that descends into the living area.

"Woman, yeh want a cup of coffee?" he asks.

"No," I bite.

"Tea?" He treads across the carpet toward the kitchen to the west. "I've got Chamomile—"

"No."

"Jasmine—"

"No."

"Earl Grey—"

I pause. "No."

"Uh huh," he mumbles to himself, watching me from the sun-lit kitchen, decorated in white marble and steel. "It's my own blend. Are yeh sure?"

At that, I glance at him and take a deep breath. "I doubt it can come close to my rooibos, but I'll try it."

He looks smugly impressed, his dark eyebrows arched, his lips drawn down for a brief moment. "Thank yeh for lowerin' your standards long enough to grace my tea with your lips." Coll places a teakettle on his stove and turns it on. After preparing his tea leaves in a steeper, he rests a cup near the stove and turns back to me. "So. Are yeh goin' to stand there, or do yeh want to take a few more steps and sit down?"

My feet shift and I clear my throat. "I'll have a seat. Thank you." My face flushes and I walk into the living room. The moment my back is turned, I shake my head discreetly. It's not simply the fact that he's being arrogant and rude. I could handle that. It's more the fact that right now I'm scared. I'm scared of telling him what I know. I'm terrified of being here, and I'm acting like a complete idiot.

In the kitchen, I hear the teakettle start to whistle and it's immediately removed from the stove. Coll mutters something and his voice echoes in the hollow corner of the kitchen.

"What?" I ask.

"Nothin' . . ." his voice is calm. Almost detached. I turn around when I hear him moving toward me. "Here yeh go." Coll offers me the simple white teacup and I gently take it from his hand. Seeing that I've got it steady, he moves around the hard leather seat and relaxes next to me—not even on another seat.

I wrap my hands around the mug and rehearse a charm in my head, lowering the temperature of the tea quickly. At that, I lift it to my lips and drink. I sense a subtle blend of bergamot citrus swirled with rose petals and Indian vanilla. It's good. Too good.

"So, Doctor Grim. What can I do for yeh?"

I take another snip. "I take it you remember what I was talking about at the club the other night. I mean, it wasn't quite as important as what the boobs next to you had to say, but you did manage to pull yourself away from their banter long enough to chime in."

Coll squints at me and takes a drink of his coffee. Prompting me to drink my own tea.

"Yeh said somethin' 'bout *gungnir* and the end of the world. I'm not sure how I can help yeh with that."

I try to glance at his left hand—attempting to see the straight line marked into his palm again—except, he's using that hand to hold the mug. I need to get him to switch hands. I need to make sure I'm talking to the right person, because if I just spit out the revelation that I'm a witch without being absolutely positive, I'll have to freeze two people and run all in the same day. With another drink from the tea, I set the mug on the nearest table and reach over for my bag, which I've set on the floor. From inside, I pull out the rune stone and hold it tight within my palm.

"I don't know if you know this, but your dad came to see me over a week ago. Did you?"

"Did I, what?" He acts more closed off than before. The arrogance is gone, and what's replaced it is a still coolness.

"Did you know?" I try to hold back my irritation. "Know he had come to see me?"

Coll watches me carefully. "No."

"He came, asking about the weapon. I told him it was a legend. A myth."

He shrugs. "So? Do yeh need to get in contact with my da? Is that why you're here? If that's the case, I could have told you to jump in the Thames."

"I take it you don't have a good relationship with your dad? Or is it mommy issues?" I lash out.

Coll's eyes darken and he stands up. "What are yeh?"

"What?" I rear back. "What are you talking about?"

He leans over and sets his coffee on the odd-shaped center table. After waving his hand over the tops of the candles, the wicks ignite in an instantaneous burst of flame.

My mouth, once watering from the rich swirl of flavors in this jerk's tea blend, becomes dry. I slowly swallow, watching the light of the candles dance around. He knows what I am—because he's hexen.

When I look back up at Coll, he's frowning at me and breathing hard. "That should 'ave scared the hell out of yeh. You're a hexen."

"How did you know?"

"I put a spell on the tea."

I slowly look to the mug next to me, wondering what he'd done to it. "What did you do?"

"Nothin', apparently. Human women usually become more," he shifts his jaw, searching for the right words, "affable towards me with that spell."

I rear back, shock and abhorrence leaking into my emotions, and stare at the cup. "Did you magically try to *roofie* me?"

"In a manner of speakin'. Now, what do yeh really want?"

I toss him the stone and fold my arms, liking him less and less by the second. My voice has a vicious bite to it—one I don't even try to hide. "Your dad brought me that. Anything look familiar on it?"

Coll's eyes linger on me before he looks down at the chunk of rune stone. "It talks about the spear of Woden."

"What else?"

His eyes flicker across the rock, trying to find what I'm attempting to point out to him.

"Try looking at the right corner."

It only takes a few more seconds before I feel the tension in the room begin to elevate. He's seen it. He recognizes the symbol in his own hand. By the time he looks back up at me, I have my right hand lifted in the air, the circle on my hand burning white in the center of my ivory palm.

"I recognized you when I saw your palm at the club last night." I nearly stop myself from saying this last part since it steps all over the point I tried to make earlier about not leaving the club because of him. "That's why I left. Coll, I think you and I are part of a prophecy. It . . . pains me to say this, but I need your help."

*   *   *

Coll hasn't moved for the past thirty minutes while I've explained everything I've learned over the last week. Well, everything I'm willing to tell him. He looks off to the side, lets a deep breath out, sets the rune stone on the center table and leaves the room. I watch him casually march up the circular staircase, back across the overlooking balcony and into a room at the west south end of the penthouse. All of this is followed by the closing of a door.

"Okay? I didn't realize we were done." I lean over and grab the stone, grasping it tight while loitering with confusion.

Should I just . . . leave? What if he's gone up to call Michael? Slowly, I drag my feet over to the staircase. I wait a few more moments before grabbing the handrail. Just then, the door above opens and I back away to watch Coll start down again. This time, he's wearing a black t-shirt—obviously having given up seducing me. He pauses halfway down the second he sees me at the bottom of the stairs.

"Five years ago," he says, his voice husky, "I got a package in the mail. A simple envelope. No return address. No sign of who sent it to me. Inside it held a note and this." He holds up a small key.

"What does this have to do with the rune stone?"

"I'm thinkin' . . . a whole hell of a lot. Here's the note." He walks the remaining steps and stops in front of me, holding out a white piece of paper. I take it from him and unfold it. At the top of the page is a symbol I've come to see far too often over the last week: Woden's Cross. My family crest. The handwriting is too familiar. Painfully familiar.

Collens, you don't know me. But, I know you, boy. One day, a hexen woman will approach you, with this symbol. Give her this key, and give her my love.

"Dad," I whisper, recognizing the chicken scratch and the way he always overused commas. "Why . . . why did my dad send this to you instead of me?"

He shrugs. "I don't know. Yeh want it?"

"Yes, please," I say scathingly.

Coll drops the key in my hand. "So, are we done?"

I look back at him. "That's it? What about everything I told you?"

"Look, I know yeh might get into the magic hexen shite all the time. For me it's just a painful memory of my family, so I do everythin' I can to stay out of it. If yeh want to chase after this mythical . . . staff, then please do. Just leave me out of it? Okay, girlie?"

"You know how this works, don't you? Our ancestors didn't just sit down and write fun stories to get a laugh. These things are prophecies and whether you like it or not, you're a part of it."

Coll shakes his head and chuckles. "Not if I don't want to be. And the sooner you get that into your head, the happier you'll be. This is my da's world. And apparently, this is your world. And I mean this with every offense I can muster: I'd rather shove a red-hot poker up my arse before I chose to be associated with either of yeh. Now, if you'll excuse me, I have a lunch appointment with a bank client I need to get ready for. Lift is that way." He motions to the other end of the room.

This time when he leaves me standing alone in his living room, he doesn't come back out. I wait around for about five minutes before I pick up my crap and storm out of the building.

NINE

"EVIE?" I SAY, THE MOMENT I HEAR THE OTHER
end pick up.

"Taran! I heard you were in England! You didn't even tell me
you were leaving!"

I lean back in the café chair I'm relaxing in, studying the key
in front of me. The street is busy with workers leaving their jobs
for lunch and tourists taking a break from their sightseeing and
shopping. All while white billowing clouds temporarily cover
the sun. "Sorry. It was kind of a last-minute decision."

"Well, how is it? A much-needed holiday, right?"

Considering that I've barely eaten or enjoyed a good night's
rest since I got here, I shake my head. "If only," I mutter.

"Ew. That bad?"

"I'm here researching that spear I told you about.
Only . . . I've come to find that it's not a spear. It's a staff, and
my dad is involved somehow. Actually, he's more involved
than I thought, and I'm supposed to stop the destruction of
my hexen kind, and *Mórai* told me all about this prophecy
involving me and this guy, who's the most egotistical shithead
I've ever met, and now I have this key that my dad sent to him,

meant for me, and I have no idea what it goes to, and I'm—" I pause, taking a breath and attempting to calm my mind. "I'm about ready to lose my mind."

After a long awkward pause, she finally responds with, "Well, is that all?"

I sigh, tapping the key on the café table. My vegetarian sandwich is drying out next to me, and all the ice in my sparkling water is melted. A surge of emotion rushes to the surface and I take a deep breath to keep it from overwhelming me.

"I know it sounds childish, and maybe not, I don't know. I just want my dad, Evie. I need his help." I pause, thinking of him, and watching a drop of condensation travel down the side of my ice water. "I miss him."

She goes silent on the other end. Although I hear one of her children scream in the background, she softly responds to me, "I know."

"I mean," I brush a rogue tear from under my eye, "it's been almost twenty-five years since he died. Because of the last three months, though—I just can't unsee it. It's like it all happened last night. It's not enough that I have to watch him die every damn time I fall asleep. Now I find out he left me this key with absolutely no clue as to what it goes to." I growl. "Why did he send it to that idiot, instead of me!?"

"What does the key look like?"

"Small. About two inches long. It's a digital key with laser points on it. Very DaVinci Code looking."

"Send me a picture."

I pull my cell away from my ear and take a picture of the key before messaging it to her. "You got it yet?" I ask, putting the phone to my ear.

"Just did. Hey, darling," she says aside, "does this look familiar to you?"

I hear her husband Josh clearly enough that he must be sitting next to her. "Oh yeah, that's a security deposit box key. All the newest models have digital keys like that. Ask her if there are any other words on it."

A security deposit box? Dad died over twenty years ago. How in the world can he be sending me a modern security key?

Unless of course, maybe he didn't.

I run my hand through my hair, my fingernails clawing into my scalp.

"Taran . . ."

"No," I reply. "No words. Nothing. How . . . how could my dad have sent me this? In 1993 digital laser keys like this didn't exist. *Dammit*. I can't believe he wouldn't help me. Selfish prick."

"Okay, that's the second time you've called your dad a prick or an idiot. Would I be safe in assuming that you're not actually talking about your dad when you do that?"

"No. I'm sorry. It's just that man I told you about." I drop the key on the table and brush my bangs out of my eyes.

"Is this man attractive?"

Coll's face lingers behind my eyes. "Why would you ask me that?"

"It's a legitimate question. So, is he?"

The tiger's eye shade of his irises, the sharp edge of his jaw, and the perverted smirk he sported while his eyes scanned a particular set of breasts last night all come rushing back to me.

"More so when his mouth is shut."

"Taran, you realize you can't go getting crushes on annoying European men. You have your own exotic Latino back here, remember?"

At the mention of Alex, I close my eyes. "Actually, no. I don't," I reply. "And I do *not* have a crush on an annoying European man."

"What? What do you mean? Are you and Alex having problems?"

"Not anymore." I take a deep breath and look up at the cars passing by, the pedestrians chatting. "We broke up."

Evangeline sighs on the other end. "I'm sorry, girl. I didn't realize. I mean you never told me! How could you not tell me something like that?!"

"It's not a big deal. It was mutual. He came to see me the day I left. I think we both realized it wasn't really working. You know, like it usually is with me."

"I guess the good news is you can chase after Mr. Hunky European Man. He is hunky, right?"

"Well, he believes he is." I don't want to talk about Coll. "Look, Evie, I'd rather not spend more time in this country than I have to. Before I can even *start* searching for Bryden, I've got to find out where the hell this key goes. Can I call you again, later?"

"Absolutely! Be safe, love."

I hang up and pick up the key again, examining its surface. Nineteen ninety-three. That's when I watched my dad die while I hid in a cupboard. If he'd made a trip out to England just before that date, I'm looking for a bank that was in business then, and most likely here in London. I tap my cell phone against my bottom lip. I open my home screen and do a quick search on the browser.

"If I were Dad . . . where would I go?"

I look through the list of banks. The Bank of England, London Crown Bank, Alpha Bank London, ICICI, Clydesdale, Citibank. the second one of the list catches my attention. London Crown Bank. Where have I heard that recently?

Then it clicks.

I heard about it at the club the other night. When Coll showed up, he said he'd been with a man named Adrian at London Crown. Dad would have used this sense of déjà vu— this "coincidence"—to direct me to where I need to go. Not just because he's hexen. Because he's my dad. It's what I would do.

I stand, grab my bag, and speed walk toward the nearest bus stop. After a short fifteen-minute ride on the double-decker, I jump off and walk into the main branch of the London Crown Bank. The first thing I see is a rotund reception desk in the center of the lobby with offices to the sides and a teller desk to the right. When I reach the desk, there's a man talking quietly with a young woman, both of them standing in front of the nearest computer screen, pointing and discussing the information glowing across it.

"Excuse me?" I butt in. "Where could I get help with a security deposit box?"

The man stands up and I immediately read his name tag: Adrian Weber. His brown hair is shaved close to his head, though it's thinning on top. Very Jason Statham. His green eyes are a dark olive and his face is thin like a runway model's.

"I can help you with that," he says with a flat expression, just like every other stereotypical stuck-up caricature of the British. "Thank you, Rebbeka." He addresses the young woman and she turns back to her computer to continue working while he steps around the counter and looks me up and down.

"Are you looking to set up a security deposit box?"

"Access one," I say, holding up the key. "Although I'm not sure of the account number. It belonged to my father. He's since passed away. I don't suppose that's an issue, is it?"

"Not at all. We have protocols for instances like this. Please, follow me. We'll get you taken care of."

I follow him to the right until he stops at another side desk and he pulls up a seat for himself while accessing the computer. "Name?"

"It would probably be under Alaric Grim," I say while taking my own seat across from him.

He types in the name and frowns. "I'm sorry, no."

"What about . . . Taran Grim?"

Adrian's eyebrows lift and his gaze slowly moves up toward me. "From America? Taran Grim?"

My accent should have made that obvious. Instead of being snarky, I nod.

"Ah, so you're the woman Coll was telling me about."

"Excuse me?"

"Collens Donovan. He's a friend of mine. I got off the phone with him during lunch. He works here you know. I wasn't expecting you to come into our bank."

"Oh," I say curtly. Great. I storm out of his home and the first person he calls is the one person available to help me. I'd rather not know what bullshit he tried to toss on Mr. Weber here. Knowing how he likes to spin stories to his advantage, I can only guess how Adrian must be thinking of me right now.

"So, how do you know him?"

"University," he answers, his fingers clicking away at the keyboard. Adrian's lip curls in the corner. "Don't worry. He's not all bad."

I drone an unconvinced "Hm," while he types in my name, his long fingers moving quickly over the keys. "Somehow I doubt that."

He chuckles and his search results pull up. "Yes, here we are. Account 2539-James Bond."

"James Bond?" I lift an eyebrow.

"Double-O seven," Adrian clicks his tongue. "It's been open since 1993. Does that sound correct?"

"You had digital keys back in '93?" I say, lifting up the key again.

This time Adrian actually smiles. "No. Five years ago we updated our system and sent all new keys to our existing account holders. It seems . . ." he squints at the screen, "that your box came with a proviso that any updates to your account, along with a letter be sent to . . ." he scrolls down and this time he truly stops and looks up at me, curiously, "Collens Donovan."

At the sound of his name, yet again, I frown, my jaw dropping languidly to the side. Right. Of course he'd be listed in this. I can't shake that asshole.

"It actually says his name?" I ask, feeling a headache coming on.

"No, just the address. I know that's his place. I didn't realize your families knew each other."

"Apparently." Or my dad dabbled in a lot more futuristic magic than I would have assumed.

Couldn't he have just . . . picked someone else? Okay, I know it's not up to him. By the spirits, couldn't someone have handed me a better man to work with? Fate? The powers that rule all? I don't know. Just anyone other than Collens Donovan.

"Well," he clears his throat looking deeply and genuinely surprised, "I'll just need you to answer a few questions for me before I take you to your box. Don't worry, it's due to the security measures set when the account was opened. Unfortunately, I'm not allowed access to those questions, so I'll need to get help from one of our branch managers. Can you wait here?"

"Sure." I nod.

Adrian leaves me sitting in the large open area of the branch and enters a door to the south. A few minutes pass and I spend the time picking at the cuticles of my nails—a bad habit I've tried and failed to stop since high school. My thumb nail drags and cuts into the pressed back cuticle skin and the faint noises of footsteps, ringing phones, and conversations drone in the background.

"Miss Grim?" a deep male voice pulls my attention away.

I turn around in my seat to see Michael Donovan looking back at me. He's dressed in a neatly-pressed gray suit. His blue tie matches the pocket square and the cornflower color of his socks just peeking out from under the cuffs of his slacks.

What is he doing here?

"Mr. Donovan. Wow," I swallow and feel my pulse rush the moment I stand. "How are you?"

"Curious. What are you doing in London?"

"Visiting friends," I lie with a plastered smile to the man who's searching for the exact same artifact I'm investigating.

His eyebrows jump. "Friends?"

"Yes. Um, my old college buddy, Pete and his wife. In fact, the same man who referred you to me."

"Ah. Yes."

"So," I break the unexplainable tension, "what are you doing here?"

"I bank here," he curtly replies. "That, and my son works for this institution. I hoped to catch him after lunch. And what are you doing here? Surely the ATM machines outside are more convenient for tourists?"

His eyes are scrutinizing, almost gleeful and excited, and the only thing I want to know is why. Why does he look so joyful to see me here? Only, it's like no other joy I've ever seen before.

I've never been a good liar. I could say I'm here to simply withdraw cash for the day. Like he said, though, I could have done that from any random street ATM. I could say something about how I know someone here. Even that would be painfully obvious that I'm lying. I feel like I'm standing here just looking like a complete idiot. I, at least, need to say something.

"Taran Grim?" a woman says, approaching with Adrian on her heels. Her dark blonde hair is pulled back into a ponytail and she gives me a bright smile. "Are you ready?"

I'm saved. I take a deep breath then turn around quickly and smile. "Yes. I am." With one last look at Michael Donovan, who's now probing me with his gaze, I smile wide and back away. "I'm sorry. I have to go. Have a great day!"

With that, I skip a step to meet with the bank manager and Adrian, leaving Michael Donovan's eyes to follow me until I walk around the corner and glance back at him. When I do, he's gone.

* * *

I'm led down a bare hallway lined with office doors and a single, large, steel vault. After another turn, they take me into a secluded room where a single desk with a computer waits for us. In front of the plain wooden desk—devoid of any pencils, frames, or other usual office accessories—is a simple, black, padded chair. Adrian stays in the hall while the manager takes a seat at the computer and I sit across the desk from her.

"My name is Millie Thompson. I understand this is your first time accessing the account, correct?" she asks.

I nod in agreement.

"And it once belonged to your father who has passed away?"

"Yes."

"All right, well, let me tell you how this will work. This will be a series of three questions specifically set up by the person who arranged the account. I'm assuming it was probably your father. If you can answer them, you'll be granted access to your security box. If not, you'll be politely escorted out of the building by our security team. It's simply a measure of insurance laid out in the account's protocol."

"All righty. Let's hope my dad made them really easy," I joke. The manager doesn't find any humor in my words or tone and she simply stares at me. "Sorry. Go ahead."

Millie scrolls down and reads from the screen. "Alina's favorite ice cream?"

"That's a weird question." I shake my head with a frown. "Why would my dad ask that? She doesn't like ice cream."

"Correct." She smiles politely. "The next question: More-eye calls you . . ."

I inwardly roll my eyes at the slaughtered pronunciation of my grandma. "*Mo sféar.* Or just *sféar.*"

"Correct. Next question: The itsy-bitsy spider ran . . ."

A dart pierces my chest and for the briefest of moments I can't take a breath. Dad sang it to me every night before I fell asleep. I bite down on my lip to keep my eyes from misting. I may have only been three or four-years-old, still, I remember Dad coming into my room on the nights he actually came home. After my bath, after brushing my teeth with the Cinderella toothbrush, and getting a final glass of water, he'd sing nursery rhymes to me before bed. Everything from Georgie Porgie to Rapunzel. Others, simple folk chants or songs of our ancestors. Each story or song special to me in their own way; only one of them I'd consider my favorite. And it had nothing to do with the subject matter or the tune.

Truth was, I never sang the *Itsy-Bitsy Spider* correct because Dad always used his hand and wiggly fingers as a spider to crawl—

"Into my little hand."

"Correct. You've been granted access to your box."

We step into the hallway and the manager passes me back into Adrian's care, informing him of the box number I need to be escorted to. He starts to take me down another hallway and toward an elevator. At first, he's quiet, and then he turns to me. "Sorry if we interrupted your conversation back there," Adrian says softly.

"What? Which conversation?"

"Michael Donovan," he replies out of the corner of his mouth.

"Oh, no!" I smile. "If anything, you saved me."

"Ah, so I can imagine. I've heard enough about him from Coll to know Michael Donovan is not the ideal conversationalist."

"Yes," I nod. "Thank you."

It's at this moment that I have the closest thing to a brain-gasp I can get. First, Emilia's reaction to me mentioning her father's name in the club, then fast forward to Coll's very antagonistic retort in his flat: *This is my dad's world. This is your world. And I mean this with every offense I can muster . . . I'd rather shove a red-hot poker in my eye before I chose to be associated with either of you.*

Why didn't I realize it before? Michael isn't just any treasure hunter or historian.

Michael is hexen.

With a hexen son, it would make sense—even though it's not necessarily a given. Coll could have easily been the product of a hexen-human marriage, like I am, with a magical mother.

This is my dad's world.

I'd completely missed it when Coll initially threw it in my face, due to him being such an ass. Now to hear this from Adrian too. A normal "daddy-issue" shouldn't necessarily leak out beyond the family lines.

Apparently I've been justified in allowing myself to be wary of letting the patriarch of the Donovan family know of my research into *Craniarann*. If he knew I'd become aware of the prophecy. . . .

Then, another thought hits me square in the chest.

Michael has to know of the mark on his son's hand. Which still begs the question if he knows about mine. Is that the real reason he came to see me in California?

"Here we are," Adrian says, leading me into a small security-coded room with three walls, top to bottom containing built-in security deposit boxes. In the center is a small table and a chair on each side. "If you need me, just press the button on the wall over there," he points to a location behind me and I glance back, "and I'll come help you."

"Thanks."

"You're very welcome."

After Adrian leaves and shuts the door behind him, I set my bag on the table then move toward the box, the key gripped in my hand. What if Dad set up an additional security measure and . . . what if he expected my craft to be more mature? More developed?

I tentatively rest my hand on the head of the key, thread it into the box's hole, and close my eyes. Taking a slow breath, I turn the key and hear the inside of the box unlatch followed by a beep. Nothing else happens. I'm not sure if the tension in my body decreases or if I'm simply numb. No matter. I pull back and open the box.

Nothing.

All that's inside is a white paper envelope with a slight bulge in the corner. I reach in and grab it. Immediately, a white cloud escapes the envelope and mists my face. It smells heavily of amber and patchouli. A mix of my dad and *Mórai*. I squint and blink, pulling my hand out, continually breathing in the mist. After a moment the mist dissipates, and I can no longer smell it.

Dad cast a genetic sensory test on the envelope. I've never performed one, nor seen *Mórai* engage in one either. If I hadn't actually been me, the mist would have eaten the flesh of the one who opened the box. No wonder Dad insisted on me opening the box.

Braving the box once more, I pull out the envelope to find my name scripted on the front:

TARAN

My fingers brush over the penned letters and swallow. Quickly, my fingers loop underneath the envelope seal and rip it open. Inside is another small key (I roll my eyes—perfect. Just what I need. Another puzzle.). It's not new like the laser key. It's older and accesses some kind of storage locker. The wide, orange, plastic-tipped end has a number on it: 12. Again, with the number 12.

The envelope also holds another piece of paper. A letter. I set the second key on the table and pull back the chair while I unfold the note.

Taran Bug,

Oh, my daughter. I'm sitting here, listening to you play with your PJ Sparkles in the next room, and thinking, where do I even start? I guess, first of all, I'm probably gone, if you're reading this. And just thinking about that, breaks my heart.

Look, I know you're confused. And, I don't blame you. But if you're reading this, then odds are, you know what you're looking for, and you just don't know where to go next. Right? While there's a lot that you need to know, about what's going on, I feel like no letter that I write, will ever be able to explain all of it to you. I've never been a great writer.

You might be wondering how I arranged all this. Don't tell your grandmother, but I cast an outlook hex, in order to help you out a bit. Darker magic, I know. I just couldn't think of any other way. The man I sent the key to? You know, Collens I believe, is his name. You can trust him, Bug. Just don't ask me how I know. Let's just say I saw some things, in your future, I'd rather pretend I hadn't seen. I am your father after all.

Bug, I wanted to protect you from this. I learned of the prophecy years ago, so when you were born, I recognized your birthmark. And I wanted nothing more, than to protect you from it. I promise. I wanted to do my job, as your dad, and keep you from ever having to face him. Not Collens, I mean. But HIM.

You have to know that.

In order to do that, I sought out an old acquaintance of mine: Radolf Wolf. He's a descendant of the Ruhmactir line—the shapeshifter hexens. Just like Collens, who will, by the way, give you what you need. You just need to figure out how to approach him better.

See, over these last few years, Radolf helped me find everything, except for one thing: Craniarann.

I found it. I know where it is. And you're going to hate me for this, but I can't tell you where it is.

Except to say it's safe. And I'm going to help you the best I can.

Taran, your number one priority is to protect Craniarann.

I'm leaving this key for you. When you figure out where

my journals are (and you will) read through them, do what you do best and find the trail I'll leave, and believe me when I tell you how much I know you can do this.

Taran Bug, I am so proud of you, your accomplishments, and your talent. You have the power to do this. Just promise you won't lose yourself like I have. There are more important things in life.

Above all, protect yourself from Radolf. He'll be watching for you. You'll recognize the tattoo on his left hand as the cross of Ruhmactir. Lastly, when in doubt, listen to yourself and no one else.

All my love,
Dad

I flip the page over again and again, hoping there's more to it. That's it. That's all he said to me. "Dad, no." A stream of tears falls from my eyes and I quickly brush them away, flipping over the letter once more. That can't be everything. Where are the damn journals?

"Think, think," I say to myself. *Mórai.*

I reach into my bag and pull out my cell phone. After dialing my mom's number, I wait for someone to pick up on the other end.

"*Mo sféar*," *Mórai* answers. Her voice is soft. "Are you safe?"

"Yes, I am."

"Thank the ancestors. I felt . . . a darkness around you."

"I'm fine," I assure her, though my thoughts travel to Michael

Donovan. "Listen, I found a key. Dad made arrangements for me to find it and it apparently gives me access to his journals. I just don't know where he would have put them. He didn't tell me where they are, I don't know what the key goes to. How do I find them?"

"You know what to do."

I shake my head. "Why do you keep saying that? Hell, you and Dad it's like talking to the Riddler. No!" I hiss, "I don't know what to do."

"Talk to the ancestors. They're protecting you. I made sure of it."

I shake my head, taking a deep breath and pinching my lips together. *Móraí* hangs up on me.

I'm right back where I started. Another note. No answers, except for this Radolf. Who apparently has a tattoo. Aside from that, I know no more than I did before I walked into this bank.

Why couldn't dad have just told me? He knew and he didn't tell me.

I look at the letter again. A page and a half and he couldn't just slip in one extra line?

I can't do this. I'm not prepared, I'm not equipped, and the time needed to do the appropriate research would take . . . years, at least. That includes the fact checking, finding secondary resources, compiling the information, and still— all the while—wondering why my dad couldn't just tell me everything I need to know.

My leg bounces up and down on the ball of my foot and I

fold the letter up, shoving it into my bag. I press the button on the wall next to the door and then grab for the handle, hoping Adrian will meet me and direct me the rest of the way out. The moment the door flies open, Adrian nearly runs into me.

"I'm so sorry, Ms. Grim. Are you finished?"

"Yes. Can you show me out?"

"Absolutely."

He smiles and offers his hand out to point the way. I follow his direction and walk down the bare hall.

"So, did you find what you need?"

"Not remotely."

"Really? What was in there? Sorry, I actually shouldn't ask."

"It's not a problem," I reply, my feet tromping across the floor. "It was just a letter."

"From whom?" he asks, opening a door for me.

"My dad. Nothing he couldn't have just told my mom to give to me. In fact—" I stop after walking through the final door Adrian is propping open. I find myself frozen just inside the main lobby, thinking things through. Dad was wrong. I can't do this, and some stupid prophesy can't make me. "I think I'm going to go home. This trip has just been a waste from beginning to end."

I sigh and offer him a passive smile when I notice he's frowning.

"I'm sorry to hear that," he says, slowly shutting the door behind him.

"Yeah, me too. Anyway, thanks for everything."

"Even though you didn't get what you wanted?" he asks.

I chuckle lightly. "Even though. It was great to meet you." I hold out my hand and Adrian shakes it warmly.

"And you too. But, uh. Can I make a suggestion?"

"Sure." I hike the strap of my bag up my shoulder.

"If your father considered that letter important enough to keep in a safety deposit box. It's probably more valuable than you think."

TEN

I RETURN TO THE HOTEL AND MAKE MY WAY UP
to my room. After tossing my things onto the bed I run a hand
through my hair again.

No. I don't care. I'm done. The ancestors and all their
combined magic couldn't force me to keep going. Prophesy or
not, I'm done. I have a list of other things I'd prefer to be doing
this summer and searching for a mythical stick in England—
one that's already been found by my father, mind you—is not
even close to making the cut.

Who was I trying to kid? I've spent the last twenty years
focusing on boys through high school, and studies through
college, and recorded history in my career that I couldn't even
spend five minutes to prepare myself for this.

Dad found *Craniarann,* and he was not only intelligent, but
practiced. And yet, I'm supposed to do this on my own.

I guess that's not exactly true. I'm being tasked to work with
Coll Donovan, and I'd rather shoot myself in the foot—with a
harpoon covered in hot sauce and vinegar. I'd rather work with
just about anyone else. Even this Radolf Wolf.

That's not true either, I think, sinking down onto the bed. If I did that, I'd be spitting on my Dad's work—his sacrifice.

I look over at my bag and reach for the letter jutting out of it. After unfolding it, I skim over the handwriting once more. Dad wrote me this letter for a reason. Even that bank guy friend of Coll's tried to tell me that.

Listen to yourself and no one else.

All right, Dad. I'm listening. And myself is saying I just need to go home because I am way over my head.

The woman required to complete this prophesy should be a woman so tied up in the old magic that it is a part of who she is. That Taran should be able to connect with it, recite it, and taste it with every breath she takes.

I should be a much stronger hexen than I am, more knowledgeable of my family history, and more even tempered. Worse, my failure to connect to who I am could ruin everything.

I specifically remember the day *Mórai* told me, "Our family is our immortality. We live through our children."

If my sisters and I are the last Grims with knowledge of our heritage, we're in massive trouble. If I just let it go, while it may not be an apocalyptic *Deireanhexe*—our kind would go extinct. Gone.

Would that really be the worst thing?

Mórai would slap me if she heard me thinking that. Honestly, I kind of want to slap myself.

I came here for a reason. I've forgotten why that is at this point. Still, I made the decision to follow this—to find out who I am and what I'm intended for. The only way to do that, is to learn everything I can very, very quickly. The only place I know that has what I need is back in Idaho.

Using a quick summoning spell, and praying to the ancestors that *Mórai* doesn't find out what I'm up to, I conjure her grimoire to me. The oiled leather, the age-stained pages, and the smell of patchouli immediately appear in front of me.

After summoning all the crest candles I possibly can from my apartment back home, carefully arrange the off-white candles into the shape of Woden's cross on the carpeted floor. Then, with a wave of my hand I light their wicks with gently dancing flames.

I step away from them. Far enough that the fire can't reach the thick book in my outstretched hands. I can hear *Mórai's* voice in my head before I open my mouth: "To gain knowledge is a steady event. Like a babe learning to walk. You must understand what your feet are there for before you attempt to balance on them."

I don't have the time to sense my feet though. Falling over is a risk I'm going to have to take. If I'm going to transfer every spell and potion recipe in this book into my memory, it's going to require a bit of recklessness.

I take a deep breath and open the book. The pages crackle with the movement and I survey the room, feeling like I'm being watched. It must just be the guilt of stealing *Mórai's* family grimoire. The grief is worse than the guilt from my own mother.

Thumbing through the pages, I find the spell I'm looking for and stabilize the book in my left hand while my right hovers over the pages by a few inches, cocked with splayed fingers at a two o'clock angle. Hopefully, if this works, every spell, every hex, and all the jotted notes within the book's pages will transfer to my memory, allowing me to utilize them all at will.

I breathe out slowly.

"Kénlas arn min shisern, pase i une chumig. Machéan doie ang curen ane draíe da hæirein."

Magic and energy swirl and twist around my fingers, fluttering the pages of the book in my hand. Again, I repeat the spell.

"Kénlas arn min shisern, pase i une chumig. Machéan doie ang curen ane draíe da hæirein."

I open my eyes on the last *hæirein* and the mark on my hand starts to glow, illuminating the pages beneath and shining through the back of my hand. My heart pounds and images flood my mind. Spells, memories, potions, teas, information taught to me long ago—lessons forgotten, knowledge I've never had.

"Kénlas arn min shisern, pase i une chumig. Machéan doie ang curen ane draíe da hæirein. Kénlas arn min shidsern, pase i une chumig. Machéan doie ang curen ane draíe da hæirein!"

My words become more powerful, entwining with the colors, words, and writings invading my own intellect. A burning erupts from the palm of my hand and the pages of the book ignite in a powerful flame. Black ash and embers of old pages float in the air while the fire ignites. I pull my hand back and drop the book on the floor.

Like a light switch, the information that came to me so

easily evaporates. I hardly notice it in my desperate attempts to extinguish the fire that's consuming the millennia-old book that belongs to *Mórai* and the entire Grim line of Hexens.

"Shit. Shit, shit, shit!" I say, smothering the pages with the hotel bedspread I've yanked down on top of it. Smoke radiates from underneath the blanket while I keep my weight on top of it, hanging my head and cursing myself for ruining the oldest relic that belongs to our family.

Shit.

The history. The spells.

Mórai is going to kill me.

My cell phone rings and I lift myself off the smoking pile long enough to answer it. The name on the screen makes my heart plummet into my stomach.

"Hello?" I answer with a shaking breath.

"Have you learned your lesson, *mo sféar?*" *Mórai's* crackling voice responds from the end of my mother's landline and I bite down hard on my lip before answering.

"What?"

"How many times must you hear it? To gain knowledge is a steady event. I'll be taking my book back."

I look down at the book. The lump underneath the comforter is now gone.

"Taran," her voice is hard. "You had your chance to learn long ago. You must do this on your own. There are no shortcuts, no quick spells. You made the choice."

"I know," my voice shakes. "I'm sorry. Is the book all right?"

"That was a bit of illusionary work on my part. It's fine."

I take a deep breath, and exhale.

"How did you know I had it?"

"*Mo sféar,* my large leather book disappeared from in front of me while I wrote in it."

My eyes close in both relief and shame. I can just see *Mórai* sitting at her desk, her fountain pen scratching away at the pages before the book disappeared and her pen collided with the wooden tabletop.

"I'm sorry."

"You should be. And this better be the last time you ever steal from me, do you hear?"

Immediately, I feel like I'm nine-years-old all over again. Alina's knocked over the last bottle of third eye draft and *Mórai* is yelling at both of us for horsing around in front of sacred and valuable things.

"Yes," I nod, wiping at the beads of sweat on my forehead.

"Good." It's the last thing she says to me before the line cuts. She's hung up.

I pull my phone away from my ear and toss it on the bed. I don't remember a single thing that filtered in during the spell, and all I'm left with is a hole of guilt sucking in my chest. And I'm pretty sure the hotel comforter is charred. I lean over and pick it up, checking for sure, only to find that there's not a single mark on the blanket. I hold it to my chest and breathe again.

"Thank you," I whisper to myself.

After tossing it back up onto my bed, Dad's letter catches my eye once more. I'm right back where I started. Lost, small, and entirely unprepared. I lean over to pick up the paper and stop. I look down at my hand, the birthmark brilliant and white on my palm. For some reason, I have this mark. Something about who I am, and what I'm capable of must somehow make me prepared to handle this.

A spell flutters into my mind and I stand tall.

Where did that come from?

I look back at the comforter, wondering if the spell I just cast actually worked. A guidance hex. Of course. *Mórai* herself told me the ancestors protected me. If that's the case, they'd also be guiding me.

Using a motion spell, I push the bed to the far wall and re-light every single crest candle. If this one doesn't work, I'm screwed.

After grabbing the second locker key out of my bag, I bounce it around in my hand before settling myself into a kneel at the north end of the circle. I take a deep breath and set the key directly in front of my knees.

The dark room, lit solely by the circle of twenty candles that edge the small key on the floor, feels cold and empty. I close my eyes and try to still my beating heart from the excitement of the burning grimoire and the anxiety of hoping this one will work.

I feel the air around me begin to move even before I hold out my hands or open my mouth. Anxiety tingles in my fingertips while I hold them nearly a foot over the warm flames of the candles.

I blow out slowly through my relaxed lips, connecting myself to the movement of the air.

"Tacht, tacht. Folay die rinnea im Feue. Lave, Lave. Siste i atme, kenne die rinnea," I whisper. *"Ó somme til Winte. Ó doma toh hayer. Ó stranzer toh cinsire. Es ruhte in doman."*

"Tacht, tacht," I repeat again. *"Folay die rinnea im Feue. Lave, Lave. Siste i atme, kenne die rinnea."*

The letter rustles on the table, the blinds clash against the windows, my hair begins to wisp around my face.

"Tá er anse, visay veje dom beala seo, som vi forlo a mui an lámhái." The blaze of the candles explodes underneath my hands and a gust of wind rolls through the hotel room. I begin the spell all over again. Three times it needs to be said. Three times to break though the spiritual wall. *"Tacht, tacht. Folay die rinnea im Feue. Lave, Lave. Siste i atme, kenne die rinnea."*

The volume of my voice rises, and the chaos escalates. I feel the flames of the candles dancing underneath, tickling my skin. My head spins. I have to keep going. The words pour from my mouth with fervent soul, willing the spell to direct me, show me what I need to understand.

The final words echo in my ears—or throughout the room—I can't tell the difference. Each syllable is intense, and my voice takes on a deep and raspy tone while energy saturates my skin and being. I feel as if the room is spinning around me like a carousel and I'm a passenger hanging on for my life while wind whips around.

My eyeballs flutter, and the words resonate in my head. My fingers twitter and flinch.

As the floor starts to tilt, I force my hands to remain

steady. The walls seem to turn on their sides and immediately, everything goes black.

*   *   *

Deep breath in. The air smells of grass and early summer twilight. When I breathe out, a humid summer breeze kisses my cheeks. My eyes slowly open to a brilliant white orb in the sky above me. The incoming moon blinds me and I raise my arms to block its intensity.

How did I get here? Where am I?

I push myself into a sitting position and look around. A grassy field surrounds me with a thick density of trees to my right. Beech, elm, and brush.

"Rheda!" a voice calls in the distance. I look around—strands of bright red hair wisping across my face—to find a woman trotting through the grass, holding her skirts up to help her walk over the tall growth.

"Yes, mother?" I respond, not in English, nor in old English, Irish, or any other language normally spoken today. It's our language.

"Your father is waiting. The ritual!"

"Coming!" I say, understanding each word uttered from my lips. I pick myself off the ground and hurry toward my mother, a woman I immediately recognize to be the legendary Frig.

Wait, why do I consider her my mother? She's not my mother. She's someone else's mother. And where did my red hair come from?

The grass tickles my bare legs and feet, creeping underneath the thin sackcloth I'm lifting up, like an overzealous date. When I reach the woman I call mother, I take a closer look at her. Her dark black hair is similar in color to my own—my real hair. Her nose is long, and her eyes a piercing shade of green with flecks of gold around the iris. Curly and almost ratted, her hair claws at the moving air. She grabs at my wrist in a firm, yet loving way, her eyes softening and then turning away, pulling me in the direction she'd come from.

"Have you prayed to the ancestors?" she asks.

"Yes."

"And you are ready?"

I take a deep breath, not knowing what it is that I'm getting ready for. "Yes. *Zonne* has accepted my offer."

"Good." Her hand leaves my wrist and weaves down to my hand, her fingers lacing with mine. "Come."

We march steadily up a shallow hill and when we mount the ridge, I look down into the valley below. A series of homes with smoke billowing out of the roof vents encircle a central village area. In the center is a stone table lined with sticks laid in precise patterns and carved with runes.

Surrounding us is a deep breadth of forest. Trees extending far as the eye can see. The evening moon is becoming brighter with the coming nightfall. I notice the shadowy clouds in the sky, the shapes they make. The energy in their figures and movements.

Mother pulls me down the hill and into the large village. A rhythmic drum pattern and the soft chanting of the clan hits my ears. At the head of the stone table is a large man. His black beard reaches the center of his chest, his broad shoulders draped in the adornment of raven's feathers all laced together like a thick cape down his back. Even if my consciousness didn't recognize him, I'd still know him anywhere: Woden. The head of our clan—our coven, the symbol of our family crest.

Mother takes me to the foot of the table and turns me to face her. I notice she's joined the chanting of the other coven members while my own mouth remains closed. She strips the cloak off my back and leaves me standing there in a beige sackcloth with an underskirt. Another woman approaches us with a carved bowl filled with black ash. Mother puts her hands in the ash and then strokes the soot through my hair, trailing her fingers in patterns down my face, neck, and arms.

After offering her hand, Mother takes me to the north side of the table and turns me to face the outer circle of chanting villagers. Then, she slowly retreats and stands next to a man who offers her his own cloak. When he fully turns to face me, I gasp inside my head.

Collens Donovan. No, that can't be. It's not exactly him. The features, the golden amber-brown eyes, the jet-black hair, the oval face with high cheek bones all says "Coll." The only thing that sets them apart is this man's two-month beard growth, and a scar that runs across his left eyebrow and into his hairline. I guess the shape of the ears and maybe the ridge of the noses are different too. The Coll I know has a wider nose ridge, whereas this man's is shorter, sharper.

He steps closer to me and looks down, his mouth chanting the same words the surrounding village is rolling off their tongues. My eyes graze over the others, and I realize it's not only my family and his. The tribes, the covens, are supported by the ghosts of ancestors—their spirits surrounding the circle.

The man who looks too much like Coll Donovan throws his head back and looks up into the sky. At this moment, the sun sinks behind the horizon and the full moon presents itself in a glowing majesty. The Coll-a-like reaches out and grabs my shoulders, his eyes still fixated on the sky. I look down at his arms to see the hair along his skin getting thicker and growing rapidly. He groans in pain. His fingers claw down my arms and he bends over in agony. Before his fingernails reach my wrists, they sharpen and dig into my skin like knives. Finally, he falls to the ground, breathing hard.

I look down at my arms to see the pink imprint of his human nails, trailed by the ruby red marks of his claws. When I look back at him, a pile of clothing is lying in shreds on the ground, and a midnight-black wild dog shakes off the hand-made wool top he'd been wearing. A set of golden brown eyes stare back at me with a hunter's focus.

Of course. He's not Coll. It's Ruhmactír. And his magic is more powerful when he's in his animal form. Which means the other tribes that are here are the Geris and the Ravns.

I search through my mind, trying to recall the knowledge I have of the pre-Roman paganism of the Celtic tribes. Facts and stories *Móraí* and Dad would have told me. The table, the chanting, the shape-shift magic . . . Woden. All of it is mounting toward something, I just don't know what it is.

"Daughter."

I turn at the voice to see Woden's deep violet eyes piercing through me. He motions toward the table and I walk up the two steps until I'm on top. I then lay back and look into the night sky.

The blood along my arms drips onto the table and I feel it tingling, an energy lacing up through my skin.

With that feeling, a memory comes into my recollection. Of course. I don't know why I didn't immediately recognize this. It's the symbolic sacrifice of Rheda. The woman scholars call "the victorious," lifted onto the offering table, in the name of *Zonne,* the first Hexen, in an attempt to prophesy the end of times. *Deireanhexe.* The story I spoke with *Mórai* about before I left.

I look up into the eyes of my father, Woden. In his hands he holds a staff. It's the first time I've ever seen it with my own eyes. It's simpler than the drawings and concept art make it out to be. A long stick carved of beech. Smooth from years of use, with delicate carvings of nature, and a single symbol above the handgrip: the cross. His chants join the others and his hand stretches out over my body. The energy from Ruhmactír's scratches spreads into my ribs and up my neck. When I feel it hit my vocal chords, I inhale a large frosty breath of air.

When I speak, my voice is disembodied and hollow—like someone held an open glass bottle over my mouth. "*In the time of the death of the gods, the council of Woden will enter into the Great House to give greeting,"* my voice rakes. *"Then will be said of his Majesty Zonne to the seal-bearer at his side, 'Go and fetch for me the flail. It is time for the end of hexen.'*

My breath continues to wheeze, the prophecy flitting from my lips, words that will be written and preserved for centuries. The prophecy nears its end, and the lines, *"Right will come into its place and Wrong will be thrust to the afterlife. Fated will be he who will see it, and he who will serve King Geri,"* are spoken. At that moment, Ruhmactír leaps on top of the table, a branch of fire in his jaw. Something about that line has ignited a frenzy in him and he lunges for Woden.

The spell ends before the final line is uttered, my lips hanging onto the words, "King Geri." The gasps of the tribe can be heard across the valley. With one roaring leap, the massive Geri clan leader attacks my father. The energy still courses through my body and I hear the final words of the prophecy in my head, though they never pass over my lips. I push myself to a position where I can see what's happening. Father casts a spell at Ruhmactír, blasting the dog through the air nearly fifty feet. When he lands, the animal skids on the ground, slamming into one of the nearest homes and collapsing the south end. The shifted hexen shakes it off and bolts for Woden who's fighting off Frec.

All around the table, the tribe of my family and friends begin to turn on one another. Half of them shape-shifters, the other half alighting with energy and power given to them from the ancestors. Spells are cast, large beasts attack, and in the midst of it all, I pull myself off the table and set my bare feet back on the cold black earth.

With my hand outstretched, I cast and feel the combined energies of Ruhmactír and my father coursing through my skin and permeating the air like a warrior's arrow. It's too late. The spell hits Ruhmactír, his jaws now clamped tight on my father's neck. The dog spins away, ripping out precious flesh and blood. I hit him again, a rage boiling in my stomach. Ruhmactír shifts his shape before slamming into a large protective rune stone that stands at the end of the village. The stone cracks and his naked body digs into the ground.

The fighting ceases and I step forward, approaching the shifter hexen carefully. I can't see his pale white chest, now only featuring a heavy layer of hair, rising or falling. Next to me, another man pulls himself off the ground and glares at me— one of the fallen shifters and a member of Ruhmactír's tribe. His arm is nearly hexed off his body.

"Listen to me. All of you," I say. "There will befall a time where our kind will cease to exist. The only path to prevent *Deireanhexe* is banding. It has ne'er been high hexen battling shifters. In all the centuries, our people have been one. If you choose to continue with the fulfillment of this prophecy, you'll answer to me, the power of my ancestors," I look down at my fallen father, Woden's blood spilling out onto the earth, "the power of the High Hexen, and the energy of the shifter flowing through my veins."

Not a soul moves. With one last glance at Ruhmactír on the ground, I feel the earth begin to move beneath my feet, the moon twist in the sky. Gravity conquers my body and I'm pulled toward the soft cold earth beneath me.

* * *

Pounding within my head draws my eyes open and I stare at the ceiling above me. The matte white paint stares back at me, a blank canvas that seems to have a memory of its own—a way of saying it will always remember what I just witnessed. A look into my family's past, the day the great Woden died, the end of Ruhmactír, and the prophecy that would one day take an unpracticed professor halfway across the world in a ridiculous attempt to stop it all from coming true.

I sit up, a lancing pain in my spine, and a dry throat that feels like I've been screaming for two hours. I groan, and twist around to release the cracks and pops within my back. All around me, the once-lit candles have been half-spent, the melted wax pooled in dried blobs on the hotel floor.

I expected the spell to show me the answers I need. Nothing I saw would even give me a clue leading to the locker it accesses. Realizing this makes me shake my head.

I pull my knees in toward my body and even more joints pop and snap.

One thing is absolutely sure. I was right before; I need Coll. He's a known descendant of Ruhmactír, and his magic is necessary to amplify any heavy craft lifting. Not to even mention the mark on his hand.

I snicker. "I can't go see him again."

Even so, there's only one person who can actually help. And he has made it cut-and-dry clear that he'd rather die than do so.

With a shift of my jaw, I start thinking about Dad's letter. *You just need to figure out how to approach him better.*

Aside from the fact that Dad apparently knew I'd have problems with him, he knew I could do this with the right . . . style.

ELEVEN

"MORNING, MISS," KARL THE DOORMAN SAYS AS
I walk up the stairs.

I nod, confidence painted on my face, accompanied with
a plastic smile. Oh, ancestors . . . I hope this works and I can
actually get him to talk to me.

"Good morning, Mr. Davis," I reply. "Is Mr. Donovan
home?"

"To be honest, Miss, I don't know for sure. I just started my
shift," he says. "Would you like me to call?"

"No, that's all right. I'll just go up, if that's okay."

"Fine by me," he smiles, opening the door for me.

I thank him and he allows me access into the main reception
area of the apartment building. Once in the elevator, I count
down the floors nervously, the elevator ascending. Coll told
me he never wanted to see me again. Well, not exactly. Still, he
may as well have and here I am barging into his home all over
again with the one thing he really said he wanted nothing to
do with: magic.

When the elevator doors open to Coll's apartment, I step
into a deathly-quiet living room. After only a few moments,

someone shifts in the kitchen. I round the corner to find a tall woman with golden blonde hair falling in silk sheets down her back. Her sheer white blouse shines a spotlight on the black bra underneath, and her assets look tighter than concrete. All of a sudden, my usually twig-like thighs feel massive, and whatever strength the spell from my tea gave me has washed away.

She leans over the sink and runs some water for a few seconds before turning it off and shaking her wet hands.

"I know you're there." She turns around and looks at me with dark chocolate eyes, her Irish accent warm and soft. "Can I help yeh?"

Startled, I clear my throat. "Is, um, Coll here?"

She frowns. "Why?" At this, she fully turns to face me. Her eyes, more sunken than most, are painted with a smoky shadow and dark eyeliner, both framed by sharp and dark eyebrows. A dusty rose shade accentuates her lips, while her nose slims through the bridge with a small button at the end—everything a perfectly soft contrast to her sharp chin.

"It's purely business. You?"

The woman smirks and walks around the kitchen island. "I shack up here every once in a dark moon."

"Oh." Then, I repeat it again with a little more understanding. "Well, don't worry, I'm not interested in him the same way you are."

At this, she laughs out right and places her hand on her hip. "Believe me, I'm sure 'bout that," she bursts with a lingering chuckle. "He's not here right now. There was some business he needed to take care of last night."

"Do you know when he'll be back?"

"He was supposed to return about two hours ago. I was just leavin'."

I nod. Sure, you leave your date in your apartment for hours on end, alone . . . I'd leave too.

"I'll come back then. So sorry to bother you."

After turning back around, I feel her eyes linger on me. The elevator door shuts behind me, and I rest my forehead on the wall, shaking my head back and forth on the cold metal. I'm going to have to call him. Walking in on his model-like dates in the morning is not my ideal way of contacting the man who's supposed to help me prevent the annihilation of my race.

Once the elevator opens, I hurry out, say a quick goodbye to Karl, and jog down the steps, skipping the last one. I feel a storm brewing inside of me. One of embarrassment, one of irritation, and charged with a lightning storm of resentment. Although, what I have to be resentful of isn't really clear to me. Maybe Coll's ability to simply brush off his heritage, his power, living like everyone else around him—at least the one percent of the human population that share his proclivities for money and time wasting. If I'd taken that path instead of chasing down this ridiculous scavenger hunt my father set up for me . . . I wouldn't even need to be here.

I run my hand furiously through my hair and round the

corner. The streets are crammed with cars, the sidewalks overflowing with people. It's a "miracle," I suppose you could call it, that I even see him shuffling down the street. Coll's hair is disheveled, his face long and pale—he looks exhausted.

"Someone's been burning the candle at both ends," I say with mustered kindness, approaching him.

"Jayz." He stops in his tracks and sighs. "I thought I got rid of yeh."

"And where have you been all night?"

He seems to think on it, choosing his words carefully. "Ran into this right pretty bird out on the town. Took me back to her place and feckin' flattened me."

"Ah, the walk of shame," I give him a smile that translates the disgust I feel.

"What do yeh want?"

"You know what I want," I respond with a sweet smile.

He squints and runs a hand over his shaggy scruff. "Okay. But I have to warn yeh, I like to be on top."

"As if I'd ever let you touch me."

"If it's not a shag, I'm not sure what else I could help yeh with. I'm pretty sure I made myself clear when I said I wanted nothing to do with yeh-know-what and a certain note and key."

I skip a step to keep up with him. He seems to be walking faster now. "I already made out the key. It was a safety security box. London Crown. I believe you have a friend who also works there with you."

"Yeh met Adrian?" his eyebrows lift in curiosity.

"He helped me access my dad's box. Want to know what was inside?"

Coll's tone is one of disinterest and conniption. "Do I have a choice?"

"Another key."

Coll leaps the few steps up into his building while I trail behind, giving a brief smile to Karl for a third time before following Coll into the building.

"I came earlier to see you about it. Unfortunately, it seemed you already had company, though."

"I often do. You sure you don't want to give this a ride?" he asks, draping his hand down his body. "Obviously, I have references."

All right, that's it. I grit my teeth. "Oh, so do you often leave women alone in your apartment, or only on nights when you have a second option available to you?"

His fist grinds into the elevator button and he whirls around on me. "Yeh think yeh have me all figured out, don't yeh?"

"It's not hard to see through something so shallow."

"Lady, yeh really know how to butter up a man, don't yeh?"

"Who says I'm trying to butter you up?"

"Gee," the sarcasm drips off his tongue with a shrug, "this is goin' to make my answer so much easier. Not that it was goin' to be any differ'nt before the unwarranted personal attacks."

"What answer?" I say, the door opening for us.

"Yeh want teh know if I'll help yeh in your hexen quest. Right?" After walking inside, he turns around to look at me.

I just notice how dark the circles are underneath his eyes. His hand reaches out and tries to close the door. I stick my hand in between the sliding doors and he rolls his eyes, slamming his thumb into the button again. Once more, I block the doors with my hands and he lifts his lip in a snarl.

"Do yeh want me to hex yer hand off?"

"I want you to listen to me."

"Why?" He folds his arms. "Give me one good reason why I should listen to yeh. Yeh broke my phone, yeh lied to me . . ."

"How did I *lie* to you?"

". . . yeh insulted my chivalry . . ." His Irish accent gets thicker and heavier.

"*What* chivalry?"

". . . I'm completely wrecked, *and* your tryin' to drag me back into a world I've been avoidin' for the past twenty years. So, if you'll excuse me. I'm exhausted, and I just want to sleep."

This time, I jump onto the elevator before the doors start to close, forcing them back open again.

"Oh, saints. Woman . . ." he growls. "Get off me elevator."

I dig in my heels and fold my arms. "*Stop* calling me 'woman,' douchbag, and listen to me."

"While that sounds like a whale of a time, I'd rather drown meself in cowpiss. Now, get off." His eyes start to glow with a red-hot burn.

"I can make that happen. All I need is a couple minutes of your time."

Coll glares at me, and the same asshole who screamed at me

in the airport shows through. The next thing I know, he pushes on the elevator button again to close the doors and leans back against the wall.

"You're bringing me up with you? Thank you."

"Like a parasite, it seems I can't get rid of yeh. Yeh can keep talkin', but I'm goin' to bed."

After a few floors, the doors open into his apartment and I follow him out.

"Oh, and I sleep naked." He turns around to face me, then waltzes back around. "Just so yeh know."

"Collens?" the woman who claimed she was just about to leave jumps up from one of the couches in the living room and looks at both of us wide-eyed. "How," she eyes me, "how did it go?"

"Well enough," he sighs. "It's done. For now."

"What's done?" I ask.

"Saints, woman, do you have to know everythin' goin' on in me life?"

I stop and close my mouth, realizing I have, in fact, stepped too far over my boundary.

"Hello, again," the woman greets me.

"Hi."

"Collens?" she looks to him. "Aren't yeh goin' to introduce us?"

"Oh, jayz," he rolls his eyes and walks into the kitchen, his voice floating behind him while he reaches into the cupboard for a glass. "Sera, this is a woman who won't leave me the hell alone. Woman, my sister, Sera." He reaches for a bottle of whiskey and pours himself a glass. At his introduction, I turn to Sera, remembering everything I'd said to her.

"My name's Taran Grim, in case that was hard to translate. You're douchbag's sister?" I ask, my eyebrows lifting.

She grins. "Shockin' right? From time to time, my big brother allows me to crash here when I'm wrecked or just don't want to go home."

"Well, you wouldn't have to worry about goin' home if you'd just quit your job and go somewhere else," Coll nearly barks at her. Though it's said with quite a bit of warmth.

Sera sighs and walks around the couch. "I've already told yeh. I can't."

"Why not? Emilia got the hell out and never told him where she went. You can too. If he's still showin' up at your work, yeh can even crash here until yeh find a new job."

"He doesn't know where I live. It's really not all that bad, Collens."

He snorts disapprovingly into his glass and sips another swig of whiskey. "Right. And what I did last night was host a nice polite adult conversation with him."

I almost blurt out "With whom?" before I catch myself and purse my lips. If they wanted me to know what the hell they were talking about, they'd tell me.

Sera sighs and tries to shift topic. "Collens told me about yeh."

"Me?" I point to myself.

"Mm hm," she hums in answer. "You're a professor?"

"Yes. My focus is occult practices in ancient Germanic and

Celtic societies. Mainly its effect on the culture and beliefs of the time."

"Which would make sense, because you're a hexen too."

Hearing her blurt it out, takes me back a bit. I manage to gain my bearings quickly and my eyes dart to Coll. "He told you, huh?"

"He's told me enough. Of course, it helps that I've never seen a woman get under his skin this bad. You may easily be the first that couldn't be molded and tricked into submission. Lucky for you, the best way to avoid that is to have a little firepower of your own."

I clear my throat. "I get under his skin, huh?"

"Like a ringworm." He murmurs into his glass.

"It's early," Sera says. "Yeh probably haven't had breakfast yet."

"No. And I don't really want it," Coll answers.

"I wasn't talking to yeh." She turns to me. "Can I make yeh anythin'? I'm a whiz at makin' potato cakes. I can even chop up some tomato and prepare some sausage."

At the mere mention of sausage, my stomach grumbles. "I'm vegetarian, actually."

"Then beans and toast!" she exclaims.

I can't stop my mouth from salivating. It's been a while since I've eaten a solid meal. Between the airplane food, the research, and uneaten food from yesterday, *Mórai* and my mom would probably tell me I'm about to wither away into nothing. It doesn't help that I can't seem to put an ounce of feminine fat around any of my "curves" no matter how many potato chips and bowls of cookie dough I eat.

Although, I can imagine that the last thing Coll Donovan wants is to have me over for breakfast. With that, I look over at him and he sets his glass on the counter, turning around and folding his arms. His eyes glaze over me and then rest on the floor. Since there seems to be no objection, I smile. "I'd love breakfast."

"Brilliant!" Sera hops up into the kitchen and starts pulling food out of the fridge. I quickly notice she doesn't use an ounce of magic to prepare it. Everything is done by hand. The chopping, the frying, the mixing. After a few minutes, Coll excuses himself and I realize he's actually going up to his room.

"Where are you going? We still need to talk."

He stops and shoves his hands into his slacks' pockets. "Right. I was hopin' you'd forgot."

Across the room, a buzz echoes throughout the apartment and Coll walks toward the kitchen and approaches the intercom. "Yes?"

"Mr. Donovan, Adrian and Garrit are here."

"Great," he whispers offline. He then pushes the button again. "Send 'em up." When he turns back around, he shrugs and his face conveys everything except a genuine apology. "Sorry, woman. I have guests on their way. Guess you'll have to wait."

"Believe me. I will."

His face falls again, and I swear I see a juvenile scowl on his face. He turns to greet the elevator that's suddenly opened behind him. From within its golden enclosure, two men step out. Adrian, dressed in what looks like his typical bank work clothes—a navy blue suit with a simple crimson tie and pocket square—his hair buzzed short like usual, followed by Garrit who's sporting a pair of jeans and an untucked white button-up shirt with white sneakers. Garrit's expensive gold watch glints in the apartment lights before he shoves his hand in his front pocket.

"Emilia told us what happened," Adrian's smooth voice cuts through the apartment.

"Good, that means we don't have to talk about it." If I hadn't been watching him so closely, I don't think I would have noticed Coll nod toward me ever so slightly, the words pouring carefully out of his mouth.

"Ah, good morning, Dr. Grim." Adrian beams at me, his dark straight-forward face switching gears faster than a driver on a speedway.

"Good morning. You don't have to bother with that 'Dr. Grim' business. Just call me Taran. You're not one of my students, you're not one of my colleagues, and this is not one of my classes."

"Could 'ave fooled me." Coll leans across the bar in his kitchen.

I turn to directly face him. "And what does that mean?"

"I thought it was quite obvious. What's next? Sendin' me to the headmaster's office? A whack on the bum with a switch?"

Garrit whistles. "And we thought the storm had settled. Didn't realize you'd brought it back with you."

"What storm?" I ask.

169

"Bloody hell, yeh just don't know when to leave it alone, do yeh?" Coll frowns at me.

"Breakfast is served!" Sera announces, warning her brother with her eyes before setting an elegant plate of beans, tomatoes, toast, and potato patties in front of him. "And don't yeh dare touch it." She smacks his hand.

Coll juts his jaw out, waits for Sera to turn away, then eyes me. He sticks his finger in his mouth, then swirls it around in the beans before licking it all off.

"Jayz," Sera shoves him. "Are yeh six-years-old? I'm sorry, Taran. I'll make yeh another plate." She reaches to take the plate away and I step forward to stop her.

"No, don't," I say, never taking my defiant eyes off of the man toddler behind the bar. "After all, just because some dog marks his territory, it doesn't actually make it his."

Sera tries to protest, but I grab the fork and plate before she can reach it. Glancing back at Coll, I find him still glaring at me haughtily. Using the fork, I gather a bunch of the beans and shove them in my mouth, never breaking eye contact with the man across from me. Slowly, Coll inches toward me and leans over.

"Yeh know what's happenin' right now?"

I keep chewing, swallow, and nod. "Yup. I'm vaccinating myself."

Behind me, I hear one of the other two men snicker. At a flick of Coll's eyes, the laughter stops, and I keep throwing bites of breakfast into my mouth. Despite Coll's trace saliva on my meal, Sera really knows her way around a kitchen. The food is absolutely delicious and I tell her so.

"Thank you, Taran." She smiles.

"Well, it should be amazing. She's a chef at Café Marguerite," Aiden says, stepping up behind me.

"What?" I nearly lose the tomato piece on my fork.

"You have anything for me to take on the run?" Aiden asks. "If Coll's fine . . ."

"I'm fine," Coll leaves the kitchen, avoiding me.

"Here." Sera hands him some potato cakes in a napkin and he graciously accepts. After saying a few quiet words to Coll, both Garrit and Aiden wish me a good day and they take off without another word. Sera and I chat while I finish off one of the most amazing breakfasts I've ever had, and when I'm done, I turn around to see that Coll has completely escaped. Most likely up to his bedroom where I'm pretty sure I'm not welcome. Sera stands at the sink, rinsing pans and dishes, and I'm not sure exactly why, but the words simply fly out of my mouth.

"So, what happened last night that Coll apparently doesn't want to share with me?"

Sera sets a plate inside the high-end dishwasher and turns to look at me. "He'd kill me if I told yeh."

"Despite how I feel about him, something tells me he'd never do a thing to you."

She smiles, and considers my request. "I suppose half of it *is* my story."

"What do you mean?" I lean over the bar.

Sera stops and fully turns to face me. After folding her arms and glancing up the stairs to the second floor of Coll's flat, she leans against the counter and takes a long breath. "Are yeh familiar with our father? Michael?"

"I've had a couple meetings and run-ins with him."

"I'm sorry."

"Michael and Coll don't get along, do they?"

"Try Michael and our entire family. Look," she glances up again, "I don't think I have the right to tell yeh our entire history. As far as last night goes, though, my father came to the Café after I got off work. He's been . . . pressin' Emilia and I to embrace our legacy and both of us have refused. Like Collens, we want nothing to do with our father or his life."

"Wait," I hold up my hand, "your legacy? What do you mean?"

"I feel like if I went into those details, I'd have to reveal more about Collens. So, that's all his to tell. If he chooses to."

"I understand."

"Yeh know," she folds her arms, "my own history with Michael is a lot less intense than Collens'. Something I'm very grateful to my brother for. Whenever our father tries to intrude into our lives, Collens comes runnin'. And it's usually a bad experience. Hexen family feuds are not like human family feuds. There are more weapons at our disposal than words, passive aggressive actions, and guilt. Michael and Collens Donovan are expert at utilizin' them, and it's never a pleasant experience."

TWELVE

AS SERA TALKS, THE PIECES CONTAINING answers about Collens Donovan start to fit together little by little. While it still doesn't explain why he such a pain in the ass, I do start to see a man deeply protective of his sisters—the dark back story still elusive to me. From what I can gather, any time Emilia or Sera text him, he drops everything, day or night, just to keep their father away from interfering in their lives. When he does, it's explosive, intense, and dangerous. Dangerous to the point of physical danger.

"And that's why Garrit and Adrian came over this morning. They know about the relationship between the two of them?"

Sera nods.

"Everything?"

This time she shakes her head. "Well, I'm not sure how much he's told them. There's one thin' I do know: Collens refuses to talk about our hexen ties. I doubt he's said anythin' to Garrit or Adrian. For all they know, Collens and Michael just . . . let their fists do the talkin'."

Upstairs, a door opens and closes. Both Sera and I jump. She returns to the sink and I turn around in my seat to see

Coll stride across the open hallway and saunter down the stairs, each step still looking labored and heavy for him. I notice he's changed out of last night's clothes and he's now wearing a pair of gray sweat pants and a zipped gray hoodie where it's clearly visible that he has no shirt on underneath. When he reaches the bottom of the stairs, he sees me sitting near the island bar and looks defeated.

"You're still here?"

"I told you I wasn't leaving until you talked with me."

"I guess that's my cue," Sera softly says. "Collens," she walks toward him and grabs his wrist, "thank yeh, again. And for allowin' me to take over your flat."

"Anytime, Sera-bear." Coll hugs her while she plants a kiss on his cheek. Avoiding looking in my direction, Coll guides his sister to the elevator and she winks at me before leaving.

I take a deep breath, watching this quiet exchange. It's obvious they love each other very much. Not only because they're siblings but because the influence of their family environment has formed this unbreakable bond between them. Suddenly, my thoughts travel back across the seas and over mountains and plains, finally resting on my own sisters—two women to whom I barely speak with any more. Two families pressured to accept the old ways, scrambling to escape and forge their own way in a modern world. And yet, I barely know my sister who's prenuptually agreed to never use magic around her husband or children, and another sister lost in avoiding the rest of us best she can.

"Yeh want to talk?" I'm jerked out of my thoughts and I

look at Coll who's now walking by me and headed toward the couches in the living room. "Talk." He sits down, his back facing me.

Everything tumbles around in my brain. The bank, the letter, the key, the vision. All of it like a train, running at top speed through my brain and I have no idea where to start. I slip off the seat and cautiously move to a seat opposite Coll. His arms are propped up on the back of the couch, his gaze dark, and his sweatshirt perfectly framing his chest down to the waistband of his bottoms. My cheeks flush, and I distract myself by looking off to the side. The sight of his grand piano catches my eye and I take a second look.

"You play the piano?"

"Yeh harassed me on the street, stalked me into my flat, and hijacked my mornin' to ask me if I play the piano?"

My eyes roll back to him. "Of course not. You just don't seem like the piano-playing type."

Coll frowns at me. "What's the 'piano-playin' type'?"

"Someone with class, intelligence, and talent comes to mind." After all, he may be respectful toward his sisters, that doesn't change the fact that he's a grade-A dick.

His eyes narrow into slits, then I watch them swivel over to the piano and back to me. A couple of seconds meander by and he stands, stalks over to the piano, pulls out the bench, and lifts the top over the keys.

"You don't have to play *right now*," I clarify. Coll just glares haughtily at me. With a few pops of his knuckles, he gently places the pads of his fingers on the keys and inhales.

Silence fills the apartment.

What follows next, makes my jaw drop. A melody so light I barely even recognize its floating fluidity over the top of an agile and intricate foundation. It's ghostly and yet tender. Each note grazes against my eardrums like serene kisses, brushing against my cheek and lulling me into a soft whisper of security while I stand up and walk slowly across the apartment of this narcissistic maggot.

While the base and his left hand begin to quicken, the top flits like an airy dandelion seed drifting through a breeze, lazily catching small lifts of wind and curling through clouds.

Abruptly, the music stops, and I swallow, feeling my nerves tingle. A stillness sets over us.

"Coll, that was . . ."

Like a flash storm, his hands beat into the piano keys furiously, the base line angrily pounded out with a similar intricacy while the top hand flies feverishly with a spell of beautiful minor notes that should clash horribly with the base, yet complement it to perfection. His long fingers touch and mold into the keys in ways I never would have imagined.

My eyes linger on his face—steeled and set like stone. A canvas of hardened, cool collection covering a heated . . . my lips part and my cheeks flush, my thoughts escaping me.

His lips slowly move—part and close—brushing against the air as if he's mouthing a set of words against some silken surface that . . . silk . . . skin . . . his lips . . . .

Why can't I finish any of these thoughts?

As the music starts to subside, the heavy base arches and

thrusts in fervor against the delicate right hand that seems to almost bow in passion.

Heat rises to my chest like fire and I place my hand over my neckline to hide the embarrassing splash of pink color that I know is spreading across my skin.

The music pouring from underneath Coll's left fingertips worships the melody, feverish and urgent, melting and blending into a sensual movement that I can only compare to heaving melodic breaths. The top hand, moving lighter than air fills my senses over and over, bending and twisting against my ears, intensifying my pulse. Notes sliding against notes, chords against chords forcing each note into a powerful carnal apex.

The notes start to trail off, trickling down with bouts of quick gasps from the base until it runs down into a soft roll of oscillating breaths until it dies into a still and peaceful silence.

My heart beats in my chest and all I can do is stand frozen, hoping my legs don't give out underneath me. The final notes echo in my ears, my eyes glued to the piano keys that are no longer moving, while the music lingers inside me. My heart pounds, and all I want to do is rip off my shirt and—

"Hey."

My fingers stroke the dip of my own small cleavage absent-mindedly. I can't even remember the thoughts once clear and vivid in my mind that are now gone.

"Dr. Grim?" Coll's fingers grip his own knees and I can't take my eyes off them. That music. That undeniable composition of musical sex that absolutely—

"Woman!"

I jerk myself out of my stupor to find my eyes locked on Coll's.

"Huh?"

A satisfied smirk pulls at the corner of his mouth like it's tied to a fishing line.

I clear my throat and take a breath. "Well, you might have the talent going for you. The other elements are still in question."

"Right." He doesn't look convinced in any sense of the word. "So, are we done here?"

A simple "sure" gets caught in the back of my throat, a moment of stupor that's, once again, made me forget why in the hell I followed him up here this morning.

"Nooo."

"Sh-nooo? What does that mean?"

I smile and lift my finger, shaking it at him. "Ooo, you're good. You're really good."

"Women tell me that all the time."

"No. I mean, you're good. You may claim you hate the hexen way, but you sure use a lot of your genetics to get what you want."

Coll swivels around on the bench to face me, his pectorals flexing. "I don't know what you're talkin' 'bout."

"Twice now, you've tried to distract me. Make me forget why I came. I know what you're doing."

He lifts his hands in self-defense and sarcastically admits, "Yeh got me. I just can't stop usin' magic." After a pause, he slams the lid of the piano closed and glares at me again. "Listen to me, woman," he spits, "when I say I want nothin' to do with my hexen side, I mean it."

"Except when it benefits you."

"Especially when it benefits me. I like to know I don't have to cheat to get what I want." He stands and looks down on me. I can smell the clean scents from his recent shower emanating from his skin. Cypress and sandalwood, and just a faint trace of ginger. My heart pounds again and I lick my lip, looking into his intense eyes. "Now, explain what yeh need so I can get yeh out of here."

The fog lifts and the anger at him and anxiety of the spell comes rushing back. The memory of my vision, the things I've learned. "I found the security box."

"I know, yeh already said that."

"Inside," I turn and head toward my bag that's been resting on the counter in the kitchen, "was a letter from my dad and a second key." I pull out the two items and bring them back over to Coll, thrusting them into his hands. He opens the letter and scans it. "Coll, whether you and I like it or not, we've been tied together for some purpose. I got that letter and key and I felt even more lost than before. I mean, this man, your relative is coming for me. If he's still alive. Knowing that, knowing I'm caught up in all this mess of magic and prophecy and darkness has made me feel so confused that the only way I knew of finding any answers was by casting a spell."

Coll looks up at me from the letter.

"So, after I left the bank yesterday, I went back to my hotel room, conjured the candles from my apartment back home and tried to get answers about the key and where it goes. I didn't get the answer I wanted, and in fact, I came away with a lot more questions. The spell I cast sucked me back to the day one of the prophesies was revealed. The day my ancestor, Rheda Grim, was symbolically sacrificed to receive the prophecy. You were there."

"What?"

"Well, not you personally. Your ancestor who, by the way, looks too much like you for it to be normal. Ruhmactír. He and your clan were part of the ritual. Before the prophecy and the spell could be completed, Ruhmactír heard everything he needed. He attacked—"

"Woden. I know. Killed him."

"You know the story?"

"Of course. Though, I'm sure our family tells it from a much different perspective. From our point of view, Ruhmactír was the savior. He ended the tyrannical reign of Woden and took back the lands and property that rightfully belonged to us in revenge of the death of our people."

"It was a time of peace, Coll."

"Obviously not." He takes a deep breath, looks back over the letter and frowns. "What does this part mean? 'I know yeh can trust him. Just don't ask me how I know . . . Let's just say I saw some things in your future I'd rather pretend I hadn't seen?'" Coll lifts his eyebrow. "Did your father see us shaggin'?"

I rip the letter out of his hands. "Over my dead body."

Coll looks at me with a sly gaze and licks his lips. "Show me."

"Excuse me?" I bite back. "Show you what?"

"What yeh saw. I want to see this vision."

"I . . ." I'm taken back. "I'm not sure I know how to do that."

Coll shrugs off his sweatshirt and drops it on the piano bench, leaving me to stare at his bare chest. Manwhore.

"I think I can help with that." He strides across the room in silence to a set of cabinets and pulls out a worn, black, leather-bound book. Not requiring an invitation, I follow him up the stairs and across the hallway. Before entering the far south door, he stops and rests his hand on the door knob.

"Just so yeh know, this is not an invitation to come up whenever the hell yeh want. Unless of course, you're naked. I'll let yeh in if you're naked."

"Keep moving, douchbag."

He nods and opens the door. Inside, I see a simple king-sized bed with a black duvet, two black bedside tables, each with their own chrome lamp. A single painting hangs over the bed. The profile of a woman in a black dress, her hands hanging to her sides. Black against white. Nothing else is in the room. So simple, I'd consider it completely bare.

Coll mutters a word and immediately a collection of lit crest candles appear on the floor. Each of them are imprinted with the symbol of Ruhmactír's clan: the wolf cross—an upside down cross with serifs at each point, saving the primitive wolf head at the top. Each flame nearly stands still in the dark room, and the layout of the candles replicates the symbol imprinted on their sides.

"This way, Dr. Grim."

"Please," I say, "enough. After I barged into your home. I think it's okay if you called me Taran. Unless you want me to keep calling you douchbag."

Coll smiles. It's more of a sense than anything I actually see, though his eyes do slide from me quickly.

"All right, woman."

I roll my eyes.

He nods his head for me to meet him at the tip of the wolf's cross. He kneels down and sets the book next to him. I look down and realize it's a grimoire. Hand written spells, images, runes, and instructions glare back at me. They're old. Older than anything I have in my cruddy notebook, and definitely older than Coll.

"You have nothing to do with your hexen line, huh?" I squint.

"You'll need to kneel across from me, here." He ignores my prod and motions to the spot in front of him. I step over the crest candles and brace myself, kneeling down onto the floor. Coll follows quickly after, glancing at the book for a moment and then looking me straight in the eye. It's slightly unnerving.

"So is this your own grimoire?" I ask, my voice uncharacteristically soft.

He nods. "My grandmother left it to me. It's over three hundred years old. Don't," he voice is firm, "knock over one of me crest candles and set it on fire." With the last few words, I finally see a playful jest in his face.

My lips peel apart and I feel a pinch in my stomach thinking about my own family grimoire that I thought I torched.

"What?" he asks.

I shake my head and purse my lips, brushing him off. "Nothing."

"If you say so," he smirks. Then, his voice drops a few extra tones, "Now, you'll need to position your hands like this."

He reaches forward and places one hand on either side of my face, his thumbs resting on either side of my nose, his pinkies closest to my ears, and his pointer fingers in the divots of my temples. "This connects my eyes, ears, and olfactory senses to your vision. Got it?"

I nod and he slowly moves his hands away from my head. I replicate his hand placement, and, realizing I need to be closer to him, slide my knees until they're touching his. I take a deep breath, a wave of cypress, ginger, and sandalwood filling the recesses of my senses. Coll's after-shower smell bogs down my mind, making me clear my throat so I can get a decent breath. There's a glint in his eyes—the side of his mouth slowly tipping up.

"What's the problem now?" he asks.

"You wear too much cologne," I mutter, getting ready to place my hands on his head.

"I've got news for yeh, woman. I don't wear cologne."

I roll my eyes again and place my hands and fingers in the correct places alongside his face and ears. Then, looking down at the book near our knees, I quickly memorize the short spell.

Mina til mina. Eje til eje. Mala af bille. Mar sina re lom.

Mind to mind. Eye to Eye. Exchange of image. So sayth I.

I lick my lips and breathe again, gently closing my eyes. "*Mina til mina. Eje til eje. Mala af bille. Mar sina re lom.*" With my "m" hanging in the air, Coll takes a breath and matches my words. "*Mina til mina. Eje til eje. Mala af bille. Mar sina re lom.*"

When the energy in the air doesn't shift or tremble, I open my eyes. The candles adjacent from us continue to softly flicker; the air remains stagnant and lifeless. Frowning, I increase the force in my voice, and try again.

"*Mina til mina. Eje til eje. Mala af bille. Mar sina re lom.*"

This time, Coll's eyes flick open and he joins me for the second line, his own face filled with curiosity.

Again. Nothing.

"What's the matter? Why isn't it working?" I ask.

"I'm not sure."

I lower my hands and he turns to flip through the grimoire, looking for an answer or a step we may have missed. I reach up to scratch my temple and when I lower my hand, the round white scar on my palm screams to get my attention.

"Wait. I don't think it's a problem with the spell," I whisper.

"What?" he says, flipping back another page. "Maybe there's another spell we need to try first."

"There's nothing *wrong* with the spell."

Coll finally looks at me. I reach over and grab his wrist, forcing his palm upward and exposing the straight line that's glaringly red in the center of his hand.

"Our hands are in the wrong place," I tell him.

Brushing my fingers down the center of his palm and down his wrist, I feel a surge in the air around me, confirming my suspicions. Beneath the pads of my fingers I feel his pulse thrumming in a controlled beat. I slip my left hand into his right in the same way until our hands are interlocked, our palms meeting, and holding tight. At the brushing of my hands against his wrist, his pulse beats harder.

"Taran?" he finally says my name.

Without answering, I look up at him.

"Did you just . . ." He looks at me skeptically.

"Did I just what?"

He smiles and I swear he tightens his grip on my hands. The more he thinks on it, his smile fades and he faintly nods. "Never mind."

What does he think I did? I frown, keeping my thoughts to myself, and form the words in my mind once more. "*Mina til mina. Eje til eje. Mala af bille. Mar sina re lom.*"

"*Mina til mina. Eje til eje. Mala af bille. Mar sina re lom,*" Coll joins.

The flames of the candles drift away from us, reaching for the opposite wall.

"*Mina til mina. Eje til eje. Mala af bille. Mar sina re lom.*" I say alone, smiling. This time, my hair whips across my face and I feel a warmth building underneath my right hand—my marked hand that's matched to Coll's. I quickly look down, taking another breath, and Coll does the same. Our hands are blazing white.

"*Mina til mina. Eje til eje. Mala af bille. Mar sina re lom!*"

Our voices deepen and intensify, and the light growing between our hands explodes, engulfing us and dragging our perception into my own memory.

* * *

The heavy scent of Coll disappears, leaving a trace of fresh grass and early summer. There's a chill in the air, foreshadowing the fall of the sun behind the horizon. After a shaking breath, I push myself up to a sitting position and look around. Coll's nowhere near me, which must mean he entered someone else's body.

"Rheda!" the voice of my mother calls once more. Her jet-black hair whipping behind her.

"Yes, mother?" I respond again, in the same form of Hexen.

"Your father is waiting. The ritual!"

"Coming!" I quickly stand and run toward Frig.

Like before, the same grass tickles my bare legs, poking through the sackcloth dress I'm wearing. My mind whirls with ideas of where Coll is, and my first guess is his own grandfather, Ruhmactír.

Her voice is like honey, something I completely missed in the last vision. "Have you prayed to the ancestors?"

"Yes."

"And you are ready?"

I take a deep breath, this time, fully prepared for the chaos that's about to ensue. "Yes. Zonne has accepted my offer."

"Good. Come."

We tread up the hill and at the top I can see the large village below. The smoke swells out of the roof holes, and the stone table in the center square.

Frig pulls me down the hill and I attempt to look into the eyes of each village member I walk by.

Where are you, Coll?

The drum beats rhythmically, the clans chant around us. Woden waits from me at the head of the stone table, and even this second time around, he's imposing and dark—like a black-bearded anti-Santa Clause, with leathery cheeks, no round belly, and biceps like rocks.

Frig leads me to the foot of the table like before and swivels me around. She chants, stripping the cloak off my back and leaving me standing there in the simple sackcloth. The next woman, shorter with honey blonde hair, brings the carved bowl of ashes. Frig places her hands in the ash and then strokes the soot over my body once more.

When she finishes, I'm once again led to the north side of the table. The moment I turn around, I catch the eyes of Ruhmactír, and in the recesses of his golden amber eyes, I see a flinch. He recognizes me. Coll's inside of him.

He steps closer to me and looks down, continuing the chant of the village. No longer does he smell of sandalwood, cypress, and ginger. That's all been taken over by ancient smoke and body odor. This time, instead of looking over the village, I affix my eyes on him, realizing he's doing the same to me. Ruhmactír, or Coll—I'm not sure what to call him—throws his head back, looking up at the sky. Coll reaches out, his grip tighter than before, and grabs my shoulders, his eyes now engrossed with the moon. Just like before, the hair on his skin gets thicker and grows, making him moan in pain before his fingers claw my arms. Coll bends over in agony. His fingernails, now claws, dig into my skin. He falls to the ground, panting.

"Daughter." Woden's deep violet eyes pierce me. He motions toward the table and I step up the two stone stairs until I'm on top. I sit down, looking over to the side for Coll and lay back on the table. He's growling out of sight, and an animalistic whimper escapes from him on the ground.

I feel the blood along my arms drip onto the table and it tingles, an energy lacing up through my skin.

Above me, Woden holds the staff in his hand, chanting with the village and clans. The moment he holds his hands and the staff out over my body, the energy from the scratches Coll caused to my arms spreads into my ribs and up my neck. Again, it hits my vocal chords, and I inhale the cold air before my voice erupts with a deathly hollowness.

"In the time of the death of the gods, the council of Woden will enter into the Great House to give greeting," my voice rakes. "Then will be said of his Majesty Zonne to the seal-bearer at his side, 'Go and fetch for me the flail. It is time for the end of hexen.'

My breath continues to wheeze the prophecy. Then, as before, Coll leaps on top of the table, a branch of fire in his jaw, and lunges for Woden.

I push myself to a position where I can see what's happening. Woden casts a spell at Coll, blasting the dog through the air nearly fifty feet. Coll again attacks Woden the moment he's distracted by Frec.

With my hand outstretched, I cast and feel the combined energies of Ruhmactír and my father coursing through my skin and permeating the air like a warrior's arrow. It's too late. The spell hits Coll, his jaws clamped tight on my father's neck.

I hit him again, feeling an anger that's even stronger than the last time I experienced Rheda's life. Ruhmactír shifts and again, collides into the large rune stone.

"Listen to me. All of you," I say, waiting for Coll to stand up—even though I know he won't. "There will befall a time where our kind will cease to exist. The only path to prevent *Deireanhexe* is banding. It has ne'er been high hexen battling shifters. In all the centuries, our people have been one. If you choose to continue with the fulfillment of this prophecy, you'll answer to me, the power of my ancestors," I look down at Woden, "and the energy of the shifter flowing through my veins."

The earth shifts beneath me, the moon twists, gravity takes over once more, and I fall into darkness.

THIRTEEN

MY BED IS WARM. FIRM AND COMFORTING.
Beneath me, it rises and falls with my own breathing. I reach
around to pull the covers back onto me. I can't find them. Just
the firm edge of the mattress. Despite the comfort, I moan,
sounding more ghost-like than calm. The sound of a car
honking outside threatens to wake me up, and I refuse to let
it pull me out of this comfort zone. My hands run along the
mattress, only to find that it's firmer, hairier, and smaller than
I remember.

"Jayz, woman. Yeh look good plastered to my chest."

Adrenaline shocks me awake and I shoot up, falling away
from the man I've been laying on top of. Coll slowly props
himself up on his elbows, his dark hair plastered to one side of
his head with the imprint of the hardwood floor on the right
side of his face. Across his bare chest is a red stamp of where I'd
been lying.

"What happened?" I ask, spinning around in my crouched
position. "How did I get here?"

He grins. "I know yeh've wanted to shag since yeh saw me,

but I have to say," he cracks his neck, "that might be one of the most innovative lays I've ever had."

"What?" I bark.

Coll laughs. "Relax. Nothin' happened. At least," he yawns, "I don't think. We must've passed out on the floor after the spell ended." He pushes himself groggily to his feet, getting his balance before offering me his hand. I reach up and allow him to pull me to my feet. My head spins and the floor sways to the left. Using my other hand, I reach out and grab Coll's arm to keep from falling.

"Feelin' me up while you're at it?" he asks, flexing his arm.

I immediately let go, almost regretting it, tumbling a little to the left. "Are you always this much of a prick?" my voice croaks.

"Oh, come on. You and I both know yeh wanted me the moment I played my piece for yeh. And when I say 'piece' I don't mean my—"

"You wrote that?" I ask, squinting at him, a thin stream of sunlight breaking through the curtains.

For the briefest of moments, his façade fades and I swear I see a hint of insecurity in his face. Quick as it broke through, he covers it up doubly fast. "If you're impressed with that, you should see what else my hands can do."

"Ugh, I need a shower," I mutter, stepping over the candles, many of which blew out while we were under the spell. Only a few melted nearly to the ground. It's a wonder the apartment didn't catch on fire. I walk out of the bedroom and down the hallway before I reach the spiral staircase at the end. Once at the bottom of the stairs, I hear Coll's footsteps traipsing down the hallway, coming to meet me.

"So, is that it?" he asks, jogging down the stairs. "Yeh fondle me and take off? That's not very lady like."

"Who says I'm going anywhere?" I eye him, backing up into the kitchen. I turn around and start looking for his herbal tea blends. Where's that Earl Grey? I open up cupboards, pushing things aside.

"The press to the left. Bottom shelf."

I turn to glance at him and notice the position of the sun outside. It's in the east, and much lower than it was when I first arrived.

"Coll. Either that spell reversed time, or we've missed an entire day."

He furrows his dark eyebrows and looks down at the smart watch on his wrist. "No shite. You're right. It's Mondee."

"Have we been passed out for nearly twenty-four hours?" I gasp.

"Looks that way." He walks up beside me and flips open the cupboard I've been looking for. Inside are jars of tea mixes. The Earl Grey he gave me before, a black that looks like dried figs with lavender and vanilla, a green amaretto, and a red chai with . . .

"Are those flattened cardamom seeds?"

"It produces a stronger flavor."

I look throughout the rest of the cabinet, realizing that there are herbs in here not usually meant for tea, or cooking for that matter.

"Why do you have hyacinth bulbs and moonseed berries in here?"

Coll lifts an eyebrow and folds his arms. "I thought yeh were just lookin' for the tea, not goin' through my personal items."

My voice remains calm, biting back at him all the same. "You're a prick, you know that?"

He rears back and a smile seeps across his face. "Look at the pot callin' out the kettle."

I sidestep his jab and close the cupboard, mimicking his Irish accent. "'I don't want anythin' to do with yeh or my da.'" I fail miserably at it. "*You* said you didn't practice."

Coll lifts a finger. "In my defense, I never actually said that I didn't practice."

I close the cupboard and face him. "You did too."

"No. I didn't."

"Did."

"Didn't."

"Did!"

"Are we going to keep doing this, or will I need to record myself and play it back for you on repeat?"

I sigh, frowning at him. "I don't understand you. Why would you lead me to believe you didn't practice?"

"Easy. I wanted yeh to go away."

"So . . . all that garbage with your father—"

Coll lifts his finger again and wags it once. "Stop right there. I'm still not talkin' 'bout him. Can I get yeh some tea? Or have yeh changed your mind?"

I shake my head. "Oh no. You can't brush me off like that.

He came to talk with me about the very thing I'm now looking for. The *same thing* my dad dedicated his life to finding and protecting. I need to know why Michael is looking for Woden's staff, and I need to know why you hate him so much."

"No, yeh *want* to know. There's a difference."

"I don't care how you define it. So, fine, I *want* to know. Now, tell me why in the hell you can't stand him."

"No," he says, moving around me, looking for a mug. When he finds it, he places it on the counter and waves his hand over it. Steaming coffee fills the inside, smelling of hazelnut and cinnamon.

"That's not good enough for me."

Coll sips the coffee and hisses, putting it back on the countertop. "Needs cream." He snaps his fingers and whispers, "*baen*." The surface of the coffee swirls with milk and he sips it again.

"Perfect."

"Coll!" I press again.

This time, he at least looks at me, an expression of contrived bewilderment painted across his features. "What?"

"Tell me what's going on."

The playfulness drops from his eyes and he sets the mug on the countertop. After pressing his lips and looking around the apartment, he leans back, folding his arms across his bare chest. "Yeh want to know the history behind me and Michael?"

"I at least want to know why you let me believe you don't practice. And I want to know how much you and your father are actually working together. Because, like I said, my dad spent most of his life—no," I correct myself, "he *gave* his life, protecting me from this. Now, I might seem intrusive, nosy, and, in your words," I growl, "*bitchy* to you, but this is personal for me. If you know more than you're telling me, I deserve to know. Now."

Coll takes a deep breath and nods. "Michael's been searchin' for that damn staff since the day I was born, it seems. I don't remember a minute that went by when he wasn't away on some dig, or buried in his office with books. So, yes. I've known he's wanted it. But," he narrows his eyes, "if you're askin' if I'm workin' with him, the answer's no. You're headed arseways with that question."

"So why did you tell me you don't want anything to do with hexen magic?"

"Again, I never said that."

"Yes, you—"

Coll holds up a hand. "I said, and I'd like to quote, 'I'd rather shove a red-hot poker in my arse before being associated with either of you."

My mouth, still hanging open from being cut off, slowly closes and I come within two inches of his face. "You did say that. You also said, *and I'd like to quote,* 'I do everything I can to stay out of it.'"

He shrugs. "Tomahto, tomayto."

"Not really." I shake my head. "So, why distance yourself?"

He looks away from me and frowns. "Michael wanted me to be a certain type of son. The one that embraced the old traditions, knew the history, and would join him in the practice.

Due to . . . our own history, I decided never to associate with him again. So, I," he drapes a hand down his body, showing it off and forcing me to back away, "adopted an alternate life, full of modern enjoyments, money, spirits, and women. I enjoy it to the fullest, and have zero regrets."

"Except, that doesn't seem to be the case."

Coll tilts his head, still putting on the playboy vibe with a casual smile. "Explain."

"You *do* embrace the old traditions. You know more than I do, you're more practiced. You *know* the history and understand it. And underneath this persona that you may or may not actually be, you seem—" I think back to the vibrant poeticism of the notes he played and the feverish intensity my body responded with, "—you seem deeper than what you portray. So, you know what I think?"

"No. What do yeh think?"

I narrow my eyes and step closer to him, the smell of ginger and sandalwood entering my senses. My heart pounds heavily when I look up at him and I swear he just leaned in closer to me. It almost makes me rethink what I'm about to say.

Almost.

"I think you're exactly what your father wanted you to be, and *that's* what pisses you off."

With that, the playfulness dies. The lift in his lip, the juvenility in his eyes, and the relaxed stature disappear, and the man I'm standing with is austere, distant, and his body language stiffens.

"I didn't realize yeh were a shrink."

"I'm not."

"Then yeh'd best keep your nose where it belongs, and out of other people's lives." He pushes himself away from the counter and leaves me standing in the same place. Irritation—and a hint of guilt—makes my heart thump. While I know he won't talk about his dad with me, I still need some credible information, and there's only been one person who's been willing to give me what I ask.

*   *   *

I flip through my cell, looking for the right name. It would have to be within walking distance, I would assume.

"Where are you?" I whisper to myself.

"Well, if you don't know that question, you might want to reconsider stepping outside," the doorman says. Karl smiles at me pleasantly and holds the door.

I laugh, despite the tension in my shoulders and neck. "Sorry, I'm just trying to find my way. Do you have any idea where Mr. Donovan's sister lives? Sera?"

"I don't, Miss. Sorry."

I nod and walk outside, looking up the sidewalk where I saw Coll sauntering the morning before. "I'll find it," I say in an afterthought to Karl. "Thank you!"

He tips his hat and I continue walking down the street, my hair pulled into a somewhat manageable ponytail and my face still cool from the cold water I splashed across it. While I know

Coll is at least willing to help me, I know he'll never—if at least, be way too reluctant—to share his history with his dad. If Michael Donovan has been searching for *Craniarann* since he was a young man, there's a chance his path crossed with my dad's. The question that plagues me is why my dad never mentioned him. Or maybe he has in his journals, and I haven't yet been able to find those. If Dad worked with a Radolf Wolf to find the staff, a man who is supposedly another descendant of Ruhmactír, then it makes sense that the Donovans would know him.

Crap.

I stop walking.

I should have asked Coll about Radolf. Maybe he's a distant cousin, or even an uncle. Well, I am headed to see Sera. She'll know just as well as Coll, I'd suppose.

Carrying on, I stick my phone back in my purse. After taking a deep breath, I whisper the words, "*Tóa mi Sera Donovan.*"

My vision tunnels and everything around me becomes blurry, except for a clear and contrasting path in front of me. Almost like a virtual reality photograph with a focused blur around the edges. Careful to watch for movement to my right and left, I walk through the clear tunnel and pursue the spell's direction toward Sera Donovan. It takes me down a right, then a left, then through a winding road through some very tightly wedged apartment buildings before it zeros in on a black door with a brass knocker on it.

The moment I'm a foot within the door, the spell ends and the blurred tunnel evaporates around me. My fist raps on the door, and then I groan at my obvious lack of sight today. There's a knocker. And a doorbell?

I wait for a few minutes, listening for any movement inside the house. When it seems that no one heard me, I reach over to push the doorbell. Footsteps pound down the stairs and the next thing I know, an older woman, about my mom's age, is opening the door. Her hair is pulled into a French twist and she looks at the door and then at me.

"Can't open a door?" she asks.

"Excuse me? I'm just looking for Sera Donovan."

She sighs and steps back. "She's in the upstairs apartment. I just gathered her rent."

I stick my head in, realizing that this is a two-story apartment with an adjoining hallway. I could have just walked in on my own, which is probably why she's a tad irritated and wondering why I can't manage a door on my own.

"Oh. Sorry. So, she's home?"

The woman motions up the stairs with a nod. I thank her and quietly jog up the stairs until I'm standing in front of the top door. The number 2B is stamped on it. My knuckles tap on the wood and immediately the door opens. Sera's exhausted state immediately changes into a smile once she sees me.

"Hello! Taran, right?"

"Yes," I smile.

"What are yeh doin' here?" she asks, inviting me inside. I follow her direction and step through the door while she holds it open. Inside, the main living area is full of color and patterns. The walls are a rich teal, while the focal point is a fuchsia arm chair. Gray and white striped curtains hang from the small window and a modern light fixture is the perfect balance to the rows and rows and rows of books.

"Well, actually, I have some questions for you. I'm not bothering you, am I?"

"No! I don't have to leave for work for another three hours." She shuts the door and turns with a smile. "I'm not sure what answers I have for yeh. I'll do my best. Do yeh want an Earl Grey? English Breakfast?"

"Earl Grey, please."

Sera zips into the kitchen and while she pours me a cup, I move to the black couch sitting at the other end of the small living area. When she returns, she offers me an adorable yellow teacup and saucer then sits next to me on the couch.

"What did Collens do now?"

I laugh, cradling the hot cup in my hands, pulling the homemade tea bag around by its string. "Nothing. Actually, after you left, I managed to get him to talk with me."

"Not surprisin'." She smirks.

"What does that mean?" I ask.

She sighs. "Nothin'. So, what can I answer for yeh?"

I clear my throat after sipping the tea, instantly recognizing Coll's own blend of herbs, and set the cup on the nearby side table. "I realize this is a touchy subject with your family, and I'm not asking for all the details, I just need to know what I'm dealing with."

Sera nods with understanding. "Yeh want to know 'bout Michael."

"Yes. Before I get there, I have to know: Do you know a man by the name of Radolf Wolf?"

She frowns and bites down on her lip in thought. "Wolf?" she asks. "No, I can't say that name rings a bell. Who is he?"

I take another sip from my teacup, wondering how much I should reveal about why I'm here and what I'm doing.

"My dad left me a letter in a safety security box and he told me about a man named Radolf Wolf that supposedly helped him find *Craniarann*—which, if Coll's mentioned me like you've said he has, I'm sure he's has told you I'm searching for it."

Sera clears her throat nervously, then nods.

"This man he mentioned was a descendant of Ruhmactír, who also happens to be your ancestor."

She nods again, listening.

"He then told me that I needed to be careful because Radolf was coming for me. In fact, I don't know for sure, but I think he's the same man who killed my dad."

"Wait," she points at me, "your da was killed because of this?"

"Yes. I was very young. Despite that, I still remember it all."

Sera shakes her head and grimaces. "Hold on." She seems to be trying to grasp some sort of bearing before she responds with, "Your da died, and you're still lookin' for it? This thing," she says *thing* like it's revolting, "is somethin' that's consumed Michael's entire life. He's nearly given up everythin'. And it seems your da did too. I mean, to give your life like that, for somethin' so insignificant. It bothers me. How can yeh be doin' this?"

"It's hard to explain," I admit. "The other day I was ready to jump on a plane and head home. Then I realized this is something I . . ." What? I ask myself. What's really got me attached to this? My father's death. The intrigue of seeing my own hand on a set of ancient runes? The trances? The lost time and the prophesies? It's all of it. Most importantly, I'm doing it for me. For the tug that pulls at the magic within me, telling me this is more than just a silly stick.

"This is something I have to complete," I finally finish. "My father died protecting me from this, and at the same time, prepared the way for me because it's something I'm meant to do. Even though it's not necessarily something I want to. "

We sit in silence for a moment, me knowing she probably doesn't understand. Then, I look at her and ask, "You swear you never met a man with that name?"

She nods.

I think on that for a brief second before asking, "How much, exactly, has Coll told you about why I'm here?"

She smiles and then bites her lip again. "Everythin'. At least everythin' you've told him up until I met yeh yesterdee. I know Michael came to see yeh in the states, and I know you're lookin' for the staff of Woden. I also know 'bout the marks on your hands, I know your da left an envelope and key for Collens to give yeh. You're—" she hesitates and then continues, "you're not angry are yeh?"

"How could I be?" I smile, though feeling a little irritated that Coll refuses to share anything with me while he tells his sister everything *about* me. "Heaven knows I'm prying into your family life enough to reciprocate."

Sera smiles warmly. "So, what do yeh want to know?"

Without beating around the ever-present bush in the Donovan family, I blurt out, "Should I be worried about Michael?"

The smile on her face falters and she exchanges it for a pursed set of lips while looking down. When she looks back up at me, she's studious. "Can I show yeh somethin'?"

I nod, a little taken back. "Sure."

Sera stands up from the couch and moves over to the black metal entertainment center. From a selection of disk cases, she pulls out a particular one and pulls out a DVD. After setting it in the player and turning the television on, she wanders back over to me, the remote-control dangling in her hands.

"I'm not goin' to tell yeh 'bout Collens's history with Michael. Like I said before, that's his story to tell. But, on the other hand, I think havin' some insight into our father might help yeh a bit."

I reach over for my tea again and take a sip. "Was he neglectful? Abusive?"

Coll's sister bites lightly on her lip, then turns to the television and pushes a button on the remote. The video plays and I instantly come face to face with a little blonde girl making faces into the camera. She must only be about two or three.

"Sera!" a man laughs, obviously the person behind the

camera. "Sera, back up, yeh li'le monster. I can't see everyone else!"

Sera giggles and runs away. Behind her is a sandy beach littered with pebbles. There's also a collection of blankets that have been messed up with sand all over them, a cooler, and a woman sitting on the blanket, breastfeeding her youngest daughter.

"Da!" The camera man gets plowed into from behind and the camera jostles. I hear him growl like a monster and try to resituate the camera once more. When he picks it up, I find myself looking into the face of a young Coll. He's got to be about five, standing there in just a pair of red swimming trunks, his pale skin peaked with goose bumps from the cold. I have to fight back a smile when I see the crazy cowlick over his left temple.

"Can I hold it?" he asks his father.

"Sure. Yeh know how teh work it?"

"Uh huh," Coll enthusiastically nods.

I glance over at Sera, and she's watching me. Not the television.

When I look back, Michael has set the camera in his son's hands and he shifts over onto the blanket next to his wife. She smiles at him before he brushes her black hair away from her ivory cheek and kisses it.

"Ew! Da!" Coll struggles to steady the camera.

"Oh?" The young Michael's eyebrow lifts, just like Coll's does, and he gets a wicked look on his face. Purely playful.

"Yeh think that's gross, son? One day you might not hate it so much."

If I was drinking my tea, it'd be coming out of my nose right about now. That's the understatement of the century.

Michael pulls his wife's face around and they both kiss longingly, baby Emilia struggling and kicking in her mother's arms.

"Gross!" the camera drops to the ground and I swear I hear Michael drop a soft F-bomb under his breath before he hurries over to it. The video ends, and I'm left staring at a blank screen.

I turn back to Sera and she avoids my gaze, her blonde hair draping in front of her face. She tucks it back behind her ear. "There are a lot of issues with Michael Donovan."

"I don't understand. The Michael I saw in that video loved his kids—his wife. What changed?"

Sera finally looks me in the eye. "One thing yeh need to know about Michael Donovan is that this video is the only proof I have that he was ever a decent hexen bein'. It's the only memory I have of him that doesn't make me want to peel my skin off my body."

"Sera, what happened? What did he do?"

"A lot of things," she says, staring at the floor absently. "One of the largest bein' that . . . we all think he killed our mother. The very woman you just saw him kiss."

FOURTEEN

MICHAEL KILLED HIS WIFE? MY EYES SLIDE AWAY
from Sera and I sink deeper into her couch. When I heard
the Donovans dealt with *family issues*, I was ready to hear the
words "overbearing," "negligent," "manipulative," or maybe
even "domestic abuser." After what I just watched, I'd never
guess Michael Donovan was the murderer of that woman.

"How do you—" I stutter, "why do you think he did?"

Sera looks away from me with a sigh. Her bright face has
become shadowed. "About the time that Collens turned six, he
says Da became . . . differ'nt."

"His memory of that is clear enough?"

She nods in a sad and reflective sort of way. "He says it was
a stark enough difference to notice. He says even mum could
sense a differ'nce in him. In fact, Collens still claims that mum
took him aside once and warned him never to be alone with
Michael. It was shortly after, that she disappeared and Collens
became even more antagonistic toward him. Michael sent out
the police and even some search parties. A while later, she was
declared officially dead. After," her voice becomes distant, "after
Collens turned fifteen, he ran away—takin' a large sum of his

inheritance with him, mind ye—and quickly emancipated himself from the family while finishin' school and getting his degrees."

My eyebrow crooks upward. "He has more than one?"

Sera cracks a smile. "A job too."

"Well, I knew that." Still, I feel genuinely shocked. I play it up teasingly. "What does he do when he's not walking around topless in his apartment and jet-setting around for the 'bank?'"

This time she giggles. "Oh, jayz. That man's more talk than anythin' else. Well, he actually works as a financial consultant for high-profile accounts at the bank. Like yeh just said, usually he's not there, and often he has to travel."

"Ah," I look off into the distance, thinking about our initial run-in at the airport. I glance back at Sera, who's now smiling at me. "I thought you said you weren't going to tell me about Coll's issues with Michael. Or . . . talk about Coll at all for that matter."

"Well, I'm still not givin' yeh tons of details," she sighs. "And especially the things I know he wouldn't want me to tell. Yeh know, this isn't just his story either. See, he still kept in contact with me and Emilia after he left, knowin' on some level that we'd be all right until we turned fifteen and . . . knowin' he couldn't yet take care of us on his own."

I hold up a hand and make her take a pause. "What do you mean fifteen? Why fifteen?"

"That's," she looked off into the distance, hesitating to continue, "that's when we come into our hexen powers."

"You don't have them from birth?"

"One of the drawbacks of being a shapeshifter hexen, I'm afraid," Sera gives me a sad smile. There's something else there, a part of the story she's holding back. This time I decide to let it go, watching the memory flit across her face. It's something that hurts, even still, and I can sense it. Though Sera might be around my age, there's a child-like fear in the depths of her adult gaze that I don't dare prod.

"I suppose . . ." I finally mutter, "it would be a good idea to continue avoiding Michael, then."

She looks back at me and nods. "Knowin' what I do 'bout my da, that would be my suggestion. But, I have to warn yeh, if you're lookin' for the same artifact he is, I doubt you'll be able to avoid him much longer."

* * *

"Thank you so much for this," I say, lifting my purse to my shoulder. "You've . . . helped a lot."

"I don't know 'bout that," Sera leans on the doorpost.

"Are you kidding me? At least I know I've been justified in avoiding him. Plus, I feel I might be able to better handle Coll now, at the very least. A bit more patience wouldn't hurt."

Sera purses her lips and nods. "Of course. Just don't tell Collens I said anythin' to yeh," she chuckles. "Oh, he'd kill me. He'd kill me good."

"Again, I highly doubt that," I smile, and I mean it. "If he kills anyone over this, it'll be me. In fact, if he knew I was here he'd probably have my head."

Sera smiles. "I think yeh might be wrong 'bout that."

I tip my head, realizing this isn't the first time Sera's been hinting at something. For some reason it makes me brave enough to say, "You keep saying stuff like that. Why? Has Coll said something about me?"

"Collens doesn't talk about his women with me. Not usually," she corrects. "You're the only one he's ever mentioned. Granted, it's usually nasty and he's cursin' like a dockhand, but I know me brother. I know 'im very well. Better than anyone, actually." She winks at me before giving me one last goodbye and shutting the door behind me.

Discomfort glues me to my spot for a good ten seconds.

I wonder exactly what Coll's said to his sister. All the winking, all the hinting, and all the "you're the only one he's every mentioned" talk creates this odd twinge inside my chest. I can't tell whether I like it or not.

I finally turn and my shoes clunk down the staircase. Before I open the door that spits me back out onto the street I take a deep breath. It's a bit busier now. Delivery trucks, bike messengers, and pedestrians scuttle back and forth down the streets and sidewalks.

Still, all that chaos and noise and the only thing I can focus on is: Michael Donovan. Murderer. Possible murderer at least.

No wonder his kids hate him.

"Dr. Grim?"

The sound of Coll's startled voice makes me not what to move, or even look in the direction he's coming. I cuss under my breath.

"What in the hell are yeh doin' here?" he asks, cautiously.

I steady myself before pivoting to the east. He's standing a decent six feet from me, his eyes darting back and forth between me and the door I just exited. Dressed in a pair of toffee slacks, an oxford-blue vest, steel-color shirt collar, and a leather jacket, he looks every bit the cool collected patrician he normally exudes. If it weren't for the ice burning in his gold eyes and the tense tendons in his flexed jaw, I'd probably take a jab at the fact that his jacket collar is popped on only one side—destroying his well-kempt image.

"I came to ask Sera some questions."

"Questions," he spits, his voice darker, yet still polite. "What kind of questions?"

I pause for a bit, looking for the right words, and finally I just let them out, controlling them in an effort to preserve my life.

"Look, you wouldn't tell me what I wanted to know and I needed to ask someone. Michael came to me in California looking into," I lower my voice, "*my family heirloom*, and the moment I got out here, I kept finding out that everyone was deadly afraid of him! I didn't know if it was just me feeling eerie about him, or if there was a legitimate reason I needed to stay away. You refused to tell me what was going on. I had to know."

"You had—" he cuts himself off, looking at the woman passing him. "You *had* to know?" When he speaks the second time, his voice is hushed, still holding onto a certain amount of respectability.

"Coll, my dad died because of this. *My* dad. The man

who sang nursery rhymes to me every night. The man who shoved me in a cupboard to protect me from his killer. The man who took me out for ice-cream every Tuesday, if he was actually around. The man who's not entirely unlike the Michael Donovan I just watched on Sera's DVD upstairs. Now, I don't know what made him change so much that you think he killed your mom. But, certainly you understa—"

The look on Coll's face sours and he steps toward me. "You saw what?" his voice is cold and livid.

I look up into his face, kicking myself. "Sera showed me the video of your family on the beach."

"You saw it?" Now, he's right up in my face. "She told yeh?"

"I didn't ask to see the video, if that's what you're implying."

Coll breathes hard once, twice. "DAMN!" he shouts. "Who gave yeh the right?"

"Sera, that's who!"

Coll steps away from me, running his hand through his hair, making it look disheveled and wild. When he turns back, his energy intensifies. "Yeh say your da died? And what? Yeh want to subject my sisters to the same fate? Yeh drag Sera into it?! Yeh visit her without my approval, and pry into *our family life?*"

"Your approval?" I bite back. "What are you, the jail keep?"

He marches toward me, shoving his finger in my face. "I risked my life to keep her and Emilia safe, and you track her down just hours after leavin' my house?"

"Minutes, actually," I glare up at him. "And you know what would have stopped me from coming?"

"I don't give a shite."

"You could have answered my questions!" My voice drops after a dozen eyes focus on me. With an intense hiss, I continue, "I don't need your life story and your deepest darkest secrets, but I do have to know about your father."

Coll's face turns red and he leans in closer. "That monster isn't my father. Not anymore. And now, yeh could have lead him directly to her door. God knows he's lookin' over your shoulder all the time."

That revelation chills my bones. "He's what?"

"*Besaint ag skjoth,*" he mutters, clapping his hands together and widening them slowly in the direction of the house. Like a shimmering mirage, I see the spell take its place—a barrier around the apartment building.

"What was that?"

"No matter how hard yeh try, your never gettin' in that home again. Yeh hear me?"

I hear thunder crack in the heavens above and I step closer to Coll, anger boiling beneath my skin. "Are you threatening me?"

Now, only an inch from my face, he hisses. "I'll kill yeh next time yeh contact her. That's not a threat. It's a guarantee. Yeh can pull my arse into this day after day, but yeh go after my sisters and there will be hell to pay. Do I make meself clear?"

"Screw you, Donovan." Lightning flashes across the sky.

His eyes flicker to the sky and then quickly snap back to my face. "Yeh put my sister in danger again . . ."

"I can promise you that won't happen."

"Damn right," he growls.

"And it won't," I cut off the end of his word, "be because I stop talking with her. I might come back, although I can't guarantee it. I won't be bullied into staying away from a person who's willing to talk with me—who's willing to help me, unlike you."

Hiking my purse into a more secure spot on my shoulder, I cuff his arm and storm past him. Plenty of cuss words and thoughts tumble around in my head. Most of them even beginning to sound like a chant that beats along with the pounding of my feet on the concrete sidewalk.

Once I'm a safe distance from him, I pull to the side of the nearest building and lean against the wall, allowing myself to breathe.

Sera Donovan underestimates her brother's wrath and protectiveness. All she sees is some troubled teenage kid that's still looking over her—not a blind fury that refuses to be reckoned with. The energy pulsating off him was enough alone to shake me to the ground. I could feel it down into my blood stream. Only—I come to grips with the emotions I was feeling, the energy around me—he was *terrified* more than anything else. That fear of hearing that I witnessed his family's most tender moment and yet again clawed my way into a subject he believes is beyond my needs immediately switched on his lawless anger.

Then again, if I believed my dad killed my mom, I'd probably do everything in my power to keep my sisters safe too.

I shake my head, closing my eyes.

That man brings out the worst in me, and the worst part is

that I always turn things into a massive hurricane every time I talk with him. Like poking a needle into a bear's hide.

"Good job, Taran," I whisper to myself. Moments ago I got him to agree to perform a spell with me, and I here I go. I just had to antagonize him.

While I may have just wrecked any immediate help I would have received from Coll, the fact still remains that I have to find out where to go from here.

I reach into my bag and shuffle things around, feeling for the locker key Dad left me in the security deposit box. My fingers brush against its plastic end and I pull it out. I would try and cast a "last placed" spell on it. Only, it'd just take me back to the bank. It's been too many years since it was used, and any attempt at trying a "return to home" spell would fall flat. As far as the key knows, the bank is its home. The only thing I can do is utilize the ancestors again. Heaven knows where they'll transport my consciousness this time.

I look up and down the street, trying to look like I'm searching for a cab or oncoming cars. The truth is, I don't want to run into Coll again. He's nowhere in sight. Most likely inside Sera's apartment, yelling about me and what a cow I am, flailing his arms in the air ready to punch something. I wait a few more seconds and then start toward the busier street. My chance of grabbing a bus or taxi will be better out there. I need to get back to my hotel. This next spell better work.

FIFTEEN

DEEP BREATH IN, RELEASE AND GAG. THE nauseating smell af human waste, rotting cheese-like bacteria, and sour excrement fills my nose, causing me to choke on my own tongue. Inside my hand, I can feel the key gripped tightly. Although I'm still in the hotel room—the glow of soft candles surrounding me—I hear the faint clipping of horse's hooves on stone and sludge, the pattering of rain, the cry of desperate men and women. I feel the cold bite of air on my skin and sense of death and suffering in the air.

Light filters in through the cracks of my eyes and when I'm finally able to see what's around me, I jerk back, slamming into a rock wall. The sight nearly makes me scream. A congregation of bodies chained to the walls around me look like skeletons with skin and shreds of fabric barely covering their sharp angles and sunken crevices. I'd like to think they're all dead, looking that sharp and hollow. After seeing some of their chests rising and falling, I know it's not the case.

"Where am I?" I whisper to myself. The words don't come out. Only a gurgle from my throat—the raw flesh inside it grating in pain.

"Quiet, witch!" a man bellows in a British accent, and the clash of some object beats against metal rings in my ears.

Witch?

I survey the damp stone room, taking in the rest of the surroundings. I'm in a jail cell and outside of the iron bars is a man dressed in a dark doublet—sitting in the shadows. His wide cotton cuffs and the ruff around his neck decorate his appearance. While his shoes are caked with mud, his stockings and garters are clean and pressed like his breeches. His face is covered in a thick black beard and a halo of pipe smoke circles his head like a cloud of city smog. I'm not sure I dare think about what year I'm in. By the man's accent, I'm most likely in England. Though, even that may not be true. The one thing I'm sure of, he thinks I'm a witch, and what's worse . . . I am. I'm in my ancestor Natty's memory.

The one thing I don't understand is why I'm still sitting here, chained up.

There are spells to get me out of this. So why haven't I used them?

Immediately, my mind goes to my mother—no, not my mother, Natty Grim's mother—her father, her two brothers and five sisters. Seven aunts. Five uncles. Most of them hexens. Some of them human by marriage.

That's why. That's why she never used her magic. To end the hunt and protect her family.

I glance down at my body and shiver. It's emaciated and reeks of sweat and other . . . odors. In the corners rats squeak and peep—in the center, they nibble on the flesh of those who are no longer breathing. Or at least, those without the strength remaining to kick them away. I jerk back in disgust, my chains jingling.

Outside of the cell, a squeal of hinges preludes a thud of stomping feet traveling down wooden stairs. When the men come into view, I count about seven of them while they file into the small room outside of the cell. I squint to get a better look at a book that one of the men is holding, attempting to read the elaborate wording and art on the cover.

IN FORME OF A DIALOGVE.

Dæmonologie.

I suck in my breath. I know that book. It was one *Mórai* gave me as extra reading back when I was about twelve. It wasn't until I was in college that I really started to study the reason behind its history and existence. Written by King James VI in response to his own experience and investment in the North Berwick trials in the 1500s, *Dæmonologie* was the manual all witch hunters used to test and try witches. It explains the marks, the experiments, the implications of witchcraft and hexens and the reasons for persecuting . . . and killing witches under the canonical law. It's full of lies. And an entire population believed it, making it all the more dangerous.

That means it must be at least 1597, if not later.

My breath stills.

Natty was caught and hung in 1612 during the Pendle Hill trials. It was an experience that hung on our family's shoulders for eight years. Eight years of cloaking spells and protection hexes before they finally left Britain and our homeland forever.

I'm living Natty's last moments.

Quick, I think to myself. *Where was Natty killed? What building is this?*

I know this. I know I do. If I can figure it out, I might be able to understand why she's brought me here. Obviously there's something here that has to do with a modern locker key. What is it?

I jerk to attention when I hear iron grind against iron. The key turns in the lock and the next thing I know, the cell door is being pulled open. Four men enter, their eyes dark and yet . . . fearful at the same time. One man, smelling of ale and fish, leans over to unlock the cuffs at my wrists that keep me attached to the wall while other men approach the other living prisoners to unlock their shackles. Not missing a beat, he kicks me in the ribs and yanks me back into a sitting position.

"Thou wilt see, witch, what hell hath in store for thee," he growls. "Learn what wilt happen to ye when ye hex my cattle! Stand!"

The muscles in my legs won't move and I prepare for another kick in the ribs.

"Stand!" He kicks.

I collapse to the ground, telling myself I have to stand. Do it. Do it.

"*Nyrte,*" I whisper to myself. Again, I don't know if the strength spell actually rises over my lips. Still, I feel my legs take hold underneath despite my struggle to pull myself up. Each step out of the jail cell, each stumble up the stairs feels like it may be the last thing I ever do. Somehow I'm able to push my body forward without any additional prodding from the men. Another large door opens and we're herded out into the gray overcast of the day.

Puddles of rain have pooled on the ground, mixed with cattle manure, pig entrails from the butchers, and the contents of chamber pots. At the top of the nearby moors across town lies a sturdy gallows, welcoming each of us witch each step that takes us down the road, closer to our deaths.

Taking a quick opportunity, I glance behind me to get a good look at the building we've been kept in. It's a castle.

"Move along!" one of the men roar.

I grit my teeth and continue limping across the cold wet rocks and dirt. Each of us are marched down the pathway from the castle, making a straight course for the local town. Far in the distance, I can see it. Gallows Hill. I know it from Natty's memory. Just the sight of it causes my heart to feel like lead against my lungs.

I stumble along, being prodded and shoved by the villagers who have started to approach the main road through town. Each of them scream and hiss at us when we walk by. Old vegetables and hard bread pelt my body. Curses, hand gestures. The moment I look over at them and show them the burning power behind my eyes, they stop and back away, only becoming brave enough when the musket-wielding man next to me kicks the back of my legs and sends me flying into the ice-cold mud.

I pull myself to my feet and the guard up ahead stops in front of the local pub, holding the door open. We're led inside, and it's empty. All except for the bar tender who has laid out a glass for each of us, filled with ale. My thin fingers shake uncontrollably. I reach for the glass and lift it to my lips, the edge clinking against my fuzzy teeth. The ale slides down my throat, moistening my lips and sending me off with the only good will the town is willing to muster before my neck is snapped in two.

The moment the last drop of ale is swallowed, we're all escorted back out onto the streets and paraded through the rest of the town, the villagers coming up from behind and following us the last dark steps until we're brought to the steps of the gallows. There are four nooses for four women. The first, Alizon Device—innocent, uneducated, and human—steps up, followed by her mother Elizabeth Device, and Anne Whittle. All three of them horrible human beings. No more hexen than I am a horse. I'm the last. My body shakes with chills. A crowd of angry villagers surround the platform, yelling and throwing chunks of wet dung and mud at us.

The moment the damp rope loops around my neck, my jaw sets like steel and I look up into the sky. How much longer will this vision last? How much—

The floor drops out from underneath me and there's a clear and definite snap.

* * *

I gasp, pushing myself into a sitting position. Without waiting another beat, I crawl over the candles that have now been blown out, their smoke curling and twisting in the dark hotel room. I reach for my laptop, keeping the image of the castle in my mind, and quickly type in: PENDLE WITCH TRIALS, CASTLES.

After a few seconds the results pop up and the top few results directly link me to the Lancaster Castle. After searching the castle's webpage, I come face to face with the image of the building Natty Grim was imprisoned in before she was hung in August of 1612.

"Lockers, lockers, please tell me there are lockers here." I flip from page to page, looking for tourist information. It's still a working castle . . . with access at the gate house. After a few more pages, I find what I need to know.

"Storage lockers are available," I read out loud before shutting my laptop and dashing for my phone. My head spins, still lost somewhere in the memory of my vision, and I have to sit down on my bed, cradling my forehead while I dial the number I begged from Pete. It rings once. Twice. Three times.

"Hello, this is Collens Donovan with London Crown." Coll answers.

"It's me. Taran. I need you to—"

The phone cuts off.

I growl to myself and press the send button again. One ring. Two. Three. Four. Five. Six.

"Come on," I whisper.

When he doesn't pick up the second time, I dial the number

again and wait for the rings. Six before the voicemail jumps in. Again, I dial the same number. This time it only rings twice before prompting me to leave a message. Great, so now he's intentionally rejecting my call. Redial once more. The phone is only able to get in one ring before it's silenced.

"You son of a—"

This time, I send him a text message: *I'm going to keep calling until you pick up.*

I call once more after waiting a minute and this time, he answers on the first ring. "How did you get my number?" he bites.

"Coll, I know you're angry with me and you don't want to talk to me. I get it, and . . ." I grit my teeth, "I'm sorry for what I did. But I finally know what the second key goes to."

"Piss off," his voice cuts through.

"Don't!" I yell. "Don't you dare hang up on me! I need you to come with me to Lancaster Castle."

He sighs. "When will yeh get it into your head, woman? Yeh trespassed into my family's life. Yeh don't *need* me to do anythin'. Yeh want me to, and that's a big difference. Don't call me again."

"Coll, I swear, if you hang up, I'll . . . I'll curse you with the eternal limp. And I'm not talking about the way you walk."

All I hear is a soft shuffling from the other end. Then, everything goes silent. I wait. Not a breath, not a peep. I can't even tell if he's still on the line.

Still nothing.

"Did you hear me?"

I pull my phone away from my ear and look at the timer. The call is still ongoing. He has to still be on the line. When I put the phone back to my ear, Coll takes a deep breath and exhales.

"You think no one's threatened me with that before?" he clips.

"Well, it got your attention, didn't it?"

"Talk, woman."

I pause, making him wait a beat before I respond. "I think the key belongs to a tourist locker at Lancaster Castle."

"And yeh want me to go with yeh?"

I nod. Then, realizing he can't actually see me, I say, "Yes. Since my dad knew you'd be working with me, I feel like you need to come. He may have set up security measures that I need your help with. I can't be sure, and I don't want to drive all the way up there and then find out that I can't get in."

Again, I hear him sigh. "And yeh promise you'll leave my sisters alone?"

"We'll talk about it. But, you have to actually be willing to talk about it. You ignore my questions again and any truce that we have will be dissolved."

"Dammit, woman," he hisses. When no further protests come from his end, I look across the room to my purse.

"Should we meet at the castle, or would you like me to call a cab and meet you at your apartment? I can pay for a cab the full way or you can drive."

"Drive?" he scoffs. "Can't we just *tiaseal?*" Apparate, travel through space, appear and disappear.

I take a deep breath. "I would. If I could."

"Yeh . . . can't?"

"Don't sound so excited about it," I warn him.

"Then," he sighs, "can't it wait 'til tomorra? It's a five-hour drive. If we left now, we wouldn't arrive until," he goes quiet, "twenty-three hours."

Shaking my head, I answer, "Every moment I waste is another moment your dad gets closer to finding out what I'm up to. I can't risk it, can you?"

This time, I don't have to wait long for him to respond. "If that's the case, I have an idea. Stay at your hotel. I'll pick yeh up in twenty minutes."

"Pick me up? Are you volunteering to drive?"

"Not on your life. It's time yeh learned to be a hexen. Which is why we'll need the space. Twenty minutes, Grim."

Sixteen

THE ELEVATOR DINGS AND I LOOK UP THE moment the doors slide open. The lobby is buzzing with hordes of tourists, many of them with backpacks slung over their shoulders or bulky hipster fanny packs drooping from their waist. I squeeze through, saying the occasional "excuse me" attempting to reach the car that's parked out in the drop-off zone of the old hotel. Once outside, I hug my body against the chill of the summer night and look around the cabs, buses, and shuttles, looking for Coll.

There, leaning against the side of a white Mercedes C-Class is Coll. His arms are folded and he's dressed in his same toffee-colored slacks with a Calvin Klein t-shirt and a leather jacket, his white shoes pristine as the color of his car.

"Took yeh long enough," he mutters when I cross the few feet between us.

"You called me twenty-five minutes ago."

He shakes his head and turns to open the door for me. "If I were yeh, I could have been down here in two," he answers.

"Good for you." I give him an overly sweet smile and pat his shoulder before climbing in the car. The black leather bucket

227

seat hugs me underneath and Coll shuts the door the moment I'm in.

After he gets back in and starts the engine, Coll peels out and looks over at me. "So, are yeh going to tell me what gave yeh the idea to go to Lancaster Castle at night? Or am I supposed to guess?"

I turn and glare at him, annoyed. "I cast another guidance spell. I wasn't sure what else to do. This time, the spell took me to 1612."

"What's sixteen twelve?" he asks, keeping his eyes on the road.

"It's a date. You don't recognize it?"

"Should I?"

I hum and look out the window. "I guess you wouldn't. Seeing that since Ruhmactír and the Ravn clan stole Bryden from my family, killed Woden, and drove us out. The Grims then forced to live among humans. Hazards of the lifestyle."

He snorts and I swivel back to look at him.

"What?" I ask.

"It's been over three thousand years. Are yeh still bitter about that?"

"I'm just explaining why my people weren't protected like yours."

"For your information," he turns the wheel and I watch a sign for Richmond Park pass on the left, "the line of my forefathers was also cut off from Bryden. A protective hex dematerialized Bryden the moment the last of the Grims were either forced out or killed."

"*Or* killed?" I ask.

Coll sneers, his eyes straight ahead. "It's unfortunate your ancestor went out the way he did."

"What are you talking about?"

"Víðarr," he pronounces it correctly with the "th" sound, "the son of Woden went into hidin' in the forests surrounding Bryden after the battle. After sneakin' back into the village that night, he was found out, beheaded, and then his body was dragged away. Our people quickly found that everythin' around them was decomposin', fallin' into rottin' bits, and sinkin' into the eart' around them. Bryden was cursed for us." Coll looks over at me again. "My ancestors survived among humans just as yours did."

Woden protected his homeland from treachery. Though this brings a strange sense of warmth to my heart, it's equally unnerving. It means he never fully trusted the Geri or the Ravn clans.

"Sixteen-twelve," I answer with a calmer tone, "was the year of the Pendle Hill trials. My ancestor Natty was one of the people killed. The only witch they actually managed to capture. She was held in Lancaster until the day she was hung."

"Why didn't she save herself? Yeh and I both know she could've."

"To protect the rest of her family. If they'd seen her actually perform a magic spell to free herself, the rest of the Grim family would have been in danger. She would have exposed them all."

The car rolls to a stop and Coll puts it into park. "So? Why not use magic to kill their attackers?"

"And where would that have left us? Feared, even more than we were? Hunted? Used?" I take a breath and turn to him. "It would have created a war they didn't want to fight, and they all knew it."

Coll hums and then opens his door to leave. I copy him and exit out the left side of the car, looking into a grove of trees, their leaves blowing and shimmering in the dusk wind. Coll strides toward the trees and jogs down the small embankment that I neglected to see in the dark when we first pulled up. Following after, I watch my feet, careful not to trip on a fallen log or step into a hole.

"Where are we going?" I ask.

"There's a glade through here. At night, it's secluded enough to give us some privacy."

I dash forward a few paces to catch up and shiver, smelling the faint mist of a coming rain. Up above the clouds are darkening and painting over the faint blue of the remaining sky. After ten minutes or so, Coll helps me down a fallen log and we both break through a wall of trees to find ourselves in a grassy clearing. Nearly ten paces toward the center, Coll turns to face me and narrows his eyes.

"All right, what do yeh know about the *tiaseal?*"

"Honestly," I shake my head, "a lot less than I should. I know it's more difficult than it sounds, and there's a danger to performing it."

Coll thoughtfully touches the tip of his tongue to his teeth. "While mainstream fiction may have gotten a lot wrong about us, there is some truth to the 'splinchin'' danger. Although, if yeh manage to only magic a portion of your body, there's no magic to puttin' yeh right again. You're dead. Aside from that, there's a risk that yeh could end up lost in ether—neither here, nor there. You'd just be lost for eternity, which is one of the reasons yeh should have learned this spell when yeh turned twenty. Your mind would have been mature enough, yet still pliable to believe yeh could do it."

"I was in college when I was twenty."

"That's no excuse. So was I."

I take a deep breath. "Well, that was nine years ago. I can't go back and fix it."

"I'm just telling yeh, it's goin' to be harder than yeh realize."

"I got it!" I bite back. I take another deep breath and exhale loudly through my nose. "Just tell me what I need to do."

Coll folds his arms. "First of all, yeh need to meditate. Feel the energy that's radiatin' through every nerve endin' in your body—become aware of every inch of yourself. The pulse in your veins, the tingle at the tips of your fingers," his voice becomes softer, calmer, "the heat behind your knees, the current wavin' through your brain, and even the gravity keepin' your feet to the ground. If you're not tapped into every bit, you'll leave part of it behind."

I nod.

"Next, you'll need to have a clear vision of the place you're travelin' to. Visualize Lancaster Castle, the grounds surroundin' it, and the area you want to be."

"I've never been there."

"Did yeh see it in a vision?"

"Yes, but that was in the sixteen hundreds. I have no idea what it looks like now."

Coll reaches into his back pocket and unfolds a piece of paper. "Lucky for you, I came prepared." When he shows me what's on the paper, I see the castle and the pathway surrounding it. "That," he points to a corner pathway, "is where we'll meet."

"What?" My eyes widen and panic sets in. "Aren't we going to practice?"

He rolls his eyes. "Of course. Don't get your knickers into a twist."

I breathe a sigh of relief and numbly nod.

"First thing's first. Hold me hands." He reaches out toward me, palms up.

"Why? Don't I have to do this alone?"

Coll snickers and his eyebrows pop. "I'm only helpin' yeh meditate and connect. Hands," he asks again.

My nerves send shockwaves through my arms and chest and I plop my hands into his.

He looks mildly unimpressed. "Not like a dead fish," he mumbles, locking his thumbs around my hands. "Jayz, it's like gripping wet cod."

Putting a little more strength into my grip, I narrow my eyes at him. "Wet?"

This only makes him smile more. "Close your eyes," he tells me. "I'm goin' to engage your magic with me own. It's called an *infe spioris*. Is that . . . all right?"

I nod, closing my eyes and trying to center my focus. Using

my core, I reach out to my toes and the nails, making them a part of me. Next, the—

I feel a set of hands rest on the top of my head, the thumbs caressing the skin of my forehead. My eyes shoot open and I jump back from Coll. "What was that?" I croak.

Coll raises his hands in defense. "That was just me."

"I know, but your hands were holding mine. How could— how did you place them on my head at the same time?"

"Is that what it felt like to yeh?"

"Yes," I gasp at the shock. "What is it supposed to feel like?" I ask.

"It feels different to everyone. I should have warned yeh. Yeh realize I wasn't actually touchin' yeh, right? Well, I wasn't physically touchin' your head at least. Can we try it again? I'll be more . . . aware."

I nod while Coll holds his hands out again. With a shaking breath, I close my eyes once more and attempt to center my focus. The moment I begin to feel the energy in each breath I take, the *infe spioris* begins again. The hands—his hands, yet, not his hands—rest alongside my head, the thumbs— his thumbs—gently grazing along my forehead, and then his fingers travel through the strands of my hair. The sensation is like nothing else I've ever experienced; like each strand of my hair can feel his stroke. His hands cradle my jaw, rubbing against my ears, the lobes, and then his fingers drift over my eyelids. Softly, the touch travels to my cheeks and runs down my nose, trailing off over my lips sending a tingling current through my skin.

I visualize an inner light pulsing into a brilliant glow with each inch his hands journey over. Down my neck, across my collar bones. Warm energy shoots down my arms, his hands skimming my shoulders and down my back. Each beat of my heart seems to make the light grow brighter, my connection to my body growing stronger the farther Coll goes. His hands travel around my waist, stroke up my stomach, and roll along the slight bumps of my rib cage. I flinch the moment his touch pauses beneath my chest and I even hear him breathe deeply in front of me. The graze of the *infe spioris* around and away from my breasts is fleeting. The sense of his metaphysical trigger is still enough to illuminate those untouched parts of me just like the rest of my body. The spell travels down my arms, wrapping around my elbows and every inch of my forearms, wrists, and individual fingertips. From there, his touch travels to my hips, rounds behind and travels down my thighs from behind, brushes to the front and cups my knees before running along the backs of my calves down to my ankles and finishes by brushing each toe.

With my whole body focused in, I feel his warm breath against my ear. "Repeat after me. *Tiaseal.*"

My voice is airy and light, yet more grounded and heavy all at the same time. "*Tiaseal.*"

"Picture me car. The ground yeh stepped onto when yeh got out."

The image of his Mercedes instantly comes to mind.

"Say it," he speaks again. "Once more. *Tiaseal.*"

"*Tiaseal.*"

A hole drills into my chest, driving me backward and the light that was glowing inside me instantly extinguishes and I feel his grip leave my hands. My feet crunch underneath me and my eyes shoot open. The evening moon is now hanging starkly in the sky while the last remnants of the day fade into the horizon. When I turn to the side, I find myself standing next to a white Mercedes, and Coll is nowhere in sight.

"That was perfect."

At the sound of Coll's voice, I spin around to see him just behind me.

"Although, you did leave this," he holds up my shoe and smiles, "behind." He hands it to me and, in a daze, I lean over to slip the pointed ballet flat back on. "You ready for round two?" Coll asks.

From the time I engaged the *tiaseal* spell, I haven't breathed. I finally inhale and it comes off a little more like a gasp. "Round two?"

"Your final exam."

"We're going to Lancaster Castle? Now?"

Coll nods. "Yeh catch on fast, woman."

My cheeks flush hot and I look down at his hands, remembering the feel of them all over my body. "Um, same, uh . . . process?" When I look at him again, he's squinting at me, lost in thought. Slowly, he nods. "Unless yeh feel you can focus on your own."

While I'd want nothing more than to tell him I can take care of myself, the image of my spliced body—half of it bleeding out near his car, the other half dangling from a tree—shocks me back to reality and I shake my head. "I'm not sure if I trust myself yet." Quickly, I pull the folded piece of paper, the image of the Lancaster Castle, studying the spot Coll wants me to travel to.

Coll steps closer and takes my left hand in his. "If it makes yeh feel any better, I didn't really enjoy the *infe spioris* any more than you did."

At the thought that Coll hated touching me, I jerk back, only slightly noticeable, shoving the paper haphazardly into my back pocket with only one free hand. "Well, I apologize. I didn't exactly ask you to do it, did I?"

Coll smiles. "I meant when my instructor taught me. Felt like wind rushin' through my body, and everythin' smelt of cranberries. Damn things make me retch."

"Oh." Shame and embarrassment only hang on for a brief spell before I ask, "Your instructor?"

He nods, taking my other hand. "I'll tell you 'bout it later. Close your eyes."

For a moment, I see a fleck of jest in his gold eyes before it disappears and his focus takes over. I close my eyes waiting for the *infe spioris*. It begins at my head, then immediately ignites my entire body.

* * *

I hobble forward and reach for something to steady me, only to find there's nothing around and I stumble to the ground. "Ugh," I groan, pushing myself back to my knees and brushing the dirt off my hands. A moment ago I'd been standing in a dirt lot next to Coll's car, and now—

I take a good look around to make sure I ended up in the right place. Everything around me is silent. Between the natural music of crickets in the grass, and rustle of leaves in the trees, there's no one else here. I look back to the left and take a deep sigh of relief. At least the castle is nearby. I may not be in the place I intended. For this only being my second time engaging a *tiaseal* spell, landing a hundred feet off base isn't that bad.

After pushing myself to my feet, I brush my pants and jog toward the castle. There's a small parking lot to the west of me, which means the gate house must be nearby. Just past that, should be the corner within the gate where Coll wanted me to meet him.

I have to hurry. Odds are, he's going to think I spliced myself and he's now in a hectic panic. Of course, not after feeling a jolt of glee that he won't have to deal with me anymore.

I arrive at the gatehouse and try the first door. Locked.

"Oh, come on," I whisper. With a simple lock, I'd probably just try an unlatching spell. Technology has started to throw a kink in my magical abilities. While I could possibly try to knock out the power, there might be a chance that some other backup generator might kick in. Granted, this is a historical building and not the secret service. I'd just rather not go to jail tonight if I can avoid it.

One more door. Locked.

"You've got to be kidding me."

The only other option I have is trying to travel the short

distance to the other side of the security fence so I can get inside. I step back and reach into my back pocket for the crumpled picture. Memorize it, I say to myself. That's the corner we need to go to. That's the destination. Folding it up nicely this time, I stick it back in my pocket and close my eyes. I don't have Coll this time to help me focus and connect with my body. I have to do it myself. Starting at my head, I key into my energy, my hair, my skin, my face, limbs, organs, and every nerve. The feeling of light illuminating under my skin clues me into knowing I'm connecting what I need. When I feel everything focused, I remember to move my lips and say, "*Tiaseal,*" bringing to mind the image of the castle pathway.

An odd, yet familiar hole burrows into my chest, pinching tight and pulling me backward, dousing the light and pulling my feet off of the hard pavement. The moment I feel earth underneath my shoes once more, I open my eyes and glance around.

"Oh my gosh, I made it," I mutter. I breathe a sigh of relief and look around for Coll. He's not here. "Coll?" I harshly whisper into the night.

No answer.

"Where is he?"

A distant pop rings in my ears and I turn to the left where a single shadow is moving along the path. It could be Coll. It could also be a security guard. Deciding it's best to stay hidden, I jump behind the nearest wall and keep my breathing still. The sound of footsteps crunches on the pathway, and I wait for the figure to come into my line of sight. I squint at the person approaching, and when I see the same jacket and Calvin Klein t-shirt in the dim light, I sigh and step out.

"It's you," I breathe.

Coll jumps and spins on me, his eyes wide and his breathing harsh. "Where the hell have yeh been?" he gasps. "I waited for five minutes and when yeh never came, I went back to look for yeh."

"I wasn't there, though."

"Damn right! I thought you'd gotten severed and mangled somewhere!"

"Well, I'm not," I mutter, looking down at myself to prove that I'm okay. "I think you can chill out now."

"Shite." He runs a hand through his hair and shakes his head. "Don't ever do that again."

"Sorry. I ended up a hundred feet or so away from the gatehouse and I had to travel inside the walls."

Coll pauses and steps closer. "Yeh did it on your own? Without help?"

I tilt my head. "I didn't really have a choice, did I?"

"Yeh could have waited."

"For you? Please." I walk up to him and look to the front gate. "The lockers should be in that smaller building there, I think."

He nods, still keeping his eyes on me. "After you."

We both walk toward the second welcome building, Coll temporarily eliminating security cameras along the way. Once we're inside, I pull the key from my own jacket pocket and scan the first row of lockers.

"Which one? They all seem," I look down the next row, and the next, "to have keys already."

Coll squints his eyes to study the lockers and hunkers down to get a better look. "Your da probably realized they would have eventually replaced any key that went missin' for a period of time. He'd have to place two spells on the locker." He looks up at me, and I realize just how much his eyes shine in the darkness—like a wolf's.

"Two spells?"

"One to imitate the look of an existin' key, and the second to draw attention away from it so no tourist would want to use that particular locker."

"So, how do we find it?" I ask.

Coll stands again and faces me. "Yeh said your dad may have set up security measures that you and I need to crack together, right?"

"I don't know for sure. I was just guessing."

"And . . ." he wags his finger at me, "your dad would have known that about us. He already saw us working together, hence why he was able to tell yeh I could be trusted."

"Well," I roll my eyes, "as far as he knew."

Coll glares playfully at me and looks around. "What if you're right? What if the only way to get the locker to reveal itself—"

". . . is by using our connection?" I finish.

Coll nods.

"How?" I ask pointedly.

Reaching out toward me, Coll takes my hand, the one imprinted with a circle and holds it in his marked palm. A gentle warmth spreads up my arm and I watch him carefully. "What if we simply cast a 'reveal' spell?"

"*Afslochtan?*" I ask.

With that, the marks in our hands illuminate and a beam of light shoots out from within our grip. My head jerks to the side to see where the light has pointed to, to find a locker that I swear wasn't there before. Both Coll and I drop our hands and I step up to the row of lockers, counting the number of rows and columns. There are ten lockers on the top row, there used to be nine on the second, and ten on the third. The second row used to have a . . . what was it? Something else was there. I can't remember what it used to be. Now, I'm standing here, looking at the number twelve locker that was once unnoticeable.

A key already rests in the hole. When I reach out to grab it, my hand passes straight through it. "I'm going to guess we've found the right one," I mumble, looking to Coll.

He lifts an eyebrow and nods at it. "Let's open it."

I reach into my jacket and grab the key Dad left me in the security deposit box at the bank. Pretending there isn't a key already in the lock hole, I stick the tangible one into the slot and it slides inside. After twisting it to the right, the door unlatches and I swing it back. Inside is a bound set of books. The top is leather bound and thin, the second has a very seventies vibe and has an olive-lime green cover, while the last three are almost matching sets of composition notebooks. I reach in and easily pull them out.

"Let's get out of here." I breathe, tucking them under my arm. "We can study them later."

"Good idea."

I leave the key where it is and Coll and I stalk back to the corner near the castle where we initially met. Holding the books tight underneath my arm, I close my eyes. Then, I feel a tug on the books and I look at Coll.

"What are you doing?" I ask, seeing his hands on the books.

"Yeh just barely learned how to travel. I'm not sure you're ready to carry extra objects with yeh."

"And you think I'm okay handing these off to you?" I shake my head. "You must be insane."

Coll looks at me disdainfully and takes a step back. "Yeh still don't trust me?"

"It's not that I don't trust you."

"No," he shakes his head. "You don't trust me."

I clear my throat and look around. "All right, honestly, no I don't. It's not personal."

His eyebrows lift in mock surprise. "Oh, good. Because here I was thinkin' this was about yeh not trusting me as a *person*. Glad to know it's just me as a business. Look," he rubs his mouth with his hand and glances down at the bundle in my arms, "I know it's hard for yeh to understand, but I actually do want to see yeh return to London in one piece. At the very least, I want to make sure those books make it too."

"Coll—"

"Taran." He steps forward again until he's nearly breathing on my face. I hold his gaze and scowl at him.

"They're my dad's. I can't . . . let *anyone* hold them."

"Yeh mean yeh can't let Michael's son hold 'em?"

"That's not what I said."

"Yeh didn't have to," he hisses. "Sod it. I don't care."

Before I even have a chance to say anything else, he disappears, traveling back to London without me. Like a match flickering to life, I tap into my body, close my eyes and whisper, "*Tiaseal.*"

SEVENTEEN

WHEN I TRAVEL BACK TO RICHMOND PARK, I arrive in an empty lot. Coll is gone, and so is the Mercedes.

"Son of a bitch," I mutter under my breath. The bastard just left me here. I hold the pile of books tight against my chest and look down. All of them made it back . . . except I'm missing my shoe again. I cuss and center myself better before traveling back to my hotel room. Once inside, I toss the bundle on the bed and run my fingers through my hair, trying to remove all the tension just by pulling it out through the strands.

I've lost him again. This is the second time in one day that I've managed to ostracize the one person who's supposed to be able to help me get to the bottom of this madness. Of course, it doesn't help that both of us are acting like childish . . . children.

I groan, sink onto the bed, and reach for my cell that's still sitting on the nightstand where I forgot it. I've missed four calls. Two from Mom, one from Evie, and another from an unknown number. Since there's no message from the unknown number, I'm not even going to worry about it, and I'd rather not deal with my mom right now. After pushing the right button, I wait for it to ring twice before the voice on the other end answers.

"Y-ello?" Josh answers the same way he always has.

"Hey, Josh. Is Evie there?"

"Actually, she just got in the shower, Taran. Can I have her call you back?"

"Is that Taran?" I hear a hollow voice call from the background and the shift of a shower curtain. "Gimme! Gimme!"

Josh chuckles. "Actually, she's right here."

"Thanks." I sigh and lay back on the bed.

"Taran?" Evangeline asks. "Is that you?"

"Yes. Sorry I didn't answer earlier. I didn't have my phone with me. By the way, are you talking to me naked?"

"Of course," she laughs. "How are you, sweetie?"

"I . . . don't know. Every time I feel like I'm getting closer to figuring this out, I take two giant steps back. I'm just," I groan, "I want to go home, I just—I don't know where home is anymore. I feel like I know too much now and I'll never feel at peace to go back and I'm too pissed off to continue."

"Uh oh. All right, girl. Spill it."

"Babe?" Josh calls in the background, "where's the new package of diapers?"

"The nappies?" she responds.

"Yeah!" he yells back.

"Back in the closet!" She then focuses her attention back on me. "Sorry. Go ahead."

"You know the asshole I was telling you about?"

"Ooo, yes! Mr. Hunky European Man. What about him?"

My eyes travel the length of the hotel ceiling. "Did I tell you he's got the other mark on his hand?"

"What?" she clips. "No! You absolutely left that part out. Tell me everything!"

I rehearse the full details of what has happened with me and Collens in the last forty-eight—or is it seventy-two—hours, including the spell we cast together that took us back to the attack on Woden, my presence at his sister's apartment, the traveling practice at the park, the break in at Lancaster Castle, and the fact that he completely abandoned me because he was pissed that I couldn't hand over my own father's journals.

"And so here I am, standing alone in this massive park in the center of England all by myself, he's taken off, and I'm . . ." I lift my foot up in the air, staring at my bare foot, "still missing a shoe, and I have to travel by myself back here to my hotel room. And the worst part about it—

A knock on my hotel room door stops me mid-sentence and I push myself into a sitting position.

"Just a second. I think the maids are here."

"Maids?" she asks. "Isn't it like midnight over there?"

"Yeah."

I stand up and walk over to the door, looking out of the peep hole in the center. There's no one there. I open up the door, thinking that perhaps the hotel staff was going around with notices or bills or something. When I do, Coll Donovan appears directly in front of me.

"Hey." His face is long, and his eyes hardened like amber. "Can we talk?"

"Evie?" I say into the phone. "Can I call you back?"

"Please tell me it's Mr. Hunky European Man."

Coll presses his lips.

No. Please, no. There's no way he actually heard that, is there?

"I'll call you tomorrow." I hang up and look back at him. "What are you doing here?"

"Can I come in?"

I place my hand on the doorframe blocking his path. "Let's see, you left me alone at Lancaster Castle, and when I got back to the park, you'd also left me alone there. So . . ." My childish side pretends to think about it and then blurts out with a solid, "no."

He nods and after sticking his hands in his pockets, he looks down the hallway. "Fair. I jest wanted to come over and make sure yeh got back."

"I'm back. Is that all?"

"I also," he looks like he's really struggling to sink this low, "wanted to apologize. I'd, uh," he looks down the hallway once more when one of the guests exits their room and walks past us, "really like to do so inside."

The smell of warm food wafts down the hallway and I stick my head out far enough to see a member of the hotel staff rolling a tray of room service meals toward us. Not only does it make my stomach grumble, but I realize humiliating Coll in a hotel hallway isn't necessarily the best way to continue working with him either.

"Fine." I step back, allowing him to walk in and close the

door on his own. While he does, I head into the main part of the hotel room and sit down on the bed again, tossing the phone near the pillow. I refuse to the be the first to speak, so I watch Coll walk in and his eyes immediately dart toward the books on the bed near me. He doesn't make eye contact with me, or utter a single sound. I purse my lips, looking at him with a gaze that asks, "What in the hell are you waiting for?"—before I remember I need to control my temper and see what he's even going to say. Mentally, I try to prepare some comebacks to what I can imagine he's going to say. Unfortunately none of them are biting or exactly witty.

This shameful, quiet, speck of a man is not the same person I dealt with yesterday, or even an hour ago. His entire demeanor is different, reminding me more of the man he's tried to hide for so many years: the man Michael Donovan wants him to be.

It almost hurts just to look at him.

"Look," he finally says, standing still, "I'm sorry."

"For what?"

He now looks at me. "I should have understood how attached yeh are to those books. I wanted to help, to put aside our family differences, and I didn't consider . . . anythin' else."

"Is that all?" I ask, leaning back.

"I shouldn't 'ave left you there."

"Which time? When you left me behind at the castle, or when you got in your damn car and drove away?"

"Both."

I ease myself a bit more, not quite feeling like a snake ready to strike. More like the team on an opposite end of a tug-of-war, ready to pull back the moment the buzzer sounds.

"Okay?" I say, almost questioningly, more skeptical than I meant it to be.

"Yeh don't believe me?"

"No, I believe you. I just didn't actually hear a full apology."

Coll's face flushes red and he looks away, his nostrils flaring. "I'm sorry I left yeh alone, and I'm sorry I tried to take your books."

I hum, my bite returning while I sit up again, "That doesn't really sound like you mean it."

"Jayz, woman. What do you want from me?"

I shrug, "I don't know. Maybe you could actually look me in the eye? Maybe you could look as if you're not ready to leave me alone here the moment I accept your apology!"

At that, Coll glances at me. "Yeh don't want me to leave?" It's said with a true earnestness, and not some haughty playboy attitude.

"Yes." I correct myself. "No, I mean. I just . . . I don't want you to just get what you want and go. It doesn't feel like you truly care about what you did."

"Yeh think I don't care?" At that, he takes a step closer to me and I glare at him. "I was an arse, yeah, but after I got 'bout five minutes away from the park I turned around and went back. It scared the shite out of me that yeh might have been severed in half! And that has nothing to do with yeh losin' the books, or Michael gettin' his hands on 'em. I was worried about *you*."

Every limb of my body tingles and I swallow the pride

bubbling inside my chest that started the moment I saw him on the other side of the door.

"That would be a first," I spit back, folding my arms—an instinctive reaction to everything else he usually says.

"Yeh really think that?" he asks.

"Prove me wrong," I quip. "You say you're sorry. You say you're worried about me. So tell me. Be honest for once and tell me—what makes you think Michael killed your mom? Because I already told you, my dad died looking for *Craniarann*, searching for it in order to protect me. If Michael is dangerous as you're making him out to be, I need to know. My life may depend on it."

A flash of anger burns behind his eyes and he breathes hard and deep. His proximity makes it easier to smell his cypress and sandalwood. I feel the negative emotions—the anger, the irritation, the frustration—within me dissipate and I shake my head. I finally realize why he uses sandalwood. It clears negative energy.

Anyone would need that in dealing with him.

"That's not goin' to be a problem," he finally admits softly.

"You can't promise that. My dad thought he'd be all right too."

Coll takes a step closer to me. "Do yeh trust me?"

"What does that have to do with Michael?"

"Just answer the damn question."

"I don't know, Coll." I do my best to keep my voice calm and steady. "I haven't had a lot of positive experiences with you. And, to be fair, I don't know anything about you except that you have two sisters, you're a shifter hexen, you have a massively screwed up family history, and that you work at the bank with Adrian—although I have no idea what it is you actually do."

He nods, his eyes scanning my face. "Then you're sayin' we're still strangers. And I don't tell strangers about my da. All yeh have to know is that I won't let him bother yeh. Yeh have my word."

"That's not good enough." My voice snaps more than I intended it to.

"My word isn't good enough? *I'm* not good enough?"

"I didn't say that! Why would you care anyway? You don't even like being around me!"

Coll's mouth slowly closes and he steps back. "I suppose that's fair. Yeh know, I came over here to apologize for the way I've treated yeh. I've done so. And I think it's time for me to go." He turns away from me and walks for the door of my hotel.

"Oh, hell. Don't leave like that." I reprimand him, standing up.

"No?" he whips around, his eyebrow cocked. "Yeh want to know why I care about me or my word not bein' good enough for yeh? Then answer me this; why don't yeh want me to leave? If yeh can't answer that, then I got to tell yeh, I'm tiring of this shite. Yeh beg me not to leave, and yet yeh still don't trust me?"

"I'm not begging," I say under my breath.

Coll grunts and twists the doorknob.

"Stop! It's not just you, Coll. I don't trust anyone."

He frowns at the wall, refusing to fully face me. His hand is still plastered to the doorknob. "No one?"

"Coll, my last five relationships ended because each of them realized I wasn't invested. I don't let anyone in, not unless I have a good reason to. I never let *them* in, I never trusted them with anything, and that's why I'm in this stupid country searching for a magic weapon with no one else to help me except myself! Here's the thing," I center myself again, "if I had my way, I wouldn't even be working with you now. Because I see through your games, and your shit, and underneath all of it you're still not the kind of man I'd want to do any of this with."

Coll noticeably flinches.

"You can't even help me get to a place where I *can trust* you. A place where I can depend on you. So, yeah. You know what? Your word isn't good enough. It's just words and they mean nothing."

After a five-second pause, he releases the doorknob. "I never said anythin' 'bout a relationship."

"Neither did I," I breathe.

"Yeah," he nods. "Yeh just did."

"No," I widen my eyes, "I merely related my experiences with other people. This has nothing to do with wanting a relationship." I back up and twist my fingers around each other. "Are you really that self-centered?"

Coll takes two tentative steps toward me and I compensate by backing up once more. He licks his lips and studies me. "You're lyin'."

"Prove it. Oh, wait. You can't, 'cause your roofies don't work on m—wait what are y—"

Before I can finish the sentence, he's crossed the remaining distance between us and has me pressed up against the wall, his mouth opening against mine. His thumbs dig into my pelvis. His knee firmly planted between my legs. While he flattens me against his chest, my mind drifts back to the park and the *infe spioris*. While hands have been on me before, in a way, this is different. This is tangible, it's real, and it seems that my heart knows it. I can't push him away.

I don't want to.

Coll strong scent of ginger intensifies, more so now than before, and my studies come back to life in my mind.

A perfect additive to love spells, ginger can be used to fuel passion. Ginger is energetic, fiery, and adds power to any magical activity.

I breathe harder, kissing him back trying to make myself believe that he hasn't done all this on purpose. But, oh—Coll's fingers slide below my waistband, his tongue drawing across the roof of my mouth—dear angels of heaven.

He's using ginger, I remind myself. This isn't real. It's not . . .

"Stop." My raspy voice comes out in a whisper while I simultaneously reach up to thread my fingers through his hair.

As if commanded, Coll steps back at the same moment I lean in, preparing to continue exploring his mouth with my own. I stumble forward and he pushes me away. After putting adequate distance between us, he squints with confusion. Time ticks by silently while we both stare at each other, neither of us wanting to be the first to move or even speak.

"Yeh say stop," he finally whispers like a thunder clap in the still of night, "and yet yeh want more?"

"No," I answer. "It's . . . it's the ginger you're wearing. Not me. And you know it."

I replay the kiss in my mind, sensing the faint trail of ginger still lingering on my clothing. What would have happened if I hadn't told him to stop? What would I have done?

"The ginger?" His voice is almost . . . silken.

I nod, still breathing deeply. "Your herbalism may work on other women, but I recognize what you're doing. You've really stepped over the line this time."

Coll slowly looks away, his head gently bobbing in understanding. "The ginger," he repeats. With that, his head bob morphs into a shake of disbelief and he steps toward the door, grabbing the knob. "I'm sorry."

I turn away and look over at the bed. Immediately, the journals and books catch my eye and I feel a lump in my throat. Dammit. I still need his help to find *Craniarann*. One way or another.

"Coll?" I'm still breathless.

He turns, giving a glimpse of his profile.

"For some inexplicable reason, fate seems to have assigned us a task. The truth is, I can't do this by myself. I need your help studying the journals." The next question is something I have to force myself to do. "So, will you meet me tomorrow at the university? Just studying. Nothing more than that."

He sighs, contemplative. Almost resistant. Yet, he answers with, "Sure."

"Eleven?"

He nods. Then, he opens the door and steps forward to leave. Immediately he stops and fully turns around. "By the way. That's pure ballax."

"What is?" my voice is gravelly and dark.

"Ginger may be used in love spells, but it only works if there's an existin'," he pauses and then emphasizes his very last word, "*relationship*."

At that, the door closes behind him and I'm left in a dead silence, my blood burning. It's then that I realize he's absolutely right.

EIGHTEEN

"WE NEED TO TALK," MY VOICE CRACKS. I ROLL
my eyes, and then focus them on the wall of the study room
in the university's library again. I arrived twenty minutes
early, driven by my own anxiety about seeing Coll today. Now
I've been staring at a dreary gray wall having a pretty serious
conversation with it.

I repeat, "Coll, I need to talk to you."

No, that doesn't really emphasize how serious this issue is.

"Coll, you have a problem and I think we need to talk about
last night." That won't work either. It's like I'm attacking him.
Unless of course, maybe I should. Isn't it my right? He did try
to take advantage of me.

"Hey, can I ask you something?" I whisper. "Why—"

Why what? What would I even ask him? Why did you smell
so damn good? Why cheat and use ginger? How can I want to
kiss you so much, knowing what an absolute blowhard you are?
Why do I want to rip your shirt off your body, slide your pants
off your ass, drag my lips across . . . .

I clear my throat and bring myself back into reality.

Most importantly, how in the world could ginger work on

me like that if we're not in a relationship? We can't be in a relationship, can we? That's just . . . .

"I hate that man," I say to myself, my eyebrows jumping upward in docile admittance. I mean, the first time I ever sat down in his apartment he tried to magically drug me into liking him, and now?

I glance down at the handwritten grimoire I've brought with me. The one I used to take notes on during my childhood studies with *Móraí*.

- *Ginger has an elemental association with both fire and earth when used for different purposes.*

- *Ginger is energetic, fiery, and adds power to any magical activity*

- *Can be used in spells to "speed things up" (note: BOOBS)*

I shake my head and chuckle. I must have been thirteen or so when I wrote most of this. Worst of all, to the side I'd drawn a sketch of ginger root. It still just looks like a lumpy turd. I scan down the list of notes until I see it again:

- *A perfect additive to love spells, ginger can be used to fuel passion to existing ties*

There it is in glittery, purple, gel pen ink and white paper. "Existing ties." That means the power of the ginger wouldn't have affected me if there hadn't already been an element of feeling between both parties.

Relationship.

I close the notebook and take a deep breath. It doesn't matter. I have more important things to worry about than Coll Donovan and our supposed relationship.

Hell, how could we even call it a relationship? Most of the time we've spent together over the past week has consisted of both of us yelling and bitching at each other.

Actually, I rationalize, that does sound like a relationship. At least one belonging to an old married couple that—

"Ah!" I exclaim in disgust at the words "married couple," shoving the notebook away. Its pages flutter and twist, the book shooting across the table. I have to tell him there's nothing between us. Before we can do anything else, we have to get this settled. Finding *Craniarann* is most important, and keeping Michael Donovan off our trail is imperative to our safety. Figuring out whether or not the school douchebag has a real crush on me or not is the last thing I want to be focused on each time I interact with him.

Out in the hallway, a man laughs and it grabs my attention. Pete. Another man says something to him and the voice is too distinct to ignore: Coll.

"*Flagibet,*" I whisper. Instantly, my hearing amplifies and I'm able to detect what the two men are talking about without leaving my seat in the study room.

"That sounds like Taran, all right," Pete says.

What sounds like me?

"I tell yeh, Pete. Sometimes," his voice drops even lower, "sometimes she's got me completely buckled and I want nothing more than to—" He goes silent and I wait. "You know? Then, other times I just want to tell the universe to beat her up its hole."

Pete chuckles again. "She leaves you feeling like, how do you put it? 'Shit beaten up in a bucket?'"

"That's it."

"Well," Pete sighs, "just so you know, she's one of the most knowledgeable and dedicated colleagues I've ever had the pleasure of working with, not to mention one of my favorites all round. Don't let her get on your nerves too much. She's just testing you."

"What like a child?" I whisper to myself in irritation. Then, the more I think about it, I nod. Yeah, that's kind of how I've been.

"I suppose. She's in the room down the hall?"

"Waiting just for you." Even without seeing him, I know Pete's grinning.

I quickly lean forward, open my grimoire, and mess up the books a bit more to make them look like I've been deeply studying their contents for the past half hour instead of talking to a wall. The second I have my butt back in my seat, the door opens and Coll walks in, followed by Pete.

"Look who I found, Taran," Pete says, leaning against the door frame. "He says you're expecting him."

"Yes, I am," I give them both the most genuine smile I can manage. "Thanks, Pete. Mr. Donovan, it's good to see you again.

"You too . . . Dr. Grim?" Coll cocks his eyebrow, both of us resorting to more formal titles.

"Come have a seat."

I notice Pete give Coll a wide-eyed look that was meant to be shared between them before he turns and walks out, pulling the door to a close behind him. I open the first journal—the top leather-bound one—and slide it to the left where Coll can get a better look at it without taking my hand off.

"Before we start," I say, my voice betraying the confidence I'm trying to play off, "we need to talk about last night."

Coll sits down in the chair next to me, spreading his legs and folding his arms. The tiny feminist inside me gets irritated at his "man spreading" and I clear my throat, glancing back at the book for a moment.

"Last night?" he asks. "Oh, yeh mean when I kissed yeh and yeh asked me to stop although yeh actually didn't want me to. Then yeh basically accused me of druggin' yeh again because I wear a homemade cologne. Yeh mean that?"

"Yes, Martha Stewart," I attempt to hold back my bite. It doesn't quite work. "You manipulated me."

Coll narrows his eyes. "Explain."

It's my turn to widen my eyes. "You need me to explain?"

"Please."

"You used *zingiber* on me!"

Coll licks his lip, scrutinizing me. "First of all, I always wear ginger. I happen to like its aroma. Second, let me give yeh a little herbalism lesson, *Doctor*. Have yeh ever recognized the other herbs I use?"

I nod. "Cypress and sandalwood."

He hums. "Good girl. You're not entirely stupid, are yeh?"

The moment I feel my skin flush in fury, he holds up a hand to placate me. "I'm sorry, that was uncalled for. Yeh just—bring it out in me."

"In all fairness, I think we both do."

Coll nods. "Let me ask yeh, though. Do yeh know what they're used for? The cypress and sandalwood."

"Sandalwood and cypress both aid in calming the mind. I suppose it helps when you're trying to take advantage of someone if they're not thinking logically while their passion escalates all at the same time."

Coll leans forward and I sit further back in my chair. "Wrong. See, cypress has a calmin' effect . . . to aid those who're trying to overcome a loss. It also facilitates a connection between the user and the afterlife. While sandalwood helps to exorcise negative energy. Want to do the math on your own? Or should I spell it out for yeh?"

My mind travels back to my conversation with Sera in her apartment before Coll found me and blocked me from ever being able to enter again. She'd told me exactly why they're all terrified of Michael. They believe he may have killed their mom. If that's the case, there's a slight possibility that Coll uses the cypress to help himself cope with the loss of his mom, while also enabling him to void out the energy of Michael's presence . . . should the opportunity ever come up.

I bite down on my lip, nervously picking at the cuticles on my fingers.

I take my eyes off the book where my gaze at some point glazed over in thought. When I look back at Coll, his face is straight and still contemplative. He's been watching me carefully think through everything. The moment our eyes meet, I can tell he knows I understand.

"Your mom," I acknowledge. This makes him faintly nod. "And the ginger's just because you like the smell? I'm supposed to believe that?"

"Believe whatever you want, Taran," he says, almost defeated. It's probably only the second or third time he's ever said my name instead of referring to me as Dr. Grim, Grim, or "woman." The fact that he's actually using my name gives me chills.

"You never use my name. At least, not often."

This takes Coll off guard and he looks down, avoiding me. I start to think maybe I shouldn't have said anything when he opens his mouth. "So yeh noticed?"

"Some egotistical 'git' calls you 'woman' repeatedly, and I guarantee you'd notice too."

Coll smiles and looks up at me. "What? And 'Mr. Hunky European Man' is any better?"

I nearly gasp and drop my eyes. "You heard that?"

"Crystal clear."

"Yeah, well," I clear my throat. "At least yours doesn't make you feel like less of a person."

This time, he pulls his legs together and leans forward. The movement draws my eyes back to him.

"And 'Mr. Hunky European Man' is supposed to make me feel like more than just an object?"

I purse my lips and nod, realizing he's right.

"Taran," he says my name again. His golden eyes feel like a laser. "I never meant to make you feel like less of a person. If I'm bein' completely honest—" He breaks the thought and shakes his head. "Never mind."

"To be honest?" I prod, quietly.

Coll studies me. "I'm afraid that if I start usin' your name, I won't be able to stop."

My throat tightens. My pulse quickens. "What?"

"Oh yeah." He nods. "I mean, I'd have to add some pretty hateful expletives to go along with it. So, it just seems easier not to say it."

Even though I sense a complete tone of jest in his voice, I grab a book and slam it on the table in front of me. "You're an ass."

He laughs to himself, reaching for one of Dad's notebooks. "Probably."

"You . . ." I hesitate, pinching the edge of my finger between some of the book pages, "you swear you weren't trying to take advantage of me?"

"I'd never do that to yeh, Taran."

I think back to the tea he'd given me and I glare at him with a snort.

Understanding what I'm thinking about he nods, "That tea never would have made yeh do anything yeh didn't want to. Had it worked, yeh just wouldn't have hated me so much. I dare say yeh would have actually liked me."

I take a deep breath and push the book closer to him, adding, "I never hated you."

He genuinely looks shocked and he opens the journal in his lap. "Could 'ave fooled me. So," he changes the subject, "what 'ave yeh found?"

Feeling a little blindsided by the abrupt change, I take a deep breath. "More than I thought I would. It's all in other languages and out of order. Knowing my dad he probably did it on purpose."

"With Radolf Wolf on his tail, I don't blame him."

Did I tell him about Radolf? I frown. I don't even remember any more. The last week has sped by in a blur. It doesn't help that days and hours keep disappearing.

He must see the confusion on my face because he follows it up with, "Sara told me. Plus, I remembered your father's letter."

"Ah," I continue. "Anyway, some of what I've been able to make out we already knew. There are depictions of the Himilæsa, which confirms what my *mórai* told me before I left. That Bryden is home to the gate of the afterlife. There are also indications of future events, lots of sketches of the incomplete cross of Woden as well as our hands . . ."

Coll glances up at me. "Incomplete?"

"It's what he calls the 'hand cross.' There's another prophecy I read that calls it the Hexen's Cross."

This time, he flips a page of the journal while looking at my hand. "I've been meanin' to ask. Why's your mark white?"

I turn my palm over and look at the circle running around my palm. "It used to be pink, like yours. But, my *mórai* performed an ancestral prayer before I arrived. The effect left my mark white. I think it's somehow been infused with the memories and experiences of my ancestors. It could be what's been allowing my guidance spells to simply take me back in time, allowing me to see what they saw and feel what they experienced. I think that when I go looking for answers, the only way they know how to answer is to show me a clue, a glimpse of the past to lead me where I need to be."

Still turning pages, Coll keeps his eyes down and studies the handwriting and sketches my dad left behind. He turns another page and this time, he holds the page closer to his face to examine the tiny scrawled handwriting. His golden yellow eyes travel down the words quickly and then turn up toward me.

"Have yeh seen this part?"

I stand up and lean over, looking at the page he's got pinched between his fingers. The print is upside down from my view so I try to tilt my head to read it.

The spell.
Rheda.
There's a connection—something I'm missing. I have to go back and take another look, but I do not think the spell was ever completed. We have the full prophecy, but there is no way, that the connections were completed.

"Connections?" I ask, looking at Coll. "I haven't gotten to this part yet. What connections is he talking about? I mean, he's right, we have the full prophecy from Rheda. There have been many since, even though hers was unique. *In the time of the death of the gods*—which we could probably interpret as *Deireanhexe*—*the council of Woden will enter into the Great House to give greeting.* Now," I turn the book toward me. "If I'm right about this, the council of Woden could possibly mean the two of us. A 'body of persons,' so to speak, designated to act in an administrative capacity who *enter into the Great House*— which I think is in reference to Bryden—*to give greeting.* This use of the word 'greeting,'" I continue, "I believe means an act of respectful regard. So, in other words—"

"You and I will enter Bryden to continue what Woden's clan started. In a respectful way," he adds.

"Yeah, I suppose. Maybe there's more to it, though. Um, *Then will be said of his Majesty Zonne to the seal-bearer at his side, 'Go and fetch for me the flail. It is time for the end of hexen.* We know, of course, that Zonne was the first hexen, and a hexen ancestor that our kind almost considers a god. The seal-bearer? Now, I'm not sure who that is. Whomever Zonne commands, he basically decides it's time for us to die."

"Great," Coll responds sarcastically. "That was about the moment when Ruhmactír attacked Woden isn't it? If I remember correct?"

I think back through the first time I watched through Rheda's eyes the death of her father, Woden. "No. *Right will come into its place and Wrong will be thrust to the afterlife. Fated will be he who will see it, and he who will serve King Geri.* King Geri is most likely a direct reference to Ruhmactír, the clan's leader. So, the prophesy is warning those who are in the wrong that their fate is sealed if they serve King Geri."

"Wait," Coll eyes me, "so, yeh think the prophecy suggests that the Geri clan, my clan, will be thrust to the afterlife? Because we're wrong?"

"No, just those who serve *him*. King Geri. Isn't that what it's saying?"

Coll squints and licks his bottom lip. "Geri isn't a person, it's a clan name."

"So, maybe the head of the Geri clan. Ruhmactír," I suggest again.

"When did we get the rest of the prophecy? They would have finished out the spell, right?"

I shake my head. "Not exactly. When I was in Rheda, experiencing her life, the entire prophecy came to her mind in the moment. Though she never finished reciting it, it's likely that she wrote it all down after the fact."

"What does the rest of it say?"

Off the top of my head, I can't remember what I'd read. Sitting in a small pile to the right of me are the rest of Dad's books and journals. I quickly flip through the three composition notebooks, and find lots of spells and research, and not the prophecy. Then, in the olive-lime book, about a third of the way in, the words catch my eye and I start to read the last part.

"*Right will come into its place and Wrong will be thrust to the afterlife. Fated will be he who will see it, and he who will serve King Geri. The learned man shall pour wine—*"

"It will come to a final end," he finishes, looking over my shoulder. He becomes quiet and looks back at the leather-bound grimoire in his hands.

"What are you thinking?" I break the silence.

Confusion, depth, and then a flash of insight outlines Coll's eyes, yet the relaxed nature of his spread legs, lazy arms, and steady breathing make me question whether he's thinking anything at all.

"Coll?"

"Taran, do yeh realize what we've just learned?"

I shake my head. I don't even know what he's talking about.

"Your ancestor Rheda never got to finish reciting the prophecy."

"I know that," I nod, wondering if he has a point.

"If she didn't get to finish recitin' the spell durin' the ritual, that means the spell was never actually completed."

I glance down at the book in his hands and shrug. "What's your point?"

"I'm not sure yet. I'm pretty sure it means we're not leaving here anytime soon. Your da wrote that down for a reason. Come on," he stands up and lays the book open on the table, reaching for another of my dad's notebooks, "let's get to work. We'll need to get Peter in here with additional shite."

NINETEEN

THE HOURS PASS, AND BETWEEN PETE BRINGING
us takeout meals, books, and making copies of pages and pages
of ancient books and history collections, I can see it in his
face: he's feeling more like a secretary than a college professor.
Still, in the hours that have been spent searching the history
of our people, neither Coll nor I have been able to get more
information regarding an unfinished spell.

I glance at Coll over the edge of the giant leather-bound
collection of Norse occult history between the ages of 1000
BCE and 1 AD. Through college, and even through my graduate
years, I've met too many men like him. At least . . . too many
men I thought he was like. Money-obsessed man-whores that
used their profession—or lack thereof—physique, and charm
to talk the panties off younger women. Or, at least women
dumb enough to fall for their crap. Just like the younger, more
naive me. I've been spending the last week corralling him into
that same cesspool of ex-boyfriends and assholes.

My lips tingle, and my thoughts drift back to my hotel room
last night. Coll's teeth dragging on my bottom lip, his hands
exploring the contours of my skin.

"Taran?"

"Huh?" My eyes limply glaze over Coll's hand gripping Dad's journal.

"Can't get your mind off last night can yeh?"

My mind snaps to attention and I look up at Coll. He grins, and that smile only deepens the moment my skin flashes red.

"Wait a second, here." Out of the corner of my eye, I see him lean forward, the book dangling from his fingers. He stares me down. "I was jest teasin'. Am I actually right?"

"At least we know where your mind is. Can we get back to work?" I ask. "Have you seen the . . . the—" I snap my fingers nervously, looking for one of the large anthologies Pete brought in earlier.

"You're right," he admits. "That *is* where my mind is."

I swallow and reach for another inconsequential book.

"If it makes yeh feel less . . . flustered. It's *all* I can think about." Coll puts his feet up on the nearest chair and pulls another book into his lap.

"What do you mean?" My hands flit from book to book. I can't even remember what I was looking for.

When Coll doesn't immediately answer, I stop looking and glance at him. He's just watching me. Calmly. It's unnerving, and my first instinct is to reach for another book. Oh, hell, just grab one!

"I didn't even wear my cologne today. Didn't want to be accused of takin' advantage of yeh."

I clear my throat, standing straight. "I thought you didn't

wear cologne." When I finally look over at him, he's still staring at me, only now a smile is slowly spreading across his lips.

"So I lied. Or—" he playfully arches his eyebrow, "am I lyin' now?"

I brush my hair over my shoulder, deciding to satisfy him and play along. "What if you're just lying all the time? I'd never be able to trust you."

He thinks on that and bobs his head in thought. "*Or* I'm always tellin' the truth."

"If you're always telling the truth, then you can't be wearing cologne and NOT wearing cologne. It doesn't work like that."

"*Or* does it?"

"It doesn't. And *don't* say 'or' again. It's annoying."

Coll closes his mouth and smiles. "Yes, Dr. Grim."

I flip open the nearest book, making a split-second decision to search for more information about the Ravn clan. My finger drifts down the rough page, gleaning for the right words and information. Finally, I stop and heft the book into my arms, sitting down into my chair again.

In Irish lore the war goddess Badb is featured in the myth of Táin Bó Cúailnge, the focal tale in a collection of stories known as The Ulster Cycle. After taking the form of a crow or raven she causes terror amongst the forces of Connuaght in the battles of Ulster and the legendary hero Cú Chulainn. It is also said that the Morrigan, in the form of a raven, perched on Cú Chulainn's shoulder at the time of his death at the gate of the Himilæsa.

"Morrigan," I whisper. I know that beast. Dad mentioned it in one of the notebooks.

"Adrian knows what I am."

I look up from the book and stare at Coll. This time he's not looking at me, but at his own hand.

"He knows you're a hexen?" I ask.

"For the last ten years." He takes a deep breath and drops his hands over the arm rests. "We'd met in university while we shared the same dorm. He caught me shiftin' once and I came clean. Surprisin'ly, he didn't run. We've been good friends since."

At hearing this, I think back to the morning Adrian and Garrit arrived in Coll's apartment after the night he'd been out, Sera waiting patiently inside. "Garrit too?" I ask.

Coll's eyebrows jump. "Yeh figured that out?"

"That night you left Sera in your apartment, that had something to do with Michael didn't it? And they knew?"

His face goes hard and he looks away from me. "Yeh really don't miss anything do yeh?"

"No. I sometimes do. Sera told me a little."

"That bitch," he smiles lovingly and I know he doesn't really mean it.

I wait a beat before I speak again. "My best friend knows about me too."

Coll looks up at me, closing a book softly and using his finger to hold his place.

I nod. "Her name is Evangeline. She's got four kids," I laugh, thinking about my usual phone calls with her—one or two of the youngest screaming in the background, another calling "mom" repeatedly, "and they're all a handful. Actually her husband is a banker. That's how I found out Dad's first key went to a bank."

"Her husband knows about you too?"

I shake my head. "No. I've heard him say on a number of occasions, though, that 'there's something creepy' about me." I smile. "He means it in a friendly way, even though he notices I'm . . . odd."

"And it took him how long to figure that out?"

With a flash, my eyes dart to him. When I see him smiling down at the book in his hands, I realize he's playing with me. "Ah, ha. You're trying to be funny. Too bad you're not." I click my tongue and reach for Dad's composition notebooks again.

The air-conditioning kicks on and Coll chuckles, looking up at the air vents. "What?" he says. "Can't handle the heat?"

"I did *not* turn on the AC."

"Right," he mutters.

I close the book and glare at him. "Do you really think you're that great?"

"A tourist from New York once called me Señor Sriracha. So . . . yeah, I do."

"Are you sure it wasn't Señor Sickening?" This time, it's my turn to smile. It quickly turns into a yawn that I try to cover with my hand the same time Coll laughs. "How—" I attempt to speak before the yawn ends, "how long have we been here?"

Coll looks at his wristwatch and says, "nearly thirteen hours. It's almost midnight."

I look at the door. "And Pete didn't come to kick us out?"

He stands up and walks over to the door, opens it, and looks out. "Hallways are dark. I'll be right back."

At that, he closes the door and leaves me alone. I try to remember how the day got away from me so quickly. I remember lunch. Pete brought both of us fish and chips. Well, he brought me chips. Then . . . was there dinner? I look over at the small trashcan. Oh, yeah. The pasta. I'd been reading through Dad's grimoire at the time and I don't remember much going on during that hour.

Lightly, I set the books back on the table, none of which I've actually read or looked at since pulling them into my lap during the last half hour. Thirteen hours of study and the new things I've learned I could fit into the palm of my hand. The first is that Dad was horrible at organizing his thoughts. What he may have tried to pass off as "organized chaos" was nothing more than simple and basic insanity. Second, Dad and I both have come across the term *Morrigan*. I remember it from my studies in grad school. Other than that, it's the first time I've seen it in conjunction with my current searching. Recalling the lessons I've learned over and over, I know it's not a coincidence. Hexen's don't have coincidences.

Third, Rheda didn't finish the spell. The only problem is that neither Coll nor I have have been able to figure out what the repercu—

The door to the study room opens, cutting off my thoughts. Coll stands there, shaking his head. "Locked. We could travel home, or keep studyin'. What do yeh say?"

I place my tired face in my hands and lean on the table with my elbows. I don't think I'd have the energy to travel even if I needed it. My eyeballs are sore, and we have books everywhere. Books I don't want to close or lose should someone put them away tomorrow.

"I know how yeh feel."

I look up to see Coll pull up a chair and sit down, pinching the bridge of his nose with his fingertips.

"What if we just stayed here for the night? We could keep an eye on the books so no one put them away in the morning or lost them, and I wouldn't risk bodily harm in traveling in an exhausted state."

"Dr. Grim," he rumbles, "are yeh tryin' to shag me in the university library?"

"You'll, of course, sleep on one side of the room, I'll sleep on the other."

"Diplomatic as always."

I roll my eyes and turn to push the chairs next to me against the wall after hearing Coll mumble something else, I whip around with an, "Excuse me?" ready to roll off my tongue only to find that he's hexed the room into a bigger space. With the wall now pushed out an extra ten feet, there's now a familiar queen-sized bed where the neighboring study room used to be. The black comforter and same nightstands rest in their proper place, and now Coll is taking his shirt off.

"What do you think you're doing?" I ask.

Coll tosses his shirt onto the bed and places his hands on his hips. "I told yeh I sleep in the nude."

"I mean," I clear my throat, "what are you doing conjuring your own bed and pushing out the wall? This is a university. I was just suggesting we summon a few blankets and pillows."

"Ah," he grins, "so yeh have no problem with me sleepin' naked."

I smirk. Hard as I try, I can't come up with a retort. The only thing really going through my head is how much . . . I actually do want to see him naked.

Stop it, Taran.

I turn around and attempt my own spells, creating some space for myself. Next, I set one of the chairs next to the wall and take a shot at the first mutation spell I've ever done since I was seventeen.

"*Mutaraigh leabenett.*"

The chair back widens slowly into a simple vintage headboard the size of a twin bed, and I curve my hand around to pull the design out away from the wall while the legs shorten, the chair bottom shifts into a mattress, and the footboard appears. When I wave my hand in front of me in the shape of an arch, the mattress covers itself with a basic white comforter with a single pillow.

Taking a final look at the bed, I place my hand on the mattress, realizing it's still chair-seat hard. A softening spell plumps up the interior and I have to admit, sitting down on it at least, it feels more comfortable than my bed at home.

Smiling to myself, I look at Coll. He's sitting on the edge of his own bed, watching me with a set of bright eyes and a smirk. Fortunately, he's still got pants on.

"That's the first time you've ever done that, isn't it?"

I nod. "It's been a while since I practiced. Well, practiced regularly that is."

"I'm impressed."

I scoff. "Spare me the sarcasm."

"No." His voice is firm, snapping his fingers and dimming the lights. "I mean it. Yeh have natural talent. It's somethin' I've never had."

At that, I nod appreciatively and kick off my shoes and climb into the small twin bed. When I roll over to my side, I look across the room. Darkness bathes the once-florescent-lit study room. Coll's faint silhouette is like a shadow. I watch him take his pants off, his back turned to me, and he sits down on his bed, running his hand through his hair.

After a few more minutes, I realize Coll's head is actually turned toward me. My heart beats fast and I quickly turn over in my bed so I'm facing the wall.

My fingers gently pinch and grace the soft edge of my pillowcase and I swallow hard. I can't see any details. I grip the edge of the pillow, every inch of me wanting to feel him touching me again, for a lot of reasons I don't understand. He's an ass. Completely savage. And worst of all, he's gotten under my skin.

TWENTY

MY BREATH SHAKES. EACH EXHALE ECHOING
against the wood walls of the cabinet. Despite the heavy smell of
chamomile, my tiny pulse rushes out of control. Someone pounds
on the door and I peek through the crack of the cupboard to see
Dad slowly walk toward the sound. A whimper escapes from my
throat and this time, Dad turns around and puts a finger to his
lips. "Stay here, Taran," he says. "Don't make a noise, don't move,
don't speak, don't even cry. No matter what you hear."

The moment I see the flash of red, I scream.

I bolt upright in bed and grab onto the blankets, the wall,
anything to steady myself. A hand grips my wrist and supports
my back and I whirl around to see Coll crouched down next to
me, his eyes wide in worry.

"Taran? Are yeh all right?"

My breathing shakes, my fists clench the sheets while my
knuckles turn a ghostly shade of white. I never scream. I
saw . . . Something. Something that terrified me. Beyond the
death of my dad. Why did I scream?

"Taran?" Coll says my name again.

The nightmare was the same. The same as always, but the

end—the end made me scream this time and I don't know why. I don't remember. Dad shoved me in the herb cupboard, he answered the door, there was a flash of red, and then I must have seen something. I just don't remember what it was.

"Taran!" This time Coll shakes my shoulders and I turn to look at him. "Jayz, woman. What's goin' on?"

"Sorry," I whisper, wiping at my eyes. "I," my voice breaks, "I have the same nightmare every night." While I try to still my breathing, I smear the tears around on my fingers before I glance at the cheap clock on the wall. It's two in the morning. I was right. My dreams are waking me up earlier and earlier. It makes me wonder if they're trying to urge me on toward something I don't yet understand.

I place my hand to my forehead and wipe off the wall of sweat that's beaded against my skin. After closing my eyes to ground myself, I look over at Coll.

"Tell me."

"No."

"Taran."

I clear my throat and take a long steady breath before shaking my head. I've not yet told Coll about my nightmares. The memories that visit me every night, haunting every inch of the darkness behind my eyelids. I feel compelled, though. Like I'm being urged to let him in on my secret.

Then, I can't stop it, and I start to tell him. "Every night, I dream of my dad's death."

I rehearse the entire nightmare to him. Every nuance and detail that becomes sharper and sharper with each sleep, and the feelings, memories, and emotions my younger self had felt. The more I talk, the deeper Coll's eyebrows dive and the darker his eyes become.

When he finally looks like the beast he can shift into, I swear I hear him growl. "So why the scream?" he asks.

"That's the odd thing. I've never screamed before. I've never been shocked awake like this. I can't remember what it was—what was different this time. The moment I woke up, I forgot why. Maybe I saw something new. Maybe I felt something. Or maybe—" My words cut off and I sort through the possibilities, one sticking out more than the others. "Maybe I blocked the intensity of the pain out over the years and now my magic is . . . forcing me to feel it all over again. I don't remember screaming when I saw Dad die. I only remember fear. Just paralyzing fear."

"Or, yeh recognized the killer."

My heart jumps and a surge of adrenaline prickles the hairs on my arms. "What?"

Coll frowns deeper—if it's even possible—and he releases my wrist. "I've seen everythin' yeh just described."

"You've seen my dad's death?"

"No," he shakes his head. "Not his. I've seen someone be killed in the exact same way." Coll pulls himself up until he's sitting on the edge of my twin bed. "The red light? I've seen it. It's what's called a *tás*. A death spell. Although, when I saw it, I didn't realize what it was."

Chills trickle down my arms and legs and I wait for Coll to speak again. Though, I'm not sure I need him to. For a man who's still coping with the death of his mother, possibly at the hands of his dad, I can guess where he's going.

"It leaves a stale feelin' in the air," he continues. "Like every livin' strand of energy has died. Doesn't it?"

I nod.

He nods along with me and leans over, resting his elbows on his knees. I notice for the first time that he's got his pants on again—even if they're not fully fastened. "Michael used that spell over twenty years ago. When I walked in the room, Michael was alone, there was no one else with him, but I could feel it. He'd killed, and somehow he'd hidden her."

"And he told you she disappeared."

Coll nods. "Taran, what if Michael was the one who killed your da?"

"I suppose, it could be possible. Dad never mentioned a Michael Donovan. He told me about a man named Radolf Wolf, though."

"Wolf? Taran, my family hosts a long long line of *canis* shifters."

"I know, and my dad told me that Radolf was a descendant of Ruhmactír. That doesn't mean that you—" I catch myself, unwilling—or not wanting—to state the possibility that Coll's father killed my own for a stick.

And don't think the image of a wolf playing "fetch" hasn't crossed my mind.

"It doesn't mean Michael was the one. We don't know that."

Coll's shoulders slump and he looks over his shoulder at me. "I've never heard of anyone else usin' that spell. Not since Heilyn

Wolf in eight fifty-one B.C. He was an ancestor of mine. Killed all his children except for one son: Weylyn. It was because of that that the hexen community distanced themselves from the line of Ruhmactír, leavin' us exposed more than before."

"I—" I begin.

"Aonghus, Weylyn's son moved the clan to the island of Ireland after that. Remained there for centuries. Clear up until I left."

I know maybe four different stories from my own family line. No more than that. The fact that Coll knows so much about his heritage shakes me and a form of guilt waves over me. A true granddaughter of Marlis Grim would know these things. "I can't believe you know so much about your family."

"In order to protect myself from them, I've learned everything I can," he says flatly.

My fingers itch to reach out and touch him, instead I twist them in the sheets. "Do you really think Michael is involved?"

Coll nods. "More than that, call it paranoia if you want, but I've nearly convinced meself he's the only one who could have killed your da. It's easy to lie 'bout your name. Knowin' Michael, it wouldn't surprise me."

"Even—" I pause, wondering if I should continue. Eventually my curiosity wins out and I form the words. "Even though this would have taken place before he changed? I was three. You would have been five . . ."

And then my words trail off. He would have been five. Right around the time that Michael supposedly killed his wife, my dad was murdered in our home.

"Right," Coll nods. "Yeh can see the possibility, can't yeh?"

I lean back against the wall, my pillow acting as a prop for my back. The thought of Michael Donovan, perhaps taking on the name of Radolf Wolf, killing my father, and then turning around and killing his wife makes me feel sick. He sat in my office, he looked in my eyes and smiled, then had the audacity to ask for my help.

All of a sudden, I feel like I'm a child stuffed in a cupboard all over again.

"I don't remember much about him. Just a couple hazy memories," I mutter in a haze.

"Yeh still love him?"

I nod. "I vaguely remember this man who was very loving, smart, and good. I think most of that comes from the things my mom told me over the years."

"Is she a hexen too?"

A snicker erupts from my throat and I cough it down. "Oh no. The most magic she can perform is turning a spoon into rubber by bouncing it in between her fingers. No, she," I think back to the stories mom and *Móraí* have told me, "she met Dad in high school. She always said, 'Alaric Grim was the oddest and hottest boy I'd ever seen.'"

I laugh again and Coll smiles along with me. "Like father, like daughter."

Blush rises to my cheeks, and I find myself glad we're sitting in the dark. "They stayed friends through grade school and then when they went to college, they both ended up at Boise State where they actually started dating. It was at that time that

Dad told her what he was. He apparently didn't want to go into a relationship with anyone, especially her, and feel like he couldn't share who he really was."

Coll leans back, bracing himself with straight arms. I briefly glance at the trail of dark hair underneath his belly button and the unfastened waistline of his pants. "How did she handle that?"

"Wow," my eyebrows arch sharply, "it took her a while to come around. In fact, she says she didn't talk to him for about two weeks, and she might never have talked to him again if her tire hadn't blown along the road that summer. He came driving up behind her about twenty minutes later." I grin again, looking down at my hands. "She always accused him of hexing her car so he'd have an excuse to see her again, and apparently Dad never denied it, though he never confessed either."

The chuckle that accompanies Coll's grin is like a magnet, forcing me to beam with him.

"Jayz, you're lucky."

"Not to overstep my bounds, you know things were good with your parents once."

Coll nods. "They were. Obviously my mother married Michael for some reason." He goes quiet. I've learned my lesson. I don't press him about Michael unless it actually involves me. Just knowing that Michael may have, and most likely did kill his wife, it leaves way too much to the imagination when I think about how he treated his kids.

At the same time I break out with, "You look tired," Coll mutters, "He tortured me."

We both look at each other and while I stare at him with shock—although, why I'm shocked, I'm not sure—he looks confused.

"Are yeh sayin' I look like shite?" he attempts to joke with me. All I can do is shake my head.

"He tortured you?" I finally ask.

Coll resigns to telling me what he's been holding back and the moment he starts to talk, I can almost see a weight lift off his shoulders. "It was part of my trainin'. After Mum died, my days consisted of grade school, then everythin' after I got home was dedicated to studyin' magic. I usually only got 'bout five hours o' sleep a night. For a kid, that sucked."

I nod in agreement, letting him continue.

"It was the year before I turned fifteen that things really got bad. Yeh see, shape-shiftin' hexens gain the majority of their powers at puberty."

"I think I remember Sera saying something about that."

"Of course she would," he sighs.

"Don't worry. It's all she told me."

He seems to think on that, and after a pause, he continues. "That final year before my comin' of age was spent tryin' to prepare my body. Stretchin' it out, so to speak. So, what Michael would do was crack a cricket bat against my ribs to prepare them. He'd . . ." he pauses without looking at me, just staring at his hands, "he'd lay me out on an old stretchin' rack, beat me with a cat so I'd know what it felt like to have my skin pulled from my body."

I swallow deep, feeling disgust bubble in my stomach. "A cat?"

Coll clears his throat. "A cat o' nine. It's a whip."

A whip. He took a whip to his own son.

"Then, after it was all over, he'd make me heal meself with a spell and we'd go back to work studyin' magic, history, spells, hexes, potions. Everythin'."

"No wonder you left at fifteen."

He nods. "I went t'rough my comin' of age—it was basically my da and about half a dozen other shifters chantin' 'round me while I transitioned for the first time—I attacked one of 'em and killed him." Coll snorts. "I don't even remember his name. Then, I ran. Used my magic to claim my inheritance that Michael previously set up for me, and I never looked back."

"What about your sisters?"

"Ah," he says, and for the first time I realize I'm leaning into him, though I don't change anything, "the moment each of 'em turned fourteen, I got 'em out. Performed hexen-block spells on 'em. While it may not have been my decision to make— keepin' 'em from receivin' their craft—I did it for their safety."

"That's why Sera made breakfast that morning without using magic. I thought it was odd."

Coll sighs and nods, staring across the room to his empty bed. "She can't even do the rubber utensil trick."

I try to crack a smile, but the atmosphere is too heavy, and I can't. Then, I do the only thing I can think of. My head lightly drops and I lay against his bare shoulder. The smell of ginger is missing, and it's absence creates a small hole in my chest. Still, the remains of sandalwood and cypress delicately linger on his skin.

Without a lot of thought, my hand reaches over and I run my fingers down his forearm before slipping them over the palm and between his own. Coll's head barely moves in my direction—far enough that his jaw briefly touches my forehead. With a light squeeze of his hand, I briefly shut my eyes.

Then, in the recesses of my exhausted mind, I swear I hear him breathe in, smelling my hair.

Coll grips my hand firmly and places his other one tightly against my thighs before pulling my legs across his lap.

I don't know how long we sit like this. My consciousness ebbs and flows in and out of sleep. When I feel my head rest on a soft pillow, my body stiffens and I wake up in a startle.

Coll pauses, leaning over me, and sits up. He hushes me and brushes the hair away from my face. "Go to sleep. I'm gonna head back to me own bed."

I reach out for his hand to stop him.

"Please stay," I whisper, my voice groggy and distant.

"No, yeh don't want that. Trust me."

I hold his hand tighter and pull, seemingly climbing up his arm until he's pulled down next to me. My eyes fall closed again when his head falls onto the same pillow. He's tense, and warm.

A chill runs down my arm and I tuck myself closer into him. Why, I don't exactly know. I'm more asleep than I am awake at this point. In that moment, his tension dissipates and his arm reaches around me and pulls me in tighter.

"Stay," I whisper, subconsciously to him. Or perhaps into the void.

Coll's breath warms my face and a single simple kiss lingers on my temple. "I'm here."

*　*　*

A groan rumbles from my chest and I attempt to roll over only to find I'm lying face-first against the study table. I quickly sit up and look around. Books surround me on every surface, including the chairs. The beds in here last night are gone, and I have the imprint of a flat table against my face.

"Did I just . . ." I whisper out loud, wondering if anything I remember from last night is real.

Laughter bellows in the hallway and I bolt to my feet before Pete and Coll walk in. If it weren't for Pete's new set of clothes and the two cups of beverages in Coll's hands I'd swear I'd traveled back about twenty hours or so.

"I hear you both got locked in last night," Pete says, a grin on his face. "And from the looks of it, it was a long night."

I glare at him and run a hand through my long hair to try and smooth it out like a regular person. "Go screw yourself, Pete."

Coll snickers. "I got yeh an Earl Grey," he says, handing me the tall paper cup in his right hand. I inhale the rich aromatic fragrance of the tea and instantly recognize his handiwork. It's Coll's own blend. After a quick whispered spell, the tea cools down enough that I can drink it and I take my first deep sip.

Like a wave rushing through me, I feel my exhaustion lift.

"Well, you two. I can't condone staying here another night, so I hope you've found everything you need." Pete folds his arms.

"Actually, I think we're nearly done here." Coll sips his own drink. "Shouldn't be more than another hour."

"Good." Pete winks at me. "Good luck you two."

I force an irritated smile and wave him out the door. The moment it's closed I look around the room again. "I can't believe I fell asleep again," I say, taking another sip and charming my hair into a sleek curled wave. "I usually can't fall asleep after my nightmares."

Coll hums once and sits down in the nearest chair. His lack of verbosity grabs my attention and I slowly sit down myself, watching him.

I squint. "You didn't . . ."

He looks to me questioningly. "What?"

"Did you put a sleep charm on me last night?"

Coll smiles. "Not in the slightest. You fell asleep easy enough on your own."

Could he be more cryptic?

I'm about to ask, "What in the hell does that mean?" when it all starts to rush back. I, of course remember waking up in a sweat, talking with Coll about Dad, about Michael, and his sisters, everything Michael used to do to him . . . and then . . . the rest of it hits me. I remember laying on his shoulder. A sliver of my memory recaptures a moment where he laid me down on my pillow—I wouldn't let him leave.

Oh, dear spirits.

It's coming back. I'd grabbed his arm and pulled him back next to me. I may even have pulled his arm around me.

"Oh, shit," I whisper.

"What was that?" Coll asks, picking up a book and bringing it over to me. The smile on his face tells me he doesn't actually need me to answer—he wants me to.

"Coll, did I ask you to sleep with me last night?"

"Well, I wouldn't exactly call it the best bonkin' I've ever had, but it's pretty damn close."

"We didn't have sex," I say bluntly.

"No, but let's say we did. How might that have gone?"

I purse my lips into a smile. Relief warms the terror that flash-froze my veins. "You're a pig. I'm sorry for making you stay with me, though."

Coll pauses. "I'm not." This time, his tone is sincere. He sets the book in front of me and I realize it's one of my dad's composition notebooks. "Look here. After I woke up this mornin', I did some independent study. I think you'll find this interestin'."

Curiously, I look down at the book and start reading.

Not finished—the laws of old dictate that what is started should be completed. It's the same concept in knots and ties.

"What does this mean?" I ask. "What are you thinking?"

"Well, read this too." Coll hands me a book. One that Pete showed me the first day I came to ask him about the Hexen's

Cross. Coll points to a specific spot on the page and I instantly recognize it. The words are part of a prophecy I've already read:

Hexen will battle the invader. The betrayer.
Ruhmactír clashes with his heir and descendant of Woden
who wields Craniarann.
Woden is swallowed alive in battle.
There the daughter of Vitharr, proclaims on
Horse's back: Woden will be avenged in Bryden land
Where Craniarann rests.

My eyebrows furrow and I look up at Coll. "Yes. I already know *Craniarann* is near Bryden. What are you saying?"

"It's somethin' that's been pesterin' me since last night. If the spell was never completed, the old laws would have been disturbed. They dictate that what is started must be completed."

I finally see what he's getting at and my eyes widen. "Like an unfinished knot, there'd be a loose end. A tear. Because the prophecy wasn't recited in full during the course of the spell, then there would have been a rupture in the energy." I stand up and quickly rush toward another book, picking it up and flipping through. It's the green book of my dad's. When I find the right location, I slam it down on the table and push it toward Coll.

"My ancestor, Víðarr, you told me he snuck back into Bryden after Ruhmactír and your line took over the ownership of the land, right?"

Coll nods, his face taking on an air of excitement.

"I wondered why he'd do that. What reason could he possibly have for leaving his family, his children, his wife, and sneak back into a land infested with enemies. He went back for a specific purpose."

This time when Coll looks at me, his eyes are bright. "He hid *Craniarann.*"

"He knew he had to hide the staff—the very staff that opened the doorway to the afterlife and granted the owner incredible power over life and death—in a place no one would be able to find it. He had to hide it right under your family's nose—where they wouldn't even think to look. My ancestor hid the staff in the fissure at the rune table. Coll," I continue, "my *mórai* was right. We have to go home."

TWENTY-ONE

WORKING WITH COLL TO CLEAN UP THE STUDY
room flies by so quickly, I hardly remember it. We push the
study table and all the chairs back into their positions and then
look at each other after Coll's phone starts to ring. He whips it
out of his back pocket and answers it.

"Who is it?" I ask.

"Garrit," he whispers. "Hello?"

I wait, trying to hear Garrit's voice coming out of the other
end of the phone. I can't make any of it out without casting a
spell.

"Brilliant. Keep an eye out for her for the next few hours."

Pause. Coll looks at me.

"Taran and I are headed out to Betchworth Castle."

Another pause, and Coll doesn't look away.

"We think she might find some answers for her . . . project.
I'll have to get back with yeh later. Tell Emilia that if she has
any issues with Michael while we're gone, she needs to contact
you. I may or may not be . . . within reception range."

Another pause while Garrit responds.

"I know, but we won't actually be at Betchworth. I promise I'll explain later."

Coll hangs up the phone and looks around the room. "You ready?"

I nod, excitement and nerves griping me.

"You don't look like it," Coll says while I reach over for my trench coat draped over the back of the nearest chair.

"It's just that, I feel like I may be too stressed to really focus on connecting with my body. What if—"

Coll cuts me off by placing his hands on either side of my face and gazing deep into my eyes. The moment he touches me, the light inside me bursts into a living flame and I instantly connect with each cell in my limbs and core. His golden irises burn with a fiery darkness. "You can do this."

The image of my family's old home near Betchworth pops into my mind. It's an image I don't recall ever seeing before, and I quickly realize that ancestors placed it there. Widening my stance to keep my balance this time, I close my eyes and recite the single word, "*Tiaseal.*"

* * *

The moment I open my eyes, my head spins. Standing directly in front of me, framed in by heavy green trees, is the ruined stone castle of Betchworth. My mouth is dry, and I look around for Coll. Directly to my left he appears out of nowhere and I feel the plop of a small raindrop on the crown of my head. Looking up, I see faint clouds beginning to swirl. Nothing really threatening. If anything, it looks like it just finished raining.

Neither of us says a word, we simply stride toward the front of the castle, knowing exactly what we're supposed to do, while the thought of, "I have no idea what I'm doing," whirls around in my head. The thing I know is that the Grims never lived in the castle. They lived near the castle, south of the parish of Brockham.

Bryden.

My feet tromp over the bushes and around fallen trees. When the sound of voices and laughter reach my ears, I lift my hand in a stalling gesture to Coll and we wait. I watch through the trees near the south wall of the castle where a path travels toward it. A small group of tourists round the bend, their backpacks secure, their cameras and selfie sticks hovering above their heads. I look to Coll and he shakes his head. We're not going to be able to enter Bryden while they're here.

Shit.

I look back up at the sky and the clouds. They're already whiter and thinner than they were when we arrived, the threat of a downpour vanished. But . . . if that were to change suddenly, and without warning, would the tourists stick around?

A quick glance down at the people, then back up at the innocent blue sky with its wispy stretches of white clouds. I slip my trench coat on and slowly look back up into the sky. The word *sturfa* floods my mind and without a second thought, it floats over my tongue and past my lips. In a mad fury, the clouds darken to black and tear open. A flood of rain and thunder drops and between claps of heavenly explosions I hear the tourists shriek below. Water runs down my face, plastering my hair to my head, neck and shoulders. The water pooling into mud near my feet soaks into my cuffs, weighing down the pants on my hips. The moment I see the tourists run out of sight again, their backpacks held up over their heads, a hand grips my shoulder and I whirl around. Rain beats against Coll's smiling face.

"That was you, wasn't it?" he asks, shouting through the rain.

"How do I know that spell?" I brush my wet bangs out of my eyes. "I've never heard it, I've never even used it!"

"It's inherited."

"What do you mean?" I frown.

"Damn. Yeh really don't know anythin' do yeh?"

I shake my head. "It's depressing, I know. My *móraí* always tells me how disappointed she is."

Coll chuckles, most of the sound of it lost in the loud downpour. "The Grims control the weather and nature. Didn't you know that?"

With that, he jogs over the wet mud and terrain and I follow him, moving slower so I don't slide down the gooey terrain and slick ground cover.

"What you do mean? You can't do that?" I ask.

"Huh?"

"You can't do that?" I say louder.

With a shake of his head, he yells over his shoulder, "I don't have a drop of Grim blood in me. I couldn't cast a spell like that even if wanted to." He steps onto the path that's now littered with puddles, rain drops splashing into them like miniature asteroids. Thunder rumbles over our heads and I look up. I could turn it off, but the tourists may come back.

"I thought you knew. That day I found you outside Sera's flat, and we started fightin', yeh started shakin' the sky and I noticed. You know, for being a professor who's studied the history of her people, you don't know as much as I thought yeh would." He holds out his hand and I take it, stepping over a log and jumping down onto the pathway to join him, my feet sloshing over the mud.

The truth is, he's not wrong. Four years of graduate work and I spent the entire time researching the human view of the mythology and history of paganism. Not since my undergrad years had I ever even cracked open my family grimoires, genealogical charts, or talked with *Móraí* about our history.

"Disappointed?" I ask, brushing wet hair off my face.

Coll shakes his head, water droplets hanging from the tendrils hanging over his forehead. "No. Just surprised."

"What else do you know?" I ask loudly, rain pattering around us, the thunder rumbling,.

There's a brief moment between thunder where I think I hear Coll laugh. "What do yeh mean?" he shouts back to me.

"What do you know about my family? About why we left? Why—" I nearly trip over an exposed tree root, "why the Geri and Ravn clans were conquered?"

"Well, I know Woden became High Hexen in fourteen-twenty-eight B.C. after the civil battle of clans. Though, I'm not sure how the battle began. In the aftermath," Coll grunts, jumping over a three-foot stone wall remnant, then helps me over, "the Geris and the Ravns agreed to a treaty in which they'd be under the subjection of the Grims in exchange for sparin' their lives. I also happen to know that our three clans were not the only ones around during the time."

I step over a large puddle, my heel sinking into the water and I shake it off best I can. "There was another clan?"

"Well, you know the Druids, right?"

I shake my head. "Druids were human imitations of us. They weren't actually hexens."

"Yes," he bobs his head, "and no."

We both walk up to the main steel gate running around the ruins and Coll hunches over to give me a boost. After easily lifting me over, he climbs over himself and we both look around.

"What do you mean, 'no?' The Druids came years after the fall of our heritage lines and the closure of Bryden. Well into the common era years."

"Those Druids, yes. You're right. The Druids most people know today were migrant humans who stumbled upon the societal remains of another clan."

"Another clan?" I stop in my tracks.

Coll turns around and stops. He pants and brushes his sopping hair off his forehead. "The Geris shapeshifted, right? The Ravns controlled thought and memory, and the Grims managed nature and the weather. The original Druids—by the family name of Druw—came from Cornwall and had the ability to manage the spiritual." Coll's eyebrows bounce once and he continues into the heart of the Betchworth ruins.

"The spiritual?" I call, walking after him. "What do you mean by that?"

"The Druws had the uncanny ability," Coll grunts again, stepping over a toppled tree, "of bein' able to converse with the dead."

I stop again, placing my hands on the trunk of the felled tree Coll just jumped over. "Talk? With the dead?"

"Where do you think Woden got *Craniarann?*" Coll smiles briefly after looking back at me and keeps walking. "I'll give yeh a hint, he didn't make it himself."

I breathe hard, pushing myself over the tree and trying to keep up with Coll in the flood of rain. Wisps of warm vapor curl out of my mouth and kiss the cold air.

I always knew Woden never made *Craniarann* himself. Although the legends claimed dwarves made the "spear" for him, I always questioned whether that meant actual little people, or if some other sort of hexen existed. Hearing the name Druw does put all of it in perspective. Druw—Dwarf. The names are similar. The translations and understandings must have been twisted and miscommunicated over the years.

"Do the Druws still exist?" I ask. "I've only ever known the Grim line and the descendants of Ruhmactír."

"*That* I don't know. I was trained by a Ravn. I've never seen a livin' Druw."

I stop, yet again, this time to catch my breath. Coll was what?

Coll pauses to look back at me. "What?" he asks.

"You were trained by a Ravn?"

He smiles. "Her name was Angelica Crowther. I believe she was one of the last. She also happened to be the person who taught me to *tiaseal*. The cranberries. Remember?"

I blink water droplets from off my lashes and I look at the ground. "And she had power over memory and thought?"

"It was one of the first questions I asked her. Wanted to know if she could erase my memories of Michael. She refused. Said I'd need 'em."

My feet slowly slurp over the ground again, the things I've just heard swirling like mad. It would all make sense. If the Grims controlled the natural earth, the Geri clan control of the physical body, the Ravns control of the intellectual mind, and the Druws the control of the spiritual realm, there would be an overarching circle of completion to the balance of power. Unfortunately, typical of hexens and humans, they fell into the pit of pride, one group raising themselves over the others leading to battles, wars, and death. Now, there are so few of us, we should technically be classified endangered.

After hopping another fence, Coll and I help each other down a slight slope and find ourselves at the base of Betchworth.

"I think this is it," I whisper, looking around.

"What?" Coll shouts at me.

"I think this is it!" I say louder.

"What do you mean?"

"Look." I point to the difference in foliage. If I hadn't been paying attention, I might not have even seen it myself. Behind us, the trees are thick, green, and the ground cover lush and full of trails of packed—and now sloshy—mud. In front of us, the trees thin out, almost sickly thin. The grass is choked off by rocks, and there's a shift in the air's energy.

"I don't see anythin' else though. How do we access it? How do we get into Bryden?" Coll asks.

I look down at my hand and then at Coll's. "It was conflict that drove Bryden into hiding—to protect it. A security measure that the Grims placed on the land. An act of respectful regard . . ." I say aloud, thinking to myself. I bite down on my lip and look at Coll. He holds his hand out, palm up. The straight pale pink scar on his skin stares back at me. I look at the faint white circle on my own palm, then reach to him with my hand, palm down, my scar joining his. A pulse travels up my arm and a glow forms between our hands. Shining through my flesh, skin, and bones, I see the incomplete mark of Woden—the Hexen's Cross.

Above us the rain pours even harder and I squint to see through the flood running over my eyelashes.

Though our opposite hands are not marked, we link palms to keep the magic of our bodies and our ancestors locked in a continual circle and look directly at each other. Coll's hands tightly grip my own and the goose bumps on my skin prickle at the warm pulse of the blood flowing underneath his skin. I swear, even in this crashing thunder and pelting rain, I can hear his steady breathing.

Like the spell to control the rain, words melt into my mouth—a spell I've never heard before.

"Datter an nature, Sone mac tíre, Cinniúi af begetre agne zeris af stolód. Ahne hor lineh, lag din i. Vie ama sul tuer, anoi almar kin."

This time Coll nods and repeats the same words, fumbling a little with the pronunciation. A third time, we recite the spell together, and after we request entrance, the ground starts to shake beneath our feet. Coll grips my hands tighter and I balance my feet on the shifting earth. Under my feet, grass blades spring to life with a savage fury and the rain above immediately cuts off. Bright wild flowers curl around my feet and the trees creak and groan, their bark thickening and their trunks swelling, growing. The foliage above covers our heads and I look up to see the leaves block out the sky.

Wind whirls against us, curling around and twisting my damp hair around in the air until I feel it dry. Whether the magic intended it or not, it feels as if it's completely erased the evidence of the storm I created.

With dry hair and clothing, I look into Coll's eyes. He's excited and terrified like me. I want to hold his hands tighter, even though I don't think it's possible.

Another crack of limbs or wood snaps in my ears and I look to the left. No one is there—the air seems to be forming homes out of nothing. The stone walls, hay stacks, grass roofs, and livestock fences appear out of nowhere. In the center, a massive stone slab with carved runes and steps rises up from out of the earth. Dirt and rocks shake off the top, falling back to the quaking ground.

Then, like a switch is flicked, it stops. My hands tensely

grip Coll's and I swear my feet are still shaking even though everything is still. A peace settles over the valley and when I look up the hill toward Betchworth Castle, it's still resting peacefully at the top of the hill in ruins. We've stepped through a figurative door that shut us off from our lives and brought us into our ancestor's, allowing us to see both at once. I take a few deep breaths and feel a tingle of relief flood my system. Now, if I could just pull my eyes away from the stone table. It's exactly the way I saw it. Almost thirty-five hundred years have passed, and it doesn't look like anything has changed. It unnerves me that smoke is still gently drifting from inside a few of the homes—like everything has been frozen in time.

I look down at my hands, blow out a shaking breath, and realize Coll is still gripping my hands. When I look up at him, he's frowning, his eyes passing over the entire landscape.

"Coll?" I whisper.

He looks back at me with one sharply lifted eyebrow. "Well, shite. I didn't expect that."

TWENTY-TWO

A PULSE BEATS UNDER MY PALM. A PULSE OF energy and magic—a residue of the spell to open the access to Bryden. Coll's grip, along with mine, releases. My hands gently slip from his, my fingertips trailing the center of his palms; his warmth trickling faintly between my fingers. In his face, I see stillness. And below our feet, I feel a strange sense of vertigo.

Our arms drop.

The weather has completely changed. Like we've stepped through the door to a snow globe. Except, instead of snow, there's a sunny sky, lush green vegetation, and the smell of untainted air—void of trace car exhaust.

"I can't believe we're here," I finally say, taking a baby step toward the village. "My whole life, I thought Bryden was in some other world—some magic dimension. It's right here," I breathe. "Right here."

"To be fair, we did have to cross a magical fence," Coll whispers.

I shrug off his comment and start to walk. To the left I see the ridge I once stood on top of. A hill Rheda and Frig climbed over before dropping down into the valley to perform the last ceremony of prophecy. I start to strip the trench coat off my back and while I do, I jog toward the hill until I build into a full run.

"This is it," I breathe, stopping at the top. "Rheda and Frig stood right here." I turn around and look down into the depths of the wild flowers and tall grass. "And there," I point ahead the second Coll catches up with me. "That's where I woke up. Each time I joined with Rheda's memory I woke up right there, and Frig would come to find her and stand with her right at this spot."

Coll's eyebrow lifts and he smiles at me. "Your family."

"Not just my family. This . . . this is hexen history. I mean," I start to walk down the hill, Coll on my heels, "this village is untouched. *Untouched.* Look at the smoke coming out of the huts. The table is still there." I shriek and hop a step. "Coll! This isn't just Bryden, this is Bryden three-thousand years ago. Do you understand that historians would *kill* to see something like this? This is the village of a large clan of hexens!"

I turn around and walk backward. "You know why they performed the ceremony, don't you?" I ask.

Coll smiles at me while we walk. "Why?"

"It was an annual tradition—a custom of the Grims. The first Grim, well," I correct myself, "the first recorded Grim was killed by his own wife. She was afraid he'd bewitched their children because they all began to exhibit magical powers. They all grew up to be hexens, hated by their mother, whom they eventually killed."

"Ouch."

"Right." I nod. "From that point on, to protect themselves from outside dangers, including inside threats, they performed a ceremony of prophecy. It was a yearly foretell to warn them and preserve them. Often the revelations were simple. You know, a coming drought to combat—which, now understanding our family ability, makes more sense—" I shrug, and turn around before entering the village, my eyes wandering around, "and it also warned them of wars. Like the one with the Geris and the Ravns, which now that I think of it, makes total sense. I mean, if they were performingthe annual ceremony and the prophesy foretold of the Geri and Ravn war, it would have given my family the upper hand, which I'm sure helped Woden to become High Hexen."

Coll walks up to the stone table and sets his hand on top of the perfectly carved rock. "You know more than you let on."

"I know the things my father told me," I lean down to examine the runes surrounding the table, "I would have known more, I think, if he'd lived."

Each rune is definitely worn and old. Not three-thousand years old, more like a couple hundred years. They're a sequence of spells. Protection spells, magic amplification spells, and unity spells. I reach into my back pocket to pull out my cell phone and quickly start to snap pictures of the runes and the table itself. Then I wander to the opposite side of the table, the same side Rheda walked up during the ritual.

Coll looks off into the distance and then focuses on me. "Why didn't your *móraí* tell you more?"

I smile and look down, brushing my hand along the table's

edge. "She tried to. After Dad died, Mom wanted to raise us on her own, much to *Móraí's* disappointment and frustration. I was about ten when Mom finally agreed to move into the home my dad was raised in to help take care of *Móraí* as she got older. That's when my magic training really started. Then, I graduated high school and history recorded by knowledgeable scholars," I modulate my voice to sound a little more pompous, "became more important to me than the crazy ramblings of my *móraí.*"

I push myself away from the table and a large black object catches my eye. At the head of the table, prostrate on the ground and positioned face-down is the body of a man. A cloak of black feathers trailing down his back has been shredded. Timidly, I shove my phone back into my pocket and step closer, rounding the edge of the table.

"Oh, Coll."

It's Woden. His dead body, unchanged for three-thousand plus years, looks as if he was just killed hours ago. Ruby red blood soaks the grass and is smeared along the ground. He's been purposely repositioned face down. In disgrace.

Coll approaches, putting a hand to his jaw. "Shite. You've got to be jokin'. He's still here."

"Time has frozen here. Nothing's changed. Nothing's progressed," I murmur. "I mean, look at this place. Smoke is still coming out from the huts. Everything has just—been paused."

Pushing myself away, I turn to walk into the nearest home. The stone walls are radiating the warmth of the bright sun that's beat on them. Inside, straw beds, a "kitchen" with a fire pit smoking up through the hole in the ceiling, and a cauldron cooking over the low flames. A wooden spoon stirs on its own, no one to guide it. I step in further and finger fresh bundles of herbs hanging from the ceiling. Alkanet root, hawthorn leaf, bugleweed . . . .

There are four straw beds in all, though I know that doesn't necessarily mean only four hexens lived here. Intricately woven blankets hang on the walls, ready to be used, and the smell . . . reminds me of Jessen. Home.

Back out in the village center, I find Coll entering another home on his own. At the south end, I see the rune stone Ruhmactír was thrown into. The tablet toppled, the carvings no longer legible. Though the village was abandoned thousands of years ago, the results of a battle are still fresh. Clothing and tapestries, once cleaned and drying on lines, are squished into the earth or torn and burned. In fact—

When I get closer to one of the piles of rubble, I see a small bit of fabric poking out from the entwining grass blades. I reach for it and pull it out to find it's a ceremonial length of . . . something. I squint, examining the dyed colors of berry juice, pollen, heavy amounts of woad and other colors that have been painted onto its surface. The runes speak of protection, the ancestral prayer, and youth. Suddenly, I get a knot in my stomach. It's a blessing cloth. For a child.

"Taran."

I turn to see Coll standing at the stone table again.

"We need to look for the fracture," he reminds me.

I nod, folding the fabric carefully—a record of the broken

and torn fragments of a people that once called this home—before placing it into my trench coat pocket. "How do you think we find it?" I ask. "Will we feel it? Can we see it?"

Coll leans on the table and rubs the edges of the stone. "I'm not sure. No spells are comin' to yeh?"

I shake my head. "No." I pause, scanning the village. "Coll, something else is bothering me. Have you noticed Woden is here, while Ruhmactír is not?"

"What do yeh mean?"

"Woden. Ruhmactír. They both died here the day Bryden closed off, didn't they? If your ancestor didn't die on impact with that rune stone," I nod toward the toppled artifact, "then perhaps Víðarr killed him when he returned to hide *Craniarann.* You're the family history expert here. All I know is that the mortal records," I shake my head, "the myths claim he killed him. That Víðarr ripped Ruhmactír open by the jaw."

Coll holds up a hand. "Yeah, I get it. None of our stories mention that. All we know is Ruhmactír died that day."

"So, what did your people do with the body?"

Coll licks his lips and scrunches his face. "I don't know. Traditional wolves deeply mourn their dead. So do we."

I think of him, still wearing particular herb oils to cope with his mom's death, and I nod. "Maybe his body didn't get hidden along with the rest of the village. What if they took him?"

"It's possible."

"Since Hexens burn their dead, there's a chance he's been gone for centuries."

"Millennia," Coll corrects.

"Right." I look down at Woden. A rush of emotion fills my chest and it's so familiar. So painful. Rheda's memories fill my mind, the love she felt for him, the respect. Not unlike the bond between me and Dad. What I wouldn't give to have him back.

"Taran," Coll's voice is soft, prodding.

I nod. "I know. The pocket. We need to find it." A brush of wind catches through the center of the village and a wave of live smoke fills my nose. I look around, attempting to retrace the events leading up to Woden's death. My feet step back and squish into the soft grass edge surrounding the table. Rheda was on the table, Woden at the head. Mother . . . Frig was here—I look down at my feet. Ruhmactír was there.

Coll watches with a quiet intensity while I walk around the stone, replaying the images in my mind. Rheda was scratched by Ruhmactír before she stepped up and laid down. Woden was attacked here.

I stop.

Rheda heard what happened and she sat up to look back—I glance over my shoulder. Where was the break? Did it happen with Ruhmactír's attack? Or did it end when she broke concentration?

"What are yeh thinkin'?"

I gaze steadily at Coll. "Give me your hand."

Coll extends his hand with the mark. Instead of taking it immediately, I step to the right. Exactly where Woden once stood before his dead body was dragged to its current position. Coll hesitates, then moves closer to me. His large fingers, warm and firm, glide against my skin. The moment our palms touch, a beam of light explodes out from between our hands and I feel the atoms vibrate with currents of magic.

The space around our joined hands begins to dematerialize—the air shimmering, a power tering through it, ripping it in two. The light intensifies and turns a bright shade of burning gold radiating both toward the sky and toward the ground—as if a curtain is parting and letting the burning daylight through. I grit my teeth against the power grating against my skin, between our hands. Instinctively, it seems, Coll holds my hand tighter which only makes it hurt worse.

Suddenly, the air around our hands splits open and swallows our hands into a dark chasm, devouring the beam of gold with it.

"Coll!" I scream above the loud oscillation of magic resonating around us, seeing our clasped hands disappear together into an unseen world that has closed down around our wrists and slowly begins to suck us inside it.

"Coll!"

Coll drops to his knees, yanking me down with him, though our hands remain caught in the same sucking hole vortex. I reach down with my free hand and grip his shirt to brace myself when a bolt of lightning crashes down to the table, cracking it in half.

Rain dumps down from the heavens and wind bellows around us while we're magically connected to an unrelenting magical hole.

Coll looks back up at me and this time, his golden eyes

irises have swallowed up the whites of his eyes and they're wide and dark. My powers have ignited the sky into a violent tempest. His are forcing his body to shift. No. No. Not now. If he releases my hand, we may not be able to bring *Craniarann* back to this world.

I run my hand through his hair and his body jerks, his back breaking and transforming.

"Coll! Don't shift! I need you!"

I feel like the ground is pulling out from under me, like I'm being sucked into a world—a power—I can't control.

"Taran." I hear the words caught on the wind. It wasn't Coll who said it. My name continues to whirl around in the air, and I hear it permeate the hole that's drawing both of us deeper. It sinks down into my soul, wrapping around my bones. A set of words filter into my mind and without thinking, I force them out.

"*Fanliv hos mi. Fanliv hos mi. Táir sar en. Fanliv hos mi.*"

Coll's free hand digs into the earth, clawing at the grass and dirt that's now mixing into black mud. The howl that erupts from his throat is more animalistic than human. Against the palm of my hand I feel his skin becoming rough like the pads of a wolf's paw.

Again, I chant, "*Fanliv hos mi. Fanliv hos mi. Táir sar en. Fanliv hos mi.*"

I feel the swallowing hole slide down my arm, exposing my elbow, retreating. Our forearms appear, our wrists, and a bright burst of light once more. The golden beam still shoots out from between our hands. The moment our grip re-enters our atmosphere, the world begins to settle. The rain dissipates, the thunder quiets, and Coll shakes off the pain, regaining control of his body. With my help, he pulls himself back to his feet. I grip his hand tighter, feeling the beam of light between our hands begin to solidify. It shortens until it's only about five-feet long, and about an inch thick.

The raw power that was once grating between our palms is now a solid object—a staff, and it's gleaming gold. The wind calms, the thunder ceases, and still silence saturates the air.

I look down, making sure Coll is all right, only to see that my hand is gripping his shirt firmly. He's panting and exhausted, but still very much in his human form.

When I look back at the staff, its golden tones have died, leaving behind a dark wooden staff. Carved into its rotating knots, and images of creature and earth, is the symbol of Woden.

"Taran," Coll wheezes.

I kneel down, keeping the staff locked in both our hands. "Are you all right?"

He nods, without verbally responding.

"Thank you, children. We couldn't have done this without you," a voice with a honeyed tone breaks through the silence. A voice I didn't expect.

TWENTY-THREE

COLL FOCUSES DEEP INTO MY EYES. THE WIDE wolf-like stare is disappearing, and I can see his hexen consciousness coming back to me. When I look up over the stone table, I'm greeted by the sight of Adrian standing at the end of the stone table, leaning on the edge, watching us carefully. Coll reaches out and grips my other hand, both of us helping the other to our feet.

Adrian leans off the table and broadens his stance, his hands confidently resting in his slack pockets, his white business shirt sleeves rolled to his elbows looking the perfect picture of a man finishing a long day at the bank, ready to kick back with a soccer match and a dark pint of beer. His eyes are dark and only focused on one thing: *Craniarann*. Like a cartoonish wolf, I wouldn't be surprised if he started to drool.

"Adrian?" Coll asks.

From behind, I hear the rustle of grass and I whip my head around to see the man I've been trying to learn about for the past two weeks, the man I considered my real enemy: Michael Donovan. Next to him is a tall, dark, and pissed-off looking

Garrit. His dark skin glistens with sweat, shining every time his muscles in his face.

"Garrit?" I whisper.

At that, Coll turns to see his sister's boyfriend and a snarl exposes his teeth. "What in the bloody hell is goin' on?"

"You'd think that after training with a Ravn, you'd recognized another one when you saw them," Garrit leers.

"A Ravn?" I repeat, looking at him.

"I'll tell you what," Adrian cuts in. "Why don't you give me the staff, and I'll explain." He holds out his open hand.

"How about we curse your eyes out of their sockets and *then* you explain," I retort.

Adrian smiles. "You're right, Coll. She's perfect for you. Too bad it won't last long."

I glance at Coll. The fury on his face doesn't alter, doesn't even flinch. "How did you get in here? Why did you bring Michael? Or Garrit for that matter?"

"Adrian, just happens to be my brother," Michael interrupts. "Why wouldn't he bring me? Now give us the damn staff, son."

Adrian takes a step forward, and I lift my hand with a breathy, "*Churraick.*"

The shock spell narrowly misses Adrian and pierces the tree behind him causing the wood and bark to expand and implode. It wasn't exactly what I was going for. Now I'm kind of wishing I'd hit him. I glance at the staff. It's changing—amplifying my spells.

However, while the explosion isn't necessarily enough to

scare Adrian, it is enough to stop him in his tracks. The same lustful stare remains in his eyes, and his lip starts to curl upward.

"Good on you, Taran. I'll go by your terms." He holds up his arms in defense and holds his ground.

"Why are yeh doin' this?" Coll asks.

"Why shouldn't I do this?" he combats. "You two went after the one thing I want. The one thing I've been dying . . . repeatedly . . . to get at for too long. And now, it's right there."

"What do you mean by that?" I ask. "Repeatedly?"

Michael chuckles from his spot and I glare at him.

Adrian looks at his much, much, *much* older brother and smiles. "A little joke. Excuse me."

"You're not Adrian, are yeh?" Coll asks.

I frown, turning to look at Coll. What does he mean by that?

"Oh, no. I'm very much Adrian. At least, I'm the Adrian you've always known. I can't say the same thing to my parents, especially my human mother, Glory Wolf—sister of Radolf who just 'happened' to die before I went to Uni."

Michael snorts behind me and I turn so I can keep my eye on him and Garrit while Coll engages Adrian.

"Were you ever Adrian?"

The man snorts. "I'm surprised you never figured it out, Coll."

"None of it was him?"

I listen, waiting for Adrian's response. "Do you want the real answer or the feel-good one?"

Coll's lack of response seems to spur him on.

"I possessed Adrian the month before we met. You never knew him. In fact, there were times over the years that, I'll admit, I was afraid you'd figured me out. You see, shapeshifters not only have the power to shift into wolves, but take possession of other physical forms that share their genetic code."

"Possession?" I ask, still guarding our backs. Michael moves to the right and Garrit to the left. The moment they do, I send out the same spell and purposely target the ground at their feet. Each man jumps back to their spot following the earth's explosion in front of them.

"Thirty-four hundred years is a long time for any one body to remain viable. Physical bodies grow old and die no matter how hard we try to formulate a potion for youth. Because of that, I engaged in a form of magic . . . that for the most part, has been outlawed among our kind since the beginning of time."

Thirty-four hundred years? I turn back around to Adrian to see him grinning.

"Ruhmactír? It can't be." I shake my head.

"I'm afraid it can," he nods once.

"No, you died."

"He may have," Michael says and I spin around to watch him again, "if I hadn't taught him how to *actuve.*" This time when he moves, I don't blast him, I watch Michael circle around us, moving to join Adrian.

"Frec?" I whisper. "The brothers."

"I'd been practicing the craft with my brother and Hellia,"

Adrian's face pains, "years before the incursion between our clans. Because of Woden I never got to finish."

Through all of this, Coll remains scarily quiet and still, though I feel his hand tighten around mine and *Craniarann*. His father stands in front and to the left, his best friend to the right, and his sister's boyfriend at our backs. Men he once considered family and trusted friends now circle us, while we armed with our own powers and the strength of a staff carved and formed by the magic of the Druws.

I feel the strength of what we hold between our hands, and at that moment, the realization hits that his father never actually killed his mother. It was Frec. And Ruhmactír . . . as Radolf, *he* killed my dad. A joint effort to get what they wanted: me, Coll, and *Craniarann*.

Coll watches his former friends, darkness seeping deep within his golden gaze.

"You possessed the body of another?" I ask.

Adrian turns his gaze from Coll to look at me. "At just the right second. Although I was unpracticed, I took a risk."

I think back to my first experience in Rheda's eyes.

The spell ends before the final line is uttered. The massive dog attacks my father. The energy still courses through my body and I hear the final words in my head, though they never pass over my lips. I push myself to a position where I can see what's happening. Father casts a spell at Ruhmactír, blasting the dog through the air nearly fifty feet. When he lands, the animal skids on the ground, slamming into one of the nearest homes and collapsing the south end.

I look over my shoulder toward the collapsed home. The same structure he'd once been thrown into.

I pull myself off the table and set my bare feet back on the cold black earth.

With my hand outstretched, I cast and feel the combined energies of Ruhmactír and my father coursing through my skin and permeating the air like a warrior's arrow. It's too late. The spell hits Ruhmactír, his jaws clamped tight on my father's neck. The dog spins away, ripping out precious flesh and blood. I hit him again, a rage boiling in my stomach. Ruhmactír shifts his shape before slamming into a large rune stone . . . .

He shifted back just before hitting the rune stone. Wait a second . . . had he shifted, or was that the moment of the *actuve?*

I step forward, approaching the shifter hexen carefully. I can't see his pale white chest—now only featuring a only a heavy layer of hair—rising or falling. Next to me, another man pulls himself off the ground and glares at me. One of the fallen shifters and a member of Ruhmactír's tribe. His arm is nearly hexed off his body.

Adrian, or rather, Ruhmactír, rolls up his sleeve farther and outstretches his arm, pointing to it. "You're thinking about the spell that nearly took the arm of my cousin, aren't you? You know the story too well." His eyes light up and he takes a step closer. Coll instinctively growls in his chest and even I can feel the power coursing through *Craniarann.* Adrian stills and holds his ground. "Or you must have experienced the results of a guidance spell fueled by one of your ancestors."

"Rheda sure had a lot to show me about you."

Adrian's lips curl over his white teeth. "I haven't thought about Rheda since that day. Tell me, what did she feel when she saw me killed?"

I squint, confused at what he's trying to get at. I see a twinkle in his eye and I cast another warning hex at him. A paralyzation spell. It hits the butterfly fluttering in front of his face and it drops to the ground.

He stops, tension and care guarding his actions. Still, he smiles at me before pressing his foot on top of the defenseless insect and squishing it into the dirt. "She was that angry, huh?"

"She loved you. Didn't she?" I ask.

Adrian grins. "I'll be the first to admit, I underestimated her."

"Just as you're obviously doin' again," Coll finally cuts in.

He shakes his head. "No. I'm fully aware of the power you both hold. I'm not stupid."

"How did it work? How did yeh come to take over Adrian's body?" Coll asks.

This time, Adrian frowns, yet looks pleased with himself just like he's mentally reminiscing about his own magic. Turning on the heel of his polished leather shoe, he takes a turn to the left and I warn him with my outstretched hand. He stops. "The man you saw, Dr. Grim, the one who lost his arm. Like I said, that was my cousin. It's easier for me to possess the bodies of those who share my blood and those who possess the same skills." He takes a sidelong glance at me. For what reason, I'm not sure. "Years later, I took the life of my son, Arlin. Then his son, Dewain. Then again, his son, Daghda."

"I guess that gives a whole new meaning to 'I'm my own grandpa,'" I snark in disgust.

"You fathered yourself for over three thousand years?" Coll's voice is sour.

"He's not the only one," Michael steps around and just because I'm in a pissy mood I let out another, "*Churraick,*" and watch the ground at his feet explode. Michael jumps back and he cusses at me.

"Of course you weren't really Michael." I hiss. "The man I saw never would have killed his wife, Frec."

This gets Coll's attention and he whirls on Michael.

I nod. "When Coll was young, you possessed the body of his father. That was why Coll and his mom noticed a change."

"That bitch always got in the way."

"Because of you," Coll barks, "I lost *both* of my parents?!"

Adrian whips his finger out and points at Woden, speaking hard and controlled. "Because of *him.*"

I look down at Woden's prostrate body and nervously look back at the others.

"Hellia, my wife, *The Phantom Queen,* was taken from me by that animal."

"The *Morrigan?*" I whisper. "Your wife was a Ravn?"

"Yes. The oldest of the Morrigan sisters. Woden had her executed for breaking the pact of clans. So she signed his death warrant. Setting up the Woden clan, playing them right into our hands so many years before."

"What are you talking about?" I ask.

Adrian grinds his teeth. "Woden took the love of my life

because she rebelled against him. I'd love to show you how she signed for his death. It's too bad you have me pinned to the ground."

"Tell us," Coll barks.

Adrian glowers at his friend, his descendant, and looks back toward the forest. Changing the topic, Adrian quips, "Do you know why Woden established Bryden here, of all places?"

For once, Coll doesn't answer. He doesn't know. I filter through all the things *Mórai* tried to shove into my head over the years, hoping that somewhere along the line, she would have told me why the clans settled here.

I glance at the ground and the next thought pops into my head. I know the answer. Not because of something *Mórai* said, but because of something Coll and I had read the night before.

It is also said that the Morrigan, in the form of a raven, perched on Cú Chulainn's shoulder at the time of his death at the gate of the Himilæsa.

"The Himilæsa is here," I whisper.

Adrian looks smug, yet impressed. "You are brilliant."

"Woden didn't put a spell on Bryden to protect the village and land, he did it to protect the Himilæsa."

Coll looks at me while I keep my attention focused on the men surrounding us. "The tree. That's the real reason you want *Craniarann*. It gives you access to the afterlife."

My hand grips *Craniarann* tighter, triggering Coll's own fist around the staff. I feel it's power shoot up my arm, my fear spiking to a peak. "You want to bring Hellia back."

This time, the confident smugness on Adrian's face is

replaced by a dead chill. I see a wildness set into his features as his eyes, the olive-green irises, shift into a dark wolf's gaze. And when he opens his mouth to speak, the sharp edge of his canines almost pierces his lip. "If my wife is all you think I want, you're more naive than I thought."

TWENTY-FOUR

ADRIAN REFUSES TO TAKE HIS EYES FROM ME.
"You know, you have his eyes," he growls. "Woden's. You have no idea what it's like staring into your face and seeing him look right back at me. My wife's murderer. The thief of our lands. That self-righteous, overzealous, egomaniacal arse."

"You're right," I muse. "It sounds like your wife's death has absolutely nothing to do with how you feel. Although," I pause, watching him closely. "I have to admit, if having your wife back was the only thing you wanted, you could have easily died centuries ago and met her in the afterlife. Why avoid her?"

Adrian's eyebrow peaks. "I didn't say I was avoiding her. I just want *Craniarann.*"

"I can get you a fire hydrant to piss on," I retort. "But you're not taking it."

Adrian almost completely ignores my retort. With a dark glare, he shifts his gaze to Coll when he jumps in.

"You know, I'd like to say these past years have been a pleasure," Coll says to his former best friend. "Somehow, I just can't form the words."

"Shove it up your arse, Donovan." Adrian glowers. "You

know, I've put up with a lot from you over the years. 'Oh, my daddy beat me.' Really?" Adrian leans in. "Well, guess what? You're not alone. But wait, 'He murdered my bloody nosey mum!' Well, she should have kept her bloody nose out of it! All she had to do was raise you and your sisters. Did she even do that, Frec?"

Michael shifts over a step and he shakes his head. "If only. You should be satisfied though, Coll."

"Oh? And why's that?" he asks. I turn on Garrit who's started to shift his position.

"She thought of you. Right up 'til the end. Beggin' for me to spare yeh. And your sisters."

Coll breathes deeper and more rapidly. I slowly look over at him, hoping to calm his energy and keep him from shifting. He doesn't look back. His skin turns a violent shade of red and his voice cracks. "And you?" he rounds on Garrit and while he does, I pin my eyes on Adrian. "What do you stand to gain?"

Garrit narrows his eyes. "What don't I stand to gain? The Geri clan wasn't the only one who lost their lands."

"That was thousands of years ago, you whiney brat!" I spit. "Are you kidding me?"

Garrit flips his hand toward me and begins to mouth a spell I don't recognize. Coll blocks it with a silencing spell. Garrit chokes back on his tongue for a few minutes with a groan and fumes, his eyes wide and intense.

"A mind wiping spell?" Coll barks. "On her? I dare you to try again."

"Answer the question," I grip Coll's hand and the staff tighter.

"Why shouldn't he want his lands back?" Adrian cuts in. "It was stolen from him. The very land that empowered his people."

"What?" Coll briefly takes his eyes off Garrit. "You mean the lands the Geris once took from the Grims? The lands the Druws bargained away from the Geris? The same damn lands the Ravns stole from the Druws? Spare me the excuses. You're using him. You've manipulated him."

"I chose this."

Coll flinches at Garrit's response and I watch the two of them carefully.

"You can't open the portal of Himilæsa," Coll responds. "The result of crossin' over and bringin' any bein' back through the gate—livin' or dead—would rip the fabric of life to shreds. You'll wipe out our entire race and anyone else in your path."

"*Deireanhexe.*" The word wisps over my tongue the same moment I turn back to Adrian. He hears my muttering and faces me. For a moment, he says nothing. He just stares back at me, the corners of his lips curving upward. His tongue laps across his upper lip, preparing the moment. It's a simple action, one that sends a shiver of fear through my body.

"A warning given by a long-dead hexen line that sided with the Grims," Adrian spits, his voice speaking in a harsh cadence—one that's been polished and yet desiccated by him time on this earth. I can't believe I haven't really *heard* it before. "Every one of us have been touched by the villainy of the 'High Hexen' Grim Woden." He says the name with a mocking flippancy. "The wielder of the darkest hexen magic. The Druws aligned themselves with him and sealed their fate. They all deserved to die with their lies."

"You and I both know the Druws never lied about their prophecies," Coll nearly chokes on the next words, "As Ruhmactír, you knew them. Frig," he nods to the dead body of Woden, "his wife, was one of 'em. The Druws became Grim. Merged their clans. They didn't all die off. And neither have their warnin's. We can't let you open that gate."

"Then I guess I'll have to kill you," Adrian replies. "I've been searching for that damn staff for over three thousand years. I've done too much. I've come too far to lose her. Your black ancestor cursed our family." His eyes burn into me. "He murdered my wife! He stole our land! That staff is mine!"

Adrian takes a step toward us and this time it's Coll that hits him with a spell. Silence stifles the entire valley as it knocks him backward and deep into the soft earth. The momentary silence breaks with Adrian's ripping bark. In a flash, he rips his way out of his clothes and lands on the ground on all fours, covered in hair, the hackles on his back shooting up from his skin and reaching toward the bright blue sky. A roaring bark rips from his throat and I quickly turn to Coll. I can see his eyes quickly flash into a wide wolfish gaze and I reach over with my free hand to grab his shoulder.

"Don't! We both have to be holding *Craniarann*. We can't let go."

Coll breathes hard and his eyes return to normal. I immediately turn and point, shouting, *"Lochel!"* at the same time Coll bellows the same hex. The spell burrows deep into Michael's oncoming chest and he shakes in pain, mid-shift, and drops to the ground. His body, experiencing the pain of pins and needles shooting through his system, changes in violent waves, a doggish whimper yelping from time to time.

Again, Coll and I match our words, somehow connected through *Craniarann,* and we hit Garrit before he gets off a spell. Oddly, Adrian and Michael I feel I can handle. It's Garrit's control over thought and memory that scares me the most. I pivot my body so I'm angled closer to Coll and whisper, "You watch your family. I'll watch Garrit."

He nods and reaches out his hand once more with a powerful spell that drills into Adrian's oncoming wolfish body. Garrit shakes off the hex he'd been impaled with and immediately charges us. This time, I try something a little more unique. The basic transmogrification spell hits him square in the forehead and his body collapses to the ground in loud and violent pain. For a moment, I turn back to join Coll and we both land spells into Ruhmactír and Frec who've both shifted into their canine forms. The two brothers manage to block our magic and they instantly reciprocate with loud barks, slashing their claws in the air.

The moment their spells engage, Coll and I raise the staff forward and yell, *"Schosynt!"* the spell fed into our minds simultaneously. The staff radiates with a white umbrella of power and the spell ricochets off the protective surface and target their originators. Ruhmactír and Frec lunge to the side and I'm hit in the back with a third hex.

I fall to my knees, losing my balance. Before I can react, my face slams against the stone table, cracking my nose, my hand loosening from the staff. Another hand reaches over and encompasses my own, clamping it tight against another, refusing to let me drop my hold. Time seems to slow while I kneel in a stupor. My thoughts swirl with uncertainty, not knowing who I am, or what I'm doing here.

Crimson blood flows from my nose and I curiously reach up with my free hand and cup it to catch the flow.

Something . . . something isn't not right. Why is it not right? I ask myself, my stomach rising up into my throat—my own breathing choking me off from the panic.

I look up to see two dogs running toward me with an unleashed wildness. The padding of their large feet on the soft ground drums against my ears. I think I recognize them, the energy in their focus, the flex of their muscles and bend of their bones. Fury seemingly saturates them while anxiety flashes under my skin. Fear knocks me back and I attempt to push away from their oncoming assault.

"Taran!"

A light wind whips across my face, trailing my hair along with it. I look up at the man who spoke. I don't recognize him. The wind feels foreign, almost like a separate entity drawing away my ability to process any of this—or simply remember who I am.

"Shite! Garrit hit yeh," he hisses. He says something in

a foreign language I don't recognize. Then again, I don't recognize much of anything right now and the pain in my skull is becoming more intense. I wince at the jerk of my arm above me, being glued to a stick by the grip of the man. "Don't let go, Taran!"

Who's Taran? I want to ask. I can't seem to get my mouth to work.

The man growls. "*Cuimhure cé were hiem!*"

Energy pelts my chest and nearly knocks me off my feet. Coll continues to hold my hand, his own strength keeping me from pulling us both to the ground with the force of the spell. At the same time, he yells out another hex at Garrit, who now looks like a version of the Hunchback of Notre Dame and a black Edgar Allen Poe.

Taran Grim. My name is Taran Grim. And these men are trying to kill us. Get off your ass!

"He hit you with a memory hex. Are yeh all right?" Coll breathes.

I nod, feeling buzzed. I don't have much time to situate myself though. Over Coll's shoulder I see Ruhmactír, lowering himself to the ground, preparing to attack.

"*Argærts!*" Coll and I both yell at the same time. Where the spell came from, I don't know. It's not one I've ever heard before, and it's not a spell I've ever used. Something about the experience and the word feels spoon-fed to us at the same time—originating from the staff like so many of the other spells.

Coll casts his over my shoulder, me over his. The staff warms beneath our grip and I feel a giant tug around my midsection, whipping me back. My hand remains magically glued to the staff. The valley of Bryden shifts into a blurred focus, tunneling and changing; and yet, not changing at all. The tugging shifts into a shove and Coll and I fall face forward into the lush grass beneath our feet. At once, the traction and dragging of the air around us ends. A sliver of noise squashes into silence.

I grip Coll's shirt and he places his other free hand over mine. I feel him turn his head toward me and take a deep breath of my hair, his body tense. I take my own deep breath before my head snaps up to see where we are. Cold, like the sensation of throwing off a much-needed blanket, grips me and freezes me to the spot. Standing around us is a multitude of people. All dressed in sackcloth with blue paint patterned across their faces, hands, and arms. Images of runes and markings can be seen in black paint overtop the blue.

"Coll?" I whisper.

"*Cés oncl e set,*" a thunderous voice speaks over our heads. Coll, still gripping *Craniarann* pushes us both into a seated position, forcing me to follow his lead. Standing over us is a very-much alive Woden. He must stand more than six feet tall and his violet eyes are stormy and piercing. Confusion, anger, fear. It's all in his face, and I can feel the wave of magic radiating from him and the *Craniarann* of the past while he looms over us.

"*Hvaber ti'fuil! Hvaber ti'fuil!*"

What are you. What are you.

TWENTY-FIVE

"HVABER TI'FUIL!" WODEN BELLOWS AGAIN.

"Fi geisten ingainn a dochen!" Coll exclaims, begging for protection, while still holding the staff. *"Táir hexens. Cainde. Gake deimder. I mér Geri."* He puts a hand to his chest, indicating that he is Geri. *"Tie ine Grim."* He motions toward me, revealing my own clan. *"Ados fá mer tribkite."*

I find myself more amazed by Coll. Ancient words travel over his practiced tongue, a language spoken solely by our long-dead—now standing before us—ancestors.

Woden looks us up and down while I survey the faces surrounding us—the feeling of death hangs in the air. Coll and I were dragged back in time. Was anyone else? I can't see Adrian and the others anywhere. If they were pulled through with us, they're hiding well. Not only that, but this is not the memory I experienced before. The stone table is here, yes. Woden is much younger, though. Behind him, I can see a small six or seven-year-old version of the girl whose memories I once inhabited: Rheda. Her hair is nearly scarlet, hanging down her back wildly. This is not the ceremony. This is something different.

"Teu bús Grim?"

Coll knocks his elbow into me and I stare directly up at my ancestor.

"*Ees eja,*" Coll whispers. I grit my teeth in annoyance at him—annoyance, and quite a bit of fear at standing in front of the only High Hexen the world has ever known. A man the rest of mankind considers a comic book character or a mythical god. I feel Coll's assurance move through me. Somehow I gain my bearings. I may not know the history, but I know the language.

"*Ees eja,*" I admit to Woden, breathing hard. "He tells the truth, I am a Grim. Only, not a Grim of your time." I continue on in the ancient language. "Ancestor," I dip my head. "He speaks the truth. We are in danger. *Craniarann* is in danger.*"*

It's at this moment that Woden finally recognizes the staff set between our hands. He scrutinizes the staff in his own and frowns. "Tell me, daughter," he nearly spits out the word. "Who seeks you?"

My eyes slink to the side, looking again for Adrian or the others. Instead of finding their faces or their shadowed eyes hiding among the crowd, my eyes are drawn to the prostrate bodies of three women. Each lies still on the ground, their faces frozen with a look of steely defiance. I instantly realize why I felt the death so heavily when we appeared. The *tás.* The death spell. Woden must have performed an execution.

I shiver and my breath catches in my throat. The one in the center must be Hellia. The other two . . . I recognize.

Alina? Lotte?

How are they—

I look at Coll, unsure how to answer the demand of my ancestor.

Coll notices what I saw and he swallows. "Don't mention who's after us," he says in English. "Things must continue as they have."

Knowing this, I'm also aware that at this time, Woden would already be aware of the *Deireanhexe* prophecy. I can't lie to him. "My ancestor," I lower my head once more in reverence, speaking his tongue much more uncertainly than before, "we have been called to protect *Craniarann*. The end," I swallow, "has been prophesied. I'm afraid, this is the time."

"The joining cross," Woden says. He stares at our hands wrapped around *Craniarann*. The marks on our hands are glowing through our warming skin and inner bones, showing off a fully-formed cross of Woden to the world around us. "Then you are truly my daughter. And you," he looks to Coll, "the son of Ruhmactír."

At the mention of his name, the past version of Ruhmactír tentatively steps forward from the crowd. He looks nearly the same. So similar to Coll, and yet colder. More distant. His face is pale beneath the light layer of blue paint. Hard and resolute. I don't see the hate, the fire, and the fury I know is under the surface. Watching your wife be executed with a *tás*, while surrounded by others ready to attack your weakness, means he's hiding it. The anger, the pain, I know it's there. With the clans of Grim, Druw, Geri, and Ravn around, he knows he can't act. He must keep it inside.

It's got to be the same reason Adrian has not yet revealed himself. Unless, of course, the staff brought Coll and I alone. Though, I can't imagine this is solely the work of the staff. This day is important. It's important to Ruhmactír.

"I'm surprised to see you here," I say in my family's ancient tongue.

The Ruhmactír of the past frowns. "Explain."

He watches me look at the bodies of his wife and sisters-in-law. When I look back at him, he's still staring at me, the same intensity and fury in his eyes that I saw in Adrian's. The anger is there, the words are for Woden's benefit. Nothing else. "I am loyal to the Grims. The Morrigan sisters, my wife . . . they chose their own fate."

It's amazing to hear him speak. Not because I battled him in the form of Adrian. Because if I didn't recognize the lie in his eyes, I'd think he actually believed what he just said.

Ruhmactír's fingers twitch.

He's biding his time. Waiting. The vengeance is there. With this many Grims in one place, though, acting in hate is most likely a death sentence.

Ruhmactír glances at the nearest clan member—Grim, Ravn, or Geri I'm not sure—his face is red and callous. It's then, just behind the ancient Ruhmactír that I see Adrian. He's tucked behind one of the village homes, watching Woden with a glare that could kill.

"Woden," I reluctantly tear my eyes away from Coll's precursor, "you are in danger. And so is *Craniarann*. You must get your family and your clans out of here."

Coll must see what I have because he steps in with, "They're here."

A ferocious bark rips from the throat of a shifted Hexen wolf. The animal lands directly behind Woden. The powerful High Hexen turns and extends his hand and a silent spell pierces through the breast of the large wolf. It has to be Frec. Though, I can't tell if it's Michael, or the original.

"Noo!" a painful bellow roars over the heads of the crowd and Adrian lunges from the shadow of the cottage, shifting once more into the wolf form that gives him so much power. The dog continues to growl and bark, the hackles on his back rising into a sharp ridge.

Woden lifts his arm and the *Craniarann* he holds glows with an unearthly power. I feel the staff gripped in my and Coll's hand reciprocate the feeling—a shadow of the power of itself. A brief moment of calm expands over the village, like a calm before a storm. The air stagnates, the sounds cease, and my own inhaling breath is like a bellowing scream. Just before an exploding force radiates from Woden's hands, clan members shout to one another—cautions, warnings, and smaller spells fly through the air, Woden's power connecting with our own *Craniarann*.

Something knocks into Coll's side throwing him against me. Another spell—I can smell it, like sulfur and patchouli—flies in front of my face, hitting Coll's opposite side, hurtling both of us into a spiral.

"Coll, no!" I scream, feeling his hand slip from the staff. His frantic and furious gaze locks on me. I watch him fly north in slow motion, colliding against the rock walls of a home. I'm flung to the south, my back cracking against the edge of the stone table. An unbelievable pain shocks my back and legs while my breath is knocked out of me. I gasp for air, rolling over, struggling to get my lungs to respond with any inch of inhalation. Gnarling breaths slowly respond before I'm able to push myself up, blades of grass and mud smeared across my clothing and arms. When I orient myself, I see Garrit raising his hand once more, preparing to attack me with a spell.

I raise *Craniarann* by myself, feeling the loss of Coll's power, and belt, "*Stallifte sa kraft!*"

The spell impales Garrit's core and exits through his back with a shining black orb that disappears into the air. He stumbles backward and grips at his chest. His eyes spring open and fixate on me. With a movement of his hand, he tries to complete a spell. Nothing happens. Again he tries. When he can't formulate an attack, I lift *Craniarann* again and knock him to his backside with a light offensive spell. Garrit growls, dazed, and attempts to push himself back to his feet. His movements are unbalanced—as if he finally understands something is missing. His magic. He stretches out his hands, looking at each one, hyperventilating.

"You bitch!" he screams.

Before he can stand, I hit him with another stunner, this time, solely my own power and not the staff's. The hex is weak. Still, it knocks him on his ass a second time.

"Stay down!" I yell.

He doesn't listen and shifts his weight onto his feet. Again I hit him with a stunning spell that knocks him back against one of the cottage walls. He collapses unconscious.

When I have the time to focus once more, I look around for Coll. He's lying on the ground, his body wrapped around the corner of a stone home.

"Coll," I whisper before running toward him. My fist grips the staff and I sprint until I fall down near his side. I peel him away from the wall and lay him on his back.

"Coll? Coll, answer me."

Without releasing the staff, I feel his pulse. It's still there.

"Child!" Woden calls to me in the distance.

Frantically, I turn around. Woden hits the now conscious Garrit with a final spell, a broken shard of rock in his hand. The red glow of the *tás* illuminates the sky and the large Ravn man falls to the ground, his eyes frozen in fear.

I barely have time to register what else has happened. Woden and the Grims are now fighting off another wolf—and the entire Geri clan. It's not Adrian leading the fight—he's lying unconscious just five feet from the infamous High Hexen. No, this is Ruhmactír himself. He's shifted, and the immediate anger and pain he feels from losing his wife has triggered a desperate attempt to murder her killer.

No, this isn't right. This isn't how it's supposed to happen. Ruhmactír isn't supposed to attack Woden until years from now.

What have we done?

"No!" I stand up to run toward them and Ruhmactír twists to face me, his fur sharp like needles and dark as soot. The most powerful hex pelts me and knocks me into the stone table. The magic that cut through me was raw, painful. My fingers barely move along the grass, my muscles refusing to cooperate. The collision with the table stole my breath once more. Pain shoots through my neck in my attempt to look up. Like an eclipse, my vision goes dark, my hearing becomes mute, and my body feels buoyant, I try to feel for *Craniarann* that's not there.

I'm slipping away, and all I can do is claw at everything—anything—to stay where I am.

TWENTY-SIX

RIBBONS OF WIND PAINT PATTERNS ACROSS MY face while feathers of air tickle the skin on my neck, my arms, and my cheek. Warm sun radiates across my face and white light glows through my eyelids. A groan escapes my lips and I roll over to the side, trying to steal some more time to sleep, and maybe some shade to cool off the beads of sweat gathering along my hairline.

Another groan comes from my left and the memory of Coll's limp body curved around the corner of a building, the angry roar of Ruhmactír and his ivory teeth, the flashback of Woden and the staff, they all flood my memory and I shoot up in a panic. I'm still in Bryden. The village, the stone table—it's all the same. Only—

. . . it's not.

Woden. Woden's body is no longer here.

Magic still burns through my veins, every inch of my skin, and the mark in my hand. I lift my palm and look at it. The white circle is now transparent and I can actually see a glow of hexen magic swimming through my veins and the muscles of my hand. "What?" I whisper.

The second groan.

I look over to see Coll just inches from where my head once rested. Lying between us is *Craniarann*. It's still here. It's not gone. A sweep of relief calms me for only a moment before I crawl over to Coll and shake his shoulder.

"Coll!" I shriek. "Coll, are you awake?"

His eyes flutter open and his dilated pupils immediately shrink in the mid-afternoon sun. "Where am I?" he asks.

I sigh in relief. He's awake, and speaking. "Bryden. We're still in Bryden, Coll."

I take a look around again to see if Adrian made it back with us. Since the *tás* killed Garrit, and Woden obliterated Frec, they're no longer going to be a threat. I just don't know what happened to Adrian . . . or Ruhmactír.

"Bryden? That's not possible. Who are yeh?"

The tone in Coll's voice is enough to let me know . . . he's not joking with me. I spin my head around to look at him. "You . . . don't know who I am?"

"Should I?" He looks around, a nervous confusion resides in his eyes.

"Coll, do—" I take a breath, "do you remember anything that just happened?"

"Woman, I don't even know who yeh are. I don't know how I got here, and I don't know how you feckin' got me to Bryden, yeah? So, you'd better tell me what the bloody hell I'm doin' here."

I reach out to touch his hand and he stiffens like a snake ready to strike. I slowly pull my hand back, a sinking in my stomach growing larger by the minute. "What's the last thing you remember?"

Coll's thick eyebrows furrow and he thinks hard. "I was on a business trip. Jest got off the plane. I was at the airport about to make a call to Adrian when I got to baggage."

Baggage claim. The phone. He doesn't even remember meeting me.

How has he—

Something knocks into Coll's side throwing him against me, and another spell—I can smell it, like sulfur and patchouli—flies in front of my face and enters Coll's opposite side, hurtling both of us into a spiral.

Two spells hit him. I saw Garrit when I looked up, lifting his hand.

He wiped Coll's memory. Just before I stripped his powers.

My voice comes out in a horrified whisper. "You don't remember anything after that?"

"Woman, I was just sucked out of an airport and dropped in a farmer's field. Who are yeh?"

"Coll—"

"*Who are yeh!?*" he bellows.

It freezes me to my spot and he pushes himself farther from me. "Are yeh workin' with my da? Are you one of Michael's bitches?"

"What? No! Coll, you need to let me fix this. Let me cast a—"

Frustration and fear flood my veins and I scramble toward him. "Coll!"

"Stay away from me."

"No, Coll. *Cuimhure*—" I crawl toward him. Before I can lay a hand on him, he travels out of sight and I'm left in the field by myself, the ancient staff of Woden lying on the ground next to me like a rotten felled limb.

* * *

I reach over for the staff and grip it tight in my hands. The familiar warmth from its magic is dormant, and the energy that once surrounded it can no longer be seen. With a deep breath, I push myself up and look around the grassy knoll— taking in a quick study of the village and the surrounding area. Woden's body is no longer on the ground. Not only that, the huts—the small homes—are nearly gone. Weathered with age and thousands of years, only faint foundations remain and the stone table is gone, which means we must have changed the course of his life. Who knows what events have changed—or have been unchanged—by everything that just happened.

First thing's first: I need a safe place to hide *Craniarann*. I can't leave it here in Bryden, and I can't exactly take it out in the open, back to the hotel, either.

I pull out the cell phone in the pocket of my jacket, only to find its screen shattered and the power dead. "Shit," I whisper. Placing one hand on the surface of the screen, I whisper, "*Deiparsiú*."

Beneath the pads of my fingers and the shaking quivers

of my muscles, the glass and internal structure of the phone pieces back together and the power automatically comes back on.

"Call home," I say. When the phone rings the second time, I hear a muffled noise followed by the harsh bite of *Móraí's* worried tone.

"*Mo sféar, mo sféar.* Are you safe?"

I take a calming breath in and look around once more. "I think so."

"Do you have *Craniarann?*"

I nod. "Yes. I just don't know how to bring it home. It's a massive staff. I can't risk anyone seeing it."

"Child. You know what to do. Trust yourself. Bring it home and don't waste time. Do you hear me?"

Again, I nod, forgetting she can't actually see me. "I do, but . . ."

When she hangs up, I look at the staff and frown. I know how to bring it home safely? How?

I hold the staff tightly in my right hand and examine it. Short of shoving the stick up my sleeve, there aren't many effective ways to smuggle a large staff out of the country while keeping it safe from those who may still be out there.

Deep ragged breaths join the chorus of the gentle breeze and I look around. It's silent. Not a cloud in the sky.

Coll doesn't remember me.

And I have no clue how to get this staff home.

I survey the land, wondering what happened to Adrian. He could be dead, and he could still come back at any moment.

My fingernail digs into the surface of the wood staff and the pads of my fingers graze its surface.

Wait. I look down at the staff, my hand running a few inches down its shaft. I pause, studying it. My fingers run over a carving of a spider, woven in with the deer antlers, entwining into tree-like roots. I hadn't noticed the insect when I gripped the staff in my hands, fighting off Adrian. It's small, it's front leg reaching forward in the motion of climbing *Craniarann*. It's incredibly detailed.

"Dad," I whisper. There's a reason he picked that nursery rhyme. I rub the image of the spider gently. "You sang me that song over and over."

I grip the staff with both hands. "The itsy-bitsy spider," I gently sing, "crawled up the water spout." I lay it horizontally in the air, waiting for the right inspiration to hit me. "Down came the rain," I look up briefly, thinking about my ability to call the rain, "and washed the spider out." I feel the weight of the wood's magic in my hands. "Out came the sun, and dried up all the rain." The circular pattern on my palm burns and the answers come flooding into my mind.

"And the itsy-bitsy spider," I slide my hands in opposite directions down the length of *Craniarann*, "ran into my little hand," I whisper.

My hand. My scar is burning.

This time, I slide my hands back together in the center of the pole and whisper the words, *"Ceade san mi,"* that flit across my tongue. Immediately, I slide my hands across *Craniarann*—one to the right, the other to the left—the sections I touch begin to disappear and I feel the scar on my hand continue to burn and glow hot. I continue on until I've contacted the entire length of its surface. I release my hands and take a deep breath before turning my hand over. Directly in the center of my palm rests the straight-line image of *Craniarann*. The unfinished cross of Woden. My mark is housing the staff, protecting it.

The white coloring of my scar fades before my eyes and both circle and the *craniarann* line return to a faint pinkish hue.

Knowing, it's safe once more, I take a couple more nervous breaths before brushing off my pants and looking toward the city. Coll brought my memory back when I lost it for that brief moment. Spells flying around, and he brought me back. I have to make him remember me, the staff, and everything we've seen.

After closing my eyes, I think back to that night in the park when Coll taught me how to travel. The feeling of his magic sliding over my body. My body's energy instantly ignites and I travel from Bryden, turning around to find myself in front of Coll's apartment.

I don't even care that Karl, his doorman, just saw me appear out of nowhere.

I rush up the steps and grab his arm. He looks at me with shock.

"Karl, I need to get in to talk with Coll."

"Who—how did—how did you do that?"

"It doesn't matter. I need to talk with Coll. Have you seen him come in?"

He shakes his head and I slowly turn around, envisioning

Sera's apartment in the back of my mind. Coll put up a protective block around the outside of the building, and no matter how much I try, I can't get the image of her apartment to materialize in my mind. Like it's slipped away. Dammit. I have to think. His spell was set up to keep me from finding her building. The building. I could try a Hexen guidance spell in an attempt to connect with him. If he notices it, he might even block me from finding him.

Sera . . . Sera wouldn't recognize it. She wouldn't even know how to break the connection if she did.

I whisper the few required words, searching for her hidden magic energy, and grab hold of it before I travel toward it. Knowing I've probably sent Karl into a stroke by traveling twice in front of him, I arrive inside her building at the top of the staircase. I quickly pound on her door. "Sera? Is Coll with you?" I yell.

Shuffling from inside tells me someone is home. Whether or not Coll is with her, is another issue entirely.

The door to her apartment only opens by a few inches and I see her poke her head out, conflict and hardness in her eyes. "I'm sorry, he's not," she says firmly.

"Please, don't lie to me," I beg, seeing the lie in her gaze. "I need to talk with him."

"Taran, I'm sorry. He doesn't even know yeh. Hell, I don't know what happened, and I think I can say he's damn near lucky he remembers anythin'."

"What?"

Sera opens up the door far enough for her to slip through.

I quickly look over her shoulder to see Coll nursing his injuries on the couch with his magic, a beer on the table next to him. Sera shuts the door and slowly turns on me, forcing me to take a cautionary step back. "Fine. Explain. Help me understand why I nearly lost my brother."

I clear my throat. "Last night, we spent the evening at the library and we found out how to find the staff, so this morning we went looking for it. When we got there—" a flash of Adrian's shifting body plays in my memory, "Adrian, your dad, and Garrit had followed us."

"What?" Sera's face screws into disgust.

"They weren't who we thought they were. I know you're looking at me as if I've lost my mind, but Adrian was Ruhmactír, and your dad? The reason he killed you mother was that it wasn't him who did it. It was Frec," I pause, "Frec and Ruhmactír have been possessing the bodies of their descendants for years."

"Stop, just stop it!" she hisses.

"A fight started," I plow on, "and in the chaos Coll was hit by a memory spell by Garrit. If you'll just let me see him—"

"Stop!" she yells. After taking a few deep breaths, Sera bites down on her lips. "Look, I know how things were . . . sizin' up between yeh. Coll, never said a lick of feelings 'bout yeh. I knew he had 'em. But," she struggles to get it out, "we've been through too much already, and now this."

"Sera, I needed his help, and he agreed. If you'll just let me in for a few minutes I think I can lift—"

"Taran," her voice intensifies, straining to remain calm. "He blasted through my door askin' what day it was. He started ramblin' 'bout this field and this woman who someone must have sent after him to *seduce* him and wipe his memory. I've never been so afraid in my life. I've never seen him so terrified."

"Terrified?" I ask.

Sera finally looks at me just before the complex door opens up down the stairs. We both turn around to see Emilia step in and she looks out of breath. "What's goin' on? You called me in a panic, Sera. What is it?"

My eyes are glued to the youngest Donovan girl. No, not now. I can't look her in the eye and tell her Garrit is dead.

"Why don't you ask her?" Sera says lightly before motioning toward me with a bob of her head.

Emilia walks up the stairs, gripping a black leather clutch in her hand. She takes a breath and stops on the top stair, still standing a good six inches below me. Even so, I feel I'm only three inches tall. Up close, I can see that her hair is slightly out of place, her face pale. I can't peel my eyes away from her. How is she going to react when I tell her that the man she loved tried to attack me . . . and ended up consequently being killed by Woden, the high Hexen?

"I asked Coll to help me find something. A staff, belonging to my family. In fact, it's the same one your dad's been looking for."

Emilia's face drains, if it's possible, even further and a look of our confusion takes over. "My da?"

Sera shrugs at my side.

I rush on, continuing on with the story and apologizing

profusely for her pain the second I see the tears start to build. And I haven't even told her that Garrit is dead yet.

"You're sure it was him?" she asks, the ends of her silky golden hair quiver. "Garrit wiped Coll's memory?"

"He was a Ravn, Emilia. He hid it from all of us and when it happened, I tried to stop it, I tried to keep us both safe—and Coll did too. We just . . . I couldn't."

"So where is he?" she whispers.

"Coll's inside," Sera explains.

Emilia shakes her head. "No," she stares me down. "Where is Garrit?"

I glance sideways at Sera, who refuses to look at me. She folds her arms and stares at the ground.

"He," I start, meeting Emilia's eyes once more, "he died."

A massive tear slides down her face. Her expression doesn't shift. At least, not immediately. Slowly, her face twists into a hardened scowl, mirroring the labyrinth of overloaded emotions and thoughts that I'm sure are tearing through her. I don't like this. I don't like this at all. I want to take it all back, I want to give them good news—

"Did yeh do it?" she finally whispers.

I shake my head. "Someone else. All I did was block his magic. I swear." I pivot back to Sera. "That's why Coll doesn't remember anything. We both held the staff in our hands and—"

Sera holds up her hand to cut me off. "Stop. I don't want to hear anymore. Feckin' stories about our da," she mumbles to herself. "Emilia, go inside. I'll be in, in a minute."

The youngest Donovan barely moves her head before brushing past us and pushing the door open. It's ajar long enough for me to see Coll standing just a foot away from the opening, his hands in his pockets, his eyes narrowing on me—he's been listening through the door. I don't get a long enough look at him to really gauge what he's thinking. I lean to the right after the door closes, my final attempt to connect with him before he's cut off from me again.

"Taran," Sera addresses me, hesitating. Searching for the right words. "Things have changed. I think . . . it would be best for all of us, if yeh left."

I nod and feel my heart pound, wanting nothing more than to remove myself from this stuffy and tense stairway. "Sera, it's me. If you'll just let me in, I can perform a—"

"No," she cuts me off.

"Then tomorrow?"

"What I mean, is . . . I think it would best if yeh left England. Don't come back. No more magic, no more staffs, no more anythin'. Our lives have been torn apart by magic and the hexen world. We lost our father, our mother, and now Coll is . . ." Her voice trails off. She shakes her head and looks away from me. "I don't care," she whispers, "how much yeh think yeh can help him, or how much yeh want his help. We don't need to invite that shite into our lives anymore."

Then, with a storm in her eyes, she glares at me. "We're done."

"Sera," I plead, stepping forward. "You don't understand."

"*You* don't understand," her eyes ignite. "My brother has

done everythin' in his power to protect me and Emilia from going through the nightmare he survived, to save us, and all at his expense. Don't yeh get it? He could have lost more than just two weeks of his memory. He could have lost himself. And all for you! For some stupid wooden stick! He doesn't want to see yeh anymore, and for what it's worth, I don't want to see yeh either. Please leave, and don't ever come back."

"No, Sera, no."

At that, Sera turns her back on me and walks back into her apartment, slamming the door in my face. I swallow down the lump that's formed in my throat, my mind revisiting the dark glare of Coll from the doorway of the apartment. Casting a final frustrated glance at the dark wooden door, I hope he'll open it once more, just to ask me a question—anything. The man I've spent two weeks with, who insulted me, disgusted me, annoyed me, and tore into me. The man who touched every inch of my hexen energy and left me with a power I've never been able to connect with before.

Instead, the solid door remains closed and I'm left with the solid thump of my hollow heart.

TWENTY-SEVEN

THE SOUND OF A CAR HORN BREAKS ME FROM my thoughts. I've been sitting at the same stop sign for what feels like the last fifteen minutes. I could have sworn I was moving already, but I guess not. I clear my throat and press my foot on the gas pedal. *A sliver of magic pulses under the skin of my palm. Coll's firm grip—his long fingers, the warmth of his touch—simultaneously releases my own. My hands smoothly slip from his. My fingertips journey down the center of his wide palms; the hot trickling of his touch faintly lingering between my fingers.*

The horn-happy driver speeds around me the first available moment and I brush my hair away from my face, coasting down the road. Only a few minutes ago I was standing in my hotel room, closing up my suitcase. After a brief travel spell, I found myself sitting in the driver's side seat of my CR-V, the suitcase jammed up between my ribcage and the steering wheel as the horn blared loudly through the airport parking lot. Now, here I am, absentmindedly driving home.

I guess that's not true. Not exactly absentminded.

"Coll, do—do you remember anything that just happened?"

"Woman," I pause the memory, attempting to hear him once again call me "woman." Woman.

"I don't even know who you are. I don't know how I got here, and I don't know how you feckin' got me to Bryden, yeah? So, you'd better tell me what the bloody hell I'm doin' here."

He wouldn't even let me touch him. Collens Donovan, the man with a whorish facade, wouldn't even let me touch his hand.

Taran, stop it. You knew him for two weeks, he pissed you off, you couldn't stand him, and now it's over. Let it go.

Seriously, just stop.

I turn on my blinker and make a left.

Woden still fought when I was yanked out of that world with a spell. Who's spell? Who sent us home? And Ruhmactír, his future Adrian self, and the entire gathering of hexens were all locked in a spell-casting battle. It wasn't right. It wasn't supposed to happen like that. Did Woden live? Did Ruhmactír die? If so, what's changed? One small alteration in magical history can screw everything up.

What about Adrian?

Adrian smiles. Just the memory of it makes my stomach turn. Adrian *was* Ruhmactír. He stood right there with me and Coll. All along. I never even knew. I should have known. It should have crossed my mind.

"You're right, Coll. She's perfect for you. Too bad it won't last long."

She's perfect for you.
You're right.

I take a breath and make the next right.

Coll stands just a foot away from the opening door. His hands are shoved in his pockets, his amber eyes narrowing on me. In what? Hatred? Confusion? Anger? None of those words seem to define what I saw in his face. Even in that brief moment. No, anger isn't the right word—ensnared. Ensnared by what, I'm not sure.

I pull alongside the sidewalk in front of my apartment building and turn off the engine. After pulling my luggage out, I heft it up the stairs and through the doors. The old building I live in has no elevator, so climbing the three flights of stairs feels like a massive undertaking for the weight I'm already carrying around in my head. Instead, I stop and look around for any watchful eyes. When I feel I'm alone, I connect with every point of my energy, extending it out toward my bags, and travel up to my apartment in one breath.

Everything is as I left it.

Everything is the same.

I drop my bags on the floor, not even bothering with the clatter of items tumbling out of my satchel. I cross the room, heading for the candles resting in the center of my coffee table. The candles I continued to summon back and forth from England have shrunk in height from use, the etching of Woden's crest half-melted off the side. I perch myself on the edge of the couch with one leg curled and the other foot resting solidly on the floor. Silence saturates my apartment.

Summoning my phone from the pile of junk that fell out

of my bag, I quickly dial my mom's number and let the phone ring.

"Taran? Are you home?" she answers.

"Yeah," I whisper.

"I'm glad you made it back safe," she replies with a grateful sigh. "Marlis has been almost impossible to handle. She's been calling about you from sunup to sundown. I can't tell you how much incense has been clouding up the air in her home for the last couple weeks. It's like a perfume factory went up in smoke."

I smile weakly and lean forward, cradling my eyes with one hand. Blocking out the sunlight and the sensations from my home, I ask, "Is everyone else all right?"

"Of course, bug. I just had a phone call with Alina today. It seems that Carl just got a promotion so they're moving back to Boise."

"Really? Leaving Portland?"

"Much to his disappointment," Mom jests. "At least I'll be able to see the grandkids a little more this way."

I nod, my hand still holding my face.

"Your dad called me today too."

My lungs seize and everything goes deathly still.

"What?" My head slowly lifts and I look out my sliding glass doors.

"Your dad. Turns out someone didn't tell him she was leaving for England. Wanted to know why no one told him."

I can't breathe, my heart beating a million miles an hour. "Dad? Did you say, 'Dad?'"

"Of course. Are you all right?" she asks. "I thought you two were on speaking terms again."

And then it hits me. Mom said *Mórai called* her. Why would *Mórai* call Mom if they live in the same house? Calling from sunup to sundown. Her home? Not our home. And Dad—

I stand up, pacing toward the glass doors. "Dad's alive?"

Mom laughs and I hear her rustle something around. "I guess that's a good way of putting it. I mean after you turned three, he took off and we didn't hear from him for nearly twenty-five years. Good as dead, right? I'm still shocked you reached out to him last month."

Dad's alive. If Dad's alive, does that mean . . . Radolf Wolf, Adrian, or Ruhmactír never killed him? But why?

I drag my fingers furiously through my hair and whirl around.

The flickering of the crest candle flames freeze me to the spot and my mouth hangs open.

They weren't lit when I walked in the room. They weren't lit when I stood up and walked past them. And I never lit them.

"Mom? Can I call you back?" I mutter.

"Are you okay?"

I hang up without even saying goodbye, my eyes locked on the gently quivering flickers of fire. I don't have time for my powers to be doing this to me right now. I quickly snap my fingers, snuffing out their flames and flash through the living room, searching for a notebook in the nearest bookcase. I drag my finger across the book spines, looking . . . looking . . . looking.

I pause for a brief moment, noticing a box I've never seen before. It's large and weathered—whether by Pottery Barn or actual aging, I'm not sure. I quickly pull it off the shelf and struggle to hold it. I wasn't exactly expecting it to be this heavy. It lands with a solid thunk when I drop it on the nearest table. It's locked. I don't know where the key is.

"*Eighlase,*" I say and the lock snaps, allowing me to open the box. Inside, frayed spines, broken leather, and the smell of sweet age. Books. About seven of them. I slowly drag my finger down one of the spines and wiggle it out. There's not an imprint of text on the worn leather cover. When I open it up, the scrawl of hexen script bombards me. It's a family tree, but not ours. And this is not my book—at least not one I remember having before.

Heart flutters. Shaking hands. I place the book carefully on the table next to me and pull open the next. It's newer, but not necessarily new either. Cloth cover, maybe early 1990s. Inside is my own handwriting. The more I turn pages, the more my jaw slowly slinks to my chest. These are not spells I recognize, yet . . . I know my handwriting. Every single one of them. Worse than that, these are not good spells. The only innocent spell in here might be the Search and Find spell, but when coupled with the Future magic, the banishing spells, the revenge hexes . . . I find that a lump starts to form in my throat.

"What in the hell has happened?" I whisper, letting the book tumble from my loose grip. "Everything is different."

I look at the rest of the books. The spine of the Grim Family

History catches my eye and I remember why I came to the bookcase in the first place.

My breath shakes. I pull out the book and carry it around with me to the couch. The moment I fall into a seated position, I fly through the pages, looking for the death date of Woden. When I find the genealogical family tree, I look to the page I know he's on and scan until I see his name. Woden Grim, High Hexen. Birth: 1402 BC. Death—1297 BC.

My lips part and my eyebrows skew. 1297. He was a hundred and five?

Ruhmactír, "Ruhmactír," I repeat out loud. "When did he die?"

Leaping up from my seat, I run back to the box and scan the spines. One of them, black worn leather catches my attention—as if I know what it already is—and I grab it. Inside is the full rundown of the Geri clan from start (I open to the very last page to see his name staring back at me) to end: Sera, Emilia, and the oldest Collens Donovan; First day of January 1986. After giving myself chance to swallow down the nerves, I flip back to the first few pages and look for the entry for Ruhmactír. When I find it, I hiss in anger. Of course. 1424. He died in his early twenties. That would mean he didn't live to see the day Rheda gave her prophesy, which would mean the spell was actually completed. So how . . .

I look at the mark on my palm. *Craniarann* is still there, housed within the circular mark.

I look around my apartment. That part hasn't changed. How, how did I—

Trembling with the slightest movement, flickers of burning crest candlewicks dance. Every candle illuminated in my house. Not just the crest candles. The pillar candles, the decorative candelabra in the corner, the short tea candles resting in my bookcase. All of them lit.

"What in the hell?" I glower at the candles, my breathing intensifying, the air feeling heavy and thick.

I watch the flames, hesitant to snuff them out again. Slowly, within the curls of the warm golden flames, shapes begin to form. Shapes of runes, movements, and shadows. *Beithe*—a small T shape. *Néada*—three lines with a slashing line through them. Birch. Killing. The runes continue on, more and more. The symbols begin to interconnect, creating mental images that flash in short bursts. Messages to me.

A woman. Dark black hair like silk. Her eyes are equally black and rich. Her skin is creamy white.

A scream. A flash of red light. The *tás*.

"You will pay for this, Grim Woden," the woman's face twists, spitting the words out in an ancient tongue. *"We will have our land, our power. And you and your line will be exterminated. I vow with my own blood."*

Woden swings *Craniarann* through the air and the sky ripples with a wave of scarlet color, the raging wine colored energy bursting from the chest of the woman. She falls to the ground, followed by two other women. Alina. Lotte. My sisters.

"Taran Grim. Daughter of Woden. You will die."

I gasp, my magic snapping me back into reality. The flames of the crest candles have been spent. The wax has pooled and started to harden across the silver platter they rest on, much of it has overflowed and spread across the coffee table. I quickly grab for my phone and look at the time. And date. It's morning. I flew into California last night.

Eleven hours. It's been eleven hours since I spoke with Mom on the phone.

I'll see to it with my own blood.

That woman. I saw her. I know her. The last time I looked into her face, she lay in a field surrounded by the clans of Geri, Ravn, Druw, and Grim. Hellia Morrigan. The wife of Ruhmactír and her two sisters. The Morrigan Sisters.

I leap up from the couch, pulling down all the books from my bookcase I can. Which one is it in? One of my old university text books talked about the Morrigan. Where is it?

I drop each book on the ground, unsatisfied to simply flip through each and every one. "*Fiehe ana Morrigan,*" I command, my hands hovering over them. Each book flies open, the pages whisking rapidly until they all land on the respective pages. I scan each entry, looking for the information I remember from school.

I stop. Right here.

Morrigan, Mor *may have derivations of the Indo-European root which means "terror," and may even cognate the Old English* maere *(nightmare), and the Scandinavian* mara *(nightmare). The suffix "*rogan*" roughly translates to "queen."*

Nightmares. The images of my father's death flashing behind my eyes. The memory of the *tas.* Terror.

I rest my hands in the air over the books again and command

them to return to the shelf. In my haste, I quickly recite a summoning spell for another book and it flies out of my bags, colliding with one of the former before landing on the floor in front of me. My spell to search for lost time and blackouts takes me to a singular page inside the book that was hand-written by Dad. It wasn't in the scribbles and scratches that mainly focused on the Hexen's Cross or *Craniarann*. It was a section I'd skimmed over so briefly I almost forgot about it.

Lost time—entrance to the depths. The depths? What does that mean? I turn the page and scan the writing. I remember this part where Dad mentioned the Morrigan. Something about a gateway, an access. I thought that simply had to do with the Himilæsa. Entrance to the depths of the afterlife.

"The depths of what?" I murmur, searching the pages. And then, my breath stills.

Hellia was a Ravn.

Dad wasn't talking about the depths of the afterlife. He was talking about the depths of the subconscious.

Her powers allowed her control over thought and memory. What was it that Adrian, or should I say Ruhmactír, said? "If my wife is all you think I want, you're more naive than I thought." Hellia and Ruhmactír were working on access to the afterlife before she died. It would have given them both unimaginable power over death and life. Hellia still wants access to the Himilæsa, he wanted the power of the staff.

The queen of nightmares. She's been doing everything. Coaxing me, grooming me, driving me so subtly, I barely noticed. All those lengths of lost time, she was gaining access to my thoughts.

It's not my powers that have been putting me into a trance.

It's her. Hellia Morrigan.

And Dad, the person who can get me my answers . . . is alive.

COMING SOON

HEXEN'S
BINDING

Acknowledgements

I HAVE BEEN WAITING FOR YEARS TO FINALLY
complete a supernatural/paranormal tale of witchcraft that
I absolutely loved and I couldn't have done it without a few
people in my life. Over the course of the last five years, I've had
friends, family, neighbors, authors, book bloggers, readers, and
fans alike who have been just incredibly supportive.

To my mom, first and foremost. I know you aren't much
of a reader because you've always dedicated so much time to
raising a family, but you have been with me through this since
I told you I wanted to publish my own book. From the road
trips to book events, the long talks, the discussions on story,
character, and worlds, I thank you. Thank you for your love.
Thank you for your time. Thank you for giving every bit of
yourself to put me into a position where I could succeed. No,
scratch that. Thank you for helping to put me into a position
had the opportunity to succeed—if I wanted to take it. I love
you so much!

I also have to thank, as I do every time, my beloved writers
group. Guys, there's still not enough emotion and feelings here.

Let's work on that. Plus, I can't wait to see what each of you have in store for the book world from here on out.

To my friends (I wish I could name you all) who lifted my spirits. There is strength in numbers and I'm surely proud to count each of you among my close-knit group of numbers. This last year has been a rollercoaster and whether it was a writing curve, a life-changing hill, or a family-oriented fall, you were there.

And I can't believe I've never thanked you, so I'm going to do it now. Hayden, you are one masterful cover designer. I don't know if I ever would have gotten around to Hexen's Cross if the reception for the designs of The Enertia Trials hadn't been as amazing as they were. A good story needs a fantastic billboard, and I have to say . . . most of the people who've picked up my books, picked them up because of you. And friend, I'm so lucky to know you!

Speaking of covers, Lauren, this artwork is insanely gorgeous. I've had people actually gasp when they see it. Hexen's Cross is a good story (if I do say so myself), but your work, your ideas, and your creativity has taken this good story and turned it into a piece of magic. You deserve all the goodness the world has to offer!

I think, if I had to pick out one group of people, however, that have touched me most this year, it would have to be my readers. When you write to me, when you come to me, or message me to tell me how my stories have touched your lives, I'm speechless. You're incredibly valuable to me, my characters, and those around you. Your empathy, your love, and your devotion to fiction is not just beneficial to me, but the world. While that may sound overdramatic, I hope you know it's not. Readers are better at putting themselves in others' shoes, and because of that, I say, you will change the world. One story at a time.

J. Kowallis graduated from Weber State University's creative writing program and lives in Utah with her Mini Schnauzer, Etta. She enjoys dreaming about, flying to, and writing about distant lands (real or unreal). You can visit her at *jkowallisbooks.com*.

Connect with J. Kowallis
– Twitter @j_kowallis –
– Instagram @j_kowallisbooks –
– Facebook www.facebook.com/authorjkowallis –

CPSIA information can be obtained
at www.ICGtesting.com
Printed in the USA
LVHW03s2302070818
586326LV00002B/212/P